not the
only
sky

# ALYSSA WARREN

BLACK & WHITE PUBLISHING

First published 2017
by Black & White Publishing Ltd
29 Ocean Drive, Edinburgh EH6 6JL

1 3 5 7 9 10 8 6 4 2          17 18 19 20

ISBN: 978 1 78530 090 5

A CIP catalogue record for this book is available from the British Library.

Typeset by Iolaire, Newtonmore
Printed and bound by CPI Group (UK) Ltd, Croydon, CR0 4YY

*For my boys*

PART I

# PART I

# 1988

*"A photograph is a secret about a secret."*
**- Diane Arbus**

# MAY

They could almost be out to sea. There's the world simplified to two elements, a rectangle of sky over a rectangle of earth. There's the wind lifting pigtails parallel to the horizon, pressing thick wool coats into the shapes of bones. If it weren't for the prairie grass in the foreground, the four-year-old twins in the sepia photograph could be walking on water. The title below the photograph reads *My Family by Clea Marie Baumhauer*. It felt odd writing "Clea" when everyone calls her Tiny Mite, but Miss Wright doesn't allow nicknames.

The twins in the photograph don't go by their real names either. Though christened Luvella and Burnella no one's ever called them anything but Luvie and Bee. Other words trapped in the photograph: German words disintegrating in the twins' cheeks like bits of apple, including, Tiny Mite imagines, curse words like *kacken* and *scheisse* because the twins' parents are Vulgar Germans. (Tiny Mite doesn't understand why Catherine the Great took Vulgar Germans with her to Russia instead of well-behaved ones, but whenever she asks Bee or Luvie, they laugh.)

Tiny Mite knows a photograph doesn't show everything that's

in it. It may look like a rectangle of cardboard, but is more like a window. Standing at her attic bedroom window, she can see nothing but cornfields, but when she opens it and leans outside, sees a barn to the left, and to the right, the wrecked airplane. In the same way, she can stick her head into photographs.

Inside this particular one, she bends so far forward that through the legs of the traveling photographer she can see the one-room tarpaper shack the twins share with their parents and four brothers—cow, horse and buffalo dung piled onto its sod roof for insulation. Alongside the door stands the rusted oil barrel filled with the buffalo chips they burn when they can't find wood. Beyond, in a lilting, wooden corral, the wild horses her brothers capture, break and sell whinny and buck. Twenty steps further is the privy (in her report, Tiny Mite has clarified: *privy, n: a wooden hut with a hole in the ground where you go to the bathroom and are lucky if you get to wipe with a corn cob much less a newspaper. Also known as an outhouse, thunder box, Johnny, crapper, stinker, comfort station, washroom, shithouse and latrine.* She hopes "shit" won't count as a swear word since she put it in a proper dictionary entry.)

Once she's inside a photo, Tiny Mite zooms in on things. In this one, she knows from the rough texture of the twins' dresses that they're made from bleached flour sacks. Deep creases in their leggings reveal black boots laced too tight.

Some photographs are crystal balls, this one in particular, and if Tiny Mite squints, she can see the twins' future. Behind the tarpaper shack, on the empty prairie, a farmhouse will rise, white as a baby's first tooth. Two stories, four front windows and a wraparound porch. A shelterbelt of sapling ash, pine, elm, oak and box elder will grow around it. A well will be dug, its yellow water laced with iron and silt. A barn will appear, large enough for ten horses, a hay wagon and threshing machine, and soon after that, a milk house, smokehouse, blacksmithing hut, silo and corncrib. A pump connected to the creek beyond the right edge of the photograph will irrigate fields of corn and alfalfa.

Grasshoppers will come and devour everything.

Two pages of her report are covered with drawings of locomotives derailing on grasshopper grease and locusts chewing the puffy sleeves off her great-grandmother's black taffeta dresses. A brontosaurus-sized grasshopper, its spine crenelated with nails and drill bits, bites off the head of a farmer wielding a pitchfork. A thought bubble above the oversized reptile says, "Brains! My favorite!"

Thought bubbles are Tiny Mite's new big thing. She'd like to draw some over the twin girls' heads, but other than *kacken* and *scheisse* she doesn't speak German, and she wasn't supposed to take the picture out of the family album, much less paste it onto her report.

Sperm can't talk, so thought bubbles were handy in the section about her parents. She's written, "I hope it's a girl!" over her drawing of a tadpole riding a motorcycle toward a Barbie cut from an advertisement and embellished with googly eyes. Tiny Mite feels uneasy about this part of the story—last week Miss Wright made her miss recess to reiterate the difference between storytelling and lying, and though she rewrote half a dozen essays on the subject, still feels confused, because even though she's never met her father, she knows he drives a motorcycle named Harley and has her very same straight black hair. She also knows his nicknames are "Blankety Blank" and "the Goddamned Idiot," but has withheld this information on account of Miss Wright's high regard for proper names.

If Tiny Mite rubs the back of the photograph, she can see further into the twins' future to the seven plagues: after grasshoppers, drought, hail, tornadoes, floods, anthrax, bankruptcy.

There's the bank manager circling the farmhouse in a dusty bowler muttering about his hands being tied, but pointing to a fixable wheel here, an outdated but sellable kettle there. He motions toward the coyote pup the twins washed out of a den for a pet and tells the auctioneer to try and get something for it.

The day after the bank manager's visit, the twins, their brothers and parents hitch a ride from the lost farm to the nearest town, Big Bend, South Dakota, with a neighbor hoping to sell a grandfather clock. For fifteen miles, the twins lie alongside the clock in the flatbed of the truck, their ears against its smooth wooden sides. The neighbor fetches a tenth of what the clock is worth, but gives their father some coins when he sees the boarding house they're moving into on the muddy side of the river bend. Though their mother finds mouse droppings in the holes in the mattresses, the bathroom down the hall has plumbing. Accustomed to breaking a layer of ice off the water bucket winter mornings, the twins are so enthralled with separate hot and cold faucets they make a game of seeing who can hold her finger under the scalding water the longest. On the third day, however, the landlady catches them and twists their earlobes until they burn. "And speak English!" she snaps, letting them go.

On the sixth day, the twins' father breaks his back under a runaway piano working for a moving company. Prostrate on a canvas stretcher, he shakes his fist at the sky. "Name's Adelbert, not Job!"

On the seventh day (though her story is one hundred percent true, Tiny Mite has used biblical wording to make her report truer and avoid missing recess), four men in denim overalls carry Adelbert to a tent revival where the collection is taken with milk pails. Though he doesn't rise like the cripple lowered through a roof to Jesus, the Lord touches Adelbert's heart, and his earthly reward for being born again is to meet a man who teaches him to fix tools, clocks, watches, and eventually, radios and small appliances.

If Tiny Mite rubs the back of the photograph, holds her breath and walks in a circle, she can see the thirteen-year-old twins pacing through a foggy dusk, paid to wear sandwich boards that read: Dance At The Ark Tonight. At sunrise they'll jump from the river's pink granite bank and dive for bottles thrown over the dancehall's balcony the night before. Eight bottles in each bony set of arms, they'll run to Camelback Bridge, and in the shade of its rusty girders, sell them to a bootlegger named Clete Blubbers. One day he'll be short of change and give them a brand new deck of cards.

The day after that Adelbert will find the cards, call them the devil's bible and throw them into the fire. Good thing he doesn't know about the Ark or the bottles—the twins' mother covers for them because God let the bank take their farm and now she cleans too many houses, boils too many sheets and darns too many clothes to concern herself with the devil.

If Tiny Mite rubs the back of the photograph, spells *ABRA-CADABRA* backward and hops on one foot, she can see the nineteen-year-old twins at the county fair. There's Luvie behind a kissing booth, bra stuffed with cotton wadding, hugging a coffee can full of quarters. She calls to a ginger boy clutching the teddy bear he just won in the ring toss. And there's Bee among the passersby, who, while accepting a donation to the missionary fund, notices a blond boy in a tweed cap doing card tricks at the center of a giggling circle of girls.

When Luvie hooks the ginger boy's eyes, he drops the bear.
When the blond boy notices Bee watching, he drops his cards.
The ginger boy blushes as he picks up the hay-covered bear.
The blond boy grins as he gathers the cards into their holder.
Both boys dig in their pockets for a quarter.

And this is Tiny Mite's favorite part of the story—the four-year-old twins in the photograph don't know they're going to fall in love with these boys and dance with them at the Ark.

The ginger boy sets his prize on the edge of Luvie's kissing booth. "You in need of a cuddly bear?"

The blond boy points at the missionary fund can in Bee's hands. "You got enough in there to buy us some burgers?"

Here's another thing Tiny Mite knows: both boys will whoop Hitler's ass. One will become a pilot and earn a Purple Heart in the Battle of the Bulge. The other will serve as a gunner on Omaha Beach. Before they enlist, both boys will marry their sweethearts under a blooming crab apple tree. The ginger boy will give Luvie a handwritten book of poetry. The blond boy will give Bee the deed to her family's lost farm.

Bee, the older twin by three minutes, will become Tiny Mite's grandmother and spank her once for taking this very picture out of the family album, twice for claiming sperm ride motorcycles and three times for saying she got the information from the Book of Revelation.

Luvie, the younger twin, will become Tiny Mite's great aunt and they will all live together in the farmhouse. While passing the butter to her sister, she'll say the Goddamned Idiot is so lazy, his sperm may have needed the extra boost of a Harley to get Velvet pregnant.

"Please," Bee will squeeze her temples. "I don't have the wherewithal to think about Blankety Blank right now."

"Fine." Luvie will smash her cigarette. "I didn't say a goddamn thing."

Goddamn. It's Tiny Mite's favorite word. Though "Blankety Blank" has the pleasing rhythm of a one-legged war hero hopping to the fridge for a beer, "goddamn" sounds like a two-chop ninja move. The one time Tiny Mite uttered it Bee washed her mouth out with soap seven times and made her apologize to God seventy-seven times because seven is His favorite number. Luvie, however, gets to say, "goddamn" whenever she wants, and smoke, too. Tiny Mite's not sure if that's because Luvie brings home the bacon selling make-up and being secretary to Randall P. Henniker, Jr., Attorney at Law, or because forty-three years later, Bee still feels guilty her G.I. came home and Luvie's didn't.

*Velvet lifts the heavy black handset.* Can she make a collect call from a pay phone? How does she dial? What if no one answers? She hadn't imagined that possibility. This late, the farmhouse empty. Through the pay phone's shattered glass door, she can see the driver of the green car in the motel's reception area accepting a key from the bouffant-haired clerk.

No dial tone. Velvet rattles the receiver's cold metal tongue. Presses 0. "Operator?"

The driver crosses the parking lot toward the phone booth, throwing and catching the key, the neon sign sprinkling his hands and face with red freckles. Suspicious of the spring in his step, she resolves to call home and sit up all night in the reception area with the clerk. Help out while she waits. Dust brochures. Water plants. Greet customers. One night, at most another day. Luvie will come. Or Jiggs. It makes her smile, realizing how happy she'd actually be to see him.

Velvet presses the 0 harder. "Operator?"

"Operator. How may I direct your call?"

Velvet's relief is overtaken by shame. What will she say to Bee? How will she explain herself? Has she waited too long to call? What if Tiny Mite isn't there? What will she do if she isn't? But she must be, which will mean she's told her story first. Tiny Mite's stories are always big and this one has had an entire day to grow unchecked. What if Luvie and Jiggs refuse to help? What if Bee won't speak to her?

"Yes, operator. I need to—" Again that cry in her head: Mimi! Wait!

What has she done? Velvet pictures chocolate-smeared lips and marker-stained hands, the farmhouse empty, everyone at the police station or out looking. That cashier from the Qwik Stop shaking his head, wringing his hands, giving his statement. A social worker at the farm, pursing lips, taking notes, making threats. Everyone in Big Bend knowing, talking, judging. For once in her life Tiny Mite doesn't have to exaggerate. What if children aren't resilient? What if they don't forgive? What if what she's done—regardless of whether she carries on, or worse, turns back empty-handed—is irreversible?

"Operator. How may I direct your call?"

Velvet looks at her warped, red-hued reflection in the steel telephone. What she has done.

It's bigger than six hundred miles and ten thousand failed interviews.

Bigger than Blankety Blank.

Bigger than Peter.

*Bibbity bobbity, bobbity bibbity, bibbity bobbity boo.*
Tiny Mite runs to keep pace with the gust-propelled thought bubble over her head. *Bibbity bobbity.* Her bare feet slap the smooth cow path winding along the creek. *Bobbity bibbity.* She skids down a muddy bank, counting the witchy finger bridges the trees' late afternoon shadows make across the creek. Fourteen. *Bibbity bobbity boo.* The thought bubble catches on the branch of a dead oak and pops, spilling letters into the water. She watches the letters sink into the gray silt. Except for the Bs and Os. They float.

"Tiny Mite!"

She scales the slimy black roots of the dead oak, pulls herself out of the creek, hurdles a deer lick and weaves through a plum thicket wooly with white blossom.

"*Tiny Mite!*" The wind stretches her name into a 100-foot-long piece of taffy.

She steps on a sharp rock, but keeps running, reaching the shelterbelt of ash, pine, elm, oak and box elder surrounding the west, north and east sides of the farm. There's the farmhouse—white, two stories, four front windows, wraparound porch. There's the tallest tree, her pine, its silhouette a black pagoda against the lavender sky, her headquarters when she's a captive Chinese princess who eats paper to train as a spy.

"Tiny Mite!"

Shimmying under a wire fence, she runs across the brown lawn spotted with slivers of dirty snow. The sheets on the clothesline snap like sails in a marina. She runs through them faster, so fast, she's walking on water. There's Jesus ahead. He trips on a wave, but gets up. Now they're neck and neck. He starts to gain on her, but when he's nearly a pace ahead, falls behind to tell some fishermen a parable. Sucker! She's the winner by a mile.

"Tiny Mite!"

Just the birdhouses to go. The White House, Sphinx, Empire State Building, Monticello float high above her. The Taj Mahal, Eiffel Tower and Corn Palace, too. The second hand has fallen off Big Ben and the Statue of Liberty is freckled with bird poo, but the miniatures of the farmhouse and barn glisten with fresh white paint.

"Tiny *Mite!*"

Pink, yellow, purple and white tulips stand like beauty contestants along the concrete steps. Jumping over the crumbled middle step, Tiny Mite opens and shuts the door, the back of which bears a ladder of pencil lines, the highest, in Velvet's writing: *Tiny Mite, 8*.

A wall of double-hung windows runs along the right side of the long, narrow kitchen, cabinets on one side and a butcher's block, four-legged white porcelain sink and green pie safe on the other. Red canisters on the counter descend in size from large to small: *Flour, Sugar, Coffee, Tea*. The animals in her grandmother's salt and pepper collection gaze down from their perch on two high shelves. At the far end of the kitchen sits the red vinyl booth Bud bought from the Barrel, the diner where he and Bee dated, when it went out of business in 1962. Twenty-six years later, the vinyl is cracked, the tabletop yellowed and the jukebox as busted as it was the day Bud lugged it home, but Bee has made the nook inviting with an embroidered tablecloth and crocheted seat cushions.

Today the booth is laden with a sewing machine, pincushions and half a dozen fabric rolls. The dress dummies next to it wear two of the gowns Bee has been contracted to make for prom. Behind the headless dummies—Tiny Mite pretends they are Lady Jane Grey and Anne Boleyn—hangs Bee's large-print calendar, freshly turned to May. Luvie and Bee sit opposite each other in the booth, mugs of coffee cupped between their purple-spotted hands, watching a rerun of *I Dream of Jeannie* playing on the small black-and-white television propped on the kitchen counter with an old phone book.

"Finally!" Bee switches off the TV.

Tiny Mite isn't sure how her grandma and great aunt are supposed to be twins when they look nothing alike. Bee is made of marshmallows, has the long white hair of a fairy and smells like the mixture of apple cider and baking soda she uses to save money on deodorant. Luvie says Bee wears calico housedresses, a pink knit cardigan and her old cat eyeglasses because she's the inspiration for *The Far Side* cartoons, but Tiny Mite knows that's a joke, because Bee wears those things so Bud will recognize her when she joins him in heaven.

Luvie is made of matches and crêpe paper. Despite her weakness for Bee's deep-fried zucchini haystacks and marionberry pies, she follows a regime of one hundred leg lifts and sit-ups per morning, the consumption of half a banana and sparkling water before meals and foregoes whipped cream on her Saturday-night chocolate sundae to keep her heart-shaped figure in the pencil skirts and slim-fitting silk blouses she wears to work. Her lips and fingernails are always a matching shade of red and every Saturday afternoon she has her hair dyed and set like Liz Taylor's in *Cat on a Hot Tin Roof*. Her mole is like Liz's, too, only she doesn't draw it on with mascara anymore because she got it tattooed.

Sometimes when Tiny Mite sees Bee and Luvie sitting at a table together, a rhyme appears in a thought bubble over her head:

*Jack Sprat could eat no fat*
*His wife could eat no lean,*
*And so betwixt the two of them,*
*They licked the platter clean.*

Bee often complains about having to finish Luvie's portion in order to not waste because Luvie eats like a monkey, which sometimes leads to an argument about evolution, even though it's complete bull crap.

Bee frowns at her granddaughter, wearing nothing but a pair of underwear pulled onto her head. "Where are your clothes?"

Tiny Mite looks down at her muddy legs trying to remember where she last saw them.

Luvie runs her lacquered fingernails through the hair sticking out of the leg holes of the underwear. "Nice hat."

Tiny Mite touches the cherry-print underpants she stole from her mother's dresser. Early in the day they made a crown of rubies until she pulled her pigtails through the holes to make horns for a Viking helmet.

"Take those off," Bee commands, "before Jiggs sees you indecent."

Tiny Mite doesn't tell Bee that Jiggs not only saw her, but thought her outfit so funny he took a pretend photo of her posing in the creek, after which he, too, became a Viking and they sailed toward Greenland until they got in a fight over the last orange, and terrified to lose his last tooth, Jiggs led a mutiny, obliging

Tiny Mite to slay him as an example to the rest of the crew, but instead of throwing his corpse overboard to electric eels, she showed mercy and laid him to rest in his trailer at the edge of the farm.

Gazing at the magic marker tattoos drawn all over Tiny Mite's arms and legs, Bee recalls her meeting at Tiny Mite's school the previous week, in which Miss Wright threatened to hold Tiny Mite back a grade.

Bee had gripped her purse. "We have a free lawyer."

Miss Wright had sighed. "I'm not saying I'm going to or even *want* to—"

"If Tiny Mite's so dumb, how come she reads the encyclopedia and can name ten varieties of tapeworm?"

"You misunderstand me. I—"

"I don't think so," Bee had snapped, "and now you've got me on the subject, why would Tiny Mite read extra books and do projects that aren't real homework if you were doing your job?"

"I'm not talking about her intelligence or potential, although I do believe they're undermined by her daydreaming and unpredictable insolence. What I'm most concerned about, what I need you to understand *today*, is that Clea is socially immature. School, as you know, serves not only as an arena for learning, but also one of socialization."

Bee waved her hand. "What a bunch of New Age bull crap."

Miss Wright frowned. "The principal informed you Clea tried to perform an exorcism on a schoolmate today?"

Bee beamed. "That's my girl."

"She dragged the boy across the playground and threatened to put him in some kind of box."

"Not him," Bee explained, "the *demon*. Sometimes rowdy ones won't budge, even when you declare their submission to Jesus. When that happens, you return the fire by throwing them in a box wrapped in chains and stuffed with angels reciting the Word."

"I'm sure you'll agree," Miss Wright coughed, "that playing exorcism is hardly an appropriate form of play, especially when the playmate is epileptic. He nearly choked—"

"Spitting and coughing is normal, a sure sign the demon's coming out. I upchucked once. Demon of pride and I'm not ashamed to admit it."

Miss Wright reddened. "You don't condone Clea's behavior?"

"It's not her fault the demon keeps manifesting! If the doctors could only see beyond the flesh to the spirit, they'd quit misdiagnosing this poor boy—"

"This isn't the only incident! Last month Clea pinned Benny McCullough under the monkey bars and ripped off his shirt!"

Bee laughed. "They were playing Adam and Eve."

"Your attitude strikes me as disconcertingly, irresponsibly delusional."

Bee slapped Miss Wright on her knee. "Don't get so worked up over a harmless Bible story."

Miss Wright regarded her knee as if Bee had smeared manure on it. "I find it highly inappropriate that you use the Bible to justify Clea's behavior."

Bee's handbag fell off her lap as she stood, spilling its contents. "How dare you speak to me in this manner, Nancy Mae Wright!" Bee watched her can of mace roll under a desk. "I knew you from the day you were born and remember the Easter you wet your sheep costume." Bee crouched on the floor to gather her things. "Your mother and I have chaired the summer picnic committee for as long as I can remember, and now that I think of it"—Bee's eyes narrowed—"she still owes me five dollars for coffee filters!" Bee zipped her purse and marched out of the school.

Staring at Tiny Mite's tattoos, imagining all the scrubbing

she'll have to do to remove them before school tomorrow, not to mention worrying about Velvet's interview and what it means that her daughter still hasn't returned, Bee snatches the underwear from her granddaughter's head. "Come home when you're called! I had to yell ten times ten thousand." She hands Tiny Mite the underwear and a pile of envelopes. "Put on some clothes and gun those buns to the mailbox before I think of a punishment."

Running to the front hall, Tiny Mite puts on the too-big underwear, knotting the side to make them fit, and laces her red tennis shoes. Bee's envelopes in one hand, her camera in the other, she heaves open the door and hopscotches around the holes in the wooden porch steps. The gravel driveway is a mile long and straight as the rows of stubby brown cornstalks that run alongside it. Dust turns her tennis shoes pink. *Click!* Tiny Mite makes the sound in the corner of her mouth as she takes a picture.

Tiny Mite knows a camera doesn't just punch things out of the world like a razor-sharp cookie cutter, but finds them like a magical magnifying glass. The slick, state-of-the-art device in her hands may look like a plain old latest issue Polaroid Impulse, but is more like Captain Kirk's transporter, and in the same way Scotty beams him to alien spaceships and planets, she can teleport, for example, to the lone bare oak on the horizon that looks like the sky's crooked, compressed spine, or time travel, for another example, to Bud's P-47 Thunderbolt, where she and her grandfather, decked out in his green flight suit, fur-lined leather hat, goggles and Mae West life preserver, shout "goddamn!" every time she presses the flashing red DEPLOY button.

Halfway down the driveway, Tiny Mite opens the envelope addressed to the Ready for the Rapture Prophecy Club and removes the ten-dollar bill her grandmother has enclosed as a donation. Luvie has ordered Tiny Mite to intercept all "damn fool waste," reasoning that if the world ends as soon as they say it will, the "idiot club won't be needing the money." Tiny Mite puts the ten-dollar bill in the back of her underwear for safekeeping. Later that evening she'll slip into Luvie's bedroom, and before saying goodnight, slide the confiscated money into the celluloid tray on top of her dresser.

Tiny Mite loves Luvie's bedroom, which smells of perfume, talcum powder and cigarettes, a heavier version of the scent Luvie carries around her like a fur stole. Nine years earlier, a year before Tiny Mite was born, Bud crashed the airplane and Luvie moved back into her childhood home, installing heavy mauve curtains over the drafty windows and hanging flocked wallpaper in a vine-and-peacock pattern. Tonight, Tiny Mite might play Sleeping Beauty on the wrought-iron bed, dance the cha-cha on the trunk at the base of it, or thanks to the rose-print carpet, not skin her knees when she jumps off it pretending to be Evel Knievel.

If Luvie's in a good mood, she'll let Tiny Mite play with the uncapped lipsticks lined on top of the mirrored dressing table like a regiment of redcoats. Though it's tempting to pretend they're saluting the handsome G.I. in the polished silver frame, Tiny Mite knows the picture makes Luvie sad and will be content trying them on. She can list the lipsticks by heart. Holly Berry, Simmering Sunset, Cherry Popsicle, Ravishing Raven, Cinnamon Cider, Crimson Kitten, Radiant Ruby, Valentine Rose.

Walking down the driveway, Tiny Mite occasionally pats her bottom to ensure the ten-dollar bill is still there. She jumps puddles. Sings. Reenacts one of her favorite episodes of *The Waltons*: Bill and Olivia's shivaree.

As Velvet drives down the pitted gravel road toward home she spies Tiny Mite near the mailbox. Moving mouth, tilted head, flapping arms. Talking to herself again. Velvet leans closer to the dirty windshield and squints. Is her daughter wearing nothing but underwear and tennis shoes? How will they talk Miss Wright out of holding Tiny Mite back a grade if she can't curb her strange habits?

Growing up, Nancy Wright persistently tried to join Velvet's lunch table and recess games despite Velvet's clique's loathing of her. Nancy had a poorly sewn cleft lip, homemade clothes, smelled like the oil in which her mother fried all their food, made sucking noises with her retainer and brought carob treats to class parties. Nancy had always been in love with Peter, too. Despite him and Velvet being crowned homecoming king and queen three consecutive years, Nancy made a fool of herself mooning over him. Peter, want these stickers? Peter, want this candy bar? Peter, want the answers to the science test? Peter, Peter, Peter!

If it wasn't bad enough that Nancy won a full ride to the state university, it was downright arrogant of her to turn down a free master's degree to return to Big Bend, a semi-deserted cow town on life support—its cord, now that the wagon trains have ceased and railway diminished, the interstate highway—to lord it over its last five hundred gasping residents. Nancy's mother brags about her daughter's respect for elders, but Velvet knows Nancy's real reason is to continue her useless vigil for Peter. And now she's Tiny Mite's teacher. Velvet could die. Sometimes she really wants to.

"Say, Velvet," Bee had said the night of the parent–teacher conference, "weren't you and Nancy Wright in the same year at school? I'll never forget the fit she had over you having twice as many friendship pins as her. Somehow her mother thought that was our fault."

Twice as many friendship pins. That part of the story was true. Velvet had had lots of friends, but wasn't it just like her mother to "forget" the real reason for Nancy's mother's outrage? Velvet tells herself not to assume the worst in people. Didn't Bee recently go to the trouble of making the ham fancy because

Velvet had half-heartedly pointed out a photograph in *Ladies' Home Journal*? Didn't Bee remove the crystal buttons from her favorite cardigan to make Velvet's cheap one look expensive? And didn't Bee stay up past midnight attaching them for Velvet's interview? And weren't eggs, sausages and apple strudel on the table by six a.m. that morning? "A good start for a big day!" Bee had chirped, her eyes like the glossy buttons of a stuffed animal, the whites too white, the lids pushed too far open, by fear as much as by an obstinate form of hopefulness, which made Velvet feel defeated before she'd even left the house.

Guilt winds its way through Velvet so tightly it recoils, replaced, as it rebounds, by Velvet's long-standing suspicion that Bee conceals Velvet's transgressions not to minimize or forget them, but to keep them fresh. Yes, people exaggerate stories, change a detail here and there, but the ludicrous discrepancies between the truth and Bee's renditions fuel Velvet's theory that they contain hidden messages, guilty sentences Bee knows only Velvet will hear.

Hence Velvet's suspicion that Bee's reminder about the friendship pins contained a hidden agenda. Was Bee suggesting Miss Wright wouldn't be hard on Tiny Mite if Velvet had been nicer when they were in school? Even if she and Nancy had been best friends, Tiny Mite would still be, well, Tiny Mite, and therefore causing trouble. Or perhaps Bee was reminding Velvet that she owed her for handling yet another dreaded parent–teacher conference? There has to be a reason why her mother, who would do a triple backbend to avoid unpleasantness, would mention so disagreeable a memory.

"Mothers forget," Luvie always says. "It's called 'unconditional love.'"

And where, Velvet thinks as she approaches the mailbox, is the unconditional love she needs to override her anger with Tiny

Mite when the secret, hateful truth is that she agrees with Nancy Wright about her daughter's behavior? Where is the energy with which unconditional love suffuses a mother when her nearly naked daughter is kicking the mailbox and singing like she's crazy? And even if she had that energy, how can she realistically curb her daughter's odd habits when Bee eggs her on talking about demons and government conspiracies?

Velvet's gone through it a million times: there's nothing she can do. As much as she longs to assert her independence, she can't afford to get her own place in Big Bend, and even if she could, now that so much time has passed, neither Bee nor Tiny Mite could handle the separation. Velvet would have to make Tiny Mite's meals, do all of her laundry, and every time she has a shift or interview, drive fifteen miles each way to the farm. Velvet leans against the steering wheel and squints again at her daughter. Is that *money* hanging out of her underwear?

Of course she's got that "camera": two checkbook boxes, a tin can and cube of aluminum foil. Its tuna smell and the black smears of paint it leaves on furniture, pillowcases and clothes don't bother Velvet half as much as the "Polaroids" Tiny Mite draws on squares of white cardboard: black plague victims, decapitated Nazis, burning witches, asteroids, tornadoes and their Volga ancestors done in extreme close-up, the edges of everyone's faces out of frame.

It doesn't help that Luvie lets Tiny Mite write lipstick messages on the bathroom mirror or check out any library book she wants, those science books for example, which Luvie should have known were too advanced and led to months of unanswerable questions: How come snowflakes are unique, but not raindrops? How long does it take my voice to reach Mars? Who got to pick the constellations? How come you can't see the Boar? Can't you try again? I'm pointing. Why can't you see it? And the morose

Billie Holiday and Duke Ellington records from *before the war*. Even in her mind, Velvet has to whisper it.

And Jiggs. Where would Velvet even start? Yes, it's tragic he's the sole survivor of the car accident that killed the rest of his family, but does she really have to consider him, as her parents have always insisted, her brother, or at the very least, a cousin, despite him being ten years her senior? Did Jiggs's father fighting in the war make him family? Was Jiggs *really* orphaned at fifteen when his aunt died? She's always suspected that Bud, wanting a son, had butted into other people's business. Even if Jiggs had been blood, was it sensible, when her family could barely afford one hired man, to employ someone mentally disabled?

Carpet samples tied around his body and fastened with bungee cords, Jiggs is King Kong to Tiny Mite's Ann. Bandolier added, Chewbacca to her Leia. His vacuum cleaner topped with a paper crown, Arthur to her Pom. Velvet still hasn't recovered from the sight of him pulling the vacuum by its plastic hose stuttering, "K-k-king B-b-Babar!" It isn't right for a thirty-six-year-old man to be a young girl's playmate, not that Velvet could ever complain, him being disabled.

"S-s-sweetie!" he calls Tiny Mite.

"Salty!" Tiny Mite calls him.

Even more maddening to Velvet are their secrets—made-up words, invisible photographs, a Morse code they do with their fingers—which make second place feel hundreds of miles behind.

Tiny Mite turns, and when she sees Velvet approaching in Bud's splurge—the rusty, white convertible on which he overspent after a land sale—jumps up and down, waving. A thought bubble appears above her head: *Supercalifragilisticexpialidocious*. After several cartwheels on the rocky gravel road, she waves again, her arm movements so exaggerated she could be a mime cleaning a window.

The sight of her daughter's unconditional love causes Velvet to slam on the brakes and cry with her face in her hands. She doesn't feel it and *needs* to, goddamn it, because the cold purple morning Blankety Blank disappeared, she swore she and her unborn baby would love so deeply their bond would compensate for her impulsiveness, uncooled love and losses, so many she gets lost in them: loss of respect, loss of pride, loss of freedom, loss of girlhood, loss of fun, loss of happiness, loss of future, loss of Peter.

Tiny Mite yanks open the rickety passenger door. "Mimi!" She scampers onto the stained red leather seat. "What's wrong?"

*Why can't she call me "Mommy" like a normal girl?*

*She's special, so you need a special name, too.*

Tiny Mite tentatively reaches forward and touches Velvet's arm, as if she were petting a lion.

Velvet's hands spring open like shutters. "I'm so silly, baby!" She forces a smile through her tears. "I was driving along, and you were right in front of me, and it's so darned silly, but I imagined I hit you, by accident, and just imagining you hurt made me cry!"

Tiny Mite's eyes widen. She would love nothing more than to pretend she has a severed leg, but remembering how her mother screamed during *Gone with the Wind*'s amputation scene, takes the story in another direction. "You *did* run me over and I got squished flat as paper, but there wasn't any blood!"

Velvet's hands spring shut and she cries harder than before. What kind of mother tells her child she imagined running over her?

Spurred on by her mother's performance, Tiny Mite continues, "And you cried and cried because I'm your itty bittiest favoritest Tiny Mite!" Tiny Mite relishes her mother's intensified weeping. It's been so long since they played an imaginary game. "But I said, 'Look, Mimi! I can do all kinds of things now that I'm Flat Stanley. I can go under the door without slamming it and I can fold myself into a paper airplane and fly myself to school and fit in your purse or your back pocket or—"

"Or you could be a blank sheet." Velvet sniffles. "Paper's so quiet."

"Sure," Tiny Mite says softly. "I could be paper."

The sight of her daughter's crestfallen face fills Velvet with such contrition and sadness—but not, she bitterly notes, unconditional love—that she gathers Tiny Mite into her arms, and ignoring the ten-dollar bill hanging out of the back of her underwear, whispers, "I'm sorry, baby."

"Don't worry, Mimi. I know it was like *Gone with the Wind*."

The nonsensical comment brings Nancy Wright to mind, and Velvet clutches her daughter as if it'll protect her from the rows of identical desks; compartmentalized plastic lunch trays; stacks of spiral-bound notebooks; sentence diagrams splitting as often as the Mississippi; and hypnotic alteration of alarm clock, teacher's whistle and school bell that trick a girl into thinking one easy year will follow another.

Tiny Mite doesn't flinch when Velvet's gold heart necklace presses too deeply into her cheek, nor does she squirm when her shins threaten to snap. Squeezing hard, she takes a deep breath of her mother's delicious scent: incense, Prell shampoo, chamomile tea, Charlie perfume.

Tiny Mite feels more like an armful of kindling than a child. Velvet preferred her when she was like a loaf of bread, round and warm against her chest, toothless. She misses the light, fine hair that swirled outward from the crown of her infant head like a fingerprint, an enlarged version, Velvet used to imagine, of her own. She spent months comparing that wispy tuft with her own thumbprint, imagining their similarities must mean something significant, but whenever she felt on the verge of enlightenment, it was time to feed or rock or change or rock or wash or feed or bathe or dress or feed or rock.

Velvet nuzzles her nose into Tiny Mite's hair and inhales her dusty Christmas tree smell. "If we don't get a move on, Grandma will think the car broke down again."

Tiny Mite jumps into the passenger seat, and as she peels pinesap from her fingertips, wonders if her mother is going to be on TV. Even with her face red and swollen from crying, Velvet is the most beautiful woman Tiny Mite has ever seen, including Liz Taylor and Farrah Fawcett. The late afternoon light streaming through the dirt-streaked window has turned Velvet's feathered hair from buttery blond to gold. "Like how Rumpelstiltskin did it!"

Velvet's body tenses. "You're not making sense."

Tiny Mite drops her head. "Sorry."

Doused with fresh guilt, Velvet adds, "It's OK, sweetheart. Try and remember what we said about sentences: the words have to be linked to each other like the cars of a train. You know, discursal."

Tiny Mite cringes hearing her mother misuse Miss Wright's term "discursive," one of those big words she figured you can't say until sixth grade. After Velvet's mistake, Tiny Mite recalculates her estimate to university, where Velvet didn't go because she didn't take advantage of her gumption.

Velvet draws a fortifying breath. "How about you and I have a sleepover?"

Tiny Mite feels nervous excitement. An overnight in her mother's room, which includes playing games on the mirrored Indian bedspread, tying their hair into rag rolls, hiding in the closet to eat ice cream and listening to Blondie and Foreigner, is rare and reserved for either celebrations or disappointments requiring stiff upper lips. The invitation, therefore, sheds no light on whether or not Velvet will be on TV, which means the overnight could be fun or scary. "OK," Tiny Mite says.

Velvet feels hurt by the lackluster response. Why does she bother? She'd rather skip dinner and go straight to bed. Wanting to fall asleep with some assurance that no matter how many interviews she fails she can still call herself a good mother, Velvet rallies. "Come on, Tiny Mite, it'll be fun. I can show you where you kicked when you were in my tummy or we can count your fingers and toes to make sure they're all there. We can play Chutes and Ladders."

Her mother isn't going to be on TV. Mimi always wants to play baby games when she's sad. "Sorry," Tiny Mite says, "but I disobeyed Grandma and got grounded to my room with no escape."

Another lie, Velvet thinks, but thankful her daughter sensed her need for space reaches into her suede shoulder bag and pulls out a coffee nip. "Here you go, sweetie."

Sucking her favorite candy, Tiny Mite looks into her mother's purse and studies the romance novel inside. It's thicker than the Bible. Tiny Mite would like to know if that's a sin, but can't ask Bee on account of Velvet's borrowed novels being a special mother–daughter secret. Sperm run loose in these books, and not just on motorcycles, but yachts, airplanes, Ferraris, speedboats, bicycles, hayrides, and even church towers. The stomach of the Navajo man on the cover is sectioned into squares like a Hershey's bar. Tiny Mite would like to get a better look at him, but she's not allowed to touch these books—if the covers are creased or their spines broken, Velvet can't put them back on the shelf, which would get her into big time doo-doo with her boss at the drugstore.

Dread fills Velvet as she drives down the rutted driveway toward the farmhouse her father tried to improve with copious amounts of scalloped trim, twisted spindles and ornamental brackets. How could he blow his inheritance on this place? Even for a wedding present? And how, Velvet wonders, as she parks next to the pink Buick Luvie earned selling Mary Kay cosmetics, could her aunt, who owned her own small, but decent house in Big Bend, stand to move back in?

Bee emerges onto the porch as Velvet and Tiny Mite get out of the car. "How did it go?" she calls, her voice high and tight.

She knows, Velvet thinks, pushing down her skirt. She hates the relentless wind, always reaching up her clothes, wrecking her hair and chilling her to the bone, even in spring. In a normal place, May would be warm and green, but in Big Bend filthy slivers of snow still dot the muddy ground and the only real green comes from the flaking water tower along the train tracks. In four weeks, however, the weather will be so claustrophobically hot and humid, Tiny Mite will fill all of the troughs in the barn with a garden hose, and even Luvie, dressed in one of her elaborate homemade bikinis, will take a dip.

Watching Velvet crush an ice pocket in the driveway with her heel, Bee guesses the TV job's a no-go. Should she hug Velvet, or would that only annoy her more? Bee nods toward the end of the driveway. "The car stalled again?"

Velvet kicks a rock. "Don't worry. It only took a second try to start up again."

A thought bubble appears over Tiny Mite's head: *Was that a lie or is Mimi still pretending there was an accident at the mailbox, and therefore, storytelling?* If only Miss Wright could see how hard it is to tell. It's almost as confusing as trying to remember whether God wants her to be in the world, but not of the world, or of the world, but not in it.

Bee grasps one of the pineapple-shaped ornaments Bud affixed to the ends of the railing. "If you say it's fixed."

Tiny Mite notices a crystal button missing from Velvet's cardigan, and worried Bee and Mimi will fight about it, scampers up the steps toward Bee to attempt a diversion. "What's for dinner, Grandma?"

"Spaghetti. I told you to put on clothes. Aren't you freezing to death?"

"No," Tiny Mite lies, trying to gather warmth from her grandmother's apron.

Velvet sighs. "It was down to me and another girl, but I put a snowflake on Tampa and a sunshine over Seattle."

Bee shakes her head. "Tiny Mite claims the Sahara was once an ocean, and if that's true, it could certainly snow in Florida."

Another gust ruffles Velvet's hair. Swatting it out of her face, she adds, "The other girl had half a college degree." If they could just get out of this wind, maybe she could think straight.

"She probably had a steak dinner with the station manager."

Velvet hates it when Bee refers to sex as a "steak dinner," but touched by her mother's protectiveness, lets the comment slide. "The girl had a demo tape and Liz Claiborne suit."

"Her parents must know the station manager." Bee feels encouraged by Velvet's nod. She wants to say, there's nothing wrong with you, it's they who lack the ears to hear and the eyes to see, but says, "It's who you know in this world. If your father had said 'yes' to that Hollywood agent, you could have had whatever TV part you wanted."

Velvet frowns. Bud often told her about the agent who spotted him having his boots shined on his way home from the war. He was in such a hurry to get home to Bee that he turned down the audition flat. Velvet always sensed regret in his retelling and often imagined how different their life could have been in Hollywood. Her mother has never left the state. One time Velvet got up before sunrise, said she was going to a job interview and drove a mile past the state border just so she wouldn't have to say the same about herself. "You should have let him."

Bee wobbles. "I was only making a point about how things work in the seen world." She'd like to inform Velvet that Bud never asked her whether she'd like to go to California, and given the chance, would have said "yes" to wearing kaftans and sipping punch by a pool all winter, but Velvet also criticizes Bee for being too submissive, so for the sake of peace, says nothing.

"You really should have let him, mother."

A thought bubble appears over Tiny Mite's head: *Uh-oh!* "I need my suns back!" she shouts, referring to the magnet-backed weather patterns she made out of construction paper so her mother could practice being a weather girl on the refrigerator.

Velvet's hands shoot to her ears. "I left them at the station!"

Tiny Mite makes her fiercest angry face. "How could you?"

"I didn't think you wanted them back."

"What?" Tiny Mite whines.

Bee covers her ears. "Honey, you can make more. Anyone hungry?" She wishes everyone would just go inside and eat.

"I can't make more!" Tiny Mite rips herself from Bee's apron. "I'm out of glitter!" She points at her mother. "I used it all for you!"

"Baby," Velvet pleads. "I'll buy you more."

"Even if you did," Tiny Mite cries, "they wouldn't be the same!" She's lost in her story now, unsure how much she cares about the suns, clouds, tornadoes and lightning bolts. Real tears make it confusing. "I made them just for you," she bawls, "and you left them in the hands of people who are *evil*!" Tiny Mite throws herself onto the gravel driveway and kicks and screams.

Rolling her eyes, Velvet starts up the steps.

Bee blocks her. "Aren't you going to discipline your child?"

Bee resents all the spankings Velvet leaves to her when a grand-mother's got a right to being the softie.

Velvet sighs. "You know it's useless, mother. Let her tire out."

Luvie appears in the doorway in her bathrobe. "What the hell's going on out here?"

As she slips into the house, Velvet nods toward Tiny Mite. "Tantrum." That actually couldn't have come at a better time. All the way home she's dreaded giving Bee the bad news and enduring a fattening dinner peppered with uplifting proverbs and Psalms. Now the ordeal is over. "I'm going to bed."

Another failed interview, Luvie thinks, watching Velvet trudge up the stairs. Luvie would feel sorry for her, well, more sorry, if her niece weren't so masochistic. Luvie pats the pocket of her robe, reassured by the palm-sized rectangle of her flask.

Bawling, Tiny Mite pounds the ground, pebbles stuck to her red fists. "I want my suns!"

Bee leans down to her and whispers, "Please don't make me punish you. We can get more glitter tomorrow."

Tiny Mite screams.

Bee grasps her ear. "I've already spanked you today and grounding is pointless, so if you don't stop it this minute you're looking at no spaghetti." A threat Bee hopes will work, spaghetti being Tiny Mite's favorite dinner. "Please don't make me take away your dinner, sweetheart. You're too darned skinny."

Tiny Mite wants to get off the ground. She wants to stop crying, wear clothes and eat spaghetti, but her eyes keep crying and mouth keeps screaming and she doesn't know how to make them stop. She accidentally kicks Bee's shin.

"That's it!" Bee winces. "Now I can't give you dinner even if I want to because I've laid down the law!" She hobbles up the steps, and as she passes Luvie at the threshold, barks, "Someone's got to be firm in this house!"

Luvie pats her shoulder. "No one's blaming you, Bee." She pulls Tiny Mite's coat off the hook by the door and goes down the steps. "What's gotten into you?" she whispers, wrapping the coat around Tiny Mite's shoulders. "They didn't fight *that* bad, did they?"

Tiny Mite sobs, lost.

Sighing, Luvie glances back at the farmhouse, a goddamned gingerbread house thanks to Bud. Luvie would gather Tiny Mite into her arms if it wouldn't undermine Bee's punishment, so she lifts her off the ground and taps her bottom. "Up to my room and under my quilt. I'll save you something, and if you don't break anything, you can pick a Johnny Cash."

A red, neon sign looms: Starlight Motel. Just as Velvet
guessed: the green car pulls into its empty parking lot. One-story,
L-shaped, brick building. Rows of dark windows and doors.
In the glass reception area, a lone clerk sitting on a stool, the
scalloped outline of her bouffant hair a black silhouette against
the TV's flickering blue light.

Bee, Bee, Bee. An ache Velvet hasn't felt in years: wanting her
mother. Maybe she should abandon her plan? Quit before she's
done more damage? Apologize? Beg for help? The darkness, her
exhaustion, the sensation of the car decelerating—all deflate her
will. And yet isn't this why she waited until now to call? Because
how can Bee help her from six hundred miles away? She can't
turn back. Maybe the motel's clerk will call for her? Deliver the
message she'd struggle to keep simple—I'm all right, sorry for the
chaos, everything's under control—because Velvet couldn't do
it now. All she wants to know: Where is Tiny Mite? Is she OK?
Does she hate me?

The green car breaks in front of the motel's reception area,
and before the driver has shifted the gear to park, Velvet is out,
running. Bee, Bee, Bee. Spray of red molten stardust, the parking

*lot slick with sleet. Velvet shivers, her untied black shoelaces trailing through blackened slush. There, underneath the Starlight Motel's flashing sign, a phone booth. She runs inside and shuts its smashed glass door. Light broken. Trash underfoot. Smell of urine. Outside the bubble of the green car, in the dark, in the cold with no coat, in a town she can't name, her plan looks absurd. Bee, Bee, Bee. Her mother may be six hundred miles away, but she'll know what to do.*

*Velvet scoops coins from the bottom of her purse. How much is a long distance call? How should she dial? She shoves coins into the cold slot. They fall onto the floor, too dark to see where. Hand back in the bag, searching. Through the door's shattered glass, Velvet can see the driver in the motel's reception area stroking his gold tie, chatting up the clerk. Requesting two rooms? Or one? Though numb, her fingers can still feel it: his touching hers in the popcorn bag between the front seats.*

*Crouching, waiting for a pulse of red, neon light, Velvet sees something dark—gum?—jammed into the coin slot. Standing, she sees the driver hand the clerk a platinum credit card. Card that is not his. Suit that is not his. Car that is not his. Bee, Bee, Bee. No more coins. She'll call collect. Good plan. Everything is going to be OK. Deep breath. Velvet lifts the heavy black handset.*

# Velvet lies on her bed staring at the mobile overhead:

mosaic diamonds made from broken soda bottle glass in eleventh grade home economics. *Golden Girls* laugh tracks from the living room below clash with the Johnny Cash playing next door. Velvet reaches for the radio on her bedside table and tunes it to the student radio station at State. Though faint, its music is far preferable to the local options: country, gospel, weather. Velvet puts on her headphones and closes her eyes. It's a form of meditation, separating the music from the static.

Whenever she fails an interview, Velvet gazes at the mobile, trying to visualize the lost opportunity turning out of view. Done. Gone. Next. Despite her positive intent, her mind turns to Blankety Blank. Where is he? How does he live with himself? How can he get away with this abandonment? How can she find him? Make him pay?

She's written every T. Wayne in the Modesto phone book and gotten no reply. She's written every Wayne in his hometown of Peoria and gotten no reply. She's written every Canadian tree-planting company she can find in hope of receiving a lead. She's written every national park in the State of Washington with the same goal and gotten the same result: nothing. Does Blankety Blank even live in Modesto? Was everything he said a lie? Not until he left did she realize how little she knew about him. They always shot off into the future. Where they would go. What they would do.

The one lead she has yet to explore: the Sturgis motorcycle rally. He had just come from it when they met, and despite his recounting of gang fights, bar riots and stunt accidents, intended to make it a tradition. Bandidos. Outlaws. Mongols. Warlocks. Vagos. Pagans. Iron Horsemen. Free Souls. Sons of Silence. Highwaymen. Hell's Angels. He thought the motorcycle gangs sounded like cool bands. One, he told her with awe, poured gasoline onto the road, lit it on fire and took turns driving through the flames. Another, he laughed, blew up a rival's outhouse with a pipe bomb.

Every August since, Velvet has gone crazy at the possibility of Blankety Blank being less than a hundred miles away and never checking on his child's well-being or sending support. The times she has nearly attended the rally and defied Bee—armed with newspaper clippings about strippers, topless biker chicks, nude beauty contests and campground orgies—Velvet felt half-relieved to stay home, reassuring herself with a job she'd just gotten or intended to pursue. But with the trail gone cold? And her opportunities in Big Bend spent? Could she ever possess that level of gumption?

*Swell of two white circles, the green car filling to*
*bursting. Five hundred and eighty-eight miles from Big Bend,*
*the full-beam headlights of oncoming traffic illuminating tiny*
*fingerprints Velvet failed to scrub off the lower left-hand corner*
*of the passenger window.*

Think of it as a vacation.

*What kind of mother would say that? Actually use the word*
*"vacation?"*

Nice man. Good girl.

*So he seemed nice, but was he? Knowing him for less than half*
*an hour, how could she possibly know? How could she have*
*trusted him? Made an assumption based on anything Jule—thief,*
*gambler, pothead—would do? And if he wasn't nice? Would*
*Tiny Mite know not to be good girl? Not to trust? Not to obey?*
*Not to be quiet? When her own mother told her to do the exact*
*opposite?*

*Another set of headlights expands in the windshield, two inter-*
*rogation bulbs demanding: Where is your daughter?*

*Not* here *here.*

*All day long she's pictured a call to the farm. Tiny Mite collected. Some upset and concern, but dinner as usual, bath as usual, TV as usual, but what if she's wrong?*

*Not* here *here.*

*Worried and ashamed, Velvet covers her face, relieved when the headlights pass, releasing her to darkness. Alongside the road, rows of ghostly unlit billboards. Fast food signs. An implement center. A self-storage facility. A town.*

*Glancing over at the driver, Velvet notices him scanning the signs, even though the gas gauge is three-quarters full. He wouldn't stop for the night? She hadn't imagined that possibility. Even this late, the green car stopping. The driver pats his yawn like a cartoon character. Is he her punishment? Maybe he doesn't know she knows she doesn't owe him? Maybe he doesn't know she's not a good girl? He certainly doesn't know she's already made those mistakes.*

*The green car, for her nerves to remain steady, for her plan to remain steady, must keep moving. She tells herself to remain calm. So they stop for food. She calls home, delivers the short explanation she's rehearsed all day, drinks three cups of coffee and offers to drive the rest of the way.*

*A red, neon sign looms:* Starlight Motel.

# Bee was true to her word: no spaghetti for Tiny Mite.

Though Luvie smuggled a banana and two pieces of thrice-buttered bread to her room, where she and Tiny Mite applied honey masks to tighten their jowls and listened to *A Thing Called Love*, it wasn't enough, and now Tiny Mite tosses and turns in her attic room, too hungry to sleep.

Tiny Mite gets out of bed, tiptoes over piles of toys, tablets, crayons and clothes and climbs down the ladder to the landing, where she sits on the top step and assesses the doors on the second floor. Bee's light has been out for hours, so that one's safe. Despite the flickering blue-gray light and Johnny Carson laugh tracks seeping out from under Luvie's door, Tiny Mite can hear her great aunt snoring. A dim light shines under Velvet's door, most likely from the flashlight her mother uses to read romance novels under a sheet. Tiny Mite waits what feels like the second coming, rapture, end times and eternity for it to extinguish before beginning her descent to the kitchen.

Tiny Mite hopscotches down the bare wooden staircase. One false move and she'll be a goner—even if Bee were in a coma brought on by a wrecking ball she'd hear the stairs creak and awaken. When Tiny Mite safely reaches the front hall, the moonlight shining through the window in the door allows her to round the corner into the kitchen without knocking over any of the muddy boots or shoes lined up on newspapers.

Though her stomach rumbles as she edges along the counter, sink and stove, Tiny Mite wouldn't dream of stopping in the kitchen—Bee monitors the supplies of her refrigerator and pantry with the same degree of vigilance Luvie employs for age spots and wrinkles. Gingerly lifting the can opener from its hook near the stove, Tiny Mite tiptoes to the booth and discovers, to her delight, the basement door open wide. Now she won't have to wait for an outside noise to cover its mewling hinge.

Three steps into the basement and dinner's wet smells of boiling pasta and hamburger grease are overcome by dry ones: dust, canvas, washing powder, dryer lint, sawdust. At the bottom of the staircase, Tiny Mite reaches into the hole under the last step where she keeps a flashlight and shines it across a rack of army and hunting coats, a deep freeze, bags of potting soil and the sawdust-filled crates where Bee buries carrots, beets and potatoes alongside pieces of tin to prevent them from growing eyes.

Running the flashlight over the first set of metal shelves, Tiny Mite gazes longingly at the jars of corn, onions, beans, pickles, zucchinis, tomatoes, peaches, apples and cherries Bee canned the previous summer and fall. Alongside them sit crocks of honey and homemade preserves, boxes of cornflakes and pancake mix, tins of pork and beef and crates of Coca-Cola. Tiny Mite recognizes a case of potato chips that were on sale at the Dale Mercantile the month before, but wouldn't dream of touching this food, Bee's second pantry.

Tiny Mite moves deeper into the basement along twenty shelves arranged perpendicular to the wall and filled with tins of tuna, beef, Spam and sardines; industrial-sized jars of sauerkraut, horseradish, preserved onions, lemons and pickle; and hundreds of boxed foods practically unrecognizable as they're coated with spider webs and thick dust.

One set of shelves is crammed with burlap bags full of flour, sugar, salt, cornmeal, coffee, soybeans, kidney beans, lentils and oats. Another is devoted entirely to Campbell's soup. Though the labels are nearly unreadable, Tiny Mite can estimate the location of most soups because Bee alphabetizes them. Not in the mood for cold soup, she continues to the area where Bee keeps Velveeta cheese and variety-size cereal boxes. She considers a miniature box of Special K and can of V8 before moving onto another shelf full of Spaghetti-Os. She must be careful with her selection—if she takes something from the front of the shelf, Bee might notice, but if she takes it too far from the back, it could be ten years old, as that's how long Bee's been collecting food for the apocalypse. Tiny Mite avoids the oldest food even though Bee insists expiration dates are a conspiracy between the government and capitalists to trick decent people into throwing away perfectly good food so they'll go out and buy more.

Tiny Mite knows she should feel guilty stealing rations they'll need when Christians aren't allowed to buy food, but there's a rhinoceros circling her stomach and if she doesn't feed him, his horn will rip a hole in her gut so large her intestines will fall out and she'll have to drag them around like prison chains. She settles, therefore, on a five-year-old can of Spaghetti-Os and carries it to the gasoline drum where she always sits to consume contraband. She hops onto the drum, and just as she presses the can opener against the can's tin lip, hears the basement door close.

Tiny Mite flicks off her flashlight. Darkness pounces on her, a black tomcat. With each downward step on the rickety stairs—

*stomp, stump, dump, plunk, plod, clod, clomp*—a bomb explodes in her heart because she can only imagine zombies, murderers, perverts or demons walking like that. A thought bubble appears over her head: *The Lord is my shepherd; I shall not want. He makes me lie down in green pastures; He leads me beside the still waters. Yea, though I walk through the valley of the shadow of death, I will fear no evil.* Now Tiny Mite understands why Benny's family prays pinching those pill-sized beads—when you're pee-in-your-pants scared, it helps to hold onto something.

The steps change from *stomp, stump, dump, plunk, plod, clod, clomp* to a hissing scrape against the basement's concrete floor, the claws of a demon limping toward her. Imagining its pus-leaking scales, she regrets every time she sat in church hoping she'd see one squeezing out of a repentant's mouth. God must have mistaken her curiosity for a prayer. Silly! As if she'd want to meet a demon *all by herself*, in the basement of all places, when Bee, the congregation's fiercest prayer warrior, is upstairs fast asleep!

The demon stops several shelves from Tiny Mite and grunts as it slides one of the burlap bags against the wall. Tiny Mite wonders if he, too, is hungry. She's not aware of any verses saying demons eat people, but just in case he hasn't read the Bible and tries, raises her can opener for a fight. Papery rustling is followed by a tiny metallic clack. More silence. Why isn't the demon slobbering? Can't he just rip the bag of chips open and get his munching and belching over with? Then Tiny Mite remembers demons have infrared vision. The demon has spied her through the shelves and paused in order to debate whether he should eat her limbs first and heart last, or go for it and rip her heart out of her chest to enjoy it at its still-beating freshest. When she expects to faint for real, the demon surprises her.

He whimpers.

It's not a wimpy whimper, but a single, focused note twisting like a pencil in a sharpener, like that awful sound that comes out of the radio after the man with the monotone voice says, "This is a message from the emergency broadcast system. This is a test, only a test." Just when Tiny Mite thinks she'd rather be eaten alive than endure the sound another second, it stops as abruptly as a pheasant shot out of the sky.

The demon makes a greedy seesaw sucking sound, not unlike times when a mucus glob is caught in Tiny Mite's throat and she's forgotten her hankie. In and out, the demon slobbers, shudders, slobbers, then hiccups, gasps, and hiccups again, which if Tiny Mite really thinks about it, sounds like sobbing. She squints at the darkness as if it'll clarify the sound. The demon *is* crying. Tiny Mite feels sorry for it. Maybe it limped because it's hurt? She imagines fixing its talon and taking care of it. Keeping it under her pine tree. Imagine Bee's face if she found Tiny Mite's pet demon!

The demon stops crying and lights a match. In the flame's corona, Tiny Mite sees satin lips pleated around a cigarette and two dimples, each a puddle of orange light. Tiny Mite gulps. What could make her mother cry like that? Even Scarlet O'Hara doesn't cry like that. The tip of the cigarette hovers in the darkness like a firefly. Should Tiny Mite go to Velvet? Would she be happy to see her, or think Tiny Mite was spying?

Tiny Mite feels a new kind of fear, an unraveling. Instead of smothering her, the darkness retracts, filling the basement and oozing up through the basement door, popping the roof off of the farmhouse and spilling into the cornfields, covering Big Bend, the county, the state, the United States, North America, the Earth, Mars, Jupiter, Saturn, Uranus, Neptune, Pluto, the outer reaches of the Milky Way, the Pegasus galaxy, 2.2 million light years of outer space, Andromeda, 50 million more light years of outer space, all 2,000 galaxies in the Virgo cluster, and further, but that's only as far as Tiny Mite can see.

She remains still long after Velvet has smashed out the cigarette and left the basement, waiting until she's lost the feeling in her bottom to jump down from the metal drum, turn on her flashlight and return the untouched can of Spaghetti-Os to the shelf. Tiny Mite follows her mother's footprints through the dust to a pile of bags stacked against a wall. Behind them she finds a dark opening. On the count of three, she flashes the light into the hole. Deep inside, a circular container. Careful not to stray outside her mother's footprints, Tiny Mite edges closer, but can ascertain nothing more than the fact that the vessel is a large Folgers can.

Tiny Mite's imagination careens through possibilities. Hidden money? Love letters from Blankety Blank? The birth certificate of a twin who died or was separated from Tiny Mite at birth? A secret pet? She aims the flashlight at the lid, but doesn't see any air holes. A thought bubble appears above her head: *Pandora's box!* She'd always imagined it like a bejeweled pirate trunk, but remembering that the Ark of the Covenant was stored in a plain cedar box, decides this must be it. And Velvet was silly enough to open it! Relieved to have an explanation for the terrible sounds and tears, Tiny Mite backs out of the dusty aisle and runs to her room.

*The green car resolute, boring through darkness.*
*Velvet staring at the dirty windshield, picturing the bluebird*
*that flew into the kitchen window when she was seven. Bud*
*took it away, to bury it, she'd thought, but he went to the*
*taxidermist, and on her eighth birthday gave it to her dressed*
*in a red felt hat, gray lederhosen and a staff he'd carved out of*
*wood. Its glass eyes scared her. She had wanted a Barbie van.*
*Crying, Velvet threw the bird onto the floor. Kicking the bird,*
*Bud yelled at Bee for spoiling her.*

*Is that what's wrong with her? That she's not, as she's thought*
*for years, deprived of opportunities or siblings, but spoiled? Enti-*
*tled? Cruel? Can she be the Nelly of Big Bend—now five hundred*
*and seventy-six miles away—if she lacks the ribbons?*

Wait here. Brave girl. Back in a jiffy.

*She's treated her daughter like a fly. Swatted her right out of*
*her face. Velvet catches the driver's stare in his reflection in the*
*windshield and averts her gaze to the muddy floor, where rivulets*
*of melted snow roll back and forth in the rectangular crevices of*

*the rubber mat, causing the untied laces of her pioneer boots to swell like earthworms.*

You made your bed now lie in it.

*How it hurt to read that line in Tiny Mite's writing. And yet she's wrong to blame her. Tiny Mite is a little girl, was littler yet when she wrote it, unaware, Velvet must admit, of the meaning of the words.*

Brave girl.

*She shouldn't have done it. She should have thought of another way, but what? All day long, mile after mile, she's tried to think of an alternative that wouldn't have spoiled everything.*

Good girl.

*All day long, mile after mile, she's told herself that nothing is irreversible. Children are resilient. They easily forgive. For all she knows a drive-in movie and sundaes at the Dairy Queen will suffice. Or an overnight in her room. Playing Clue, Mouse Trap, Yahtzee. Watching* Breakfast at Tiffany's. *Painting each other's nails. Braiding each other's hair.*

Back in a jiffy.

*What if she's not? What if she needs more time? What if forgiveness has a higher price? Maybe she should tell Tiny Mite everything? Yes, she's a little girl, but maybe she's old enough to understand the sea of glass mixed with fire? That the speed of this green car, despite her misgivings about its driver, has given Velvet more momentum and hope than she's felt in years? That what Velvet must do to help herself helps her daughter, too? That they're in this together?*

*Why then this sinking feeling? Fluttering in her heart. Another wave of nausea. The high beams of an oncoming car cause her to squint. It feels unbearable. Swell of two white circles, the green car filling to bursting.*

# From the sanctuary down the hall, Tiny Mite hears the

organ surging and Jiggs singing the opening hymn louder than everyone else. Jiggs is like a can of soda pop. When a song shakes him, he bubbles over the edge and no one stops him even when the song's over and he's singing an extra verse solo a cappella.

From her hiding place in the bathroom, Tiny Mite surveys the sanctuary in her mind's eye—worn red carpet, wooden pews, plastic-zinnia-filled urns either side of the pulpit, and hanging between the tall paned windows, long felt banners onto which Bee has sewn quilted, calico letters:

*Jesus Christ: Lifeguard on Duty*
*Dusty Bibles Lead to Dirty Lives*
*If God is Your Copilot, Swap Seats*
*Free Trip to Heaven: See John 3:16 for Details*

Tiny Mite knows the order of the service by heart: two hymns, announcements, a modern song with acoustic guitar, open mic for prayer requests, another modern song, a prayer, a Bible reading, a sermon, the altar call, the laying of the hands, the final prayer (finally!) and then doughnuts. If she's fast enough, she can snag a bear claw from the back table and eat it en route to the front of the sanctuary in time to get a glazed twist.

The stall door shakes. "Out of order, my foot!" Bee rips the note off the door and bangs again. "Open up, Tiny Mite!"

Tiny Mite pulls her denim skirt over her head, pinches it under her chin to make it a headscarf and cracks open the door. "Sorry, there's no more room in the inn."

Bee rams the door open and yanks down Tiny Mite's skirt. "Tell me what you learned in Sunday school today."

Tiny Mite shrugs. "A girl got made out of a guy's rib?"

"Is that so? Then how come Betty says you excused yourself during the second chapter of Corinthians and never went back?"

Tiny Mite prefers Paul before Ananias peels the scales from his eyes. After that? A thought bubble appears over her head: ZZZZZZZ!!!!! She likes the parting of the Red Sea, Jonah slurped into the guts of a whale, Jesus chucking pigs off a cliff, Daniel trapped in the lion's den, although the latter would have been greatly improved by a lion getting an arm or two because God could have grown Daniel new limbs. One of her biggest pet peeves about God is the extent to which He wastes his power. "The lesson was boring."

Bee snorts. "And you don't think Jesus was bored stiff dying on the cross for you? What's this mess?" She gathers the torn pieces of toilet paper from the floor and stacks them on top of the plastic dispenser. "By my book, they're still usable. In my day we got excited about a two-holer with a Sears catalogue in it. What are you upset about? I haven't even spanked you yet!"

"People can't wipe with my snowflakes!" Tiny Mite is also crushed that she forgot to add "two-holer" to the definition of "privy" in her school report.

Bee grabs Tiny Mite under the arm and yanks her out of the stall, through the side corridor and out to Bud's splurge, throughout which Tiny Mite screams as loud as she can so the next sermon will be about child abuse and her grandmother will have to repent during the altar call.

"Get in," Bee commands after the spanking. Once they're buckled into their seats, she hands Tiny Mite a bear claw, wrapped in an embroidered handkerchief.

"Thanks!" Tiny Mite licks the cinnamon glaze. "You should ground me, Grandma. No one my age gets spanked anymore."

"No one at school will play with you anymore, so if I ground you, it doesn't count as punishment." Bee lifts her left eyebrow. *Subject closed.*

Tiny Mite changes tack. "What does manna taste like?"

Bee squints at the paned windows of the white clapboard church, reminding herself to organize a cleaning committee. "It's cornbread, honey." Pulling out, Bee glares at the red Datsun in the next parking space, its bumper covered in stickers: *Give a hoot, don't pollute!*; *Arms are for hugs*; *Not all who wander are lost*; *CAUTION: Driver is singing*; *Discover wildlife: Be a teacher*. If she weren't in the church parking lot, Bee might give Miss Wright's smug vehicle a good bump. "Let's have a quiet contest the rest of the way home."

Tiny Mite zips her mouth and then gazes out the window, counting the one-story brick-fronted buildings they pass: bank, bakery, post office, five-and-dime, the boarded-up diner, the boarded-up florist, the dress shop that went out of business, its streaked window still stacked with naked mannequins. The crooked neon sign in the window of the Crow Bar says *OPEN*. The veteran's hall has a smashed-in door. Vines grow out the windows of the graffiti-covered boarding house where her grandma and Luvie lived after their family lost the farm.

As Bee drives through Big Bend—gleaming green John Deeres at the Fleet & Farm, daffodils in front of the funeral home—she wonders how Velvet managed to break her toe in the middle of the night. Though disappointed about the weather girl interview, she was fit as a fiddle when she said goodnight, but by morning, limping, the hem of her nightgown caked with dirt.

"I caught it on the corner of my bed," Velvet had sniffled.

An unlikely story, Bee thinks as they pass the funeral home, because in spite of the fact that the Lord had provided a proper bed for Velvet, she prefers to sleep on a mattress on the floor. Why do such strange things befall her daughter, the miracle child God bestowed upon her and Bud after seventeen childless years? Pregnant at forty! The whole town celebrated, sent gifts and placed bets. Nineteen sixty-two had been Bee and Bud's lucky year—a good crop, a daughter, financing for the plane, money for extra hired men, Bud markedly happier crop dusting than farming.

They viewed Velvet's birth as a sign they'd be blessed as Sarah and Abraham, but Bud crashed the plane and Blankety Blank appeared when Velvet was eighteen despite Bee warning her ten times ten thousand never to date boys who drive vans or motorcycles and never to wear provocative clothing—bikinis, high heels, dangly earrings, skirts higher than the bottoms of her knees, anything V-necked, anything tight-fitting, anything black.

Despite her warnings, Bee hadn't really been worried. Since the age of fifteen, Velvet had been in a chaste courtship with Peter Dale, and even if Peter had never existed, hadn't Bee's own marriage been the best argument a mother could provide? Bud had been an exemplary father, affectionate and curious about everything Velvet did. Surely he set a standard that hadn't necessitated articulation? Theirs had been a happy home, filled with Velvet's friends and activities, endless ball games, a sweetheart of whom they approved. And yet over Peter Velvet chose a long-haired hooligan from the land of fruits and nuts.

Handsome as a marble bust, but thick as a stump, Blankety Blank had a mysterious hold over Velvet. It pained Bee to watch her fight for his half-hearted attentions, concede to his trendy opinions and believe his stories about visiting shamanic healers in Brazil or swimming with whale sharks in Indonesia. Bee would overhear them talking on the porch at night, smoking marijuana stolen from Luvie's secret crop in the hot house, discussing how they'd support their baby—dealing Native American artifacts, hosting ayahuasca purges, teaching tantric yoga or starting a carob candy business—when the guy couldn't take a dish to the sink or chop a piece of wood. This was Velvet's idea of a good life?

Luvie has always advised Bee to let Velvet go, let her live her own life. Bee suspects Luvie thinks Bee considers Velvet a failure, which makes Bee so angry she could spit. How could Bee, who quit school after eighth grade, think such a thing about a daughter who made homecoming queen multiple years running? And when that pregnancy test landed on their house like a meteor, who offered to adopt and raise the baby no strings attached if Velvet wanted her life back? (As far as Bee was concerned—and on this point Luvie agreed—a baby with their blood in it could not be put up for adoption.) It was complicated, but women of her generation overcame far worse, in fact women had been putting up with men's indiscretions for centuries, so why couldn't Peter swallow his pride and do the same for Velvet? Wasn't it the thing now, for men and women to be equal?

Bee squeezes the steering wheel as they pass the Lions, Kiwanis, Veterans and Elks club signs at the edge of town. Who, she wants to shout at the top of her lungs, was supportive when Velvet decided to make a go with Blankety Blank? And who, in a spirit of open-mindedness and family values, not only encouraged the ill-matched couple (for the sake of the baby), but let them sleep *in the same room* despite them being unmarried? Out of love for her miracle daughter, Bee never uttered the phrases "unevenly yoked" or "out of wedlock" and Luvie has the nerve to hint Bee might be judgmental? Even if Velvet and Blankety Blank had married and *divorced*, Bee would have forgiven that. (She's forgiven Liz Taylor for five, but as for the two from Richard Burton—she pictures him in his Roman breastplate—grace has its limits.)

Bee sighs as they drive under the interstate and turn onto a county road. There is one thing about Velvet for which Bee feels ashamed: her chronic discontent. When Tiny Mite was a baby, Bee thought the malaise would pass, that the joys of motherhood would bring Velvet back to her gregarious, joyful, fun-loving self. Bee thought Peter might forgive her, and if he didn't, that Velvet would find another beau, but in the passing years Velvet has grown more sullen, turning down dates and opportunities to go out, shirking her chores and holing up in her room, reading or playing solitaire.

Bee blames Velvet's generation's entitlement to an easy life. Life *easy*? Who invented that kind of notion? New Agers? Hippies? Cults? Even more mind-boggling to Bee is the fact that Velvet's heartaches haven't cured her romanticism—the one silver lining that could have resulted from the Blankety Blank debacle! But it's the opposite: Velvet expects more, some form of compensation, her suffering making her doubly owed. The way Bee sees it life is hard as a fact. You look at your family and count your blessings. Now and then you go to the movies, have a pleasant chat with the mailman or enjoy a piece of cherry pie. You do not burden others with your problems. You do not blame God.

Velvet's unhappiness bothers Bee to such a degree that she fantasizes about her daughter having less annoying weaknesses like swearing, smoking, lying, or God help her, laziness, but Velvet works hard, taking every overtime shift she can find and spending her only day off driving forty miles for an interview if she thinks the odds are as high as one in a hundred.

There's something about Velvet's industriousness Bee doesn't trust, something other hardworking people have in spades but Velvet lacks. Bee thinks of tree trunks, fence posts, Adelbert's legs before they withered, the groundedness he retained even in a wheelchair. Velvet's hardworking, but not steady, Bee thinks, which explains why despite her endurance, she gets fired from so many jobs. Her employers eventually realize that while she's a good worker, she'll never care, and though many of the interviews are long shots, the weather girl a perfect example, nine out of ten go bust. Do her interviewers sense Velvet's tireless body lacks, well, spirit?

Bee hates feeling stumped about Velvet. She's always prided herself on intuiting people's inner natures and spiritual gifts, Bud being the best example. She knows full well people considered him a slipshod farmer and disapproved of his carpentry and the time he spent traveling to sell it. She caught their exchanged glances and shaking heads, but unlike them she knew he was a maker, and if cutting wood kept him from having nightmares that drive veterans to drink, who was she to complain? Her only gripe is that he didn't build a tall, spiked fence around the farm, a real crotch-ripper to keep out perverts like Blankety Blank.

Bee prides herself on understanding Luvie. It might shock people that she tolerates her sister's smoking, drinking, card playing, carousing, dancing and even fornicating. Velvet may have lost Peter, but it was her own darned fault. Luvie didn't have the choice, and truth be told, Bee not only respects her sister's ability to have fun despite the many crosses she's had to bear, one of them stepping in as breadwinner, but she also gets a kick out of Luvie's old-style rabble-rousing, reminding her of the fun she and Bud had after the war, when they thought nothing of driving thirty miles on a Tuesday night in search of a dance. How she misses the sway of brass horns, swirl of skirts and thunder of wingtips pounding the floorboards loose.

Bee glances at Tiny Mite, making handprints all over the passenger window. Bee may not understand where her grand-daughter gets her more knuckle-headed notions, that flowers, for example, wink at her, or that it's bad luck to eat the tip of a banana or that her homemade camera bites tunnels through the sky, but Bee appreciates Tiny Mite's contentedness with the farm and positive outlook, her favorite example the smiles that appear in Tiny Mite's "Polaroids" regardless of the subject's expression when she takes the "picture." Bee chuckles remembering the time she found her granddaughter burning a headless Barbie she claimed to be a witch she'd caught performing séances in the barn. She had to punish her for playing with matches, but deep down felt proud at how she zippadeedoodahs her own way down the path of righteousness.

The road steeply inclines to Bee's favorite intersection: the hilltop from which she can see it all—the river, its tree-hugged banks cutting diagonally, with the exception of its deep C-bend, across the great plain, mostly, thanks to the river, fields now, but dotted here and there with pockets of undulating dunes, covered, in May, with a short crop of yellow-green grass. To her right, Big Bend, its grain silos, water tower, steeples and buildings, snug in the C-bend in the river. To her left, the thin black line of the interstate the only break between the expanse of farms and the horizon.

As the white convertible passes the half-light half-flame-illus-trated billboard in the Cripes' westernmost field—*Are you going to heaven? Or HELL?*—Bee thinks, "big picture," cheerful she at least possesses the ability to see world events through God's master plan for the Kingdom. Though she'd never tell a soul, she gets Communism. Darwin? She doesn't work herself into a toot over that nonsense—it may take a couple hundred of years for his theories to be refuted, but it'll happen just like it did for the one about the earth being round. And while she's got plenty of gripes about the government, Bee agrees with its policy to claim UFO sightings as its own military exercises to keep the peace. Approaching Beel Junction, Bee glances toward Dale Mercantile, still standing alongside the defunct Texaco and condemned dancehall, The Ark. Maybe there's a bigger, brighter picture, even here, that only God can see?

Tiny Mite grins as the white convertible turns into Beel Junction. With its pine floors, pressed tin ceilings, old-fashioned counters and floor-to-ceiling wooden shelves filled with candy jars, antique scales, rusty tins and Coca-Cola signs, Dale Mercantile could almost be the General Store at Prairie Town. Its mother-of-pearl inlaid cash register has metal pop-up numbers and punch buttons as big as dimes. If he's in a good mood, Peter Dale lets her crank the grain mill, restack the horseshoes and strum the out-of-tune banjo that hangs alongside the front door.

Bee and Tiny Mite get out of the car. Bee feels determined to shop today. Tiny Mite skips to keep up, stopping, when Bee does, to admire a mixture of old troughs, barrels and milk pails planted with flowers. An old school bell rigged to the door ding-a-lings when they enter the mercantile. Standing behind the counter wearing a hand-knit blue turtleneck, Peter writes in a notebook. Looking up, he issues his usual smile-frown at the sight of them, swiping his wavy auburn hair from his face while slipping the notebook under the counter.

Though most adults speak in code, Bee and Peter's conversation is particularly cryptic, but being a spy, Tiny Mite can crack it.

"Morning Mrs. Baumhauer." *It feels too familiar to call you Bee.*

"Morning." *I refuse to call you Mr. Dale.*

"Was the second sermon as good as the first?" *I attend the early service to avoid your family.*

"The mercy and grace of Jesus Christ is always music to my ears." *You should be more forgiving.*

"His struggles in the desert have always moved me." *I'm only human.*

"Your flowerpots sure look wonderful." *Please don't be defensive. I come in peace.*

"We got a delivery of giant larkspur seeds." *Please hurry up and buy whatever you're going to buy so I can go back to writing poems.*

"You should come out to the farmhouse and cut some of my sweetheart tulips for your mother." *Please visit Velvet.*

"I wouldn't dream of cutting your famous tulips!" *No way in hell.*

"An egg cutter! We'll take one please." *I only shop here to promote Velvet.*

While Peter rings up the ninety-nine-cent sale, Tiny Mite studies the split spine of the faded, green, cloth-covered edition of *Leaves of Grass* lying next to the cash register. While Bee digs in her purse for coins, Peter scans Tiny Mite's face with his soft brown eyes, searching it, she knows, for signs of Blankety Blank. If having the wrong father isn't bad enough, having the right one scrutinize her for disloyalties beyond her control—black hair, square jaw, knobby knees, thick earlobes—is torture. Tiny Mite focuses on the letters on the book. G-R-A-S-S. To her relief, Peter hands her a pixie stick before excusing himself with a lie about needing to attend to something melting in the storage room.

Outside, buckled back into Bud's splurge, Tiny Mite sucks the sugary pink powder from the paper straw. Gripping the steering wheel, Bee stares at the mercantile. Flowerpots. Windmills. Porch swings. Gnomes. It all could have been Velvet's. Turning the ignition, Bee feels overcome with sadness and guilt, realizing that she's always empathized more with Peter, because when Velvet left him, it felt like she left her mother, too.

# AUGUST

# "Have you noticed, Luvie?" Bee stares out the kitchen

window, the furrow in her brow deep enough to sow wheat. "No one whistles anymore. You used to know people—milkman, mailman, garbage man—by their whistle."

Luvie wipes the cloud of soapsuds from her sister's flushed cheek. "Cold drink?"

Though nearly faint from the heat, Bee shakes her head.

Luvie sighs, baffled at how this fast of her sister's makes waiting any easier. "I thought you were allowed liquids?" Luvie reaches into the refrigerator and drinks cold ginger water straight from one of the stoneware jugs she and Bee carted to the field hands when they were kids. Luvie misses the creak of the wagon wheels. The songs that passed the time. The cornstalks high above, kings all, flies flitting from crown to tasseled crown.

"No, I can't even drink." Bee presses a hand against her stomach. "Not with Velvet making my nerves shake like a ten-foot rattler."

As she swallows, Luvie rereads the note affixed to the freezer door with bright plastic letter magnets:

*Dear Mother,*
*Gone to Sturgis. Back in three days. All my shifts are covered.*
*Don't worry* ☺
*Love,*
*Velvet*
*Isaiah 54:4*
*Do not be afraid; you will not suffer shame. Do not fear disgrace; you will not be humiliated.*
*Psalm 27:1*
*The Lord is my light and salvation—whom shall I fear? The Lord is the stronghold of my life—of whom shall I be afraid?*

Of whom should her niece be afraid? Maybe the motorcycle gangs who deal all of the drugs and illegal weapons in the state? Or the bikers who raped two sisters at an interstate rest stop? Or shot the trucker at the Conoco nine exits from Big Bend? Though Luvie shares Bee's fears, she figures the best support she can offer is confidence in Velvet. "She's going to be fine." Luvie returns the jug to the fridge. "She's got more mettle than we give her credit for."

Bee resumes dishwashing. "She's not going to find Blankety Blank at that rally."

"She might." Luvie opens the freezer and lets the cold vapor surround her throbbing head. "And if she does, it'll be a big help."

Bee turns on the faucet and rinses soap from canning jars. "I don't have the foggiest what we'd do without your paychecks, Luvie. Go back to pickle sandwiches, acorn flour and sunflower seed coffee. Remember the cattails we used to eat?" Bee misses the cool of the creek. Moss against bare feet. *Flusssteinen. Angelrute. Wassermelone.* Her grandparents and parents still speaking the native tongue.

Luvie remembers their parents telling them stories about eating cattails. "I wasn't complaining, Bee, and you know this isn't just about money." She joins her sister at the sink.

"What else could it be? Surely Velvet doesn't want to *be* with him again!"

Luvie takes the dish towel from Bee's shoulder and lays it on the countertop. "It's the pride she'll gain trying." Pulling dripping jars from the sink, Luvie sets them in rows on the towel. "Not to mention giving him a piece of her mind."

Bee grabs the newspaper from the counter and slaps a photograph of a woman walking down the main street of Sturgis in a chain-mail bikini. "Will you look at this tart? She's got dollar bills sticking out of her get-up like a stripper—in broad daylight! A Jezebel drunk on the wine of her own adulteries if I ever saw one."

Tiny Mite, who is eavesdropping under the kitchen window, is intrigued to learn she's not the only one who stores money in her underwear.

"Hubba bubba." Luvie pokes the picture as if to test the elasticity of the woman's breasts. "What do you bet those pups are real?"

Bee snorts. "Real double Ds don't pop out of brassieres like prairie dogs." She slaps the window screen with the newspaper. "Tiny Mite! I can hear you spying. Get in here!"

Tiny Mite obeys. The kitchen smells like ammonia.

Luvie frowns at her grandniece. "Why are you wearing all my girdles?"

A thought bubble appears above Tiny Mite's head: *It pleases God thus to act through a simple maid.* Nose freckled with sweat beads, she pats the outermost layer of girdles. "It's armor. I'm Joan of Arc!"

Frowning, Bee fans her face with the newspaper. "There was no Joan on the ark."

Luvie points at the girdles. "Aren't you roasting to death?" She nudges her sister. "Think she's going to get heat stroke?"

Tiny Mite shrugs. "Joan gets burnt at the stake, so I might as well get used to it." Jiggs's fate was far worse—drawn and quartered, tarred and feathered, *then* burnt at the stake—and other than the 7-Up he fizzed from corner of his mouth for dramatic effect, he took it like a true martyr.

Bee nods toward the dining room. "Tiny Mite, take those girdles off and set up the plates. We're eating on our laps tonight."

Which means they're eating on TV trays because the dining room table is covered with the maps, prophecy charts, leaflets, Bible verses and newspaper headlines Bee has brought up from the basement so she and Tiny Mite can organize them into one timeline that will illuminate the exact time and location of Christ's second coming. They will scour maps of Washington D.C. for streets laid out in pentagrams, hexagrams, trapezoids, owls and snakes—symbols beloved not only by Satan, but Freemasons, crack dealers, UFOs and the Shining Path. As they do not have maps of Moscow or Vatican City, their next mission will be to organize by date hundreds of newspaper headlines they've sorted into boxes labeled "earthquakes and volcanoes," "heat waves and blizzards," "tsunamis and hurricanes," "riots and coups," "wars and massacres," "weddings and divorces," "comets and asteroids," "UFOs/NASA/CIA," "serial killers," "crashes ALL" and "nut heads miscellaneous." After taping the headlines in order, Bee and Tiny Mite will look for correlations between dates, locations of world events and the verse numbers of prophetic passages in both the Old and New Testaments.

There's a reason for everything, Bee says, patterns everywhere if one has the courage to see and an ear to hear.

"Hey!" Bee calls from the kitchen. "You're too quiet in there!"

Tiny Mite drops the headline *30 MILLION WATCH LUKE LAURA NUPTIALS* and runs to the hutch to collect plates, silverware and left over Fourth of July napkins. Passing the headless dress dummies, one of them wearing half of Becky Trilling's wedding dress, Tiny Mite carries her haul into the living room next door.

Atop the fireplace's wooden mantlepiece sits the left camel tasseled Oxford Luvie tore off Robert Kennedy when she and some college girls stormed the stage at the state university where he gave a speech. Though this story is one hundred percent true, Miss Wright made her miss recess for making it the theme of her social studies assignment *Government and the Individual Voice.* The prissies got As for their boring essays about community service, voting and writing local congressmen. Victoria Fitch, who calls her Tiny Shite, got extra credit for dressing up as Mrs. Revere. Tiny Mite would take the Kennedy shoe to school as proof, but Luvie has declared the treasure off-limits to all but her, even for dusting, which is why it's caked with dust. Tiny Mite writes *Bee was here* on the side of it and then sets up the TV trays.

"*Fantasy Island?*" Bee suggests, carrying a tray of food into the living room.

"*The Facts of Life!*" Tiny Mite counters.

"Neither," Luvie grumbles, fanning herself with the *TV Guide.*

Tiny Mite in her girdles and Bee and Luvie in their slips watch the evening news eating goulash, beet salad and the sweet watermelon pickles Bee makes from the leftover rinds she brines throughout the summer. Tiny Mite watches Bee—cold face towel on top of her head—whose mood either lightens or darkens sitting on Bud's brown recliner, as it makes her remember something funny he did, like riding his bike through town and stuffing grass clippings in the bras on all the clotheslines, or something sad, like crashing his airplane before paying his bills. If the latter, Tiny Mite will turn off the television, jump onto the coffee table and do a show. She's really good at "Jailhouse Rock," but always adds one of Elvis's gospel songs to keep her act from getting too secular.

Bee digs two ice cubes out of her water glass, slipping one between her breasts and the other into her steaming goulash. "We should have sent Jiggs with her."

Luvie growls.

Tiny Mite nearly hops up to sing, "I'm Popeye the sailor man," but remembering Bee's recent warning about Popeye and Mighty Mouse being cannabis users, tries to think of a joke. Glancing at the empty davenport, a thought bubble appears above her head: *How come I couldn't go to Sturgis with Mimi?* Oops, she said that one out loud.

Bee purses her butter-slick lips. "Sodom and Gomorrah is no place for a child."

"I want to meet him." When neither Bee nor Luvie respond, Tiny Mite kicks the leg of her TV tray. "I want a dad."

Bee lays down her fork. "Most kids only have two parents, but you've got me, Luvie, your mother *and* Jiggs, which makes double what they got, and don't forget Henniker, your free legal counsel."

"Luvie says he's a pervert."

Bee nods. "True, but you never know when you'll get sued for breathing in this country."

"I still want a dad."

Luvie pours whiskey from a flask into her iced cola. "Someday, I'm afraid, you'll learn men are more trouble than they're worth."

"Not *all* men," Bee corrects. "Some of us find our Charlton Heston."

Luvie rolls her eyes remembering the Christmas Bud squeezed her buttock as Bee served eggnog and *elisenlebkuchen* in the same room.

"One year"—Bee rubs the arms of her chair—"it was still snowing in May."

Tiny Mite loves this story.

Frowning, Luvie pours more whiskey into her cola.

"I'd lost hope of spring ever coming, said I'd forgotten the sound of birds. Bud looked up from his newspaper," she smiles, "calm as a cucumber. Said if I didn't hear birdsong by the end of the week, he'd buy me a fur coat."

Luvie holds her glass against her flushed cheek. "Don't even *talk* about fur."

Mopping her brow with her napkin, Bee laughs. "I sure was excited—a fur coat!—but the next Saturday, I found a cage full of canaries in the kitchen."

Canaries, Luvie knows, from the Clayton pet shop owner who owed him a poker debt. Those trips all over the county with those wooden doodads of his? Surely Bee didn't believe Bud sold a thing? Surely she didn't believe all his debts resulted from poor crops? In case she does, Luvie doesn't ask, knowing all too well how many years a person can ride her own love story. Two years of marriage to Snook—even with his long absences in the war—could sustain her for a lifetime.

"Tell another one, Grandma!"

Bee gazes out the window at the daisy-filled flowerpots on the porch. "I'll never forget my wedding bouquet—lilies, roses, carnations, chrysanthemums—as big around as a pizza. On our first anniversary, Bud admitted he'd snuck into the cemetery the night before and stolen them!"

Luvie does what she always does when angry with Bud for his various whimsies and irresponsiblities: works through her list. Bud breaking his wrist pulling Snook out of the harvester before it severed his leg. Bud driving a blindfolded Bee out to the Baumhauer farm to see her wedding present. Bud at Snook's memorial service, not pulling Luvie off the ground, but sinking into the sodden grass alongside her, rocking her, the knees of his naval uniform caked with mud. "Besides more money," Luvie nudges Tiny Mite. "What do you think you're missing not living with the Goddamned Idiot?"

Tiny Mite stares at the ceiling blotched with brown rings from a bathroom pipe that burst before she was born. "Dads doze on the couch with a cap over their face?"

Luvie snorts. "While the women work."

"They make pancakes on Saturdays?"

"Your grandmother makes them any day you want."

Tiny Mite thinks for a moment. "They walk like Frankenstein when you're sad?"

"Because they never grow up!"

"They always have dimes in their pockets?"

Luvie reaches into her purse and tosses Tiny Mite a roll of quarters. "Here, sugar. Spare you the trouble."

*The green car suddenly sinister in the fading light.*
Its *new car smell overwhelming. It's lack of cracks, scuffs and stains, cell-like. Five hundred and ten miles from Big Bend, Velvet counts fence posts to keep calm. Ninety-one, ninety-two, ninety-three, ninety-four, ninety-five. Momentum. Progress. So the driver of the green car isn't who she thought he was. She's still who she thinks she is. He'd have to buy gas anyway, and did she ask for any food? Hasn't the driver said multiple times that she's doing him a favor? Keeping him company, awake, as they drive through the night? She doesn't owe him anything. One hundred, one hundred and one, one hundred and two. One long night—one fencepost at a time—and she'll be there. Half the battle. She can still do it. She has to, if only for Tiny Mite. To make it all worth it. It reassures Velvet. The green car resolute, boring through darkness.*

# Tiny Mite recognizes three reasons why this very moment

she could be a character in the Bible:

1. The sky is red.
2. The clouds are black.
3. When she hears the roaring of a thousand hungry lions she's wearing a loincloth. (First to pretend she's a leper rescued by Judah Ben Hur, then Jesus nailed to the cross.)

*He who has an ear let him hear.* Metallic roaring. She imagines lions with chain-mail lungs and nails for teeth. *Blessed is he who stays awake.* Tiny Mite gasps. Could this be the seven peals of thunder she and Bee have been waiting for? Tiny Mite goes to her attic window and scans the landscape. Two dark clouds snuff the sunset's last purple embers. Lightning strikes the horizon near the lone bare oak. Wind rips ghost tracks through the cornfields between the horizon and farmhouse. *I know your deeds, says the Lord. Wake up!* Tiny Mite tightens her loincloth. Christ is returning on a cloud accompanied by angels numbering a thousand times ten thousand! She will taste hidden manna and receive a crown of life! Jesus will pick her as one of his brides! When she realizes she'll be disqualified for not having an oil lamp, she looks for a suitable alternative until getting distracted by a yellow light at the end of the driveway, which turns out not to be the illuminated throne of heaven, but the headlight of a motorcycle.

Her father, not Jesus.

Score! Tiny Mite runs downstairs to see the handsome hippy and gleaming red Harley Luvic once described as a pinball machine on wheels, but by the time she reaches the front hall, the roaring has stopped and the ensuing silence is frightening—Bee waited night and day for Velvet to return from Sturgis and yet no gravel crunches beneath reunited feet. No hellos are sung between hugs. When she opens the door, Tiny Mite understands.

Velvet has come home on the wrong hog.

Horns protrude from both sides of the driver's black helmet. Studded dog collars ring his neck. The braided tip of his white beard is tied with a bead. Tiny Mite studies his mirrored sunglasses, gold hoop earring, black T-shirt, black jeans, black leather chaps and red leather vest embossed with a tarantula on one side and a skull and crossbones on the other, a breastplate of fire if she ever saw one. His black leather jacket bears enough spiked studs to rival a stegosaurus. A white rabbit's foot, dream catcher and various steel chains mixed with other satanic talismans hang from his belt. The silver head of a bone-handled knife peaks out from his black leather holster. Further details, the spikes at the heels of his boots and the tattoos all over his forearms lead Tiny Mite to the only plausible conclusion—her mother, sitting behind him, an angel in her white crocheted sundress and chambray shirt, is touching a real, live demon.

Its chariot confirms Tiny Mite's assessment: apart from the

naked lady painted on the gas tank, the entire motorcycle is covered in black matte paint. A coyote tail hangs from its bent antennae. Tiny Mite guesses the demon killed and skinned it with his bare teeth. His black leather fingerless gloves creak as he points at her. "I thought you were kidding when you said she was in rags."

Everyone turns and stares at the dishcloths loosely tied around the midsection of Tiny Mite's otherwise naked body. "This is the Turin Shroud," she explains, and when no one responds, exclaims, "I'm Jesus!" She expects the demon to screech at the mention of his archrival, King of Kings, Emmanuel, Holy One, but he laughs, teeth white and straight as a game show host's.

"She's just like you said, Vettie."

The demon lets down the chariot's kickstand. As Velvet dismounts, Bee springs forward. "Thank you very much for delivering Velvet home safe. We hope you have a nice trip back!"

"Mother," Velvet growls.

Bee shoots Velvet a dirty look and then smiles at the demon. "We're out of milk and my granddaughter's got to have it with supper. Would you mind driving back to town for a gallon?"

A thought bubble appears over Tiny Mite's head: *I have apple juice with supper.*

The demon nods. "I just drove 100 miles for your home cooking, mam. A few more will only make it taste better." He winks at Velvet before restarting the engine, which sounds like an explosion.

When the chariot's red light disappears from the end of the driveway, Bee pulls the dish towel from the waist of her apron and whips Velvet.

"It's not the 'steak dinner' you think, mother!"

Bee's lips quiver. "If I hadn't already seen a person like Blankety Blank, I'd have sworn this one was the Antichrist!" Bee intensifies her attack with the towel.

Luvie snatches the towel and throws it on the gravel. "Would you get a grip?" She turns to Velvet. "What on earth are you doing?"

"George wanted me to get home safe!" Velvet holds her hair in a ponytail to keep the wind from blowing it in her face. "He's helping me! He's going to contact him!"

Bee throws her hands into the air. "I don't want you finding him! I never did! I don't want anymore of these, those"—she waves dismissively toward the end of the driveway—"coming within a mile of our property. What if your father were alive to see this?"

*You're not like the others, Bluebird.* Velvet's eyes fill with tears. "Considering what's happened to my life, I don't think this would faze him."

Bee covers her ears. "I don't hear what you're saying in front of your daughter."

"I'm not talking about her! I'm talking about everything else. Why do you always take my wanting more to mean my heart is lacking?"

Bee blinks, stunned by the truth of the statement. God must have given her a child in order for her to share in the excruciating ache of His unconditional love. "All I want is for you to be happy and I can't see how that's going to happen until you stop it with this Blankety Blank nonsense and see that we can make it on our own. Be patient, Velvet. It's almost September. I'll get half a dozen orders for homecoming dresses."

"So that gets us to October." Velvet waves at the roofless milk house, leaning barn and bowed front steps. "How long can we live like this?"

Poor Mimi can't see the glory of the unseen world, Tiny Mite thinks. If only the scales would fall from her eyes.

"Daddy and I knew this farm was a sinking ship."

Some prophet, Luvie thinks. Bought a convertible instead of selling the place when he had the chance.

Bee takes a fortifying breath. "We can do all things through Him who strengthens us."

"We can't eat Bible verses, mother."

"Since when were you so poor you couldn't afford to miss a rabbit because of the price of bullets, or so hungry you ate grass?"

"Just because I didn't—"

"Or so cold you prayed your parents wouldn't freeze to death during the night?"

"I hate your prairie stories!"

Luvie puts her fingers in her mouth and whistles like a referee. "Both of you! Calm the hell down!"

"I don't care what either of you say." Velvet crosses her arms. "I'm going to find him and get what's owed me."

"I say good riddance," Bee continues, "and thank the Lord we can get by without Blankety Blank's child support check."

Velvet stares at her mother, hands to hips, feet apart, a mountain. "So maybe we get by? I want life to get *better*. Why can't you ever understand that?"

Bee throws up her hands. Where is the bottom of Velvet's unhappiness? How can it always feel like they're falling? Like their house is sinking when Jesus is their rock? "If you would only just let go and let God, Velvet. If you just had a little faith—"

Velvet puts her fists against her temples and screams.

Tiny Mite covers her ears. Judging by the fire, smoke and sulfur coming out of everyone's mouths, the demon has possessed them all, and who will break the chains if Bee has also succumbed to Satan's power?

Velvet wipes her eyes with the backs of her hands. "Don't you see, Luvie? She never listens to me."

Luvie might pelt Bee with a hymnal if Velvet's boss, Floyd, hadn't called that morning and threatened to fire Velvet for skipping another shift. What did he mean by "another"? Most days Luvie drops Velvet off right in front of the automatic doors. Luvie has withheld this information from Bee, as well as the fact that her make-up sales are down a third and Henniker has threatened to make her part-time. Furious with herself for supporting her niece when deep down she shared her sister's fear that Velvet would do something stupid, Luvie snaps, "You two are wasting precious time fighting while that hog heads back here. The truth is we could use the Goddamned Idiot's child support, so if this fellow knows where he is, I say we get that information. Don't look at me like that, Bee. He's not moving in."

Bee plants her fists on her hips. "As if I'd allow a *second* demon into my house!"

A thought bubble appears above Tiny Mite's head: *He IS a demon*! Her hunch confirmed, she feels weak, even in her loincloth. Ever since the demon arrived and possessed everybody, the Lord has opened her eyes to the spiritual warfare taking place: the tongues of her family members turned to branding irons, their red-hot eyes shooting each other with lasers. Their words are scary and confusing, like when tongues are spoken at church, only worse because she can understand them. She should be faking a heart attack or setting something on fire, but this fight has no railings and never levels long enough for her to get her bearing.

Bee collapses onto the bottom step. "We're not people who talk like this. Quick, somebody tell a joke."

It's the chance Tiny Mite has been waiting for. "What's the state tree?"

When no one responds, Bee offers, "The maple?"

Tiny Mite throws up her arms. "The telephone pole!" No one

laughs, which would normally be devastating, but a headlight appears in the driveway.

Bee jumps to her feet. "He's not coming in the house!"

Velvet raises a palm. "I promise he'll leave in the morning."

Bee seizes Tiny Mite by the shoulders. "Run as fast as you can to get Jiggs."

Velvet stamps her foot. "Mother, no!"

"I won't feel safe without a man in the house."

Luvie slaps her palms together. "Goddamn it, Bee. Why complicate things even more?"

Bee stoops to face Tiny Mite. "Listen now. Don't get wound up and talk fast at him. Tell him this is an extra dinner, that we're not changing the schedule."

Tiny Mite nods. She knows Jiggs likes his watch almost as much as Miss Wright does. Meals, for starters. Breakfast at seven. Lunch at twelve. Supper at six. Monday, Wednesday, Friday, Saturday, a frozen dinner in his trailer. Tuesday, Thursday, Sunday, whatever Bee cooks at the farmhouse.

Bee slaps Tiny Mite on the bottom, setting Tiny Mite across the prickly grass. "Whatever you do," Bee calls, "don't mention the demon!"

Hanging onto her loincloth, Tiny Mite turns into the cornfield. The air is cool between corn rows, but the earth warm and dry. Run fast, talk slow, slay the demon. The thick leaves of the corn-stalks slap her shoulders with palm branches as she passes—the people love her and so they should. She has fed 5,000 with two bread loaves and a fish. Though her lungs ache, she picks up the pace. No wimp face, she tells herself, not even for stepping on a rock. Talk slow, run fast, sweat blood. The faster Jesus runs the more they hate him. Judas, for one, slaps her in the face, but there's no time to slice off his ear. Must keep running through the Garden of Gethsemane. Must outrun the soldiers in metal kilts.

Faster, faster, the faster she makes it to that cross the faster she can die for everyone's sins and Mimi, Grandma and Luvie's fight will be erased and the demon defeated. Her side aches. One of the soldiers has stabbed her. "Father," she cries, "why have you forsaken me?" A light shines at the end of the corn row, but it's not heaven.

Luvie says Jiggs lives in a crop circle so his relatives have a place to land when they come to visit, but Tiny Mite knows this is a joke because Jiggs's family died in the car crash that dented his tongue and turned his brain from high to medium. The clearing isn't a real crop circle, either, but a spot along the road where Jiggs swerves the combine so he has a place to plant his vegetables and park his Airstream trailer. The Rottweiler chained to it barks.

"Rookie!"

Whining, tail wagging, he digs in the dirt and then licks her.

Jiggs opens the door of the Airstream, its steps folding out like those of a spaceship. Aquatic television light ripples around his silhouette—small head, broad shoulders, skinny legs, ears as big as French horns. "S-sweetie?"

"Salty!" She jumps into his arms and takes a deep breath: grain, cigarettes, cinnamon gum, Irish Spring soap.

His brow furls. "W-where did did." His jaw clenches with the frustration of so many letters tripping and falling over the rim of his upper lip. "Your c-clothes go?"

Realizing she has lost her loincloth in the cornfield, Tiny Mite starts to cry and squeezes him, the cigarette packs in his front pockets poking into her ribs. He carries her into the Airstream, sets her on its built-in sofa and disappears to the bedroom. A half-opened can of tomato soup sits on the kitchen's small countertop with a spoon poking out of it. Her homemade Polaroids cover both cabinets. A woman on television swishes her long dark curls as she says *Don't hate me because I'm beautiful*. Jiggs returns with a white undershirt and pulls it over her head.

"Grandma whipped Mimi and says we're not a nice family and they hate each other and steak dinners and prairie stories, too!" Tiny Mite cries again.

"Shush-oo." Jiggs shakes his head, his face crinkled with worry. "Con-con—"

"Confused?"

He nods.

"A Viking demon came with a big knife and a dead coyote and Grandma asked him for milk!" Jiggs holds up his palm again, but Tiny Mite gains speed. "Mimi says Bud told her bad things about the farm, but Grandma doesn't believe her! Luvie says the demon can stay with us and Grandma says no and fire's coming out of everyone's mouths!" It's raining exclamation marks. *Ting, ting, ting*. Her heart is a pincushion.

"T-teeny, I, I, I d-don't remem-mem—" Jiggs squeezes his eyes shut as if swallowing something too large for his throat— "member this g-game."

"This isn't a game!" Tiny Mite shrieks. "Right now this very minute there's a demon covered with the mark of the Beast in our driveway! The great red dragon with seven heads and ten horns is coming! Don't you see?" She pulls Jiggs by the hand. "It's the end times!"

*Green car that is not his. Credit card that is not his. Tie*
*not his. Suit not his. Shoes, cufflinks, tapes. Nothing.*
    *Four hundred and sixty-five miles from Big Bend, Velvet takes*
*inventory of her possessions:*
    *A pack and a half of Slims.*
    *One make-up kit.*
    *One pair of pantyhose.*
    *One pair of long johns.*
    *Four crumpled receipts.*
    *One watch.*
    *One Prairie Town uniform.*
    *One pair of Prairie Town boots.*
    *No coat.*
    *No money except for the loose coins at the bottom of her purse.*
    *No idea how she will achieve what she has set out to do.*
    *Thoughts racing. Body sweating. The green car suddenly*
*sinister in the fading light.*

# Jiggs marches through the cornfield, rifle slung over his shoulder.

Tiny Mite skips behind him. "Please, Jiggs, *please* do your trick to the demon. Pretty please with candy corn on top?"

Jiggs usually smiles at the mention of his favorite candy, but some filthy-fingered demon has taken his teeny Tiny Mite's clothes. He has never seen her so upset. Something bad has happened. Jiggs reaches the lawn on the side of the farmhouse, and when he recognizes the kind of motorcycle owned by the bum who left Velvet high and dry, sprints into the house.

"Wait!" Tiny Mite calls from the cornfield, but Jiggs disappears. The closer she gets to the house the clearer it becomes that Jiggs has left her a treasure hunt.

Clue #1: The demon's chariot lies on its side.
Clue #2: The top step is broken.
Clue #3: The screen door hangs from one hinge.
Clue #4: The welcome mat is askew.
Clue #5: People scream and shout in the dining room.

Clue #6: The demon stands with a napkin tucked into his black
   T-shirt, hands in the air.
Clue #7: Jiggs points his rifle at him.


Seven clues to match seven seals and seven bowls of wrath. No
wonder the demon looks terrified. With his Viking helmet off
and bald head exposed, he even looks vulnerable.

Luvie holds her arms out like a pastor blessing a congregation.
"Put the gun down, Jiggs. This is not the Goddamned Idiot. His
name is George."

"Whatever Tiny Mite told you," Velvet pleads with Jiggs, "she
lied."

A thought bubble appears over Tiny Mite's head. *I didn't lie!*
Mimi remains under the demon's influence, but Bee has freed her
mind from Satan's shackles, praying softly, clasped hands against
her forehead. It must be working, Tiny Mite thinks, because tears
fill the demon's eyes.

Jiggs spies Tiny Mite by the table in his T-shirt, and shaking
at the thought of something bad happening to her naked body,
clicks off the gun's safety.

To Tiny Mite's surprise, the demon whispers, "Dear Jesus,"
but she knows it's too late—his doom to the lake of fire has been
prophesied since the beginning of time.

Luvie jumps between Jiggs and the demon. "Who do you think
this man is?"

"H-he he t-took."

Luvie's mouth moves as he speaks, as if to draw out the words.

"H-he." The words are stuck. Tears blur Jiggs's vision. "T-took
her her c-clothes!"

George shakes his head. "Oh Lord, no. I would *never*."

Velvet glares at Tiny Mite. "I told you she lied!"

"I did not!"

Luvie holds up a hand. "George doesn't have Tiny Mite's clothes and never did. They're up in her room, Jiggs. She took them off herself, having the goddamned fool notion it would be fun to wear rags and pretend she's Jesus."

Jiggs frowns. He can't look at Tiny Mite. He asked her if it was a game and she said it wasn't. Ashamed, he lays the rifle on the table alongside a place setting, aligning it with the silverware as if it's an oversized salad fork.

Now everyone's running and Tiny Mite has to blink extra fast to figure out what's happening. Luvie runs to the table and grabs the rifle. Jiggs runs to George, and throwing his arms around him, begs for forgiveness. Bee and Mimi run toward Tiny Mite, a two-headed monster.

"You little brat, you could have gotten George killed!"

"What did I say about talking too fast?"

"Does it ever occur to you that there could be consequences to your stupid games?"

"Didn't I say *not* to mention our guest?"

"I never said anything!" Tiny Mite looks to Luvie for support, but Luvie struggles with the top of a fresh whiskey bottle.

Velvet shoves Tiny Mite. "You're always causing trouble! No matter what I do!"

Patting Jiggs on the shoulder with one hand, George holds out another toward Velvet. "Easy, Vettie."

Bee doesn't like this "Vettie" business one bit.

"I didn't say anything about clothes," Tiny Mite persists. She glances toward Jiggs, now sitting at the table with his head in his arms. "Remember, Jiggs? I didn't!"

Jiggs doesn't look up.

George walks over and smooths her hair. "We know it was a misunderstanding, honey."

The demon is the only one who believes her. A thought bubble appears above Tiny Mite's head: *I love demons! I hate everyone else!*

Holding the whiskey bottle out to George, Luvie winks. "Hell, I bet you could use a shot."

"Seeing as I've just avoided one, yes, thank you."

Tiny Mite likes the idea of giving a demon hell. It's like rubbing salt in the wound of a deer lick or spouting off to a fountain or getting torqued at an engine or hamming it up for a pig or even better—she giggles, this one is so good—turning a blind eye to Helen Keller.

Velvet flicks Tiny Mite's earlobe. "You think what you did is funny?"

Tiny Mite stares at a stain in the carpet. "No."

"Tell us what's so funny you have the nerve to laugh."

"It was a joke about Helen Keller, turning a blind eye to her."

"And what does that have to do with anything?" One of Miss Wright's patronizing expressions appears in Velvet's mind. "Do you see what I'm talking about, Luvie? Mother? She doesn't make sense."

Bee clears her throat. She'd hug Tiny Mite if it wouldn't upset Velvet. "Maybe a joke isn't such a bad idea."

"Mother!" Velvet cries.

Tiny Mite needs to act fast. "What's Helen Keller's favorite color?"

"Black?" Bee offers.

Tiny Mite doesn't hate Bee anymore. "Corduroy!"

"That's a good one," Luvie cackles, pouring herself a second whiskey.

Tiny Mite doesn't hate Luvie anymore, either. "How did Helen Keller meet her husband?"

Jiggs lifts his head from the table. "S-s-school?"

Tiny Mite never hated Jiggs. "On a blind date!"

Everyone but Velvet laughs, who's tempted to throw one of Bee's lovebird saltshakers at the freaky timeline pasted all over the wall.

"Want to hear my favorite Helen Keller joke?" Tiny Mite asks George.

He holds out his whiskey glass for Luvie to refill. "Why not?"

"How do Helen Keller's legs get wet?"

George strokes his beard. "I don't know. How?"

"Her dog is blind, too!"

"That's disgusting!" Velvet gazes into one of the boxes on the floor and reads a headline: HOMELESS MAN EATEN ALIVE BY RATS.

George tips the whiskey bottle in Velvet's direction. "You could use a drink, too."

Nervous, Velvet shakes her head. In the overwhelming chaos of the rally—the bonfires, blasting music, roar of thousands of Harleys, the stares and touts of the bikers, their women no less intimidating in leather corsets, dog spikes, bikinis, decorative nipple covers, and, in some cases, topless or wearing nothing but a G-string and body paint—George had been an oasis, fatherly in his demeanor and generous in his offer of shelter, information on Blankety Blank and a ride home. In the farmhouse, however, he looks tough verging on scary. Velvet hopes she hasn't made a mistake.

Though the meatloaf and green beans have gone cold, they sit down and eat. Jiggs has seconds. George has thirds. Bee goes to the kitchen and retrieves a red Jell-O salad layered with banana slices and topped with crushed Nilla wafers and Cool Whip.

Tiny Mite asks George, "Can you really help us find my dad?"

"Maybe." He notices the glass of apple juice by Tiny Mite's plate and frowns. "I run into him from time to time. We have a few friends in common."

Velvet wishes she could ride all the way to California with George, crossing state lines like they were nothing but cracks in a sidewalk.

Tiny Mite notices George staring at her glass of juice and pushes it toward him. "Want some? We make it with apples from our orchard. Grandma puts it on her armpits."

Velvet pinches Tiny Mite in the arm. "Can you be normal for one night, for our special guest, for *me*?"

"But Grandma does!" Tiny Mite persists. Why does everyone accuse her of lying?

Velvet stares at the wall, tears welling in her eyes. What are the odds of meeting a nice guy in Big Bend? And if she gets that lucky, what are the odds he'll stick around after meeting her family? A newspaper clipping—*HUNTER SHOT BY OWN DOG*—falls off the wall and lands in a box labeled "serial killers."

Noticing Velvet's tears, Jiggs clears his throat. He has the perfect trick to get everyone laughing again. "G-George? Y-you you a a"—he cranks his neck to the left as if the letter he needs is on his shoulder—"b-betting man?"

George lowers his spoonful of Jell-O. "Not usually, but tonight I'll make an exception."

Jiggs's lower lip covers his upper teeth when he smiles. "I I b-b-bet b-b."

Tiny Mite jumps out of her seat. "He bets you can't touch your nose with your tongue!" She loves this trick more than anything Charlie Chaplin, The Three Stooges and Laurel and Hardy did combined.

"You're on," George snorts. "How much?"

Tiny Mite claps. "A dollar!"

Jiggs nods in agreement.

George's eyes go cross-eyed completing the feat. "Sorry, you picked my one party trick."

Amazed, Tiny Mite tries to do it, but fails. Jiggs winks at Tiny Mite as he slides the bill across the table. Tiny Mite bites her lip to keep herself from giggling as she hands the bill to George. "Are you going to give Jiggs a chance to win it back?"

George shrugs. "Double or nothing?"

Tiny Mite jumps out of her seat. "We bet Jiggs can touch his eye with his tongue!"

George laughs. "How about I bet ten bucks he can't do that?"

Jiggs takes the glass eye out of his left socket and pops it in his mouth.

Everyone laughs except Velvet, who covers her face with her hands.

"Holy shit," George whispers, staring at Jiggs's empty socket.

*Shit.* Even Luvie isn't allowed to say it. Tiny Mite waits for Bee to wash the demon's mouth out with soap, but she laughs like a hyena at the bottom of a barrel of moonshine. Seizing her chance, Tiny Mite stands on her chair and proclaims, "That was a goddamned hoot!"

*The green car stopping. Velvet dreads it—gas stations* recalling the Qwik Stop, phone booths tempting her to turn back—but grateful for the opportunity to clean Tiny Mite's handprints from the passenger window, Velvet gets out and grabs a scrubber from a rusty dispenser attached to a pole.

The driver goes inside the station and returns with a brown paper bag under his arm. Gold tie flying, coat-tails flapping. "Take it easy, bluebird. There isn't going to be any glass left."

Her father's nickname in his mouth. It stops her cold. She's shared too much. The wind blows blue cleaning fluid onto her pink dress.

"Get the windshield while you're at it?" The driver gets into the car.

Velvet scrubs, shivering, vacillating, nervous as long as the green car is stopped, because stopping, despite the four hundred and thirty-two miles between her and Big Bend, makes her feel in danger of rewinding. When she finishes the windshield, Velvet *puts the scrubber into the dispenser and returns to her seat, warming her numb fingers with her breath.*

*In the driver's brown bag: hot dogs, onions, relish, fries. A treat earlier in the day, but a second time? The smell makes her feel sick, but maybe that's because the green car is stopped, she's wavering and needs it to go, go, go? Also in the bag: cheese sticks, nacho CornNuts, Funyuns, her favorite brand of popcorn. Velvet opens the popcorn, relieved as the green car rolls away from the pump.*

*On the interstate, the driver shoves a quarter of a hot dog into his mouth. A blob of bright yellow mustard drips onto his pant leg.*

*"Here's a napkin." Velvet holds it out, not wanting to touch him, give him ideas.*

*"Thanks." He wipes the stain, making it bigger. "Ah shit. Steve's suit!"*

*"Steve?"*

*The driver explains that he is driving Steve's green car across the country as repayment for crashing on Steve's couch for six months after losing his third job in a year. He is still wearing Steve's suit, loaned to him for Steve's wedding two days earlier, because Steve's mother, thinking the garbage bag containing his clothes contained garbage, threw it away. Steve's suits: for some banking job. Steve's fiancée: a chemical engineer with an MIT degree. Steve's in-laws: dentists with a six-bedroom lake home in Coon Heights. Steve's honeymoon: Paris with a stopover in England for a trip to a war museum to see the Sea Vixen an uncle flew in the...*

*Velvet stares out the blue-streaked passenger window feeling like she's falling. Green car that is not his. Credit card that is not his. Tie not his. Suit not his. Shoes, cufflinks, tapes. Nothing.*

# "You thought I was the devil?"

The deep voice snatches Tiny Mite from the darkness on her way to the kitchen. When her eyes adjust, she sees George sitting alone in the dark at the dining room table, the blankets, sheets and pillow with which he's supposed to make a bed on the davenport still folded on the chair beside him.

"Just a demon." Tiny Mite smoothes the front of her night-gown. "I swear on Bud's grave I never told Jiggs you took my clothes."

"I know you didn't, but he *thought* I did. Do I look that evil?"

Tiny Mite nods. "Your Viking helmet is pretty scary." She takes a step closer to the table. "Did it hurt to get all those dragon pictures on your arm?"

"Not if you're a Viking." George holds out his hand. "Come here and I'll show you something special."

Tiny Mite shuffles forward a few more steps, her bare toes gripping the shag carpet.

"Closer."

His thumb bears a tattooed spider. When she touches it to see if the ink has a raised surface, he flips his hand over so she can study the web tattooed across his palm, the center of which has the words "some pig" integrated into it.

"Charlotte!" she cries.

"Shhh! What are you doing here anyway? Aren't you supposed to be asleep?"

Tiny Mite shows him the can opener in her hand. "I'm going to get some food from the basement." Despite the big dinner, her stomach rumbles. "Want to come?"

"Why not?" George follows her through the kitchen, down the rickety stairs and into the laundry area full of soapboxes, plastic baskets and racks of hunting clothes. Tiny Mite shows him the sawdust-filled crates full of potatoes and large stone brining jar where her grandmother keeps cucumbers submerged under a paraffin-covered rock. She takes the flashlight out from under the bottom step and shines it down the long aisle of shelves.

"Jesus," George whispers, running his fingers along the edges of the shelves as they walk deeper into the basement. When Tiny Mite's flashlight illuminates a string of gas masks, he jumps. "Holy shit! What are those for?"

"Chemical warfare." She shines the light at a metal door in the floor. "When the Antichrist starts the nuclear holocaust, we're going down there. My bunk is under Mimi's. Want to see it?"

"Hell no."

"We have air tanks, like for scuba diving, and lots of mouse traps. Rodents will outnumber humans in the end times. Did you know that a single rat can birth up to three hundred pups a year?"

"This place is creepier than shit. You come down here often?"

"About once a week."

"What's that spooky jingling?"

"The wind slaps Grandpa's pheasant hook against the house."

When George met Velvet at a BBQ outside the Knuckle and learned she was looking for Trent Wayne, he couldn't believe his friend could leave a woman that beautiful, even with a brat in the picture. When he saw she'd brought an old army tent for accommodation, he offered his motel room, promising to crash in a buddy's motor home. She'd been reluctant to accept until he told her about his sister Peggy, drawn into the Haight-Ashbury scene at seventeen, abandoned by the father of her child and estranged from their family. Every time George bought Velvet food, he told himself he was feeding Peggy, but when it looked like Trent wasn't showing at the rally, he felt relieved, and when Velvet held his waist for miles of interstate, he wondered if despite their twenty-year gap he might have a one in a hundred chance. Then he saw Trent's brat—no question about paternity—and, charmed by her, felt even more hopeful. Throughout the evening, however, he has been starting to get the picture: the family is clearly mixed up in some kind of cult. "You didn't lure me into this basement to cut me up for some kind of sacrifice?"

"Oh no!" Tiny Mite laughs. "Rams are for sacrifices, not people, and even if you were a ram, only men do offerings. First they touch the head and say some stuff; then they cut it open and put its blood on their right earlobe, right thumb and right big toe."

"No shit?"

"They sprinkle its blood on the altar and take out the guts and burn it all with incense. The rest of the animal gets burned outside the camp on a fire. Then your sins are gone."

"They do this in front of you?"

"Oh no. Now we have Jesus!"

"That's a relief."

"Besides, Grandma says that between all the Chinese babies and aliens stealing cattle, we can't spare the meat."

"Aliens what?"

"When they run out of space food, they land their space ships in Montana and skin the left sides of cows. Their favorite is udders and whizzers."

"Whizzers?"

Tiny Mite whispers. "The boy cow's pee-pee." She leads George down an aisle, hands him the flashlight and climbs to the fifth shelf. "You like Spaghetti-Os?"

"Sure."

It's hard to see the expiration dates. A thought bubble appears above Tiny Mite's head: *Eeny meeny miny moe.* Hoping for the best, she reaches for two cans near the middle of the row. Back on the floor, she discovers that one is nine years old, the other four. Out of politeness, she hands the fresher one to George and points at the gasoline barrels. "That's where we sit and drink it."

"Sit on my lap, honey, so you don't get your nightgown dirty."

George's leather clothes creak as she settles onto his thighs. He smells like gas, cigarettes and whiskey.

His hairy arm around her waist, he opens both cans. "I've done some trippy shit in my time, but this takes the cake." He flashes the light at a life raft suspended from the ceiling. "So your dad's called 'the Goddamned Idiot?'"

"And Blankety Blank."

Velvet had painted a very different picture at the rally. "Your mother doesn't love him?"

"Oh no. She loves Peter the sad grocer who isn't my father."

"Ah." George nods, feeling like a silly old man. "Do you know how your parents met?"

"His sperm drove a motorcycle into Mimi's egg."

George winks. "Is that how babies are made? I always wondered."

"You can also bang pots and pans together at a shivaree."

"Shiver what?"

"A shivaree. The whole town does it when a couple gets hitched. After the wedding, you sneak into their house while they're at work and do funny things like short sheet the bed and rub lotion all over the sheets and stuff the pillows with crackers and booby trap the toilet. Then everyone goes back in the evening and hides in the bushes. When the couple turns out their bedroom light, you bang pots and pans together until they turn on the lights and invite everyone in for coffee and pie."

"Sounds pretty innocent."

"Sometimes the shivaree gets rowdy and the groom gets kidnapped. Benny says his dad got handcuffed and thrown into a canoe and went twenty miles downriver before they found him. Arty Acker got tied, blindfolded and thrown into the back of a truck gassing up at the Qwik Stop. He had to hitchhike home from Lincoln!"

"But what's that got to do with babies?"

"Seven months after the shivaree, the baby comes, although sometimes it can take longer."

George laughs.

Tiny Mite can't believe her luck, alone with George, all the rest of the adults asleep. "What are some of the things my dad likes to do?"

"Motorcycle rallies, Dead concerts, camping, comic book conventions."

"My dad likes comics!" She'd like to lock George in the basement and make him talk all night.

"Must. He paid three hundred bucks for an early *Spiderman*."

"Three *hundred* dollars?"

George coughs. "You know we should probably head upstairs before your Grandma catches us and locks us in that bunker."

Tiny Mite nods. "Give me the cans. I hide them in my room

and smuggle them to school in my backpack to throw into the lunch room trash."

When they reach the kitchen, George turns. "Are you sure your mother's in love with this Peter?"

"Cross my heart."

George rubs his belly. "Thanks for the grub."

"George?" Tiny Mite pauses. "I'm sorry I thought you were a demon."

"Don't sweat it, sweetheart. You weren't the first."

*The green car runs on Velvet's stories. Things she hasn't*
talked about in years.

The deaths of Bee and Luvie's four brothers: *influenza, tractor rollover, Okinawa, pancreatic cancer.*

Birthday presents from her father. *The stuffed bird for her eighth. The five-story dollhouse for her ninth. The puppet theater for her eleventh. The mini-golf course for her thirteenth.*

Bud's dark moods: *the farm inverted, sinking toward the core of the earth. How she hovered when it got bad, sat on his lap, lingered on the landing, did her homework in the barn. Stay with me, bluebird. Organized his tools. Couldn't do it without you, bluebird. She knew his mood by the way he drove, moved, sighed, walked, most keenly feeling his withdrawals from her mother, a rejection, by extension, of herself, and she did everything she could—baking, skits, presents, drawings, jokes, affection, good behavior—to deliver him back to her mother, triumphant when he stormed into the house with an armful of flowers or wrenched Bee from the stove, dipping her, dancing to whatever was playing* on the radio, or grabbing Bee's arm, raised the spatula in her hand, using it as a microphone while he sang.

Four hundred and two miles from Big Bend, riding in the green car, confessing to a stranger, Velvet wonders aloud whether her anger toward her mother lies in a deeper resentment that Bee lost Bud again and again, and that despite all of Velvet's efforts to hold their family together, Luvie gets all the grace.

Velvet wills the green car to go faster. She gazes at the fuel gauge for reassurance, but discovers it low. How she dreads it. The green car stopping.

# On her way downstairs for breakfast, Tiny Mite can

feel everything's out of sync. A stack of folded sheets, blankets and towels sits untouched on a dining room chair. Bee and Velvet aren't in the kitchen, but sitting in their wrong seats in the living room, staring at the floor.

"Grandma, where's George?"

Bee sighs. "He cleared out in the middle of the night."

Velvet stares at the note George left her. Nothing but a curt goodbye and old Modesto address she's already written to a dozen times. Now she only has generalities about Blankety Blank to go on: Big Sur, comic book conventions, City Lights bookstore, Habitat for Humanity. What kind of man builds houses for the poor in foreign countries when he doesn't support his own child at home?

Tiny Mite can't believe George would leave. She has many questions to ask about her father. She runs to the window and searches the driveway, but his bike is gone. Dew-covered spider webs dot the thick, unmown grass. The windmills stand still in the flowerbeds. The rainbow windsock hangs deflated from the ceiling of the porch.

Luvie shuffles into the living room. "George must have pushed that hog all the way to the interstate so he wouldn't wake us."

Velvet notices Luvie's robe, lopsided from the weight of the full flask in its right pocket. "I was counting on you to help me, Luvie, but no, you had to start boozing."

"I'm not going to apologize for needing a drink after talking Jiggs out of shooting your friend! You really have some nerve, Velvet, and now you've made things even worse getting fired."

"Fired?" Velvet and Bee cry in unison.

Luvie nods toward the kitchen. "That was Floyd from the drugstore. Said you were supposed to be there for inventory at six this morning."

"I wasn't!" Velvet pulls at her nightgown. It's not even nine and she's sweating through her clothes. Humid. No breeze. The air smells like pig shit from the farm up the road. "He changes the schedule and then forgets."

Luvie shakes her head. "You are a royal pain in the hunyacker, you know that, Velvet? Apparently you've also been stealing novels?"

"I only borrowed them. They were in perfect condition when I put them back."

Bee drops the cushion she was plumping. "You *stole*?"

"I'll get a better job, mother."

A thought bubble appears over Tiny Mite's head: *Up in the sky, look! It's a bird! It's a plane!* "You could work at the Dale Mercantile." Job. Tick. The sad grocer not sad anymore. Tick. Her mother not sad anymore. Tick.

Velvet glares at her daughter.

"Now there's an idea." Bee nods. "He still has regards for you."

Velvet rolls her eyes. "You think that because he's polite when you shop there. He's just grateful you put up with his dirty old store instead of shopping at the megamart in Henning like everyone else."

"I'll never shop in Henning! Those beepers at the checkout counters will be the scourge of Christians in the end times. Wait and see: when they put computer chips in everyone's hands and those of us who refuse the sign of the beast won't be able to pay for groceries, you'll be glad we can shop at Peter's store."

"Mother, I'd rather starve."

"Starve we will," Luvie adds. "My Mary Kay customers are shopping at the megamart, too."

Everyone stares at the floor.

Luvie pulls a Road Runner book out of her pocket and holds it out to Tiny Mite. "Found this on the counter. George left it for you."

Velvet snatches the book, flips through it, and when she doesn't find any more information on Blankety Blank, reads George's inscription aloud: *Dear Tiny Mite, thanks for keeping me company. Always remember you're some pig. Love, George.*

"Some pig?" Bee scoffs.

"It's a nice thing, Grandma, from *Charlotte's Web*. If you look really close at George's palm you can see it written there. He showed me the spider on his thumb, too."

Luvie narrows her eyes. "When did he do that?"

"In the basement." Then Tiny Mite remembers she saw it in the dining room.

"Jiggs was right," Bee cries, "and we *disarmed* him!"

Luvie sits on the davenport and pulls Tiny Mite close. "What happened in the basement? Did he touch you anywhere on your body?"

Tiny Mite shakes her head. "I just wanted to show him the gas masks and life rafts."

"Let me guess?" Velvet throws the book onto the floor. "You showed him the nuclear bunker?"

Tiny Mite wonders if perhaps she shouldn't have told George about aliens—Grandma says the general public isn't ready for that information.

Velvet grabs Tiny Mite by the shoulders. "What else did you say to make him leave?"

Tiny Mite wonders if she shouldn't have told him about blood sacrifices or whizzers or shivarees or sad grocers. "I didn't say anything!"

"Why do you have to make everything harder for me?" Velvet shouts, shaking her.

Bee wrenches Velvet from Tiny Mite. "It's not her fault."

"It *is* her fault! She probably snitched about the novels, so thanks, Tiny Mite, for getting me fired when we need the money most!"

Tiny Mite snatches the Road Runner book off the floor, and screaming at her mother, waves it like a preacher with a Bible. "May your eyes grow dim! May your camp be desolate! May your loins shake *continually*!"

She runs out of the house and through the wet grass, breaking every cobweb in her path, until she reaches her pine tree, the blue spruce from which Jiggs has pruned the inner branches so she can stand underneath it. Stepping through its floor-length boughs is like slipping under Mother Goose's hoop skirt, its branches her crinoline's whalebone lining. The ground is hard and dry beneath her feet. Chest heaving, Tiny Mite opens one of the metal tool-boxes she uses for storage, takes out a notebook and black pen and fills an entire page.

*I hate Mimi! I hate Mimi! I hate Mimi! I hate Mimi! I hate Mimi!*
*I hate Mimi! I hate Mimi! I hate Mimi! I hate Mimi! I hate Mimi!*
*I hate Mimi! I hate Mimi! I hate Mimi! I hate Mimi! I hate Mimi!*
*I hate Mimi! I hate Mimi! I hate Mimi! I hate Mimi! I hate Mimi!*
*I hate Mimi! I hate Mimi! I hate Mimi! I hate Mimi! I hate Mimi!*
*I hate Mimi! I hate Mimi! I hate Mimi! I hate Mimi! I hate Mimi!*
*I hate Mimi! I hate Mimi! I hate Mimi! I hate Mimi! I hate Mimi!*
*I hate Mimi! I hate Mimi! I hate Mimi! I hate Mimi! I hate Mimi!*
*I hate Mimi! I hate Mimi! I hate Mimi! I hate Mimi! I hate Mimi!*
*I hate Mimi! I hate Mimi! I hate Mimi! I hate Mimi! I hate Mimi!*
*I hate Mimi! I hate Mimi! I hate Mimi! I hate Mimi! I hate Mimi!*
*I hate Mimi! I hate Mimi! I hate Mimi! I hate Mimi! I hate Mimi!*
*I hate Mimi! I hate Mimi! I hate Mimi! I hate Mimi! I hate Mimi!*
*I hate Mimi! I hate Mimi! I hate Mimi! I hate Mimi! I hate Mimi!*
*I hate Mimi! I hate Mimi! I hate Mimi! I hate Mimi! I hate Mimi!*
*I hate Mimi! I hate Mimi! I hate Mimi! I hate Mimi! I hate Mimi!*
*I hate Mimi! I hate Mimi! I hate Mimi! I hate Mimi! I hate Mimi!*
*I hate Mimi! I hate Mimi! I hate Mimi! I hate Mimi! I hate Mimi!*
*I hate Mimi! I hate Mimi! I hate Mimi! I hate Mimi! I hate Mimi!*
*I hate Mimi! I hate Mimi! I hate Mimi! I hate Mimi! I hate Mimi!*
*I hate Mimi! I hate Mimi! I hate Mimi! I hate Mimi!I hate Mimi!*
*I hate Mimi! I hate Mimi! I hate Mimi! I hate Mimi! I hate Mimi!*
*I hate Mimi! I hate Mimi! I hate Mimi! I hate Mimi! I hate Mimi!*
*I hate Mimi! I hate Mimi! I hate Mimi! I hate Mimi! I hate Mimi!*
*I hate Mimi! I hate Mimi! I hate Mimi! I hate Mimi! I hate Mimi!*
*I hate Mimi! I hate Mimi! I hate Mimi! I hate Mimi! I hate Mimi!*
*I hate Mimi! I hate Mimi! I hate Mimi! I hate Mimi! I hate Mimi!*
*I hate Mimi! I hate Mimi! I hate Mimi! I hate Mimi! I hate Mimi!*
*I hate Mimi! I hate Mimi! I hate Mimi! I hate Mimi! I hate Mimi!*
*I hate Mimi! I hate Mimi! I hate Mimi! I hate Mimi! I hate Mimi!*
*I hate Mimi! I hate Mimi! I hate Mimi! I hate Mimi! I hate Mimi!*

*I hate Mimi! I hate Mimi! I hate Mimi! I hate Mimi! I hate Mimi!*
*I hate Mimi! I hate Mimi! I hate Mimi! I hate Mimi! I hate Mimi!*
*I hate Mimi! I hate Mimi! I hate Mimi! I hate Mimi! I hate Mimi!*
*I hate Mimi! I hate Mimi! I hate Mimi! I hate Mimi! I hate Mimi!*
*I hate Mimi! I hate Mimi! I hate Mimi! I hate Mimi! I hate Mimi!*

The page is a wall.
   The letters sooty fingerprints.
   The exclamation points bloody drips.
   A crime scene for which she feels no remorse.

*Mimi is mean. Mimi is mean. Mimi is mean. Mimi is mean. Mimi is mean. Mimi is mean. Mimi is mean. Mimi is mean. Mimi is mean. Mimi is mean. Mimi is mean. Mimi is mean. Mimi is mean. Mimi is mean. Mimi is mean. Mimi is mean. Mimi is mean. Mimi is mean. Mimi is mean. Mimi is mean. Mimi is mean. Mimi is mean. Mimi is mean. Mimi is mean. Mimi is mean. Mimi is mean. Mimi is mean. Mimi is mean. Mimi is mean. Mimi is mean. Mimi is mean. Mimi is mean. Mimi is mean. Mimi is mean. Mimi is mean. Mimi is mean. Mimi is mean. Mimi is mean. Mimi is mean. Mimi is mean. Mimi is mean. Mimi is mean. Mimi is mean. Mimi is mean. Mimi is mean. Mimi is mean. Mimi is mean. Mimi is mean. Mimi is mean. Mimi is mean. Mimi is mean. Mimi is mean. Mimi is mean. Mimi is mean. Mimi is mean. Mimi is mean. Mimi is mean. Mimi is mean. Mimi is mean. Mimi is mean. Mimi is mean. Mimi is mean. Mimi is mean. Mimi is mean. Mimi is mean. Mimi is mean. Mimi is mean. Mimi is mean. Mimi is mean. Mimi is mean. Mimi is mean. Mimi is mean. Mimi is mean. Mimi is mean. Mimi is mean. Mimi is mean. Mimi is mean. Mimi is mean. Mimi is mean. Mimi is mean. Mimi is mean. Mimi is mean. Mimi is mean. Mimi is mean. Mimi is mean. Mimi is mean. Mimi is mean. Mimi is mean. Mimi is mean. Mimi is mean. Mimi is mean. Mimi is mean. Mimi is mean. Mimi is mean. Mimi is mean. Mimi is mean. Mimi is mean. Mimi is mean. Mimi is mean. Mimi is mean. Mimi is mean. Mimi is mean. Mimi is mean. Mimi is mean. Mimi is mean. Mimi is mean. Mimi is mean. Mimi is mean. Mimi is mean. Mimi is mean. Mimi is mean. Mimi is mean. Mimi is mean. Mimi is mean. Mimi is mean. Mimi is mean. Mimi is mean. Mimi is mean. Mimi is mean. Mimi is mean. Mimi is mean. Mimi is mean. Mimi is mean. Mimi is mean. Mimi is mean. Mimi is mean. Mimi is mean. Mimi is mean. Mimi is mean. Mimi is mean. Mimi is mean. Mimi is mean. Mimi is mean. Mimi is mean. Mimi is mean. Mimi is*

*mean. Mimi is mean. Mimi is mean. Mimi is mean. Mimi is mean.
Mimi is mean. Mimi is mean. Mimi is mean. Mimi is mean. Mimi is
mean. Mimi is mean. Mimi is mean. Mimi is mean. Mimi is mean.
Mimi is mean. Mimi is mean. Mimi is mean. Mimi is mean. Mimi is
mean. Mimi is mean. Mimi is mean. Mimi is mean. Mimi is mean.
Mimi is mean. Mimi is mean. Mimi is mean. Mimi is mean. Mimi is
mean. Mimi is mean. Mimi is mean. Mimi is mean. Mimi is mean.
Mimi is mean. Mimi is mean. Mimi is mean. Mimi is mean. Mimi is
mean. Mimi is mean. Mimi is mean. Mimi is mean. Mimi is mean.
Mimi is mean. Mimi is mean. Mimi is mean. Mimi is mean. Mimi is
mean. Mimi is mean. Mimi is mean. Mimi is mean. Mimi is mean.
Mimi is mean. Mimi is mean. Mimi is mean. Mimi is mean. Mimi is
mean. Mimi is mean. Mimi is mean. Mimi is mean. Mimi is mean.
Mimi is mean. Mimi is mean. Mimi is mean. Mimi is mean. Mimi is
mean. Mimi is mean. Mimi is mean. Mimi is mean. Mimi is mean.
Mimi is mean. Mimi is mean. Mimi is mean. Mimi is mean. Mimi is
mean. Mimi is mean. Mimi is mean. Mimi is mean. Mimi is mean.
Mimi is mean. Mimi is mean. Mimi is mean. Mimi is mean.*

Each word is a brick.

She writes a fortress.

Tiny Mite opens the book from George and amends the
inscription.

*Dearest Tiny Mite, you are a superstar and dancing queen. The
Mayor of Funky Town!*
*Thanks for keeping me company. Always remember you're
some pig. (and then some!)*
*I Love, you George*

The Road Runner cartoons in George's book look nearly identical, but if she flips through them, the characters move like they
do on television. With each flip Wile E. Coyote uses a bomb from
the Acme Corporation to blow up a rock over a canyon to squash

the Road Runner, only the *super-sonicus-tastius* speeds away unharmed, and when the *famishius-famishius* checks the fuse, the bomb explodes the rock and he falls into a canyon onto another rock that catapults him head first into a spiny cactus.

At first Tiny Mite prefers flipping through the book quickly— the whir of snapping paper, the sensation of time accelerating— but as the novelty wanes and she flips more slowly, decides seeing the robotic movements within a movement is akin to Ezekiel seeing wheels in the middle of the wheel. Seeing a single action bloomed makes her feel like she's inserted her hands into the world, pushed them apart and discovered secret pockets, hidden spaces normally unseen by the naked eye. *She who has eyes.* Flipping slowly not only allows her to see actions broken down, but to understand their meanings differently. Instead of falling, Wile E. Coyote looks like he's floating down, making her imagine how other actions could be interpreted: a slap could look like a tai chi move; a jostle, a dance; Mimi's yelling, opera singing. *She who has eyes let her see.*

Tiny Mite spends the rest of the morning making a flipbook of Wonder Woman punching a cloud. She hears footsteps outside the tree. Hoping it's Velvet, she peeks through the pine needles. Pink terry cloth slippers. Bee's knees crack as she crouches to set a lunch tray on the scraggly grass bordering the tree.

"How about coming inside to help with the timeline? I found a news story about a girl with psychic powers going missing during a tornado on a date corresponding to not only three prophecies, but Marilyn Monroe's death." Bee waits a moment, and when she receives no reply, adds, "I can't place so important a clue without you. If it corresponds to as much as I'm guessing, it could be the start of a new timeline. Imagine timelines within timelines!" Bee waits a moment and then sighs. "Your mother didn't mean what she said, sweetheart."

"Knock knock," Tiny Mite says.

"Who's there?"

"Leaf."

"Leaf who?"

"Leaf me alone." Feeling guilty, she adds, "If you don't mind, please."

Standing, Bee slaps her thighs. Tiny Mite waits until she disappears into the farmhouse before sliding the tray under the tree and eating the apple, two white pickled eggs sprinkled with celery salt and a plate of hot cinnamon whirly jigs. On the paper napkin under the glass of milk, Bee has drawn a smiley face next to the verse: *Be kind and compassionate to one another, forgiving each other, just as in Christ God forgave you. Eph. 4:32.* Tiny Mite crumples the napkin and throws it through an opening in the branches.

Sitting cross-legged on the dirt, Tiny Mite gazes at her beanbag, blankets, toy tub, toolboxes and stack of Bud's *Mechanix Illustrated: The How-to-Do Magazine,* wondering if she were to learn to eat worms, grass and berries, whether she could manage never to set to foot in the farmhouse again. Opening another toolbox, she grabs her View-Master and pulls *Charlie Brown's Summer Fun* from a sleeve. Wrapping herself in a wool blanket and wiggling deep into the beanbag, she clicks through the reel until she finds her favorite picture: Charlie Brown running downhill on a flower-lined path pulling a red kite. The blue sky above the swishy trees is slashed with white and yellow pastel streaks. Charlie asks her if she'd like a turn. She says "yes," only when he hands her the kite string, a gust sucks it into the sky and as it swooshes this way and that, makes red curlicues over the yellow and white slashes.

When Tiny Mite awakens, late afternoon's canary light nests in the pine's uppermost branches. Sweaty and still angry, she throws off the blanket and digs in the toolboxes through her illegal items, including Bud's hunting knives, a Grateful Dead T-shirt that belonged to her father and a bunch of old photos of wide-eyed dead people Bee calls Memento Moris even though none of them are Japanese. They'd be even deader if Tiny Mite hadn't rescued them from the fire barrel, which is why they say "*Domo arigato*, Mr. Roboto" every time she takes them out of the toolbox. She'd inform them she's a *girl* robot, but other than *kamikaze* and *Kikkoman*, doesn't speak Japanese.

When Tiny Mite feels really scared, she gazes into the blank eyes of Memento Mori babies on satin cushions and white-haired people on wooden tables, and because nothing is scarier than them, the original scary thing doesn't feel so scary anymore. The Memento Moris are often dressed in Sunday best and propped in rocking chairs, church pews or damask-covered Victorian settees with kinked necks. The most terrifying one depicts a dead girl about Tiny Mite's age slumped between her parents on a wooden swing not unlike the one on her own porch. The girl's arms dangle at her sides, oblivious to the homemade rag doll sitting erect as a schoolteacher on her lap. Even worse than her rolled back eyes are her parents' expressions. Tiny Mite covers the faces of the mother and father with Hello Kitty stickers. She stares down the girl and then puts all of the Memento Moris away.

Digging deeper into the toolbox, Tiny Mite pulls out a plastic binder with Winnie the Pooh on the cover. At the top of the second page sits one of her favorite treasures: her name written in her mother's left-handed, windswept cursive. *Clea Marie Baumhauer*, her name up high on a sturdy shelf. She found the mostly empty baby book in her mother's closet and from time to time snuck peeks to see if any more sections had been completed, but after years of seeing no progress, smuggled it to her pine tree and filled it in herself.

> *The day we learned the great news: we did cartwheels.*
> *Our reactions: we did the cancan.*
> *The first people we told: God.*
> *Their reactions: He made a rainbow.*
> *Advice from family and friends: You made your bed now lie in it.*

Tiny Mite loves the fifth and sixth pages best, where instead of following the instructions to fill in lists of baby gifts, Velvet covered the space with two sets of ink handprints: Tiny Mite's and her own. They look like a family of black starfish.

Gravel crunches in the driveway. A door slams and a car starts. Blinding headlights prevent Tiny Mite from determining which car leaves, but when her eyes adjust, she finds the farm in the magical seam between dusk and night, everything a black silhouette pinned against the sky, a landscape made from construction paper. The paper doll world.

# Hot dogs, caramel apples, slushies, circus peanuts.

The green car is a fair. Its driver a juggler of ideas, ringmaster, future after future rolling from his lips. Maybe he'll finish his anthropology degree? Or volunteer with Greenpeace? Take banjo lessons? Learn to surf? Speak Mandarin? Start a literary magazine?

Velvet's father said maybe, too. It was their favorite word. They made space, air and sunshine out of it. Maybe they'd open a birthday party service with enormous cakes and masses of helium balloons? That was one. There were hundreds. Velvet stares out the window at the cloudless blue sky, missing him. She's been lost for so long, a balloon her father let go of when he died.

The driver waves his orange lollipop like a baton. Maybe he'll scrap the anthropology degree? Go to medical school? Learn acupuncture? Homeopathy? Backpack in Sri Lanka? Visit a monastery? Convert to Buddhism? Take up carpentry? Renovate a house? Live off-grid? Compost? Buy a metal detector? A pot-bellied pig?

His ambition and enthusiasm make Velvet's own plan feel modest and therefore attainable.

Maybe he'll finish the screenplay he started ten years ago? Take acting lessons? Go to film school? Raise animals? Pesticide-free vegetables? Open a macrobiotic cafe? Sell the kombucha he makes with the yeast starter he inherited from his grandmother?

Maybe she should revise her plan? Aim higher?

Three hundred and thirty-one miles from Big Bend. The greater the distance the brighter the maybes. The green car runs on his ideas. The green car runs on Velvet's stories.

Velvet blows cigarette smoke through the window of the red playhouse. It hurts her knees to crouch, but she'd rather not leave evidence of trespassing in the thick coating of dirt covering the plywood floor where she and Peter used to kiss until his braces wore her lips raw. In the corner, among a pile of sticks, brown leaves and faded toys, lies the deflated air mattress they jokingly dubbed "third base." She marvels that this playhouse ever felt like a hiding place when it's less than forty yards from the back of the Dales' pale yellow two-story house. They used to drag their books out here, claiming to study. Blankets, cushions and picnics, too, neither parent ever protesting.

In the years since their break-up Velvet has driven by the Dales' house thousands of times and rarely caught Peter's silhouette in the window of his apartment over his parents' garage, but from the playhouse, she can see the beer in his glass as he passes the sliding glass doors flanking his parents' family room and kitchen. Jim and Jeanie Dale sit in their usual recliners watching a pre-season football game. Someone with curly hair sits on the sofa. A woman? The thought makes Velvet sick. Peter joins the group, sitting, to Velvet's relief, in the rocking chair opposite the mystery guest. Velvet takes a final drag before smashing the cigarette against the ceiling of the playhouse. *Velvet Lynn Dale.* She touches the faded ink. Her lost self, written in Peter's handwriting.

A light switches on the back porch illuminating half the lawn. Jeanie Dale stands by the glass door, palm against her eyebrows. Scrambling out of the playhouse, Velvet bangs her head on the low doorframe and scratches her cheek on the torn chain link as she crawls through the hole in the fence. Emerging on all fours in the neighbor's backyard, she finds herself in the company of three smoking teenagers—Liddy Schnaut, Cath Grover and Mort Vandenkamp. The current rulers of Big Bend High recognize her. Cath gasps. Liddy exchanges a snide look with Mort. Velvet should give these runts a piece of her mind for throwing Tiny Mite's library book out the bus window, but instead runs, slipping on their laughter all the way to the convertible, which doesn't start until the third try.

Heart pounding, Velvet screeches away, yet can't help rounding the corner and idling past the Dales' house, its porch swing, flowerpots and garden gnomes dark. In the driveway sits an old Datsun—red, burgundy or brown, she can't tell with the streetlight burnt out. She squints at its many bumper stickers— probably a collection of pro-gun rants. The front porch light illuminates. Too humiliated to get caught twice, Velvet drives away.

She hates the night ride between Big Bend and the farm, the absolute darkness beyond her headlights turning ditches to bottomless swamps, corn rows to endless alleyways. There's the leaning gray structure of the Haverton homestead where in 1906 typhoid wiped out a family of eight within a week. There's the blinking red radio tower from which Tommy Kramer fell to his death. There's the road out to the caves where pioneers starved hiding from Indians. There's the Henderson mailbox where little Richie got lost and froze in an April blizzard. There's the half-dozen *WHY DIE?* signs posted at the entrance to tombstone road, the hilly, winding, washboarded gravel road through the dunes, where teenagers still race for Big Bend glory. There's Beel Junction, Dale Mercantile as dark as the boarded-up businesses next to it.

When Velvet pulls up in front of the farmhouse, its windows, too, are dark, even the attic room where Tiny Mite usually sleeps with her lamp lit. Velvet gazes toward the blue spruce, wondering if she's still underneath it. Earlier that afternoon, she went out to apologize, but found Tiny Mite asleep, a reminder written on her hand in black ink: *Don't forget to be mad at Mimi.* Velvet considers leaving her under the tree, but reminding herself that a good mother wouldn't be able to sleep without knowing her child is safe in bed, grabs the flashlight from the glove box of the convertible and walks toward the tree.

Velvet wants to be the kind of person who can enjoy the sight of bark, leaves and grass iced in moonlight, but finds it difficult when that moonlight illuminates the house's missing shingles, the hole in the roof of the barn, the rusty cage of the empty corncrib and the hollow bodies of three cars her father stripped for parts before she was born. With all her might she wants to see the poetry Tiny Mite and Bee see, but it's the same as it is at church— hard as she longs, she doesn't feel the faith, joy or awe others feel. Thinking about it gives her the falling, wind-in-the-ears sensation she felt when the class moved on to an equation or grammatical rule before she understood the previous one.

The cool overgrown grass obscures a badger hole, causing Velvet to trip. Cursing, she rubs her ankle, hopping the rest of the way to the pine tree. "Tiny Mite?" Velvet shakes one of the branches. "Tiny Mite!" Velvet pokes her head through the branches and shines the light on the beanbag. Finding it empty, she growls about twisting her ankle for nothing. Turning to go, she catches a glimpse of the Winnie the Pooh baby book she bought at Floyd's drugstore when she was pregnant, and furious to discover it stolen from her closet, charges under the tree to inspect it.

Years earlier Velvet printed her baby's handprints at the top of one of the pages and then added her own underneath. The other pages in the book, by comparison, seemed corny, and as there weren't baby gifts or paternal family trees to list, she decided to leave the rest of the book blank. Now she discovers it ruined with stickers, scribbles and glitter glue. Worse, the handprints have been colored in with crayon.

She used to study these hand and footprints as if they were maps, a notion she finds silly now, not so much because of the immaturity in hoping her child would transport her to a different, wonderful life, but because of the cruel fact that as her baby developed and wriggled off her lap, she became less knowable to Velvet, and Velvet, as a result, felt more lost. The handprints were maps to nowhere, she tells herself, wiping tears from her eyes, no more useful than maps to Peter Pan's hideout, so why does it matter that Tiny Mite scribbled on them?

Flipping to another page, a phrase catches Velvet's eye. *You made your bed now lie in it.* Her life sentence, written in her daughter's handwriting. Velvet throws the ruined baby book on the ground, and flashing the light onto a tub of toys, illuminates the stuffed bluebird Bud gave her for her eighth birthday—now wrapped with a chain—and a naked baby doll, its arm missing, pins stuck all over its body and face. Velvet moves the flashlight to a metal box she recognizes from childhood afternoons in the garage and barn handing tools to her father's sunburnt arm appearing and disappearing from underneath a truck or Johnny popper.

Velvet drags the largest toolbox alongside the beanbag. The hinges squeak as she opens it. Her father's Philips screwdriver is no longer snapped into the lid and all the trays that used to hold his nuts, bolts and screws are gone. Inside lies one of Bee's beloved albums of their homesteading ancestors. Velvet hates their uneven eyebrows, off-center noses and missing lips. Tiny Mite attributes their freakishness to the poor quality of the photographs, but their ancestors are expressionless to the point of looking dead, and they have some nerve, in Velvet's opinion, gazing out of their brown photos with sourpuss expressions, imposing their misery on her, when their farmhouse—the very one to which the Baumhauers have returned—smells like sawdust and fresh paint, and Big Bend, with its new train depot and post office, bustles with horses, carts full of construction materials and so many people a brothel has opened outside town. The most humiliating job on Velvet's long, unimpressive resume was her position as butter churner at Prairie Town, the mock pioneer village five exits up the interstate, where, while still breastfeeding, she got minimum wage to dress in prairie garb and pretend to be one of her dumb-faced, greasy-haired, coarse-clothed ancestors.

Velvet grabs the spiral-bound notebook underneath the album, and flipping through it in search of a cute drawing to lift her mood, finds herself in the dark forest of her daughter's anger.

*Mimi is mean. Mimi is mean. Mimi is mean. Mimi is mean. Mimi is mean. Mimi is mean. Mimi is mean. Mimi is mean. Mimi is mean. Mimi is mean. Mimi is mean. Mimi is mean. Mimi is mean. Mimi is mean. Mimi is mean. Mimi is mean. Mimi is mean. Mimi is mean. Mimi is mean. Mimi is mean. Mimi is mean. Mimi is mean. Mimi is mean. Mimi is mean. Mimi is mean. Mimi is mean. Mimi is mean. Mimi is mean. Mimi is mean. Mimi is mean. Mimi is mean. Mimi is mean. Mimi is mean. Mimi is* mean. Mimi is mean. Mimi is mean. Mimi is mean. Mimi is mean. Mimi is mean. Mimi is mean. Mimi is mean. Mimi is mean. Mimi is mean. Mimi is mean. Mimi is mean. Mimi is mean. Mimi is mean. Mimi is mean. Mimi is mean. Mimi is mean. Mimi is mean. Mimi is mean. Mimi is mean. Mimi is mean. Mimi is mean. Mimi is mean. Mimi is mean. Mimi is mean. Mimi is mean. Mimi is mean. Mimi is mean. Mimi is mean. Mimi is mean. Mimi is mean. Mimi is mean. Mimi is mean. Mimi is mean. Mimi is mean. Mimi is mean. Mimi is mean. Mimi is mean. Mimi is mean. Mimi is mean. Mimi is mean. Mimi is mean. Mimi is mean. Mimi is mean. Mimi is mean. Mimi is mean. Mimi is mean. Mimi is mean. Mimi is mean. Mimi is mean. Mimi is mean. Mimi is mean. Mimi is mean. Mimi is mean. Mimi is mean. Mimi is mean. Mimi is mean. Mimi is mean. Mimi is mean. Mimi is mean. Mimi is mean. Mimi is mean, Mimi is mean. Mimi is mean. Mimi is mean. Mimi is mean.

All the paths look alike and lead to the same dead end.

*I hate Mimi! I hate Mimi! I hate Mimi! I hate Mimi! I hate Mimi! I hate Mimi! I hate Mimi! I hate Mimi! I hate Mimi! I hate Mimi! I hate Mimi! I hate Mimi! I hate Mimi! I hate Mimi! I hate Mimi! I hate Mimi! I hate Mimi! I hate Mimi! I hate Mimi! I hate Mimi! I hate Mimi! I hate Mimi! I hate Mimi! I hate Mimi! I hate Mimi! I hate Mimi! I hate Mimi! I hate Mimi! I hate Mimi! I hate Mimi! I hate Mimi! I hate Mimi! I hate Mimi! I hate Mimi! I hate Mimi! I hate Mimi! I hate Mimi! I hate Mimi! I hate Mimi! I hate Mimi! I hate Mimi! I hate Mimi! I hate Mimi! I hate Mimi! I hate Mimi! I hate Mimi! I hate Mimi! I hate Mimi! I hate Mimi! I hate Mimi! I hate Mimi! I hate Mimi! I hate Mimi! I hate Mimi! I hate Mimi! I hate Mimi! I hate Mimi! I hate Mimi! I hate Mimi! I hate Mimi! I hate Mimi! I hate Mimi! I hate Mimi! I hate Mimi! I hate Mimi! I hate Mimi! I hate Mimi! I hate Mimi! I hate Mimi! I hate Mimi! I hate Mimi! I hate Mimi! I hate Mimi! I hate Mimi! I hate Mimi! I hate Mimi! I hate Mimi! I hate Mimi! I hate Mimi! I hate Mimi! I hate Mimi!*

*I hate Mimi! I hate Mimi! I hate Mimi! I hate Mimi! I hate Mimi!
I hate Mimi! I hate Mimi! I hate Mimi! I hate Mimi! I hate Mimi!
I hate Mimi! I hate Mimi! I hate Mimi! I hate Mimi! I hate Mimi!
I hate Mimi! I hate Mimi! I hate Mimi! I hate Mimi! I hate Mimi!
I hate Mimi! I hate Mimi! I hate Mimi! I hate Mimi! I hate Mimi!
I hate Mimi! I hate Mimi! I hate Mimi! I hate Mimi! I hate Mimi!*

Velvet tears the pages out of the notebook and stuffs them into her back pockets. What other horrible things does Tiny Mite think of her? Velvet digs through the rest of the box, and when she finds no more notebooks or a diary, kicks open another toolbox containing more old photographs. Velvet shines her light on one of an old man lying on a wooden table in a dark suit, and never having seen it before, throws it aside to inspect the one underneath. A baby in a lace dress lies on a satin cushion. Something isn't right about the baby, but then the people in these old photos always look strange. A photograph stuck with stickers catches Velvet's eye. It depicts a family of three sitting on a porch swing, the parents' faces covered with Hello Kitty stickers. Something odd about the girl sitting between them gives her goosebumps. Even the rag doll on her lap is creepy. The girl's arms dangle at her sides. Her eyes are rolled back. The girl, Velvet realizes, is dead. She throws the photograph onto the ground. Sticks crack, wings flap, shadows reach for her as she runs to the farmhouse.

Radio blaring. Green car purring, zooming, weaving between trucks, motorcycles, Winnebagos. Two hundred and ninety-five miles from Big Bend it's Velvet who's out-of-state, not the drivers of the adjacent cars, their bumpers adorned with strange, colorful license plates.

Farms and fields turn to ranches and canyons. Towns have unfamiliar names. Cheever. Maybe she'll move here and become a florist? Hutton. Maybe she'll move here and live in a cabin and knit sweaters? Ryle. Maybe she'll move here, buy a poodle, drink from crystal wineglasses and change her name to Anastasia Landon? Ketrick. Maybe she'll move here and marry a harmonica player, start a band, sing?

She thinks of Tiny Mite, this very minute most likely on the davenport, watching cartoons, eating a warm batch of cookies.

She thinks of Peter, this very minute most likely in his dad's rundown store, stocking the same products he's stocked for ten years, listening to the same radio station—National Public Radio—the dial's been tuned to for just as long, rereading books he's read a dozen times, *wishing he could see her now, moving ninety miles an hour in a brand new car, passing towns he's never heard of, scenery he's never seen, going somewhere he'll never go. And this is her favorite part—she's doing it without him. How she'd love to roll down the window and scream: I don't need you to leave!*

*Velvet dances in her seat, drums the dashboard, filling the barren, snow-dusted expanse with fantasies about the changed life she and Tiny Mite will soon possess. When the green car runs out of gas, they stop and the driver buys three new cassettes and a whole bag of food. Back on the interstate—thirty, forty, fifty, sixty, seventy, eighty miles an hour—the party continues. Morrissey, Kinks, Talking Heads. Hot dogs, caramel apples, slushies, circus peanuts.*

"Remember what a spoilsport Dean Coots was at his shivaree?" Luvie wears a daisy-patterned rain cap to protect her hair from the hot wind blowing into the Buick as she drives. "Remember him on his porch in his tighty-whities shooting at everybody?" Laughing, she reaches out the window and flicks cigarette ash onto the highway.

Velvet squints at a herd of cows vying for the shade of the only tree for a mile. "I don't go to shivarees." Over her dead body will she ever be that hard up for entertainment, even if the only alternatives are hayrides, potlucks, bingo, races on tombstone road, flattening pennies on the train tracks or—*whoop, whoop*—jumping trains. The latest kid to do so nearly held on to Gant, breaking the record and a femur, earning him a lifelong bar story, but costing him a football scholarship to State. Not that Velvet's choices—books, movies, backgammon in the kitchen of Carole Bunt, her old Sunday school teacher—are adrenaline-inducing, but after being queen of Big Bend, and a bored one at that, she prefers solitude to participating in second-rate entertainment as a third-class citizen.

Gazing into the rearview mirror, Luvie puckers and then evens out her lipstick. "Henniker knew something had to be behind that performance at the shivaree, so when he went to a conference up in Hyde, where Dean grew up, he asked around. Seems Dean's been married before and had a surprise on his first wedding night." Laughing, she turns east onto County 5.

The sunlight, despite the filter of the bug-caked windshield, makes Velvet's eyes water. People warn you not to stare at the sun, she thinks, but it's so much sky that hurts. She lowers her gaze into the ditch, thick with grass, purple thistle and the tall burgundy plumes of tobacco weed.

"Apparently when Dean and the first wife woke up the morning after their wedding, they heard snickering, and assuming it was coming from the room next door, got on with their business." Luvie elbows her. "You know how newlyweds are."

Velvet doesn't know. In her limited experience, sex wasn't a fraction as thrilling as jumping onto the back of Trent's motorcycle. He'd stopped for gas at the Qwik Stop and delivered the line—*You obviously aren't from around here*—and like that her mission became proving his assumption correct. Tall and muscular, his bone structure and shoulder-length black hair made him look like a character named "Rock" on a soap opera. He wore multiple strands of suede around his neck and his dark, hip-slung jeans made her feel dowdy in the high-waisted, acid-washed ones she'd bought on sale at the only clothes shop in town. While she rang up his gas, mints and Coke, he told her about a party he'd gone to a week earlier in LA at which he'd heard from "some cats" that Sturgis was "rad" and decided "then and there to check it out" and the trip had been "so killer" he'd decided to stay on the road. She'd read the book, right? Velvet had no idea what he was talking about, but nodded. He'd gone fifteen hundred miles to *check something out* and Peter was too chicken to go to college less than a hundred miles away? When she handed him his change—her nervousness caused her to miscount it—he squeezed her wrist, and nodding toward his gleaming red and chrome motorcycle in the parking lot, asked if she'd like a ride. She stared at the clock to buy time in which to formulate a refusal that didn't make her sound like a hick, but her shift had been over for four minutes. His deep tan made his light blue eyes more pronounced. *OK, but it has to be quick.*

"So while Dean and the first wife are making whoopee," Luvie continues, "the snickering gets louder and louder until Dean can make out specific words."

The motorcycle ride ended on a bank under the disused railway bridge spanning the hairpin in the river that gives Big Bend its name. Trent had smelled like fancy cologne, wet leaves and the rum they drank from his canteen, a potent mix combined with the sweet-smelling tar oozing from the heat-swollen railroad ties overhead.

"'Dean, baby,' went one of the voices," Luvie says in a high-pitched voice, "'I took one look at your willie and was so darned scared,' to which another voice went"—Luvie switches to a low voice—"'Scooby may be a great Dane, sugar, but he don't bite.'"

Trent's hair swept Velvet's face and prickled her eyelids. She can still picture her white underwear lying inside out in the grass next to her head.

Luvie continues her story. "The voices were making Dean madder than a hornet. He banged on the wall over the headboard, but the voices yelled, 'Scooby, down boy!' and 'Scooby, that's a good dog!' and 'Oh Moses, oh Jesus, oh Scooby-Dooby Doo!'"

Afterward, when Trent suggested a skinny dip in the brown river, Velvet had to inform him that currents and water moccasins make the river a no-go. He asked how a person cools off in Big Bend. Worried all the viable options—rain barrel, sprinkler, creek—would make her sound like a hick, she mentioned the vodka Luvie kept in the deep freeze in the barn. Smiling, he slipped into his jeans and lit a joint. She scrambled for her clothes. Worried he'd reverse his opinion of her as a "cool fox" if he discovered she didn't know how to smoke, she took the joint when he held it out to her and took a deep drag. She coughed, and because he laughed, tried to compensate by replying, "Sure, whatever" when he said, "I can crash with you, right?"

Luvie takes a final drag before throwing her cigarette out the window. "So Dean called the front desk to complain about the people next door, only the receptionist told him there were no guests in the rooms on either side of him."

Velvet leans her head on the passenger window and sighs. When Trent paused during his advances and asked, "You're covered, right?" She didn't know he was talking about the Pill. All she wanted was for the gorgeous man who thought she didn't belong in Big Bend to keep kissing her.

"And then before Dean knew his ass from his head," Luvie snorts, "Three high school kids rolled out from under his bed and ran, only Dean couldn't chase them, naked as a flocked chicken, the first wife screaming like the lead in a horror show!"

The sky, Velvet thinks, is a bully, hogging four-fifths of everything. She imagines places where it would fit in the palm of her hand, in the mountains, perhaps, or a city thick with skyscrapers.

"The boys in Hyde told Henniker the whole story. Seems Dean moved to Big Bend because in Hyde he couldn't walk down the street without someone humming or whistling the *Scooby-Doo* theme song."

Sometimes Velvet feels like she's on a bus that has careened off the road and landed in a river and she's the only passenger who notices it's filling with water.

Luvie slaps the steering wheel. "Apparently Dean shot out the shivaree because he didn't want the same thing happening to the second wife, only now that Henniker's told the story, folks are singing the *Scooby-Doo* theme song again!" Luvie laughs so hard her mascara starts to run.

Velvet shakes her head "Poor Dean Coots. First the cootie jokes. Now all this monkey business wrecking his fresh start."

Realizing Velvet hasn't been laughing, Luvie frowns. For a girl who dumped a nice boy to bring home a stoned biker, Velvet can be exasperatingly square. Luvie pokes her in the ribs. "Have some fun, honey. You're not yourself this morning."

Velvet smoothes her hair behind her ears. "I'm just nervous about the interview." Corn rows peel away from the car. Soon it'll all be harvested and the sky will be even bigger. "Why do you stay here, Luvie?"

"What kind of question is that?"

"You could get a better job any place, make more money, keep more for yourself."

"And who would I spend it with?" Luvie turns the radio's thick plastic dial in search of an upbeat tune, but finds nothing but weather reports and commercials.

Velvet guesses she's supposed to find Luvie's loyalty heroic instead of claustrophobic. "We hold you back. Honestly, why *do* you stay?"

The memory of pink ladies and sherry flips, Luvie thinks. The lindy hop and swing. The glint of candlelight on brass saxophones, trombones, trumpets. Because there is only one brown corrugated river where she and her brothers caught catfish and one garden where she and Bee tended their grandmother's *erdbeeren* and one stump where she and Snook kissed and one willow-shaded grave-yard where she could bear to be buried and that doesn't include Velvet and Tiny Mite, the daughter and granddaughter she never had. Luvie scratches the comb-shaped scar on her neck from the self-inflicted wound she received the day she got word of Snook's death, thankful Bee convinced her that no man, not even one with angel food cake for a heart, is worth dying for. And Velvet's angst-ridden generation needs her to come out and say all that? Who am I? Why am I here? What does it all mean? Foxes chasing their own goddamned tails. Looking over the edges of things they shouldn't go near in the first place. Luvie would have thought that an only child would cling to family, but maybe a person had to lose four brothers and two parents in ten years to fully grasp the value. Luvie misses her mother's brow, shiny in firelight, the clack of wooden knitting needles, the unvaried stitches in each hat, mitten and double-length scarf, the red banners of her childhood. Always mother, but that was another lifetime. This is *it*, Luvie could scream, but guessing that's the last thing a romantic like her niece could bear, says, "Beautiful day."

Beautiful? With a heat index of 120? Velvet feels exasperated. "This is not the only sky. There are other suns."

Luvie slams her palm against the steering wheel. "And all this time I thought Tiny Mite and Bee were the ones talking nonsense! What you've got to understand, Velvet, is that if we lived somewhere else, we'd have the same problems, only with different scenery."

They pass the *Welcome to Big Bend* sign no one has painted in thirty years. It's like Chinese water torture, Velvet thinks, looking at the same things day after day after day. "Please, Luvie, there has to be another reason."

Luvie waves at two teenaged girls in tank tops and denim cut-offs selling the season's last sweetcorn from the back of a pickup truck. "Maybe the goddamned awful truth, Velvet, is that I don't want to starve to death during the end times."

Velvet laughs.

Luvie pats her niece on the knee. "Now use that smile on Bob

Holt and you'll get the teller job before you open your mouth."
Luvie drives over the curb as she turns into the bank's parking
lot. She dated Bob's father for a year in the late 70s. Hopefully
his son will remember.

Velvet gazes at the ceramic gnome pushing a daisy-filled wheelbarrow alongside the bank's winding slate walkway thinking
maybe Bee was right, maybe it *was* God's plan for her to get fired
from the drugstore so she could interview for a better job without
going behind Floyd's back. Maybe she'll actually like this job.
Maybe she'll even get promoted. "You don't think Floyd told
Bob about the novels, do you?"

"No, but to hell with him if he did. Sweetheart, you've got to
get better at forgetting the past."

Velvet wonders, who thinks about the past more than Luvie?
Bee maybe. Rather than pick a fight, she smiles. "Thanks for
the ride." The bank's freshly mown strip of lawn and streak-free
doors fill her with hope. "Wish me luck!"

# The novelty of it all. Radio voices she's never heard.

Music she's never heard. The bizarre cassettes in the green car's glove compartment: Sonic Youth, Joy Division, Psychedelic Furs, Siouxsie and the Banshees, Violent Femmes, REM, Husker Du, Echo and the Bunnymen.

Strange names. New world.

How could it seem any different? For as long as she can remember: Bee, Luvie and Tiny Mite have been sucking Velvet into a time warp. At the farmhouse: black-and-white movies on the TV; Bing Crosby, Nat King Cole, Glenn Miller and Benny Goodman on the record player. Bee sets the table with upside down glasses and bowls like it's the Dust Bowl. Luvie sets her hair like it's 1955. Jiggs wears snap button shirts and mutton-chops like it's 1972. Tiny Mite praises King Edward VIII's abdication, acts out Charlie Chaplin's gags, relays the exploits of Rita Hayworth and Ginger Rogers as if she's just read them in the papers. Tiny Mite thinks it's normal to watch Laurel and Hardy at church youth events, to play, hidden under that tree of hers, with old, half-broken toys: Howdy Doody, Flossie Flirt dolls, Tiddledy-Winks, Juggle-Head, rolmonicas, View-Masters.

Velvet imagines climbing on top of the green car and screaming, her voice carrying two hundred and ten miles to Big Bend. *"It's December 1988!" Almost 1989. Almost a new decade. Almost a new millennium. Almost—it feels just beyond her fingertips—a new life. Maybe her greatest rebellion is living now?*

She thinks of the strangest cassette she found in the green car: The Rise and Fall of Ziggy Stardust and the Spiders from Mars. *She asked the driver: who's Ziggy Stardust? He laughed for a mile. Now Velvet pops cassettes into the player, taps her feet and mouths lyrics as if she knows them all. Another new song begins. Velvet reaches for the volume dial. Heart soaring. Radio bluring.*

# Bee fans herself with a McCall's pattern box.

Luvie rolls a cold can of ginger ale along her neck.

Tiny Mite puts her face close to the grill of the fan positioned at the edge of the table and chants. *Yo oh na.* The fan deepens her voice. *Yo oh na na.* She is Red Cloud, warrior chief of the Oglala Sioux. *Yo ho. Yo ho.*

Bee tugs Tiny Mite's arm. "Sit down and eat your dinner before it gets cold."

A thought bubble appears above Tiny Mite's head: *But dinner is cold!* Tuna sandwiches, pickles, raw vegetables.

Luvie plucks a radish from the glass bowl of iced water next to her plate. "Where's Velvet? I thought you were collecting her from the bank after her interview?"

Bee takes a deep breath. "I have news." She taps the side of her water glass with a butter-smeared knife. "Velvet has a new job."

"At the bank!" Tiny Mite claps.

Frowning, Bee lays down the knife. "At Prairie Town."

"Prairie Town?" Luvie lowers the radish from her mouth.

"What happened with Bob?"

"I ran into him at the pharmacy after the interview. He said she did all the math wrong."

"A teller doesn't need to know calculus!"

"That's what I said, but he claims he gave her three chances and let her use a calculator. Then I bumped into Gary Brayson filling his Model T. He offered Velvet her butter-churning job back. The Lord always provides, doesn't He?"

Luvie groans. Something about the man's too-close deep-set eyes and constant hand wringing gives her the creeps. Concerned, she presses grids into the tablecloth with the tines of her unused fork.

Bee stares at the ice cubes melting in her lemonade.

Tiny Mite claps. "Prairie Town is my favorite place in Big Bend! I'm going to work in the General Store when I grow up."

Brightening, Bee tugs one of her granddaughter's pigtails. "There's a can-do attitude."

"I don't know what to say." Luvie throws her crumpled napkin onto her untouched sandwich. "She was miserable last time."

"That's because she got blisters churning real butter. Gary says he's modernized the place, that all she has to do is move the stick up and down in the hole. Apparently the butter in the gift shop is the regular stuff in a fancy wrapper."

"All the more reason to assign butter churning to one of those stiffs!"

Tiny Mite loves the wax people at Prairie Town. They rock babies, weigh flour, saw timber and guard bank robbers alongside real people dressed as homesteaders who answer questions about how to hammer horseshoes, make soap, fix wagon wheels, sew quilts, make corn brooms, and in the case of her mother, churn butter. The best is Prairie Town's apothecary who demonstrates how to make laxatives from powdered sulfur and molasses.

Bee works over a molar with a toothpick. "I agree it's not ideal, Luvie, but it'll tide us over until she finds something else."

Luvie stands. "Where's Velvet? I'd better talk to her."

Bee feels a stab of jealousy. "In her room getting used to the idea." Standing, she grasps Luvie's flask and spikes her sister's ginger ale. "Put your feet up. I'll go."

Bee climbs the stairs and knocks on Velvet's closet door. "Honey? Are you OK?"

Nose blowing. Sniffling. "What do you think?"

Bee sighs. "I know everything's gone kerflooey, Velvet, but I promise things could be worse. Compared to when we ate jackrabbits and cattails, we really do live high on the hog." A memory causes her to chuckle. "We made our own soda pop mixing baking soda and water. Now doesn't that make a Coke something special?"

"Why do you have to make everything better, mother? If your life was as bad as you brag, why didn't you just shoot yourself?"

Bee wobbles backward. "What kind of question is that?" Bee thinks of the time her parents beat her feet with a boar-bristled brush all night to keep her from falling asleep and dying of botulism after she'd eaten from a tainted jar of green beans. She feels a similar urgency to break down the door, steal under her daughter's skin, exile her thoughts, rescue her spirit, hold her body against the earth, fortify her. "We owe it to our ancestors, Velvet, who fought and worked harder than we'll ever imagine to give us our life in this country."

"I don't owe those bug-eyed people a thing!"

Bee's bones feel like they're disintegrating when she and Velvet argue, and it's no wonder, she thinks, when Velvet's never-ending misery rattles every nut and bolt loose in her body. "You've no right, Velvet Lynn Baumhauer, to feel the way you do!" Bee meant to say Velvet had no right to *speak* the way she did, but as always when they fight, Bee feels foggy-headed, powerless and furious at her daughter for stealing things Bee regards an old woman's right—to complain, to be weak, to be coddled, and most of all, to be her husband's most grieved mourner. Velvet has no right derailing her life over Bud when she, the widow, was in her girdles by six the morning after the crash washing vases and baking popovers for mourners coming to pay respects that afternoon. "You've got no right!" Bee bangs on the door. "None!"

Velvet waits ten minutes beyond the slamming of her mother's bedroom door before leaving the closet. Tiptoeing to the window, she sits in its deep sill. Within weeks the heatwave will flip to cold. Jiggs will cover all the windows with thick plastic sheeting to insulate the house until late May, so she may as well take in the view of green cornfields, though marred by the billboard standing in the field Bud sold to Grottig and Sons the year he died. *This site marks the future home of Grottig Corporation, state-of-the-art processors of quality meat products.* Bee hadn't wanted to live next to a packaging plant, but Bud said it was a great opportunity to sell eroded fields pocked with buffalo wallows. He sold a quarter of what the Grottig Corporation offered to buy, betting he'd get a higher price if he held out for the rest. To celebrate the first sale, he blew half the payment on a white convertible, which he and his daughter drove all over the county discussing businesses they could start with their upcoming cash injection—a mini-golf course, a movie theatre, an ice-cream parlor, a birdhouse factory, a costume shop, a birthday party service, a car dealership. Mile after mile dreams exploded over them like fireworks.

Whatever they did, Velvet would star in all the commercials and they would employ Sullivan's Nod, a subtle persuasion technique Bud had read about that involved nodding during a pitch to increase sales. He practiced on Velvet. Nodding, he'd ask her if she'd like to scratch his back, and after she did, he nodded and asked if she'd like to get his shoes, which sent her running to the front hall. He practiced on Bee. Nodding, he'd say, "I have a feeling you're gonna give me a supper fit for the gods," and when minutes later she put a steaming plate of roast beef and green beans boiled with onions and bacon in front of him, he winked at his daughter and said, "See? I'm getting good at this!" Sullivan's Nod would help them sell all-important extras such as the nineteenth hole in their mini-golf course, leather seats at their car dealership or pie at their diner. Why hadn't he thought of a diner before? Or a bakery? Bee was a great cook. Maybe they could tie it in with a cookbook deal or the birthday party venture?

Maybe.

All of Big Bend buzzed with the word after the sale of the land to the Grottigs. The town council even put up a sign next to the Grottig billboard: *The city of Big Bend welcomes the Grottig family, provider of 5,000 jobs and proposed William B. Grottig Elementary.* Peter said maybe, too.

"No," Velvet told him. Growing up, Velvet had only ever seen two ways out of Big Bend: going to the state university or becoming a missionary. There was no way she was going to live in a jungle wearing outdated clothes writing letters to the home congregation requesting ramen noodles and sanitary napkins, but school wasn't her forte either. "You're too smart to stay here, Peter. I'll go with you and wait tables until we get married."

"But maybe we'll do better here?" They had a picnic by the creek on a square of AstroTurf leftover from the prototypes Bud built for the mini-golf course. "Big Bend will double with Grottig workers, meaning hundreds more mouths to feed, which if our projections are correct, could mean a second Dale Mercantile. My dad and I would both need to run one."

"Your mother can do it."

Peter laughed.

"Let him hire someone. You've already been accepted."

"Dad says I'll earn more in the four years it takes to graduate than I would in ten years as a teacher."

"Teaching isn't the only thing you can do with a math degree. You could be an accountant or an engineer or maybe even a scientist."

"I can always go to college, Velvet. This Grottig thing is a once-in-a-lifetime opportunity. I'm my father's only son. He's built everything for me, and when he retires, it will be mine."

Built everything. A crummy store in a ghost town. "So?"

"*So?* It would all be yours, too!"

"But I don't want to live in Big Bend!"

"Not even when we're married and have our own house?"

"I don't want to work in a grocery store!"

"I'm not asking you to. I'd want you to look after"—he blushed—"our children."

"Not here!"

"Wasn't it good enough for us?" When Velvet failed to reply, he added, "Don't you love me?"

"Of course, but we made other plans."

"We didn't know about the Grottigs then. We have to go with change, Velvet."

"And what if they don't build their stupid plant?"

"I've seen the floor plans with my own eyes. Chicago architects are expensive. Why would the Grottigs pay all that money to draw a building they aren't going to build? Honestly, Velvet, you're not being reasonable." He cleared his throat as he took her hand. "You're sensitive at the moment," he said, referring to her father's recent death, "but soon your head will clear."

With no alternate plan for her future or the grades to go to university herself, she broke up with him on the AstroTurf. Worst of all, she loved him. He pleaded and cried, but she stood her ground. Her beauty made her feel more powerful than his father and one hundred Grottigs. She and Peter had been homecoming king and queen three years running, and the fact that everyone talked about their wedding as if the invitations had been printed made Velvet feel like the event was fated to occur regardless of a glitch like a break-up.

News of the rift shook the town, though not its citizens' certainty the couple would reunite. They were kids and kids spun tiffs into tornadoes. Peter left daisy bouquets on the steps of the farmhouse and twelve-page love poems in her mailbox, commencing a summer of flirtation, back glances and blushes that made Velvet feel like she and Peter were putting on a play for the whole town. By the end of July, Peter talked her into going to a drive-in movie, and to prevent him from getting overconfident, Velvet made him stop at first base instead of third. Everything seemed to be going according to her plan until they went swimming in the creek one mid-August afternoon, and when she asked when he had to register for classes, the fight started all over again, only they couldn't resolve it because Velvet was running late to her shift at the Qwik Stop. Four hours later, she was on the back of Blankety Blank's hog.

After years of hooing and hawing, the Grottig Corporation never made another offer for her family's land, never built the plant, never attracted new residents, never built the promised school. Peter never went to college. Someone, Velvet thinks, as she gazes out her bedroom window, should have torn the billboards and their false promises down, although they do prove she was right, which, after all her mistakes, is her only consolation. She hopes they shout it at Peter every time he passes them in the same hand-me-down car he drove in high school.

Tiny Mite once quoted a verse from the Book of Revelation

describing the end times as a "sea of glass mixed with fire," which is precisely what Velvet's stomach turns into when she thinks about Peter. Feeling a swell rise in her stomach, she jumps down from the window ledge and scurries down the stairs. As she rounds the corner into the kitchen, the tip of the swell burns her heart. She's got to make it to the deepest part of the basement before the shards gathering in the back of her throat spew from her mouth, so that no one, especially her daughter, hears the screech grinding glass makes as it rushes through her teeth.

# NOVEMBER

# Two hours into her butter-churning shift, Velvet drops

the dasher into the hole of the oak barrel and slumps into the rocking chair by the open door of the one-room log cabin she shares with three wax figures: one kneads plastic dough on a rough wooden table, one spins cotton by the stone hearth and one works at a quilting loom under the cabin's one sooty window. None of the wax figures look down at their work, but gaze blankly ahead.

Despite the embers glowing in the fireplace, the cabin is so cold Velvet can see her breath. She should listen to Bee and wear long johns and leg warmers under her dress, but in her mind, the longer she holds out the longer autumn holds out: Velvet versus winter. In a way she's already won: some years the kids trick or treat in snowdrifts, and yet three weeks later, it's only snowed twice. Shivering, Velvet pulls the shawls off all of the wax figures and ties them around her shoulders.

Her boss, who prowls the premises pretending to be a much-feared Sheriff Shurbetter, doesn't allow his employees to wear modern conveniences that "could undermine Prairie Town's mission to be one hundred percent authentic," so she peers out the window to make sure no one is coming before pushing up the sleeve of her dress and checking the time on the digital watch she wears on her upper forearm. It could get her fired, but without it she'd drop out of human time and get lost in God's—Tiny Mite has been acting out Old Testament stories—where a day takes millions of years and people live to be six hundred. According to the digital watch, her shift won't end for another two hours and fifty minutes, an intolerable length of time to wait for a cigarette.

Rain runs down the cracked wooden doorframe and pools inside on the dirt floor. Aware of Sheriff Shurbetter's reluctance to get his antique hobnail boots wet, Velvet reaches under her skirt, takes out the crumpled pack and lighter she hides in her knee-high socks and pulls out a cigarette. Two days to Thanksgiving. Thirty-one days to Christmas. The Thanksgiving festival will include a pumpkin-throwing contest and scarecrow race, Christmas a nativity pageant. After that, Prairie Town will close for the season. Three paychecks to square one. Halfway through her cigarette, Velvet hears splotchy footsteps. She runs to the fireplace, smashes it in a metal bucket next to the woodpile, tightens the strings on her gingham bonnet and resumes her position behind the butter churner.

Two ex-classmates—Bonita Harding, still wearing her yellow-and-blue high school letterman jacket with its *Class of '80* embroidery, and Dody Schnaut, in a puffy red ski parka—run inside and shake out their frizzy hair. The strong smell of alkaline setting solution means one of their perms is fresh. Dody and Bonita go straight to the fireplace and speak with their backs to Velvet.

"So what's your big news?"

"Peter Dale is getting married."

"No way. He isn't dating anyone."

"He's been dating a whole year, in secret."

"Secret dating, my ass. He must have gotten someone pregnant."

Velvet feels short of breath. Dody, despite graduating with worse grades than her, is now a dental hygienist. The truck driver with whom Bonita eloped after two weeks' acquaintance crashed his rig four months later and left her a half-million-dollar life insurance policy. Does her dumb luck set her free? No, Bonita prefers to be the Alexis Carrington of Big Bend rather than a merely well-off person somewhere else.

Dody and Bonita turn, pretending they hadn't noticed Velvet butter churning in the corner.

"Velvet Baumhauer?"

"You still work here?"

"Her name's Purdy Smith." Sheriff Shurbetter strides into the cabin. "You got any questions about the making of our handmade butter, just shoot."

Smirking, Bonita steps forward. "How long does it take to make it?"

Velvet's cheeks burn. "Hours and hours."

"And where is Mr. Smith?" asks Dody.

Fighting tears, Velvet slams the dasher against the bottom of the butter barrel. "Out killing dinner."

Sheriff Shurbetter nods with approval. "I hate to rain on your parade, ladies, but we're closing early on account of the weather, so if you'll run along to the General Store, we're passing out free stick candy with each rain check."

Dody thanks Velvet for the "enlightening demonstration." Giggling, the two of them leave.

Sheriff Shurbetter repositions the wig on the wax figure

kneading bread. "I'll be happy to lock up your cabin, Velvet, if you'd like to join your friends."

Velvet grips the dasher to keep her hands from shaking. "They're not my friends."

"Really? They inquired after your whereabouts." He sniffs the air. "I don't smell cigarettes, do I?"

"I told them not to."

"Smokers don't get free candy in my outfit!" He rushes out the door.

Velvet takes the half-smoked butt out of the bucket and slips it into her bra. Peter marrying? There are no candidates within a twenty-mile radius.

# The beyond. One hundred and fifty-two miles from

Big Bend, all the radio stations Velvet knows, lost to static. Her heart, suddenly, a bird with a broken wing. The green car, suddenly, a mistake? It's driver, suddenly, untrustworthy? Has she done the right thing?

Velvet soothes herself analyzing the evidence:

Dashboard: free of cracks and dust.

Upholstery: free of holes and stains.

Radio dials: free of grime and missing pieces.

Rearview mirror and windows: free of divots and cracks.

Floors: free of mud and slush.

The green car's gasoline: paid for with a platinum credit card.

The green car's plastic smell: a full blast of the faint new car smell Bud's white convertible bore the day he brought it home.

The green car's driver: gray suit, gold tie, gold cufflinks, caramel leather oxfords identical to the one Luvie tore off Bobby Kennedy. Whether he's a banker, lawyer, newscaster or businessman feels irrelevant when everything about his appearance *indicates someone more responsible and accomplished than anyone Velvet has ever met.*

*Velvet strokes her seat belt, smooth as the white satin banner she once wore over her homecoming gown. Everything will be OK. Her window fills with marvels. Metal not wooden electrical poles. Wooden not metal fences. Wide not deep ditches. Blue not black mile markers. Like air. The novelty of it all.*

# Lying on her back, a bent knee gripped in each hand,

Tiny Mite screams, "Lord, why hast thou forsaken me?"

A flash of pink through her bedroom door. "What the hell is going on in here?"

Tiny Mite sits up, surprised to see her mother wearing the pioneer dress she usually leaves in the Prairie Town locker room. "I'm practicing for the Christmas play."

"With a pillow under your shirt?"

Tiny Mite removes the pillow and pulls her denim skirt over her knees. "I want to be Mary."

"Even if it *was* Christmas"—tomorrow, Velvet realizes with dread, is the first of December. Where will she find money for presents?—"Mary doesn't yowl like a coyote."

"She does during birth. I want to pep up the nativity scene this year."

Velvet scans the room. Toys everywhere. Blankets on the floor. Her favorite set of sheets tacked to the ceiling. On the bedside table—a mountain of multicolored gum wads on the ceramic gum saver. On the dresser top—nests, bones, snake skins, arrowheads, various animal skulls. In the corner—can it be?—a pile of headless, naked dolls. "For once be a good girl and go to bed."

A thought bubble appears above Tiny Mite's head: *But we haven't had supper!* Noticing deep circles under Velvet's eyes, Tiny Mite is pleased to have exciting news. "Guess what I found out at school today?"

"Can you tell me later? I've had a horrible day."

"Miss Wright's going to have a shivaree!"

Recalling Dody and Bonita, Velvet stops. She thinks of the Datsun she saw in the Dales' driveway. Surely not the red one always parked next to the bookmobile in the school parking lot? Nancy Wright? "Are you sure?"

Tiny Mite relishes her mother's interest. "Benny told me at recess."

All this time Velvet discounted the gossip about the plastic surgeon in Denver. A nose job. Scar resurfacing. "Does she look different to you this year?"

Tiny Mite nods. "Grandma says plastic is the currency of the Antichrist."

Peter and Nancy Wright? The letters of their names burn their way down Velvet's throat like a gulp of boiling water. "Who is she marrying?"

"I don't know, but Benny says at the end of the school year." Tiny Mite stops when she realizes her mother is crying.

Velvet wipes her tears with her sleeve. "What happens to Miss Wright at the end of the school year?"

"She's moving away."

Velvet's stomach falls out from under her. "Where?"

"I don't know, but if we bang pots and pans together at the shivaree, she'll have a baby!"

"No!" Velvet turns and scurries down the ladder.

Tiny Mite holds her breath until the front door slams. When

she feels this confused, she pretends to be Nancy Drew, and starting from the moment Mimi interrupted the birth of Jesus, searches their conversation for clues. What are clues? Things that aren't quite right. Tiny Mite picks up the tablet on her bedside table and makes a list.

*Clue #1: Mimi came home from work in her pioneer dress.*
*Clue #2: Mimi smelled like cigarettes.*
*Clue #3: Mimi said "hell."*
*Clue #4: Mimi forgot my bedtime.*
*Clue #5: Mimi forgot that shivarees are parties.*
*Clue #6: Mimi was angry Miss Wright is getting married.*

And why, Tiny Mite wonders, staring at Clue #6. The answer lies in another clue, something she overheard Bee saying when she got home from school: *How could Nancy do such a thing when she and Velvet were so close in school?* The solution of the mystery is so obvious Tiny Mite can't believe she had to pretend to be Nancy Drew to solve it. She goes to her desk, finds her silver glitter pen, a piece of pink paper and writes a note. Thrilled to solve her mother's problem, she climbs down the ladder and slides the paper under her bedroom door.

*The green car chucking fields, fences, trees, silos, farms,*
*tractors, trains, towns onto the road behind it, the stretch between*
*Velvet and Big Bend—eighty-four miles now—piled high as a*
*mountain. Big Bend. The farm. The crashed airplane. The speed of*
*the green car strips her clean. Prairie Town. Dody. Bonita. Nancy*
*Wright. Gone. Velvet feels like the green car's oak figurehead,*
*impervious to storms, tidal waves, gales.*

*Bee. Luvie. Jiggs.*
*She deserves this road.*
*Peter. Tiny Mite.*
*The truth: leaving him hurts more. He was right that day at the*
*playground. The smell of lilacs still sickens her, so much that she*
*poured gasoline onto Bee's bushes to kill them, but every spring*
*their blooms emerge, asserting his charge. Eight years Velvet has*
*striven to prove him wrong and failed.*

*She deserves this road.*
You made your bed now lie in it.
*Velvet wills the green car to go, go, go. Faster toward it.*
Not *here* here.
*The beyond.*

# Velvet runs to the creek through the steel dusk, cold

wind roaring in her ears. Peter and Nancy, Nancy, Nancy, Nancy, Peter? At the creek's edge she doubles over, lungs burning, and as she gazes through the leafless trees, wonders how there can be so much sky, but no air?

After a long cry, Velvet collapses onto a pile of wet leaves and reaches into her sock for her cigarette pack and lighter. Maybe Peter and Nancy aren't getting married? Numb hands shaking, she lights the cigarette. Maybe there's been a misunderstanding? Her sources, after all, are Dody, Bonita and Tiny Mite. Velvet watches snowflakes land and melt on her palm. Even if the worst-case scenario is true, maybe she can talk him out of it? Maybe if she makes a bold enough gesture he'll finally forgive her? Maybe the whole engagement is a means of testing her?

"Maybe." Velvet says it out loud to make it possible. As neither she nor Peter have dated much over the years, Velvet has nurtured the fantasy that merely pride has kept them apart, that they're still putting on a show for the town, her abstinence, her misery proclaiming: I can bear your punishment. I am still here. I am waiting. Couldn't he see? "Maybe, maybe, maybe," Velvet whispers, teeth chattering, but repeating it makes her hear the echo. Maybe isn't a key or a door, but a hallway of mirrors.

The farmhouse is dark and quiet when Velvet returns from the creek soaked and chilled to the bone. Though it's nearly eleven, she goes to the kitchen phone and dials Carole Bunt, her backgammon buddy and Prairie Town's septuagenarian soap maker. Carole answers in a gruff voice that softens as soon as Velvet says her name. Carole doesn't make Velvet state the reason for her call, but kindly gets to the point: Peter and Nancy are getting married on New Year's Day. Over the Easter break they are honeymooning in Hawaii. At the end of the school year they are going to the state university where he will start preparatory classes for a bachelor degree in science. Nancy will do a doctorate in education. Carol apologizes. Velvet thanks her and hangs up.

Gagging on glass mixed with fire, she runs into the basement, and when she reaches the last shelf, falls onto the floor. Rolling on the dusty floor in her wet dress, Velvet cries so hard it feels like she's coughing up all of her organs only to suck them all in again, raveling and unraveling, never in equal lengths, eyes burning, throat sliced, lungs scorched. Peter leaving Big Bend? She shakes, gasps, hyperventilates, hiccups.

Velvet reaches into her sock. Two cigarettes left. Deciding she can manage with one in the morning and stop for more on the way to work, she lights one. Taking a deep drag, she clings to the only consolation she can find: Peter doesn't love Nancy Wright. She's just the last train out of Big Bend, and now that her face is fixed, he can bear to jump aboard. Isn't that what Blankety Blank was to her for a few months?

After Blankety Blank left, Velvet swallowed her pride and wrote Peter so many apology letters he eventually agreed to see her. They met at the school playground one Sunday evening when the lilac bushes were in bloom. He sat on a bouncy horse. She leaned against the slide. Both kept their hands in their pockets. Peter looked anywhere but her eyes or belly. She spoke first.

"Can you love me at all after the stupid things I've done?"

He kicked the gravel and shrugged, a gesture she interpreted as "maybe"—he bounced his heel whenever he deliberated—and the grain of hope it provided after so much regret and despair made her blurt an offer that crossed her mind on the way there: if he'd take her back, she'd put the baby up for adoption.

He squinted. "You'd do that?"

She said she would.

"Are you sure?"

She said she was.

His lips curled with disgust. "What kind of person would give her baby away?"

Velvet tried to backpedal.

"What kind of mother are you?" He shook his head. "I can't believe I ever wanted you to have my children." He got off the horse. "Shame on you, Velvet Lynn Baumhauer! *Shame!*" He ran away.

And yet Velvet still wonders if she gave up too soon, her sole piece of evidence that first shrug. That and the fact that his anger seemed more rooted in disappointment than hate, in fact, if he had hated her, why agree to meet? At the time she believed emotions that strong were absolute, but now knows better. Even Luvie's grief has frayed. Deciding she'll steal a cigarette from Luvie in the morning, Velvet takes the last cigarette out of her sock and smokes it. She puts both butts in the Folgers coffee can she hides in an opening between two bags of cement.

Upstairs, as she enters her bedroom, Velvet nearly slips on a pink piece of paper. Recognizing Tiny Mite's handwriting in silver glitter ink, she smiles as she picks it up. *Dear Velvet,* she reads, *Mr. and Mrs. Wright request the honor of your presence at the marriage of their new-improved daughter, Nancy (a.k.a. Miss Wright). You've always been her favorite friend, so we hope you'll forgive us for losing your invitation and come. Be there or be square! Love, Mr. and Mrs. Wright.*

*Blur of snow-crusted fields and dashed white lines.* *Opening her window—automatic!—Velvet leans her head against the smooth doorframe—new plastic!—and closes her eyes. Cold air rushing over her face, it's like breathing underwater.*

*She thinks of the red playhouse, the air mattress, imagines Peter above her, drowning in his hands, blankets breaking over them like waves. Piles of schoolbooks around them, shoals. He asks whether she knows that ninety percent of the ocean's living space is comprised of a pitch-black zone called the abyss, only ten percent of which has ever been explored? With his hand in this spot, she's been to the bottom and back—twice. Does she know that the world's longest mountain range—which is underwater— is longer than the Andes, Rockies and Himalayas combined? She's scaled it all—without safety ropes. Does she know the heart of a blue whale is the size of a car? Hers is the size of an aircraft carrier. Does he know she's a fairy, siren, contortionist squeezing herself into a corked bottle? Bobbing twice around the world?*

*Escaping seconds before running out of air? Swimming faster than marlin?*

*She made mermaids jealous.*

*Velvet opens her eyes. Wind whisks her tears out the window. The road still there. The horizon still a door.*

Brave girl.

*Telephone poles, fence posts fall like dominoes. One day at a time. One foot in front of the other. Isn't that what Bee always says? One mile at a time. She can do this. A white bag stuck on a mile marker waves. See? Already eleven miles from Big Bend. Devil-may-care speed. The green car chucking fields, trees, silos, farms, tractors, trains, towns onto the road behind it.*

*In most parts of the state today, cloudy skies with winds gusting to forty mph out of the northwest and a chance of afternoon snow flurries.*

Velvet storms into the kitchen as Bee deposits a steaming Mickey Mouse-shaped pancake onto Tiny Mite's plate. "Why is Luvie's door locked?"

*Icy roads caused by overnight sleet.*

And why, Velvet wonders, does her mother turn the radio up so goddamned loud?

*Travel advisories for the following counties.*

Bee frowns at Velvet's dirty, crumpled Prairie Town uniform. "You didn't sleep in that?" From Velvet's red eyes, snarled hair and mascara-stained cheeks, Bee knows she's heard about Peter and Nancy, but getting fired for having a slovenly appearance will only make things worse. She sets down her spatula. "Take off that dress so I can iron it." What could be more infuriating, she wonders, than watching one's child suffer and having no better solution than *ironing*?

Velvet can tell Bee knows about Peter and Nancy by the way her mother avoids her gaze, as if she's ashamed, which she probably is. Velvet brought this on herself, which in Bee's book means she's forfeited her "boo hoo rights." Velvet bets Bee never even broaches the subject.

*Overnight a low of five with an eighty percent chance of snow.* More snow. Velvet sighs. On with frozen windshields, chained tires, masked faces, throbbing fingers. Luckless travelers without snowplows or extra tires freezing on the interstate. "I need to get into Luvie's room." Velvet switches off the radio. "I left something in there that I need for work." If she doesn't find a cigarette she will suffocate.

Bee pours two more pancakes onto the griddle, hoping breakfast will make Velvet feel better. "She's sleeping. You'll have to get it later. Up all night with the stomach flu. I need you to dial Henniker and call in sick for her."

"Flu, my foot. Try a hangover." Luvie, Velvet guesses, must have come home during one of the few intervals in which she managed to doze. She closes her eyes, so tired her bones feel chalky.

Bee flips the pancakes with one hand and feels Velvet's pale, clammy forehead with the other. "You're shaking. You must have caught Luvie's flu."

Velvet rubs her eyes. It feels like a bucket of sand is trapped under each eyelid. "Mother, please make Luvie unlock the door." She goes to do it herself, but trips over a box on the floor labeled "Heat waves and Blizzards."

Bee grabs the box, and when she can't find any place for it, shoves it into the oven. "What do you need?" She vows to keep the house cleaner. "Take off your boots so I can polish them."

Velvet snatches her purse and car keys from the kitchen counter. "I'm leaving." She can smell the pancakes on the griddle starting to burn, but doesn't have the energy to mention it. "I have to be at work early."

"Wait!" Bee grabs the components of Tiny Mite's lunch and stuffs them into a brown paper bag. "You need to take Tiny Mite to school."

"What about the bus?"

"We missed it."

"*We?*" Velvet glares at her daughter poking her untouched pancake as if she has all the time in the world. How will she buy cigarettes without Tiny Mite blabbing her secret?

Bee removes the smoking, burnt pancakes from the griddle and drops them into the sink. "I kept her back to take her temperature. You don't want her going to school sick do you? And she needed a shower and a blow dry. I don't dare send her into this weather with wet hair. We would have been on time if you'd given her a bath yesterday, or the day before. Do I have to do everything?"

Tiny Mite's school is fifteen miles away. Velvet clasps her hands together to keep them from shaking. "Please, mother. I really need you to take Tiny Mite to school this morning."

"Velvet, I would if I could, but I told Bonita I'd have her curtains finished before her mah-jong, and I don't dare risk letting her down. All the windows in her house need doing."

Tiny Mite pushes her pancake away. "I can ride my bike to school."

Bee winks at her. "In the snow? And be late for your big presentation? Nonsense. Finish your pancake while your mother washes her face and combs that hair."

Velvet marches to the booth, yanks Tiny Mite out of it and orders her to get her coat. She grabs the sack lunch and rams it into Tiny Mite's Kermit the Frog backpack.

Bee hands Velvet a set of long johns as she and Tiny Mite scuffle out the door. Deeply saddened about Peter's upcoming wedding, but terrified to say anything that will upset her daughter more, Bee squeezes Velvet's arm to convey her support.

Interpreting the squeeze as further proof her mother has relegated Peter's engagement to the unspeakable, Velvet yanks her arm away and drags Tiny Mite across the porch, telling herself to move, move, move otherwise she might crumble. "For the love of God, Tiny Mite, zip your coat in the car!"

The wind nearly prevents them from reaching Bud's splurge. This morning, Velvet thinks, as she slips on the ice-coated gravel, was supposed to be nothing more than a door through which she would step into a day with the two simple tasks of buying cigarettes and pretending to churn butter and it's not yet eight and already the day is shrunken, kinked and knotted. When will she walk through a day without having to stoop? She holds Tiny Mite under her arm to keep her from slipping. "We have to do a quick errand on the way to school, baby, but it won't take long."

Looking at her Snoopy watch, a thought bubble appears above Tiny Mite's head: *Mrs. Goode will take roll in twenty minutes!* Though afraid of being late, Tiny Mite doesn't argue, nor does she ask for help with her seat belt once they're inside the car. Mimi has traded eyes with a nasty, old rooster.

Velvet drives with one hand and bites the nails of the other. According to the fuel indicator, Bud's splurge has an empty tank. "We're running on vapors. We'll have to get gas, too." If they even make it to a gas station. It would be just her luck, Velvet thinks, to be stranded on the side of the road in her prairie dress without a cigarette.

Tiny Mite looks at her watch. Missing roll is one thing, but Benny is passing out peanut butter cups for his birthday during morning milk. "Mimi, I can't be late!"

"You're going to be late and that's that!" Velvet's mouth feels dryer than a hay bale. She digs in her purse, finds a lemon cough drop stuck to the bottom, and despite the black bits stuck to it, sucks it into her mouth. Catching the reflection of her daughter's crestfallen face in the window, Velvet swells with guilt. "Please don't be angry. I'm not feeling well." She watches the fuel gauge. "Too bad you don't hate school like I did. Then we could play hooky."

Tiny Mite would love nothing more than an adventure with her mother, but Velvet smells dirty, her clothes are messy and she keeps looking into the rearview mirror as if KGB agents are following them. "Maybe another day. I have my big presentation in second period, remember?"

Velvet vaguely recalls something about rats. She would have picked horses or butterflies or tropical fish. "Of course I remember."

Tiny Mite pats her backpack. "I brought ketchup for blood!"

Velvet will surely hear about it at the next parent–teacher meeting, but isn't in the mood to argue. "That's great, baby. Knock 'em dead."

Velvet turns on the radio, punching the preset buttons until she finds a talk show hosting a contest in which callers gargle songs, and if the DJ recognizes the tune, receive free tickets to a Twisted Sister concert. The first contestant gargles, "We All Live in a Yellow Submarine," but the DJ guesses, "Islands in the Stream." Tiny Mite laughs. Velvet switches it off.

"Hey, Mimi, did you know there have been fifty ice ages?"

"That all?" Velvet turns the defrost button to high. "Feels like more."

The Qwik Stop sign looms ahead. Velvet has boycotted it since Blankety Blank disappeared, but with her gas gauge bouncing into the negative range and the prospect of waiting ten more minutes for a cigarette growing unimaginable, she pulls into its lot, passes several 18-wheelers and parks in front of a pump. Velvet orders Tiny Mite to wait in the car and then runs into the station, the laces of her untied pioneer boots dragging through the gray slush.

Velvet goes straight to the cashier and looks around as she waits in line. Other than a new till and rotating wire rack filled with paperback books and cassette tapes, the Qwik Stop doesn't look any different than it did when she worked there. Country music still plays overhead. The Victorian clock over the hot dog machine still ticks loudly. The door still makes a high-pitched *ding!* whenever someone opens it. When the man in front of Velvet leaves, she plops her purse onto the counter. "I need one, no make it two, packs of Slims, please. And seven bucks on pump three."

"Luvie doesn't like those." Tiny Mite stands on her toes, peering over the counter.

"I told you to stay in the car!"

"But I'm missing Benny's peanut butter cups. Please get me one for making me miss roll?"

"How much are they?"

The clerk is a tall, silver-haired man whose cap says *Old Fart* over the bill. A dozen short black hairs dot the ball of his nose. He yanks at one as he flips through a notebook next to the till. "Says here fifty cents."

Velvet digs in her purse, shakes it and digs again. "Tiny Mite, you didn't take a ten out of my purse, did you?"

"No."

Velvet remembers spending it earlier that week on hair color, nail polish and bread. Hands shaking, she struggles to count her loose bills and coins. "Actually, I'll take six bucks on pump three and one pack of Slims."

"Luvie likes menthols."

"These are for a friend at work, baby. What did I say about staying in the car?"

"What about my peanut butter cup?"

Velvet squeezes her temples. "I'm sorry. Make it $5.50 on pump three, the Slims and the candy."

The till beeps as he tallies her order. "With tax that's $14.81. Need a bag?"

Realizing she's still short by more than a dollar, Velvet pulls the long johns and a pair of pantyhose out of her bag. "I'm sure I have a five in here somewhere." She finds several coins in her make-up kit, but can't concentrate enough to adjust the amount of gas to get the total right. Feeling a sharp pain in her chest, she wonders if Bee has finally force-fed her enough bacon and butter to give her a heart attack.

The clerk puts his hand on Velvet's shoulder. "Let me help." He gathers and counts the coins and crumpled bills she's placed on the counter, takes a ten dollar bill out of his own wallet and punches the buttons on the till. "That's two packs of Slims, ten dollars on pump three and one peanut butter cup."

"That's so kind of you, but I really couldn't. Make it one pack of Slims and whatever's left for gas."

The clerk winks at her. "I wouldn't want you letting down that friend at work." He drops the change from the transaction into the green plastic charity cup next to the till and then reaching into the candy display, hands Tiny Mite a peanut butter cup.

"Thanks!" She tears it open.

Velvet stuffs her things into her purse. "I can't thank you enough. It's been one of those days."

"I've had many such days myself." He holds out his hand. "Oscar."

Velvet shakes his hand. "How come I've never seen you before? You didn't actually move here, did you?"

Oscar laughs. "I'm just filling in for a hunting buddy whose mother passed."

"Jule's mother died?"

"You knew her?"

"I worked here a long time ago."

"Who should I tell Jule sends her regards?"

"Velvet, Velvet Baumhauer, not that there are any other Velvets around here. Tell him I'm real sorry about Edith. She used to give the employees homemade rag pudding at Christmas."

A teenaged boy with dyed black hair, a 50s-style overcoat and narrow tie printed with a keyboard steps in line behind Velvet and clears his throat.

Oscar nods. "I'll do that, Velvet. You take care."

Velvet pulls Tiny Mite aside and speaks in a firm tone. "Now this time I mean it. Go wait in the car while I go to the bathroom."

Tiny Mite's teeth are blackened with chocolate. "But it's cold out there!"

Velvet pinches Tiny Mite's arm. "Do it!" If she doesn't have her cigarette, she might commit murder. "If you don't obey, I'll tell Bee you have a voodoo doll."

"I don't!"

"Oh yeah? What is that baby doll with pins stuck all over it?"

"She's having acupuncture."

"Like those headless dolls in your room?"

"They're cannibal food."

"What?"

"They live in Papua New Guinea."

Velvet feels like screaming. "Go to the car this second or I'll snitch about the pictures of dead people you keep under that tree."

Tiny Mite's eyes widen. She runs to Bud's splurge and sits with her legs tucked inside her brown corduroy dress. Gazing through the mud-splattered passenger window at the stampede of dark clouds churning the sky, she searches for the odd puffy white one. Puffy white clouds are God's thought bubbles. God can't talk, so she fills them in for Him. *Uh-huh. Yup. Hmm.* When she runs out of clouds, Tiny Mite makes one with her frozen breath: *Don't got the foggiest why Miss Wright is marrying the sad grocer even though I'm supposed to know everything.* Tiny Mite overheard Bee on the phone earlier that morning. Now that she knows the truth, she hates Miss Wright. Hare-lipped traitor! She hopes a forty-pound trichinosis-carrying rat bites her in the neck.

When the teenager's keyboard tie flutters past the windshield, Tiny Mite turns and scans the gas station for signs of her mother. Oscar leans over the counter reading a newspaper, tapping his cowboy boot. The teenager starts his brown Ford Escort. Tiny Mite follows its red tail lights across the road to the Dairy Queen drive-through. From now on, she decides, she can only look at red things. Her eyes hop from the Dairy Queen sign to its trash cans and upturned picnic tables to a barn on the horizon to a *STOP* sign near the interstate overpass to a *DO NOT ENTER* sign to an uh-oh, no more red things in sight, help, mayday, mayday her eyes are falling, falling until they're saved in the nick of time by the blinking turn signal of a green sports car exiting the interstate. It turns into the Qwik Stop parking lot and backs into the pump opposite Bud's splurge. Its Missouri license plate reads: *The Show-me State.* Tiny Mite likes its two bumper stickers: *My goldfish is smarter than your honor student* and *If you don't like my driving, get off the sidewalk!* The driver of the green car gets out. Holding his gold tie against his gray suit to keep the wind from blowing it in his face, he runs into the station.

A thought bubble appears above Tiny Mite's head: *Where the devil is Mimi?*

Rubbing a peephole out of the frosty film on the passenger window, Tiny Mite sees Mimi inside the station laughing with Oscar and the man with the gold tie. She looks so different it's like the Qwik Stop bathroom was a time machine that transported her to and from a Sunday afternoon pot roast, bath and nap. Her hair is combed, face clean, make-up fresh and boots laced. Mimi and the man with the gold tie continue their conversation as they walk out of the station, Mimi leaning close and throwing her head back like a wife telling a husband about the funniest thing she saw on TV while he was at work. The man lets go of his tie to make a wide-armed gesture. The tie flaps Mimi on the cheek.

Tiny Mite tries to decipher their muffled dialogue as they fill their respective tanks. The man says something about a speeding ticket he avoided in Iowa. Mimi laughs like he told her the funniest knock-knock joke on the planet. When her handkerchief blows out of her pocket, he runs into a snowdrift to retrieve it and touches her on the shoulder with one hand as he hands it to her with the other. As he shakes snow from his pant leg, Mimi thanks him as if he saved her life. He looks at Tiny Mite and then speaks to Mimi in a lowered voice. She, too, lowers her voice. Instead of laughing, her facial expression turns sober. Turning away from Bud's splurge, they talk some more.

Tiny Mite looks at her Snoopy watch. If they leave in the next ten minutes, she'll at least make second period to give her presentation on Norwegian rats. She does a mental rehearsal: Norwegian rats are nocturnal rodents that came to America around 1755 with the settlers and ate the black rats that came with the explorers and pilgrims. The teeth of Norwegian rats never stop growing, and because rats don't have dentists, turn dark yellow and sometimes even orange. Though Norwegian rats can be found all over the United States, 60 million live in New York City, where they eat 250 tons of food and drink 62,000 gallons of water, mostly from sewers. Norwegian rats do other really gross things like pee on their food, kill other rats' babies and make obscene gestures at New York City transport workers. They eat cadavers from the coroner's office, homeless people and sometimes even their own babies (alive!). Norwegian rats spread diseases like typhoid, rat-bite fever, salmonella and trichinosis, which is a worm that eats your brain until you can't think straight and die.

Tiny Mite knows she can get an A on this report if she could just make it to school, but Mimi and the man with the gold tie keep talking. She looks at her Snoopy watch. To keep herself from crying, she counts birds pouring through the sky.

At twenty-three birds, a cold gust swoops into the car, followed by Mimi breathing hard, flushed and smelling, strangely, not only of perfume, but cigarettes. Tiny Mite tries to make eye contact with her mother—one look will tell her everything will be all right—but the rooster eyes are back. Velvet turns the ignition twice, but Bud's splurge fails to start. Normally this causes her mother to bang the steering wheel and curse, but today she whispers, "Yes." When it starts on the third try, Mimi does not put on her seat belt, but reverses, and instead of pulling onto the road, drives the convertible to the telephone booth in the corner of the parking lot. She kills the engine, reaches under the seat, pulls a lever, jumps outs, slams the door and lifts the hood, all so jarringly, Tiny Mite feels like a character in a flipbook with missing pages.

Velvet's pink waist in the middle of the almond-shaped opening between the edge of the hood and dashboard looks like a pink iris in a huge eye. After a few clinks and clanks, the waist disappears, replaced by the yellow phone book hanging by a thick metal cord, the booth's 100-pound amber pendant. *Pink eye, yellow eye, blue eye, brown, ashes, ashes, we all fall down.* Where the devil, Tiny Mite wonders, has Mimi gone now? She looks at her

Snoopy watch. If they leave now, she might be able to squeeze her presentation into the end of second period.

Tiny Mite turns, and through the car's rear window, sees Mimi inside the gas station shaking clasped hands at Oscar like he's Principal Sharpe and she really, really needs him to release her daughter from detention this one time pretty pretty please. Oscar holds up his hands up and shakes his head as if they're at the Tower of Babel and he doesn't speak English. Mimi points at her watch. Oscar gazes at Bud's splurge and shakes his head again. Tiny Mite waves, but neither Oscar nor Mimi wave back. Mimi continues to shake her clasped hands until Oscar shrugs. Mimi blows him a kiss as she runs out the door, the wind pressing her thin cotton dress against her legs as she runs to the car. Finally!

Mimi opens the driver's door, but doesn't jump into the seat. Standing outside the car she shouts instructions so quickly Tiny Mite can barely understand. *Broken. Mechanic. Ride.* The words are like rushing birds. *Wait. Patient. Now.* It's like the migration of birds has swooped down and filled the car. *Nice man. Not long. Good girl.* Their wings flap against her face. *Wait here. Brave girl. Back in a jiffy.* When the door begins to shut, Tiny Mite jumps into the driver's seat and grabs Velvet by the waist. "But it's freezing in here!"

Mimi's cold pale hands grip Tiny Mite's shoulders. "Not *here* here. In the station! Quick, quick, run inside. Oscar's going to watch you."

Tiny Mite presses her head into Velvet's stomach, inhaling her mother's smell so deeply she imagines millions of cells in her body expanding like balloons. "But I want to go with you!"

"Mitchell's car only has two seats."

"Mitchell?"

"The nice man with the green car."

Tiny Mite needs to find her mother's eyes. She tries to push her head outside the car. "I can sit on your lap."

Mimi's cold hands hold her inside the car. "Please don't make this harder than it needs to be."

The tightness in her mother's voice is scary, especially with her eyes out of sight. "But how will I get to school?"

Mimi says in an even tighter, higher, stranger voice, "You may not make it today. Try and think of it as a vacation."

"But I don't want to stay here!" Tiny Mite pushes against her mother's waist.

Mimi pushes back. "You're not *staying*, just waiting!" Tiny Mite falls backward. Mimi slams the door.

Tiny Mite watches Mimi run and get inside the green car. Tiny Mite jumps out of Bud's splurge. The green car begins to drive away. "Wait!" she calls, running alongside it. Mimi faces the driver. If she would just turn and look at her. Tiny Mite doesn't care if she has rooster eyes. "Mimi, don't leave me!" The green car slows, filling her with relief, but when she slaps her hands against the passenger window, the green car lurches forward and accelerates across the oil-spilled lot. "Mimi, wait!" Tiny Mite screams.

The green car disappears onto the interstate.

*This moment a breath held too long. The green car a rocket approaching escape velocity. Velvet wills it to go faster. Or she'll lose her nerve, crumble, for good, into the slush on the side of the road. Melt. Her life will be a slow melting.*

*The green car stops.*

*No. "Go!"*

*"Are you sure?"*

*Marker-stained hands bang the window. Chocolate-smeared glass. If she turns, the capsule will break. She will fall. Her life will be a never-ending fall.*

*No. "Go!"*

*Roar of the engine.*

*Hands disappear.*

*Mimi! Wait!*

*Velvet covers her ears. Stop! Stop stopping me!*

*The green car approaches the on-ramp. Velvet grips the dashboard, lungs aching. Almost. Almost. Blur of snow-crusted fields and dashed white lines.*

Tiny Mite's tears blur the empty on-ramp. "Mimi, come back!"

Oscar steps out of the gas station in his shirtsleeves and gestures for her to come inside. "Your mother's getting a ride to the mechanic! She'll be right back!"

Throat burning, Tiny Mite stares at Bud's splurge in the corner of the lot. Hood up, it looks like a white grand piano pushed aside, that nobody knows how to play. She considers ignoring Oscar and waiting inside it—deathly cold will hasten Mimi's return—but when a gust nearly steals her hat, she runs to the station.

The door goes *ding!* as she enters. Oscar disappears behind a door that says *Staff Only* and returns with a tower of Styrofoam cups and a folding chair. He wedges the chair into the space between the door and a newsstand stuffed with magazines and maps. "What's your name, little girl?"

"She didn't tell you?"

"She was pretty upset about the car breaking down."

Tiny Mite's throat constricts. Her eyes fill with tears. "My name is Clea."

The folding chair has a camouflage life jacket duck-taped to its seat. Oscar pats it. "Get comfortable, Clea, and I'll make you a hot chocolate."

Tiny Mite would like to sit, but fears comfort will delay Mimi's return. Standing, she counts the wooden shoes—ten—nailed to the wall by the cash register bearing the sign: *You ain't much if you ain't Dutch.* The rest of the wall behind the till is plastered with signs announcing the sale of farms and baby gerbils, church activity notices and lost dog and cat flyers.

Oscar hands her a hot chocolate with a tiny yellow umbrella poking through its marshmallow. "May I take your coat, little lady?"

Grasping the zipper, Tiny Mite shakes her head. "My mother will be here soon."

"True." Oscar whistles his way back to the register, where he turns up the country and western station and spreads his newspaper across the counter. "You need anything, little lady, please holler." His Adam's apple pops out each time he turns a page.

A thought bubble appears above Tiny Mite's head: *Oh where oh where has my Mimi gone? Oh where oh where could she be?* She sips her hot chocolate, watching for green cars and tow trucks. The gas pumps in the middle of the lot look like disconsolate robots. *With her tail cut short and her ears cut long, oh where oh where could she be?* Tiny Mite tells herself to be patient—even light takes 75,000 years to cross the Milky Way.

Oscar clears his throat. "It's already been a half hour. Any minute now."

Customers come and go buying gas, slushies and lottery tickets. Oscar neatly folds his newspaper before returning it to the sales rack. He shuffles cards and plays solitaire by the cash register.

When a talk show begins on the country and western station, he changes it to soft rock. Three times he goes outside to smoke a cigarette. A black garbage bag blows across the lot, followed by a brown paper one. The wind, according to the radio announcer, is becoming southeasterly at twenty-five to thirty miles per hour. Tiny Mite tells herself this is nothing—solar winds sweep the sun at two million miles per hour.

Tiny Mite considers getting her backpack out of the convertible so she can do her homework, but fearing distractions will allow Mimi to take longer, stays in place and closes her eyes, mentally flipping through her Road Runner book for the comfort of Wile E. Coyote moving when she cannot. *Ding!* Her eyes spring open. A woman, not Mimi, walks into the station and buys a gallon of windshield fluid. Her blue sweatshirt says *DALE MERCAN-TILE*. Tiny Mite asks Oscar if she can use the phone.

"Course." Oscar looks at his watch and frowns. "You sure you don't want me to take your coat?"

Tiny Mite is sweating, but shakes her head.

"Whatever you say, sweetheart." He leads her through the door that says *Staff Only* into a small office plastered with hunting and fishing photos. Oscar points at the phone on the desk, telling her to help herself as he's got to man the register. When he's gone, Tiny Mite opens the desk drawers and finds several issues of *Car & Driver* and *American Sportsman*. Flipping through the phone book, she finds the D section.

*Dale, Arnold.*

*Dale, Bernie.*

*Dale, Peter.*

Tiny Mite dials Peter's number, and when she gets his answering machine, hangs up and flips to the business section for another number. The rotary dial is stiff. She taps her foot as it rings.

"Dale Mercantile," says a man with a soft voice.

In order to sound more grown up, Tiny Mite lowers her voice. "May I speak to Peter, please?"

"Speaking."

"I'm calling with an important announcement. It's an emergency. You're marrying the wrong woman!"

"Come again? Who is this?"

Tiny Mite panics. "Velvet!"

Peter sighs.

"Wait! It's not really Velvet!"

"No kidding."

"No, it's not! It's Tiny Mite and I'm calling to say you should only marry your sweetheart. Velvet is really sad. She cried all night when she heard what you're up to with my teacher."

"Tiny who?"

She hangs up.

Oscar pokes his head through the door. "Didn't get through?"

Tiny Mite shakes her head.

Oscar looks at his watch. "I'm sure there's a perfectly logical explanation." He takes a five-dollar bill out of his wallet. "How about you run across the street and get us some burgers?"

Tiny Mite is starving, but hesitates. "What if Mimi comes while I'm gone?"

"I'll send her over and she can have one, too."

Tiny Mite grabs the money and runs to the Dairy Queen. She has enough to buy two burgers, two fries and a small Snickers Blizzard. Back at the Qwik Stop, she inserts two straws into the blizzard so she and Oscar can share. He lets her sit on the counter. They dip their fries into a mound of ketchup in one of the hamburger wrappers. An elderly lady hobbles into the station complaining that she can't find the full service pump. Oscar tells her the Qwik Stop is self-service, but that he'll be happy to help. While he's gone, Tiny Mite steals five of his fries.

After lunch Oscar gives her a mug of pens and a book of cross-word puzzles from the magazine rack. The clues are too hard, but she's happy to color in the blank boxes as more customers come and go buying gas, potato chips and aspirin. After she fills in the last box on the last page, she begins to write on the back cover. *This old man he played crack he played knick-knack on my back. With a knick-knack paddy whack* she'll chip away the time *writing words on every line.* Running out of space in the book, she writes *please make her come* on her palm. Tiny Mite tells herself to be patient—Pluto takes 248 Earth years to orbit the sun, and if she lived there, she'd have to wait 248 years between each birthday.

In the corner of the lot near the broken-down convertible, Oscar changes a tire for a man whose arm is in a sling. When the man drives away, Oscar opens the door of Bud's splurge and sits in the driver's seat, one leg inside and one leg out. It starts on the first try. Oscar gets out and looks under the hood. Tiny Mite wonders why he puts it down when the mechanic will just have to put it up again. She reminds herself to be patient—though God claimed to make the world in six days, it really took 10–20 million years.

Oscar returns to the station. *Ding!* "I hate to say it, sweetheart, but it's after three."

"After three!" Tiny Mite jumps off the folding chair.

"Do you have any relations I could call?"

"Grandma. Bee. Burnella Baumhauer."

They go back through the door that says *Staff Only.* Oscar dials the farm. While he waits for an answer, Oscar digs in the top drawer of the desk, and when he finds a Tootsie Pop, hands it to Tiny Mite.

"May I please speak to Mrs. Baumhauer? Hello? Yes, mam, my name is Oscar and I'm calling from the Qwik Stop. The Qwik Stop? Jule Vandenkamp's station on the interstate?"

Tiny Mite sticks the sucker in her mouth. It tastes like root beer and has a fat circle around its middle. Saturn. Her tongue runs along its craters.

"Pardon? No, mam, I'm not with Jews for Jesus. No, not Jew, *Jule* with an L like lucky. Yes, my name's Oscar Howard and pardon? No, I'm not a telemarketer. There's been some kind of misunderstanding. Your granddaughter's been at the Qwik Stop all day. Her mother hasn't returned for her."

Tiny Mite drifts out of the office and returns to her chair by the window. Twisting the sucker against the roof of her mouth, she vows, "I, Clea Marie Baumhauer, promise on my honor cross my heart hope to die for liberty and justice for all not to bite or chew this sucker so it lasts all the way until Grandma gets here. Amen." She sucks too hard, however, because by the time the pink Buick screeches into the parking lot, she tastes root beer mixed with blood.

Bee runs into the station wearing one of Bud's hunting coats over her nightgown, tomato pincushions affixed to both wrists. "Where on earth is your mother?" Bee pulls Tiny Mite off the folding chair as if Velvet might be hiding underneath it. "Peter's called her three times this afternoon!"

Now Bee has rooster eyes. Tiny Mite bursts into tears.

Leaning against the gas pump, the driver of the green car strokes his gold tie. "Where are you headed?"

Velvet doesn't want him to know she's from here. "Henning." She doesn't want him to ask where that is, to learn that it's close. "Where are you headed?"

"Modesto."

Is she hearing correctly? "Modesto, California?"

He laughs. "Is there another one?"

What are the chances? "A friend of mine lives there." She imagines finding Trent's house and kicking him in the groin when he opens the door. "For the longest time, I've been trying to figure out how to get there."

The driver of the green car shrugs. "You're welcome to a ride."

Shrugs. Like it's nothing, offering a stranger a ride halfway across the country. Maybe it is? Maybe people do that? Isn't that what that writer did? That guy she was supposed to read about senior year? Had the whole adventure on mooched rides and a dime? Wrote about it on one long scroll of paper? An idea hatches in Velvet's mind. Head and heart whirl. The rest of her body feels frozen,

*wooden, heavy, yet here she is, moving, scheming, lying, executing.*
Wait here. Brave girl. Back in a jiffy.
*Will she be? Yes. Go. Do.*
Think of it as a vacation.
*Panic. Like she's being smothered. This moment a breath held too long.*

# PART II

# 1994

*"A photograph is both a pseudo-presence and a token of absence."*

\- **Susan Sontag**

# JANUARY

# Blinking turn signals, rotating hot dogs, fluttering ties.

Unlaced boots, runny mascara, dirty slush. The same blizzard of slippery images, and no matter how many times Clea's had this nightmare, they slip away before she can yank them out of order to prevent the shrinking glimpse of Velvet's bleached hair through the green car's mud-splattered window. *Back in a jiffy.* Gray exhaust, smudged handprints. *Nice man. Brave girl.* She tries to scream. Chokes. *Think of it as a vacation.* The dream runs out of air. *Not here here!* And spits her out. Clea sits up in bed.

Her racing heart.

It feels like a twelve-pound rat was released into her chest that day at the Qwik Stop, one that circles her ribcage, scratching and clawing to burrow free, running up and down her limbs, biting, hissing, rearing, growing frantic with each closed passageway.

Years ago her mind similarly scoured her memory for clues. Did Velvet leave because Tiny Mite ate her chocolate-flavored lip gloss? Maybe. Because she stole her cherry-print underwear? Maybe. Because she ate rations from the basement? Maybe. Because she missed the bus, insisted on that peanut butter cup or didn't stay in the car like she was told? Maybe it was the fake invitation she made for Miss Wright's wedding? Or telling George about whizzers? Maybe she shouldn't have called Peter? Shouldn't have been a meddler or a bad student? Been a burden? Been born?

Maybe.

Remembering the night her mother made terrifying noises in the basement, Tiny Mite revisited the opening between two cement bags. The Folgers can was still there. Maybe the answer to her mother's disappearance was hidden inside? Maybe it contained secret letters? A diary? A goodbye note? She pulled the can out of the hole and lifted its plastic lid.

Cigarette butts.

Convinced there had to be more, she thrust her hands into them, and unable to feel anything else, spread the butts onto the floor. Nothing. At the time she wondered if her mother left because she was addicted to smoking and couldn't bear to tell Bee? Maybe she didn't want to set a bad example for her daughter? Maybe she had lung cancer and wanted to spare everyone her death? Clea's tireless rat heart couldn't stop scratching, searching, burrowing, wondering. Over and over she replayed the day at the Qwik Stop trying to break down each action, see it opened like a fan to find movements within each movement, secrets that would explain the wheels in the middle of the "maybes."

Now she knows better.

Clea reaches for the water glass on the bedside table and takes a sip. Heart calming, she stretches her legs, causing a rag doll and stack of magazines—*Cosmopolitan*, *Seventeen*, *National Geographic*—to slide off the bed onto the floor. The Snoopy clock on her bedside table says 11:48. Her bedroom smells like sweaty sneakers, Anais Anais perfume and the malted milk waffles Bee makes every year on her birthday.

Clea lies back down, closes her eyes and listens to the wind play the house like a harmonica. "Fourteen." She says it out loud, waiting a moment before deciding that other than sore breasts and the throbbing pimple at the tip of her nose, fourteen feels as uneventful as thirteen.

Last year, she and Jiggs stripped her attic room, tore down the wall separating the storage area, installed skylights and painted everything white. Clea had planned to leave the walls bare, but one afternoon lying on her bed, so bored she watched weak tea shadows stretch and sink past the baseboards, she liked the shape of one and traced it with a pencil. The following day, she traced white lashings of morning light over her bed, and all day at school, wondered how far they'd strayed outside her lines. Back home she traced the shadows on her floor. Each day she repeated the process, varying times. On a Saturday, she timed her tracings to the half hour. Three seasons later, her walls and floors resemble a tide map.

Clangs downstairs remind her how little Bee cooks of late, how much effort she's taken to mark the occasion. Clea needs to go downstairs and eat at least one waffle, but hates her birthday for being the day she weakens most wondering whether Velvet will send anything, a torment given the ease with which she usually refuses her phone calls or mail. Years ago, she got out a piece of paper and with her glitter pen wrote: *I, Clea Marie Baumhauer, swear on Bud's grave and all the graves of all the war heroes who ever lived that I will NOT SPEAK TO VELVET EVER AGAIN!!!!!!* She shoved the contract into one of her grandmother's tax folders so she couldn't change her mind.

Clea leans down to the floor and grabs the antique zoetrope

she found in the attic when she and Jiggs redid her room. Setting it on her lap, she reaches inside and pulls out a pile of yellowed paper strips. Each strip is printed with a series of black illustrations that look indistinct until she slots one into the bottom of the dark metal perforated cylinder, spins it in its wooden base and looks through one of its slits. A black windmill rotates. She replaces the strip for one featuring a juggler. She has dancers, horses, penguins and a gymnast that flips over a pommel horse. Her favorite is the crow. She slots it in and gives the cylinder a strong push. Fourteen. She watches the crow flap its wings. Four more years until she's eighteen, five more academic grades until she's free. "Faster," she whispers, spinning the zoetrope. "Faster!"

Something crashes down in the kitchen. Worried Bee has dropped something—worsening diabetes has debilitated her left foot—Clea puts the zoetrope on her bedside table and gets out of bed. The floor is strewn with clothes. Shuffling through them, she pulls on garments close to the door and climbs down the ladder to the landing where it's always a relief to see Jiggs's boots, checkerboard woolen blankets and television in Velvet's old room.

Thirteen 8x10 school portraits of Velvet line the stairwell—high school senior to kindergartener. A ghost couldn't be sharper. Velvet here but not *here* here. People used to say *you don't look anything like your mother*, which she took to mean, *shame you're not as pretty as her*. Clea used to study these portraits, willing herself, praying, to prove them all wrong by blossoming into a brunette version of Velvet, but now, sliding down the staircase in thrice-worn, hole-ridden tube socks, their dissimilarities are a point of pride. Velvet in a ballerina bun and tiara. Velvet in feathered waves and rainbow eye shadow. Velvet in silver barrettes and glitter lip gloss. *You are nothing like your mother.* In case their contrasting features aren't enough—tall not petite, gawky not balletic—Clea compensates with long, uncombed hair, clumpy mascara and copious black eyeliner she never removes, only adds. She wishes someone would take Velvet's portraits down as much as she's relieved no one has. Passing them, her mother devolving as she descends, sets Clea seesawing. Missing her, hating her. Hoping, despairing.

"Have you seen the size of her loaves?" Bee says in the kitchen.

Clea stops on the bottom step, Velvet beside her, a kindergartener, front tooth missing, white blond hair French braided.

"Look at them, Luvie, and tell me the government's not putting hormones in the beef. Where else would she get equipment like that?"

"Speak for yourself, Bee. I had DDs."

"My foot. You had Cs and a pair of socks."

"Cup size shouldn't determine a girl's suitability for Sex Week. She's got no interest—haven't you noticed how she dresses or how much she studies?—so once and for all, Bee, don't make her go."

"It's Pastor Mike's final youth outreach before the hand-off. It won't kill her to make a show of support."

"Is that blue thing what I think it is?"

Bee sighs. "Should we give it to her?"

Curious, Clea steps into the kitchen wearing a faded black Mickey Mouse T-shirt and belted pair of Bud's army trousers. Bee and Luvie sit in the booth.

"The birthday girl!" Though alarmed about her granddaughter's appearance—somewhere between homeless person and drug addict—Bee reaches into the multi-pocketed fishing vest she wears over her nightgown to avoid trips for pens, scissors, tape, tissues, magnifying glasses, postage stamps or lemon drops, and takes out a kazoo.

Luvie sings the birthday song along with Bee's kazoo.

Embarrassed and grateful, Clea claps when they finish. "Thank you." From the television on the counter, Elmer Fudd promises *West and welaxation at wast and no more wascally wotten wabbits!* Every Saturday morning, Bee turns on the TV even though Clea hasn't watched cartoons for years.

Bee struggles out of the booth, wincing when her weight shifts onto her bad foot, and limps to the stove. Pouring batter from a glass beaker into the waffle maker, she almost says, "Tiny Mite," but catches herself. "Clea, have you decided what you'd like for birthday treats?"

Birthday treats in eighth grade? Clea is horrified at the idea, but as Bee rarely bakes anymore, decides to accept the offer and hide them for the nights when they eat the last tinned sardines and green beans from the nearly empty shelves in the basement. "That would be great, Grandma. How about peanut butter cookies?" Cheaper than chocolate chip and they'll keep longer.

Bee is heartened by her granddaughter's interest. She's never sure what will worsen Clea's moods. "How many children are in your class?" She should have said "kids" not "children." Flipping the waffle, she braces herself for a whine or moan.

There are now only sixteen. "Thirty-six," Clea lies so Bee will make a triple batch.

"Wonderful." Bee carries a steaming plate of waffles to the booth, folds herself back into her seat and pours what looks to Luvie like a diabetic-killing amount of maple syrup onto her plate.

Sipping her coffee, Luvie decides not to pick a fight. Bee has trouble enough seeing another year of her granddaughter's life go by without a mother. The blue envelope isn't the only correspondence that came from Velvet, and the fact that Bee hasn't shown it off makes Luvie worry it contains bad news.

Bee frowns at Clea's too-tight T-shirt. "Didn't you find the turtlenecks I laid next to your ladder?"

Clea will go naked before wearing Velvet's clothes, but to save Bee's feelings, says, "They make me too hot."

"Men's eyes are like airplanes without pilots," Bee says. "Now that you're fourteen, it's up to you to land them, which is why turtlenecks are perfect. Steers them straight to your lovely face, which is as far south as they should be flying."

Clea stabs her waffle. At school she read *C.B.'s rack: eighth wonder of the world* carved into one of the desks in the science lab and had to choke back tears as she dissected a worm. After volleyball, Queen Priss said it was a miracle Clea's breasts hadn't given her black eyes jumping for net shots and everyone in the locker room laughed. Clea forewent the group shower to avoid further scrutiny of her body, but had to endure B.O. jokes the rest of the day.

Bee adds, "It's a young woman's duty not to lead men astray."

Luvie chokes on her coffee. "They accomplish that entirely on their own."

"Jiggs!" Bee is relieved to see him enter the kitchen with two brightly wrapped presents. She hobbles back to the stove to fry her boarder three eggs to accompany his waffle.

"Salty." Clea kisses Jiggs.

"S-s-sweetie." He slides into the booth next to Luvie and pushes his gifts across the table, tapping the largest one.

Clea opens it and pulls out the camera she made when she was a kid. "My Polaroid Impulse!" Clea laughs turning the painted checkbook box and tuna can over in her hands. "You kept it."

Grinning, Jiggs taps the smaller present, obviously a thick paperback.

Clea opens it and gasps. A brand new camera. Shiny black plastic. Automatic flash. Two rolls of 35 mm film. Four double

AA batteries. She tears everything from its packaging and inserts the film and batteries into the camera.

"Thank you!" Clea launches herself across the booth and hugs him. His white western shirt smells of Old Spice and starch.

As she returns to her seat, Clea notices a blue envelope poking out from under a stack of her grandmother's books and periodicals—*Demontracker, Is Gorbachev the Anti-Christ?* and *The End Times: Will You Be Left Behind?* Sliding out the envelope, Clea recognizes the tight, prim loops cartwheeling across the front.

Bee sets a plate of eggs in front of Jiggs, and exchanging an apprehensive look with Luvie, slides into the booth next to Clea. "That came for you *yesterday.*" *Not just on time, but early!*

Bee never misses an opportunity to put in a good word for Velvet. Clea understands why, but it annoys her. The envelope is addressed to *Tiny Mite Baumhauer.* Clea's rat heart springs upward and bites the base of her throat. *Tiny Mite?* How old does Velvet think she is? Clea still longs to open the envelope. Maybe Velvet has finally written an apology? Or explained why she hasn't visited? Maybe she's writing to announce she's saved enough to bring her out to live with her in California? Maybe she'll get to attend one of those cool high schools she sees on television, where kids walk outdoors between class? Maybe rolling in her mouth like a sweet, Clea accepts a letter opener from Bee's fishing vest and slits open the envelope.

As soon as she removes the card and sees Strawberry Shortcake holding a pink birthday cake with red-and-white polka-dotted birthday candles, she regrets opening it. Despising herself for subjecting herself to more humiliation, yet still wondering what's inside, she opens the card. A ten-dollar bill floats to the table. The text reads: *To a berry special daughter on her berry special day!* The first *berry* has been underlined three times. Other than that, all Velvet has written is *Lots of love, Mimi*. Four words. Not even one for every year she's been gone. *Tiny Mite. Love. Mimi.* Some words, Clea thinks, must be earned. *Good girl. Brave girl.* Her heart rears and spins. *Back in a jiffy.* She asks Bee for tape, and when her grandmother produces a roll from her fishing vest, Clea returns the ten-dollar bill to the card, shoves it into its envelope, tapes the flap and writes *RETURN TO SENDER!!!* all over the front and back. Grabbing her new camera, she stomps out of the kitchen with the card.

Silence in the booth.

In the front hall Clea puts on two layers of long underwear and three pairs of socks. Bee changes the TV channel and cranks the volume. *If you belonged to the world, it would love you as its own,* proclaims a televangelist. *As it is, you do not belong to the world.* Unable to hear Bee and Luvie's whispered argument, Clea zips herself into one of Bud's snowmobile suits, and then sitting on the bench opposite Jiggs's ten-slot gun rack, laces her feet into a pair of his boots. *So we fix our eyes not on what is seen,* continues the televangelist, *but on what is unseen.* Hat, gloves, a red scarf knitted by her great-grandmother. Dressed, Clea grabs the camera, birthday card and Bee's outgoing mail pile before stepping into the bright, white cold.

Strawberry Shortcake? How old does Velvet think she is? And *who* does she think she is? Some kind of priss? And that ten-dollar bill? Does she think she can buy forgiveness? *That* cheap? Clea and Bee get into fierce arguments about accepting Velvet's monthly checks, one of the reasons Clea wears Bud's clothes. Queen Priss can call her "scissor sister," "todger dodger" and "clitty licker" till the cows come home—Clea will not wear school clothes purchased with Velvet's money.

Hard packed snow squeaks under Clea's boots as she trudges down the driveway. At the mailbox, she shoves the birthday card and Bee's protest letters to a county implementing a 666 area code into the clown's mouth. The rubber flap has disappeared, so she secures them with a stone.

Clea takes the camera out of her pocket and looks around. Overcast sky. Ice-crusted road. Dirty snow banks. Scraggly fields. Gazing at the gray-and-white landscape, she feels like she's in the wrong story, an ugly story Velvet turned from color to black-and-white. Clea lies down in the ditch, one hundred and eighty degrees of sky pinning her to the ground. Maybe she'll get lucky and freeze to death.

She holds the camera to her eye. The sky looks small. The electrical poles short. Cut off from their poles by the perimeter of the frame, the five wires look like the lines of a musical score, the three crows roosted on them notes. If she could read music, the birds would sing her a song. Jiggs can read music. Intrigued by the idea of presenting him with a photograph he can play on the piano, she presses the shutter. The camera's noise causes two of the crows to fly upward. When they settle into a different formation, she takes another picture, and when they shift again, another.

*What is unseen.*

Unearthing a secret song is not unlike mapping the paths of shadows on her walls or, when she was a little girl, flipping through her Road Runner book, thinking about actions within actions and wheels inside wheels. Two of the crows fly away. *Click.* Clea likes the slicing sound. In that second, she's not *here* here.

A passing truck scares the last crow away, but Clea doesn't move the camera. It's comforting simply looking through it, wondering what it will catch—in half an hour two airplanes and a floating yellow plastic bag. These she doesn't photograph, but watches glide like fish through an aquarium. When sparrows land on the telephone wires overhead she takes a picture whenever one of them changes its position or flies away. She feels calm, the frame a trapdoor through which one of the rats in her heart escapes each time she presses the shutter. The camera rewinds the film. She inspects the shot counter. She's already taken thirty-six pictures?

\*

The world a whiteout but for the hazy gray line where sky meets land. Clea dislikes wishy-washy horizons. They remind her of blizzards and runny mascara, slushy parking lots' and frozen breath. The muddy roots of Velvet's bleached hair.

Flashes of red as Jiggs scrapes ice from the dirty windshield. After he's chipped little more than a porthole from the driver's side he checks the antifreeze and adjusts the snowplow attached to the front bumper. Jumping behind the wheel, he hands Clea two paper bags—one containing her lunch, the other, five rolls of film.

"Thanks!" He supplies her with film, no questions asked.

*Jiggs buys her a new camera and she can't take a family picture?*

*It's her camera, Bee.*

*Says she "doesn't photograph people"?*

*It's a phase, Bee. She's a teenager.*

*She takes roll after roll of birds and clouds and trees!*

"G-g-got your your c-camera?"

"I don't take it to school. It would get stolen." How many things has Victoria Fitch filched over the years? In first grade, her pencil case and stickers. In second grade, her favorite mittens. In third grade, just before swim class, her towel and underwear. In fourth grade, her diary, which, over the course of a year, she photocopied and distributed in installments to the whole school. That one still burns. Clea puts the bag of film into the glove box for safekeeping and inspects her lunch. Apple, granola bar, liverwurst sandwich. Better than sardines, which make her breath stink. Fish face! Fish fingers! Victoria Fitch always has a cute lunch. A thermos of soup or macaroni and cheese. Crust-free sandwiches. Yogurt pots. Mini muffins. A neon yellow Le Sac bag in which to carry it all. Clea removes the napkin from her own lunch sack—Bee still draws sunshines, smiley faces and Bible verses on them—and hands it to Jiggs, who stuffs it into his breast pocket in lieu of a handkerchief.

Jiggs starts the truck, gives it some gas and cranks the heat to high. They hold their gloved hands over the open vents. Cold air. Heater still broken, they cover up with sheepskins, not unlike her ancestors, Clea thinks, riding to town under buffalo hides, feet buried in hay packed around heated bricks. So much for progress. Jiggs turns on the radio. Announcements of weather-related cancellations: Prairie Lutheran deacons meeting, Hector county veteran firefighters reunion, Girl Scout troop 589, Big Bend knitting collective, Henning AA, Henning hockey, Henning parent–teacher association...

The wind whisks and swirls snow from the tops of the white banks lining the road. Clea wishes she could see this landscape with the romanticism of her childhood, but each day Velvet has been gone has torn a scale from her eyes until she now sees the farm, the fields, the sky, Big Bend, her baby book, even herself, as junk rightly discarded. She hates exclamation points. All of her thought bubbles have burst, replaced with accordion words that stretch so far she can still get lost in them for days—maybe, when, soon, perhaps, sometimes, probably, possibly, hopefully, if.

*When is Mimi coming back?*
*Hopefully soon.*

*When can I talk to her?*
*If she calls.*
*Where did she go?*
*Probably California.*

Clea stores these conversations in another accordion word: meanwhile. The longest accordion word: why.

*Why aren't you doing something?*
*God will work it out.*

She didn't want God to work it out. She wanted the adults to work it out. Now she knows better.

At the edge of Big Bend, passing the Fleet and Farm store, Clea spies a group of Hutterites hunched against the wind as they cross the parking lot. The men wear plaid shirts, overalls, cowboy hats and black coats. The women wear apron dresses over white shirts with Peter Pan collars, black-and-white polka-dotted headscarves and black coats. The little girls wear gingham bonnets. Some people mock the Hutterites, who live in isolated colonies throughout the state, calling them "backward" or "weird," but Clea admires their dignity and sense of purpose, the clarity of choosing so structured and predetermind a life. Not that she wants it. Their clothes remind her of Velvet's Prairie Town uniform, but living without always wondering where she'll go and how she'll do it? That sounds peaceful.

Continuing down the road, Jiggs and Clea pass the boarded-up pawnshop, closed-for-lunch German restaurant, dental clinic, insurance agency and five-and-dime, its windows covered with *GOING OUT OF BUSINESS* signs. Where would Velvet work if she still lived here? Catching herself sympathizing with her mother, Clea breathes onto the window and writes *NOT MY*

*PROBLEM* in the condensation, but wipes it away with her sleeve before Jiggs sees. Five *FOR SALE* signs dot the frozen lawns between Sixth and Second Streets, four of them in place for more than a year. Abel Cole, ninety-four, hand shovels his walkway. Jiggs pulls into his driveway, lowers the snowplow affixed to his front bumper and clears the driveway in less than three minutes. Abel Cole waves his thanks as they back out and continue on their way.

The glass-fronted marquee sign on the lawn of the church has been broken into. Yesterday its black letters read: *Rejoice! King Jesus is Alive! Celebrate with us! Sundays 10 a.m. Sunday School 11 a.m. Upcoming events: SEX WEEK Jan 27/28.* Today it reads: *Rejoice! Sing! Celebrate! Cum have SEX with us WEEKdays.*

Bee insists that Clea attend Sex Week. Has her grandmother not seen any of the boys at her school? Their shiny too-large noses or eyes angled at her breasts? Body odor, bad breath, loogies, zits. White bread always stuck in Bill Hew's braces. Manure always caked in Kevin Vandenhosen's sneakers. Spit always dripping from Jason Hegel's trumpet. Giggles from Curt Whiting at any mention of booby traps, breast meat or guys named Dick. The Hooper twins' hair always home-styled in bowl cuts. Jerod Stenker. Where would she even start with him? In case revulsion isn't enough, Clea once shoved a contract between her mattresses: *I, Clea Marie Baumhauer, swear to all members of the Trinity who in the beginning were the Word and through whom all things were made and have been made that I will never love a Big Bend boy, or worse, date one out of sheer boredom.*

Clea fills with dread as Jiggs turns right onto First Avenue. Her school could be in Siberia. Flat lot. Zero trees. Chain-link fences. Crumbling track. Mangled bleachers. Netless basketball hoops. The one-story building missing many of its anemic bricks.

The line of dumpsters alongside it dented and flaking beige paint. How will she get through her first lesson? The day? The week? Five more years?

Jiggs stops three blocks away.

"Thanks." Clea jumps out of the truck and slings her backpack over one shoulder. "If you have time, pretty please with candy corn on top, could you look at the convertible?" One good thing about turning fourteen: applying for her learner's permit.

Saluting, Jiggs drives away.

*

Clea stares at the snow-covered windshield, sighing, counting, tapping the edge of the glass casserole pan on her lap. On the count of ninety-eight, Luvie jumps into the driver's seat of the Buick, a whirlwind of perfume, hairspray and double mint gum, her hair freshly dyed, red lipstick coated with gloss. Turning the ignition, she activates the windshield wipers, which carve two narrow Vs out of the snow.

Clea reaches for the door handle. "Want me to scrape it?"

"Nah." Luvie puts the car into reverse. "I could drive these roads blind."

Clea fastens her seat belt. "I thought Grandma was driving me to Sex Week."

Luvie raises an eyebrow. "I met the new pastor last night."

"Really?" Luvie hasn't been to church in years. "Where?"

"Crow Bar."

"You're kidding."

Clea turns the heat to high, and as Luvie drives to town, learns about Pastor Ray's black leather trousers, 7-Up with extra lime, commitment to AA and how Jesus saved him from the alcohol and drugs that destroyed his music production career with Willie Nelson.

"So that's why you're gussied up on a Sunday afternoon." Luvie spends most Sundays in bed, hungover, napping. "Why don't you come in and register me? You could make introductions."

Luvie inspects her freshly painted red nails. "I did try to get you out of this thing."

"Thanks, but I don't mind going to Sex Week a tenth as much as I do Grandma asking Velvet for money to fix Grandpa's convertible." She resents Bee's excitement over a twenty or fifty dollar bill from Velvet, when thanks to her, the family has to manage on a third less income. "Jiggs says he can fix it."

Luvie sighs. "He can't, sweetheart, but will toil under that hood for a decade if it would make you happy."

With Luvie working part-time and her Mary Kay sales dwindling, Velvet's contributions help. Clea groans. Being dependent on her tormentor is a torment all its own. "Please don't let Grandma ask her, Luvie. I'll ride my bike to school."

"At night? In a blizzard? When the wind chill's negative thirty? I have to take Bee's side on this one. Besides"—Luvie's eyes narrow—"it's the *least* she can do."

She. Since that day at the Qwik Stop, Luvie hasn't spoken her niece's name. "I need a job, Luvie."

"When you're sixteen. Two years isn't that long."

It's an eternity. "I need more film."

"How much is a roll?"

Clea wants rolls and rolls. She wonders how many photographs she needs to take—one hundred, one thousand, ten times ten thousand?—to release all the rats from her chest. "I want to earn my own food."

"Now really."

"I'm not eating her food."

"You're eating *my* food, Jiggs's food, your grandmother's

food, the government's food!" Thanks to Velvet, the family now collects food stamps.

As they pull into the ice-coated church parking lot, Luvie nods toward the raked, orange, black-striped Mach 1 emitting a cloud of gray exhaust. "That's not the Stenker kid?"

Clea is as shocked as Luvie to see him here. The matte black spoiler, blaring heavy metal and hooded figure behind the wheel are normal at school, but church? For Sex Week? She can't imagine who could have forced him to attend. Certainly not his mother, spaced out on pills and so drunk by closing time no one in Big Bend books haircuts after three. A stepfather maybe. Jerod must be on his third or fourth by now.

Luvie shivers. "Kid looks like the Grim Reaper."

Clea's never seen him without a dark gray or black XXL sweatshirt. "He always wears the hood pulled low."

"Sorry, I shouldn't have said that about the Grim Reaper."

The Baumhauers don't speak about the Stenker tragedy, unlike everyone at school, where kids, the prissies especially, smear red lipstick on his locker, squeeze ketchup onto his car, slip ski masks onto his desk and dress like him for Halloween, not that Jerod makes things easier for himself coming to school with blood splatters on his clothes and cuts all over his hands. He never meets people's eyes or talks to anyone but teachers, and only then if spoken to, his face impassive, his low voice monotone. Despite the no-hats-in-class rule, no one makes Jerod remove his hood. His worst crime, however, is getting straight As. In that regard, he and Clea are similarly outcast, although unlike her, Jerod draws extra flack for having repeated second grade in the wake of the tragedy. Not that anyone insults him straight to his face—already six feet tall and bench pressing more than most football players, Jerod sets his course down the hallways in his all-black ensemble—sweatshirt, jeans, basketball sneakers, backpack—and everyone gets out of his way. His intimidating demeanor and stature are not lost on the basketball coach, but Jerod doesn't participate in school activities. His Mach 1 roars into the school parking lot at 7:59 and roars out at 3:01, spewing gravel onto the other cars.

Luvie scans the half empty church parking lot and frowns. "I don't see Ray's car." Her face settles into a dreamy expression. "He drives a silver '59 Eldorado."

"He probably doesn't want to step on Pastor Mike's toes."

Luvie examines her reflection in the rearview mirror. "I'll troll Main Street and see if I catch anything."

Clea squeezes Luvie's bony shoulder, fingers slipping on her silk scarf. "You're a very fetching lure." She gets out and waves the casserole pan. "Good luck!"

Luvie revs the Buick's engine, and as she pulls away, toots the horn.

Clea waits until the Buick has disappeared up Second Avenue before entering the church. The gray carpet is soaked with melting snow. The foyer is filled with yellow balloons. Christian rock plays on the speakers. The sanctuary's double doors are open, revealing new banners Bee has sewn in red, blue, orange and green felt:

*Pet your dog, not your date*
*Just say S-L-O-W!*
*There's no condom for the heart*
*Kids in the back seat cause accidents, accidents in the back seat cause kids*

Clea nods. Accidents like her. She gets in line to register behind a sophomore couple holding hands and looking nervous, no doubt about Sex Week's grand finale—the chastity ceremony, during which unmarried couples go to the altar, make vows to retain their virginity and receive silver promise necklaces. Clea can't imagine anything more mortifying. Even if Humphrey Bogart walked in, knelt in front of her and declared undying love, she would rebuff him.

"Nice to see you, Clea." Jeanette, Pastor Mike's wife, hands her a nametag and bright yellow T-shirt bearing a play on the NIKE ad: *I'm NOT doing it.* "We're asking everyone to wear these throughout the conference." Jeanette wears one over a navy turtleneck patterned with tiny pink ducks. "We're all in this together."

Together? Really? Clea wonders why the horrors of puberty have to be either whispered or broadcast in public. She trades the casserole pan for the T-shirt. "That was a great lasagna, thanks." She and Jiggs wiped the pan clean with half a loaf of bread.

"You're very welcome. I know your grandmother's in agony with that foot."

Clea smiles, grateful that Jeanette, as well as all the other church ladies who cook them dinners, attribute their help to Bee's health and not the Baumhauers' diminished income.

"Give her my best, will you?"

Nodding, Clea walks into the sanctuary. Victoria Fitch and her posse sit in the back pew, displaying last year's promise necklaces over their yellow T-shirts. "Nice plaid," Queen Priss whispers, spotting Clea in one of Bud's old work shirts.

Clea stops and stares into Victoria Fitch's amber eyes, heavily made up with purple eye shadow. "You're welcome to borrow it anytime."

Queen Priss flicks her shoulder-length strawberry blond hair. "I'll keep it in mind next time I dress as Paul Bunyan."

Clea feels a stab in her chest, but manages a chuckle. "I'll keep your make-up in mind next time I dress as Boy George."

Queen Priss chortles. "Because you would, lesbo."

The prissies laugh.

Rolling her eyes, stinging, Clea continues up the aisle and chooses an empty middle pew. She waits until thirty seconds to start time before pulling the yellow T-shirt over her plaid shirt.

Giggles from the back pew.

"What's that smell?" Queen Priss riffs on the joke she's been telling since third grade: Jerod "Stinker," not Stenker.

Unbelieving, Clea turns. The sanctuary goes quiet as he stomps up the aisle, jaw clenched, gaze on the pulpit. Jerod chooses an empty pew two rows ahead of Clea, sitting with force, as if pushed. Even Pastor Mike is unsettled as he steps to the microphone. "Welcome! Everyone's, of course, absolutely welcome. Good to see you all. Wow. Glad you came."

As Pastor Mike makes announcements and says an opening prayer, Clea looks down at her wet duck boots. What could be more humiliating than being a teenager? Everyone knowing your mother ditched you at a gas station and never came back. But other than that? Bee recently slid a Skywatch leaflet into her backpack warning her about alien reptoids with psychotronic mind powers that mimic humans so convincingly they infiltrate youth groups to impregnate Christian girls. What would have happened if the prissies had stolen her bag that day and gotten their glitter fingernails on the leaflet? Clea stares at the peak of Jerod's black hood wondering how he bears his shame. Hers feels unbearable and she didn't kill anyone when she was seven.

Sex Week's first speaker says the portrayal of sex as fun and easy in rock songs is a lie and he should know: his wife spent their honeymoon in agony.

Sex Week's second speaker dims the lights for a slide show of magnified, disease-ridden genitalia.

Sex Week's third speaker uses an overhead projector to expose the subliminal sexual messages the liquor industry sends America's youth via pornographic imagery encased in ice, bubbles and other murky liquids. He taps a pointer at the ice cube in the enlarged image of a whiskey advertisement. "Look closely and you'll see an orgy in here." Clea squints, but can't see anything. Changing slides, he redeploys the pointer. "Not one, but two couples fornicate in this nest of bubbles here." He changes slides. "In this gimlet of vodka, you'll notice a kaleidoscopic vision of a woman's, um, shall we say, *anatomy* repeated ad infinitum."

When the lights come on, everyone rubs their eyes, averting each other's gazes. A girl in the pew behind taps Clea's shoulder, cups her hand around her ear and whispers, "Jerod's got crabs. Pass it on."

Clea leans to the boy closest to her and whispers, "Henniker knocked up Victoria. Pass it on."

No one passes the message to Jerod. A wave of giggles surges to the pulpit, squelched when a man and woman step forward to sing a duet about purity accompanied by a flute. Afterward the woman says, "We know you kids are struggling and want to support you." A pianist plays a soft ensemble. Ushers move down the aisles distributing white note cards and tiny pencils. "Think of these cards as a prayer. We're going to give you a few moments to tell God your sexual struggles—no names, please—and after we collect them, we'll know how to pray for you."

Gazing at her card, Clea considers scribbling, *I can't achieve orgasm without a doughnut smashed against my face*, but that would be for the adults, as well as unoriginal—she'd read something similar in Luvie's *Cosmopolitan*. What does Clea want to tell God? At the last minute she writes, *It's not funny* and tosses the card into the collection basket. When she looks up, Jerod has turned and is staring straight at her, dark circles ringing his gray eyes. Her immediate reaction is to look away, but holding his gaze, she gets an idea.

\*

A month later, Clea gazes uncertainly at a bullet-pocked mailbox, its post bearing a profusion of signs:

*Private Road: Right to Pass by Permission and Subject to*
*Control of Owners*

*No Trespassing: Violators Will Be Prosecuted*

*BEWARE OF DOG*

*NO DUMPING*

*Warning: Electric Fence*

*Danger: Guard Dogs On Duty*

The steering wheel of Bud's splurge makes a grating rasp as Clea turns into a dirt track bordered by thick, snow-dusted pines. The heat won't turn off and no matter which direction she moves the lever, the warped wipers squeal over the windshield's arc of grime. Though Jiggs managed to get Bud's splurge going again, he warned Clea it was temporary and forbade her from leaving the farm. Now, as louder and louder clicking and scraping sounds emanate from its engine, she worries she might not even reach her destination.

A half-mile down the road, she reads two hand-painted signs nailed to a tree trunk: *KEEP OUT!* and *Warning: Pit Bull.* Clea swerves around half a dozen ice-filled holes. The track curves to the right and crosses a creek. The convertible whinnies like an injured horse as it struggles up a steep, salt-strewn slope to a lot filled with several wheel-less cars raised on cement blocks, two four-wheelers, four snowmobiles stacked double high on a rusty trailer and the orange Mach 1 she sees every day at school. Clea parks next to it, gets out and zips Bud's hunting coat up to her throat.

The air smells of pine, burning trash and cooking onions, the latter from the trailer beyond the vehicles. Three dogs—a pit bull, Labrador and German shepherd—hurl themselves against a chain-link kennel, their barking joined by Nirvana blasting from a boom box.

Clea spies the onion skillet, a hamburger package and ashtray through an open window as she passes the trailer. Following the music, she passes a clothesline shaped like a stripped inside-out umbrella, a barn covered with antlers and horns, two smaller corrugated metal buildings, a red-and-white shed that looks like a playhouse, a cracked cement half-court with a bare basketball hoop and a large, weed-filled garden surrounded by three layers of chicken mesh and barbed wire.

Dressed in a black wool cap, long john top, inside-out yellow Sex Week T-shirt, padded camouflage overalls and rubberized boots, Jerod stands with his back to her underneath an oak tree. Ropes hang from many of the tree's branches. Six of them hold three dead coyotes by the feet. Through the garden fence, Clea watches Jerod brushing the fur of one of them. Next to him, stacked in a pink plastic laundry basket, lie three skinned carcasses, a translucent film holding their internal organs together.

Clea vomits into her hands, kneels and wipes them onto the tall brown grass bordering the garden. When she stands, Jerod is watching her, hands at his sides. He frowns, and then peering beyond her shoulder, throws down his brush and rushes toward her. Taking her by the shoulders, he guides her into the darkness of the closest shed.

"It'll be OK."

Clea nods dumbly. He's never spoken to her before, much less touched her.

Through the crack in the shed's door, she watches him return to the coyotes. Shifting, she accidentally kicks a box near her foot and hears rattling. A snake? She nearly runs for it, but as Jerod turns off the boom box, a heavyset man even taller than him approaches in a brown grease-stained coverall and neon orange coat. "What's that convertible?" He jabs his thumb toward the trailer.

"Engine I'm looking at."

The man flicks Jerod on the ear. "Move it."

It's strange to see anyone touch Jerod. No one at school would dare. Not even the adults.

The man inspects the unskinned coyotes still hanging from the tree. "Same trail?"

Jerod nods.

"M44s?"

"And sheep brain."

"How many?"

"Thirty-five."

The man nods and walks away.

Jerod waits several minutes after the trailer door slams before returning to Clea. "Sorry about that." He shuts the door behind him and locks it before turning on the light.

"Stepdad?"

Jerod's eyes go dull like at school. "Mom's boyfriend." The cement brick room is full of shelves, tool chests, hunting clothes, space heaters, coolers, gun racks, crossbows, an unmade cot and a camp chair occupied by a badly scuffed basketball. She scans one of the piles of books. McCarthy, Le Carré, Michener, Salinger, King, Kerouac, Tolkien, L'Amour, Clancy, Fleming, Hemingway. At the far end of the room more ropes hang from the ceiling in front of a metal door.

"Where does that door lead?"

"Walk-in cooler."

Jerod closes the plaid curtain over the room's one window and leads her to a large sink. Though a small white sliver of soap lies in the dish, he reaches into a cabinet and unwraps a fresh bar of Lava soap. He adjusts the taps, testing the temperature with his fingertips before moving aside so she can wash her hands.

Clea once found a Lava wrapper in one of her grandfather's

toolboxes with measurements written in pencil on the back and has since used it as a bookmark. Taking the soap, she washes the vomit from her face and hands and then dries them on paper towels from a wall-mounted dispenser.

"You skin a lot of coyotes?"

Jerod vigorously washes his hands with a gritty gray paste. "Two hundred last season."

"For the meat?"

"Sell the hides."

"How much?"

"Depends on the market. Last year was good. Fur traders paid fifteen bucks a pop. This year's looking more like thirteen."

It feels strange to talk to him. She points at a row of boards leaning on a wall with skins pulled over them. "What are those?"

"Bobcats. I've only caught two, but they fetch ninety each."

"Jiggs got a badger yesterday and said something about selling it."

"Did he shoot it in the head?"

"Not sure. I think it got pretty messed up in the trap."

"If you're not there fifteen, thirty minutes within trapping, forget it."

"What does a badger go for?"

"If the hide's mint, up to one twenty."

"You hunt them?"

"Sometimes, but they're nasty. I'm more of a coyote guy."

Clea marvels at this whole other life Jerod has, school an annoying but necessary sideline, when for her it's the main event. Her jealousy of his earnings reminds her of the reason for her visit. "I've come to ask a favor."

Jerod rinses the paste. Squeezing antibacterial dishwashing soap onto his hands, he scrubs his nails with a brush. No wonder his hands look raw at school.

Her request can't just be about the convertible. It's too strange she's trespassed, and to pretend otherwise, feels disrespectful. "I'm supporting myself now, well, as much as I can."

Jerod scrubs his hands, listening.

"Grandma wants to ask my mother for money to fix our car."

"And you can't have that." Jerod dries his splotchy red hands on a paper towel. "You get those formulas Mr. Olson showed Friday?"

It's strange seeing his brow furl. At school his face is stone. Clea nods.

"I didn't calculate the coordinates of the vectors right."

Clea smiles. "You'll fix my car in exchange for help with trig?"

"I'm not sure I can fix it."

"Either way, deal." Clea offers her hand. Jerod shakes it. His hand is warm and damp.

Letting go, he nods the direction of the trailer. "Problem is."

She knows. They can't study at his trailer. Or her house. Or school. A public alliance would make things worse for both of them. "You know that rusty old truck at the river?" Clea played in it when she was little and guesses it's still there, marooned on the bank, sunken to its bumpers in mud.

"I know it. Monday after school?"

"Monday." Clea points at one of the coolers lined against the wall. "Am I crazy or did that just move?" Holes dot the lid.

Outside a door slams. Jerod flinches. "Better get you home."

"Is there a back way?" Clea doesn't want to encounter the man in the orange coat. "I'll walk home." She heads toward the door.

Jerod jumps ahead of her. "It's too far and it's getting dark." He turns out the light, opens the door and pops his head outside.

"Run through the orchard," he whispers, "cross the bridge and meet me where the electric fence meets the wooden one with a triple reflector." He steps out of the building, looks both ways and motions for her to go.

Clea runs past the oak full of ropes and hanging dead coyotes into an orchard of apple, cherry and pear trees divided with an icy, dirt track. Passing a tractor, boat trailer, wheelbarrow and pile of rusty irrigation equipment, she reaches a two-plank bridge over a steep creek. The track ends on the other side, leading into a forest. Pushing low branches aside, Clea steps over undergrowth through thick leaves, relieved when she hears a motor. At the fence bordering a pasture, Jerod waits for her on a large army green ATV with a dented roll bar and rear box full of bags, tools, snow-shoes and the plastic clothes basket holding the coyote carcasses.

He opens the passenger door. "Mind if I set a few snares along the way?"

"Be my guest." Clea gets in and finds it calming, the ease with which he navigates the icy, bumpy terrain, setting traps at the fence lines of each pasture with quick precision. "How do you know they'll run there?"

Crouching, Jerod points at clover-shaped indentations in the mud and snow. "Tracks." He nods toward a barbed wire fence. "See that bent wire? They're going under it." He coils a metal wire into a circle the size of a pizza, affixes it to a stake, pushes the stake into the ground and attaches a clip to the fence. He takes the carcass from the back of the ATV and lays it on the trail in front of the snare. "Extra incentive." On the other side of the fence he scatters sticks on both sides of the trail. "They always take the easiest route."

At the creek bordering the Baumhauer farm, a deep violet sunset casts purple shadows across the snow. Clea gets out of the ATV.

Jerod gazes beyond her shoulder.

She turns to see what he's spied—a coyote?—but it's just her family's farmhouse, looking, from this angle at the bottom of the hill, large and cozy, all of its windows alight. For years she's considered it an embarrassment, lilting and perennially in need of paint, but after seeing the squat trailer Jerod shares with his mother and her menacing boyfriend, feels grateful she'll soon be inside. "See you tomorrow."

Reaching into the rear box of his ATV, Jerod pulls out a bulging canvas sack and hands it to her.

The bag is heavy. She pulls the fabric away and looks inside. "From your orchard?"

He nods.

"Thank you."

With a dip of his chin, he drives away.

Clea runs toward the farmhouse, arms wrapped around the bag, secrets jostling like apples inside her.

*

Waxwings and sparrows burst from the leafless treetops each time Clea shoots the gun. Lying beside Jerod on the snow-dusted deer stand high in an elm, she watches the birds through his scope to ensure she misses, which he teases will ruin her shot. *Bang!* She hands him the gun, photographs the treetop, waits for the birds to resettle and does it all over again.

To thank Jerod for fixing the convertible, Clea made him a flipbook with her first roll of pictures. He smiled (a real smile, not just a faint upturn of the corner of his mouth) as its birds mechanically hopped on telephone wires. Now she has flipbooks of snowfall; a snail seesaw bouncing on a playground; groceries moving down a conveyor belt; leaves blowing across a sidewalk;

the wind inflating and deflating a bag stuck to a fence post. She made her favorite flipbook taking shots of the back of Bee's head as she watched *Wheel of Fortune* each time Vanna White turned a letter of the phrase *Make a Wish*. The flipbooks prod the stillness, dent her boredom, nudge time. The breeze of their fanning pages reminds her of riding her bike beneath trees when she was little, head back, eyes open, branches combing her hair.

*Bang! Click, click, click.*

Bullets gone, they stare into the white sky, Clea wondering how she could unscramble the hieroglyphics winter trees write with their inky black branches. An airplane passes. A raven squawks. They roll onto their stomachs and study trigonometry.

For twelve Mondays they met at the rusted truck, Jerod hopping into the driver's seat asking, "Where we going today?" They concocted locations and sights, but when the thermos was empty, spread their books on the shredded seat and worked. Then two Mondays in a row they spied a couple kissing inside the truck, so Jerod showed her this large deer stand. Though she misses their road trips and the intimate wind cover of the truck, they now have treetop picnics to which she brings themed accessories. Today she hands him her View-Master and a sleeve bearing a faded Union Jack.

Jerod reads the sleeve in a dramatic voice. "*View-Master presents in three-dimension full-color kodachrome: The Sights of London, 1965.*" He inserts the disc, and pushing the white knob on the side of the View-Master, flicks through images of Big Ben, Buckingham Palace, Piccadilly Circus and Trafalgar Square.

"I also brought *Windsor Castle, 1948*, and *The Coronation of Queen Elizabeth II, 1953*." On the floor of the deer stand she lays a rose-patterned cloth, gold-rimmed teacups and Bee's hive-shaped honey pot. "We're having Earl Grey."

"What's that?"

"A fancy kind of tea."

"And biscuits?"

"Scones." She arranges small Tupperware boxes containing whipped cream, jam, scones and cucumber sandwiches.

Jerod sniffs the scones suspiciously. "Clea scones or Luvie scones?"

She laughs. Over the past few months, some of her treats have been better than others, as they were baked by Luvie and therefore mixed incorrectly or burned. "They're Clea scones made *for* Luvie. I had to intervene when she brought Ray a carrot cake made with two cups of salt instead of sugar. We only realized the mistake when we cut the spare loaf for dessert. I thought she was going to tear her hair out even though she'd just had it set."

Jerod closes his eyes as he swallows his first bite. "The English have it so good." *You have it so good.*

Their friendship has cast a softer light on her family. Three loving adults to come home to. Mealtimes. Card games. Chats. Sometimes Jerod and his mother go days without exchanging a word. Sometimes she and her boyfriend are gone for days without explanation. Some nights the boyfriend doesn't come home at all and Jerod's mother stays up all night watching television and drinking, passing out on the sofa.

Clea hands him a jar of Bee's chokecherry jam. "Wait till you put this and cream on it." She feels proud of the spread, paid for with money she recently earned—Bee, thankfully, now lets her work two hours after school each day—ringing up wart cream, magazines and bubble gum at the pharmacy.

Jerod chews slowly, savoring each bite. His mother bakes even less than she cooks, which is even less than she stocks groceries. It's always there between them—their hunger, Velvet, Blankety Blank, his mother, father, stepfathers, the thing that happened when he was seven—but they never speak about it. They are equals—no pity or explanations required—although the enormity of his grief makes hers feel smaller, bearable almost. With him she feels less self-loathing. Her shame fits inside his.

After tea they study.

"So for this one"—Clea taps a formula with her pencil—"to solve for x, isolate the cosine term."

"Uh-huh."

"Which means..." Clea calculates the equation. "Are you paying attention?"

Staring at the ground, Jerod slaps his forehead. "I can't believe I never saw it."

Clea gazes down at the dirty cube of salt lying in the snow, wondering how many animals it has lured to their deaths. "The deer lick?"

Jerod thrusts his chin toward the pale green generator beyond it. "What better place to stay warm?" Grabbing his shotgun, he climbs down the grayed boards nailed horizontally to the side of the tree. "Come see."

Clea follows him, her thick, red, home-knitted scarf catching on the bark.

Jerod throws the shotgun onto the seat of the ATV, and from the back box, grabs a gas can and pile of canvas bags. Clea follows him across the frozen brown grass to the fence line where Old Man Pike has stacked railroad ties and stones against his generator. Jerod sets his supplies on top of the humming metal box, twists a stick from a nearby shrub and crouches in the snow.

"I knew it!" Jerod nudges some bulges in the snow with his stick. "Look at these scats."

Clea has never seen anyone get excited by yellow animal droppings.

Jerod mashes them with the stick. "They've got fur and feather in them." He stands, removes a glass beaker from one of the bags, tears it from its plastic wrapping and sets it on the generator. Taking the gas can, he pours diesel in front of the rocks and railroad ties. "Let's see what's inside." Crouching, he rolls the stick between his palms, watching the pile. "Come on, big money."

Clea feels nervous, but tells herself that if he were hunting something scary, he'd use his gun.

A flat, rectangular scaled head with elliptical eyes and forked tongue pokes its head out of the pile. "Jerod." Her skin breaks out in goosebumps as the snake slithers toward them. "Is that what I think it is?"

"Rattler." Using the stick, he draws it out of the logs and flips it onto its back. "Big one, too."

Clea guesses it must be five feet long. Its tail shakes. Its head rears. She jumps backward, and with an embarrassingly prissy yelp, shoves her hands into her coat pockets.

With the tip of the stick, Jerod pins the rattlesnake's head to the ground. Reaching down with his free hand, he clasps it behind the head and lifts it high, its body undulating mid-air. "Grab that cup, will you?"

Clea retrieves the glass beaker from the generator, puts it into his outstretched hand and retreats. She'd accuse any other person of insanity, but doesn't doubt Jerod's control as he works the beaker into the snake's mouth and presses its fangs against the plastic lid. Stepping closer, she watches clear liquid run into the beaker. "What do you do with the venom?"

"Sell it to hospitals. Henning, Clapton, Mead. They make antivenom with it."

"What do you get?"

"Forty bucks an ounce. Should get two out of this one."

Eighty dollars? She'd have to work twenty hours at the pharmacy to earn the same. "Jerod!" She points where he poured the diesel. "More are coming out!"

He turns, looks and shrugs. "Those are just bulls and garters. All breeds of snake hibernate together."

Clea jumps onto a rock.

He laughs. "They're harmless, not to mention sleepy from the fumes. And it's cold. Heat gets snakes feisty. Hand me one of those bags."

She doesn't want to walk near the snakes streaming out of the den, but worse, doesn't want Jerod to think she's scared. It takes all her effort not to scream as they slide over her boots.

Jerod unclamps the rattlesnake from the beaker, hands her the beaker and taking the sack, throws the rattlesnake into it. She expects it to thrash and shake its rattle, but it goes still. "Thinks he's back in the den."

"What will you do with it?"

"Take him home, milk him a couple more times and sell him to Reptile Kingdom. They pay good money for rattlers over four feet."

She remembers the rattling she heard in his workroom. "You keep them in coolers."

"Yup." Jerod sets down the bag and returns to the den with his stick.

"Does your mom know?"

Nodding, he flicks garter and bull snakes into the bushes as if they were worms.

"Doesn't it freak her out?"

"It freaks *him* out more, makes him kinder, if you know what I mean, so she puts up with it."

Each dangerous thing he lets her know about him makes her feel both honored and more comfortable in her own grungy story. "Ever gotten bit?"

"Couple of times."

"Was it like in the movies? Sucking and spitting out the venom?"

He raises an eyebrow. "I opted for a hospital."

"What happens?"

"You see visions like on LSD. Rainbows and yellow-brick roads."

"Really?"

He laughs. "It's like a bad hangover with fever. They let you out after a day and your hand hurts like heck for three days. Tylenol helps."

Jerod catches, milks and bags two more rattlesnakes before announcing he's lost his patience. He goes to the ATV, gets a shovel, and when he returns, wedges the den open. Inside lies a slithering ball of snakes.

Jerod catches six rattlesnakes total, three over four feet. Big money indeed. "Do you ever eat them?"

He reloads the ATV. "You can, but it's work. Lots of bones."

"Is it good?"

"It's flaky like fish, but tastes like chicken. Want to try it? I'll make a fire and cook you one right now."

"Caviar would be cheaper."

Jerod shrugs. "I catch them all the time. Seriously, you hungry?"

She's always hungry. "Not without ketchup," she jokes, "but thanks."

"Any time." He gazes at the deer stand. "Sorry to skip our lesson."

"You have snake work to do."

"We're splitting the proceeds from our catch."

"That was all you, Tarzan." Laughing, she returns to the tree.

"We are splitting it!" He starts the ATV.

"Are not!" she shouts, climbing the ladder.

Waving, he drives away.

She wonders where she'll find the money. In her lunchbox or one of the pockets in her Trapper Keeper? Though they never speak or look at each other at school, she sometimes finds a candy bar in her locker or a book in her backpack.

Back in the deer stand, Clea eats the remaining scones and sandwiches. As she drinks cold Earl Grey, she pulls the reel out of the coronation envelope, pops it into the View-Master and watches the misfiled *Wedding of Prince Rainier III and Grace Kelly, 1956.* She flicks through it three times and then packs up the picnic and books. Backpack heavy, she climbs down the ladder and walks home, camera to her face.

The white dome overhead hasn't got a nick of gray. *Click, click, click.* Each shot whittles the sky. Lately she's enjoyed walking the fields, creeks and roads around the farm, dusting the landscape with her camera, finding patterns she wouldn't have noticed in cow paths, fence lines and buffalo wallows.

At home, Clea stamps snow from her boots onto the front hall mat. The house smells like burnt chocolate chip cookies. She slips up the stairs to her attic room, reloads the camera, and without removing her heavy clothes, photographs shadows as they move in and out of the lines on the walls. These photos occasionally fit like puzzle pieces into her pencil tracings. She's taped a dozen into place and the harmonizing effect of the lines on the wall corresponding with those in the photographs has made her wonder what other images might be integrated. Corn rows, telephone poles or tree branches? Fences, creeks or cow paths?

"Goddamn it, Bee!" Luvie calls from the bottom of the stairs. "Come down and help me!"

"My foot aches!" Bee cranks the rerun of *Golden Girls* playing on the TV on the stool at the base of her bed.

"Where the hell did you put that Bible-shaped cake pan!"

*Click.* Clea photographs a shadow. She needs to be not *here* here. Ever since Pastor Ray came to town, she's been torn between wanting Luvie to find love again and not wanting Bee to experience more loss. *Click, click.* It's like the days she laid under her pine tree flicking through *Wonders of the Deep, 1954,* or *20,000 Leagues Under the Sea, 1974.* As long as she holds the viewfinder to her face, she can breathe underwater.

"Try the pile on top of the fridge!" Bee shouts. She leans forward in bed, gazing down the hall, wondering if Clea has snuck by without saying hello. Bee doesn't like this new habit of her granddaughter's, but too hoarse to yell again, slides on the red reading glasses hanging from a chain around her neck, and reaching into the breast pocket of her fishing vest, extracts three postcards.

> *Dear Mother,*
> *Classes going well! Two on Tuesday and one Friday evening. Birthday love to TM.*
> *X Velvet*

> *Dear Mother,*
> *Sorry I haven't written. Busy with an exciting new opportunity. Greenbacks coming soon!*
> *X Velvet*

> *Dear Mother*
> *Glad to hear the extra cash helps. The job isn't anything special, just pays well for once! Don't worry ☺*
> *X Velvet*

Bee lays the postcards on her lap. Velvet is taking three classes a week, yet sends triple her usual monthly contribution? Something doesn't add up. "Don't worry" has been her tell since she was a girl, that she's worried or scared or lying or all three. Would Velvet gamble? Do something illegal? The palm trees and sunsets on the postcards fill Bee with panic. Is anything what Velvet claims it is? Is she even going to college? Where is she really?

And if Bee's health were better? Would she drive out to California and bring Velvet home? The truth masked by her bad foot: she couldn't risk coming up empty. Velvet fleeing. Discovering all the addresses are duds. Having no contact or leads. Better to have Velvet by a thread than tug and lose her for good. Returning the postcards to her pocket, Bee revisits the conclusion she's come to ten thousand times: the best she can do is believe in Velvet's story and wait.

# There's a system. Check the clock. Lock the doors.

Close the curtains. Listen. Wait. Listen. Clear the table. Lay out the bills, presidents up, corners aligned. Smell them. Divide them into two piles. Left: bills for Bee. Right: bills for the can.

Mixed rolls are no longer allowed in the can. Only bills of the same value per roll. Twenty bills per roll minimum. At first she affixed one end with a large paper clip. Now new white rubber bands are wrapped around both ends with a triple twist. Rolls are placed vertically in the can, the first in the middle, all additional rolls added in a tight spiral formation. When a level is complete, the first roll of the next level is placed in the middle and the process repeated. Once rolls enter the can they cannot be removed.

Listen. Wait. Listen. When she completes a roll of ones: a glass of wine. A roll of fives: a postcard or letter to Bee. A roll of tens: a day off. A roll of twenties? Maybe she should remove all the rolls? Exchange all of the bills for twenties? Maybe that should be the new rule? Only rolls of twenties in the can?

# MAY

# Clea photographs each item before it burns in the

barrel—old homework, artwork, report cards, Bible studies, issues of *Life* and *Highlights*, Sunday school crafts, "Polaroids" she used to draw, notes from classmates, birthday cards, calendars, baby clothes. She burns most of the Memento Moris, the homemade Polaroid Impulse and any pages from the Road Runner book she couldn't integrate into the lines on her bedroom wall. She reads George's inscription before throwing it into the barrel. *Always remember you're some pig.* It's difficult watching that page blacken and shrink, but her need to cleanse herself of anything that doesn't fit into the collage is stronger than any feelings of nostalgia.

Clea lifts one of the last items out of the storage box—her baby book—and holds it against her chest. Part of her doesn't want to burn it, especially the pages with the handprints, but as she flips through it reading the lists of fantasy presents, milestones and memories she fabricated because Velvet never bothered to fill it out, her anger flares. Saddened by the sight of her scrawny, teetering, childhood handwriting—shoddy scaffolding for so much hope—she chucks the baby book into the barrel.

Flames curl around the faded Winnie the Pooh cover. Clea feels a stab of regret for not saving the handprints. Her eyes fill with tears. Her rat heart spins. What good are fingerprints that make empty promises? She tosses a stack of diaries on top of the baby book. From now on she will only store her feelings in photographs, which are expressive, but discreet. They keep secrets, but no matter how stark the image, say maybe, but so quietly, only she can hear.

"Hey!"

Clea jumps.

Luvie steps through the barn's double-height double doors, the only source of light the fire and moonlight shining through the hole in the roof. "What on earth are you doing?"

"Spring cleaning."

Luvie rubs her arms. "It's cold as a witch's wazoo out here." What kind of fourteen-year-old burns trash by herself in a barn on a Saturday night? Last night a party at the Hooper barn got so out of control, the Hooper twins, who hunt from a hole they've cut in the roof of their truck, shot out every insulator on the power poles from County 5 to the interstate. Though they're underage, the sheriff has locked them up for three days to teach them a lesson. Luvie just ran into Doris taking them a fried chicken and the two of them laughed recalling the era of Snook and Bud racing tractors down Main Street, mooning a quilting convention and entering dyed piglets into the county fair.

Luvie shakes her head watching Clea throw a stack of children's books into the fire barrel.

Earlier that week, after Clea and Jiggs left for school, Luvie suddenly felt strange, so uncomfortable she kicked off her heels and climbed the ladder to Clea's attic room. What she saw made her heart stop: the room stripped bare as a cell, wobbly lines drawn in some kind of pattern all over the walls, a strange mix of papers taped all over them—Road Runner cartoons, torn bits of maps, photographs (some hung upside down), and, most chillingly, a *memento mori*. Luvie hasn't said a word to Bee, thankful her sister is too frail to climb the ladder. They should all be inside the farmhouse right now, laughing at Clea's stories about the Hooper party, but of course she wasn't there. Luvie gets an idea. The snow has melted. The roads are clear. "Want to do something"—she almost says "normal," but catches herself—"ornery?"

Clea shrugs. "Sure."

"Good." Luvie throws her cigarette butt into the barrel. "I'm going inside for a few things. Meet me at the car in five minutes?"

Nodding, Clea slides the metal lid over the barrel.

Luvie disappears.

Clea stands in the darkness, crying over the lost baby book. She wipes her nose on the sleeve of her grandfather's quilted hunting jacket and goes outside. A black pickup truck with oversized wheels, hologram mud flaps and a double gun rack affixed to its back window sits in front of the farmhouse. With its multiple antennae and two round spotlights mounted over the cab, it looks like an apocalyptic beetle. Sitting behind the wheel, Luvie wears trousers, one of Bud's coats and a seed cap. Clea hoists herself into the passenger seat. "How come you've got Henniker's truck?"

"Bastard made me trade cars." Luvie hands Clea another seed cap. "Henniker claims this truck won't accommodate three 'clients' he's supposedly taking fishing, but the truth is he doesn't want Ruth recognizing it outside the motel where he takes his tart. She's going to that puzzle competition in Groton this weekend." Luvie pats Clea's leg. "Tuck your hair up into the cap."

Clea obeys. Henniker's truck smells like cigarettes and fried food. A box of country music CDs sits between the seats. The backsides of the sunshades are plastered with pictures of swimsuit models in provocative poses.

Luvie winces as she turns the ignition. "Not only do I have this beast all weekend." The gear grinds as she shifts it into reverse. "If Ruth sees the Buick, she'll think *I'm* shacking up with someone, which couldn't be further from the truth." Luvie tips her cap as she drives down the driveway. "I haven't done this in years."

They drive Big Bend's dark gravel back roads until Henniker's headlights catch the dull red tail lights of a van parked halfway in a ditch. Luvie passes it, turns right at the next intersection and circles back, only the second time she approaches, kills the headlights and glides forward in the moonlight. Twenty feet behind the rocking van, Luvie blasts both the truck's headlights and upper spotlights on high beam.

Through the van's back windows, Clea can see a young man's back and buttocks. The woman underneath him shields her eyes. Queen Priss! Clea laments leaving her camera at home. Priss deserves a bit of blackmail after sticking Kool-Aid-stained maxi pads all over Clea's locker. Luvie honks the horn and revs the engine. Queen Priss and her boyfriend scramble for their clothes. Luvie drives forward, rams the van's bumper a couple of times and peels away, spraying the van with gravel.

Luvie and Clea laugh all the way to the next intersection. At the stop sign, Luvie pulls a metal thermos from her purse and holds it out to Clea, who declines. "It's only hot chocolate," Luvie beams. "I'm off the hard stuff."

Though watery, Clea sips it to be supportive. "How's the Ray campaign going?"

Luvie sighs. "How do I compete with all these widows who've been baking for fifty years?"

"Forget pies. Why not join the choir?"

Luvie winks. "And let those robes obliterate my waist?"

"You both like music. Take him dancing or to one of those out-of-the-way blues joints you know, or I don't know, invite him over to hear your record collection? He might be able to help with Grandma's end times chart."

Sharing a look acknowledging how unwise it would be to bring anyone home, they both laugh.

Luvie frowns. "Your grandma doesn't like him."

"She doesn't like anyone replacing Pastor Mike." Or Snook.

"What about you? Any nice boys at school?"

"None." Clea and Jerod still avoid each other at school to protect their secret. She enjoys the constant volley required to sit on opposite sides of the classroom, lunch table, lab and bleachers. If he twirls his pencil. *Boring.* Or taps his sneaker. *Lame.* If she chews the end of her pencil. *Starving.* Or coughs. *Gross.* They sign the most in math. Pencil tap to the forehead. *Did you get that?* Bite on the lip. *No.* Yawn. *Yes.* Though Jerod is getting higher scores, they continue the ruse that she tutors him, meeting every Monday afternoon in the deer stand. In exchange, he's fixed Bud's convertible, the heating in Jiggs's truck, the antennae on Bee's TV, the arm on Luvie's record player and the power cord on Clea's radio.

"Not even *one* boy?" Luvie knows something's up. No way did Jiggs fix the convertible or shoot the buck that appeared on the porch with an arrow through its heart. "Cupid seemed at work the other day."

"Jiggs is learning to bow hunt."

A lie, Luvie knows, that Jiggs would cover, which means he knows, which given his overprotectiveness, means Luvie needn't worry, not yet. Clea's anger—her insistence, for example, on separate shelves for Velvet-free groceries—doesn't have her mother's destructive edge. While Velvet's strivings felt like blind, desperate groping, Clea's ambitions, whatever they are, feel set in steel rails no local boy could budge. Luvie gazes at Clea's outfit: mud-caked boots, overalls, yellow Sex Week T-shirt and a camouflage jacket. "I understand why you don't want to wear her clothes, and new duds aren't in the budget, but we can't let you go around in your grandfather's hunting gear. Your grandmother and I used to wear beautiful outfits. Sewed them for every occasion—hats, gloves, stockings, matching shoes, the works. What do you say we go through them and find things we can remake into clothes you could wear to school? I know it wouldn't be the latest fashion."

Access to Luvie's treasured wardrobe? From *before the war*? "I'd like that a lot, Luvie, thank you."

The truck's headlights graze the backside of a station wagon with wooden side panels.

Luvie raises an eyebrow at Clea. "One more?"

They circle and advance on it the same way they caught Queen Priss. When the time is right, Clea flips on the lights. Naked bodies twist. Hair swings. Luvie revs the engine and bumps the bumper. They laugh. The man dives into the front seat. The woman scrambles to cover her bosom with a balled-up T-shirt. The door of the station wagon opens, its naked driver wielding a pistol.

"Uh-oh!" Luvie reverses, switches the gear to drive and peels away.

The man shoots out one of the truck's tail lights. "Henniker!" He chases them down the road, shooting twice, but missing. "I know your goddamned truck!"

*

Clea walks into the kitchen on a Saturday afternoon wearing a pink dress. Shocked, Luvie sets her coffee mug on the counter. "Is that one of my old slips?"

Bee pats the sewing machine in the booth. "It was, but we put in a zip, made new straps and added that lace panel at the hem."

"It's pretty." Luvie tilts her head. "I'm not sure about the denim shirt and Mr. Roger cardigan. And how about sandals instead of those dirty Keds?"

Bee winks at Clea. "It's called the grunge style, Luvie."

Laughing, Luvie raises her mug to Clea. "You look swell, sweetheart."

Clea hugs her. "Happy birthday. Promise to nap, so you have energy for your surprise tonight?"

Tightening the belt of her robe, Luvie yawns. "I should be able to manage that."

Watching Clea and Luvie make fresh coffee and sandwiches, Bee admires her handiwork on the slip. This idea of Luvie's to remake their old clothes—Clea calls them vintage—is an answer to Bee's prayer for a renewed connection between the three of them. Ever since that awful day at the Qwik Stop, Clea, Luvie, even Jiggs, have turned their backs on Velvet, and because Bee cannot join in their hatred, has gotten ousted from their ranks. Not that she hasn't hated plenty—she's hated God, hated herself for being an inadequate mother, hated Velvet's choices, hated Big Bend's pity and contempt—Velvet such a no-go subject, people say "nice to see you," instead of "how are you?" to avoid her feelings. She cannot, however, hate her only child, bearer of Bud's eyes, chin and hair. She can't turn like Clea, Luvie and Jiggs from a ringing phone. Bee will take any conversation, any scrap of news, any letter, even if it's about the weather, even if it's just the sight of Velvet's handwriting on a check, and she'll take any contribution—a penny, a hundred dollars—if it means they share something. Bee's unflagging cordiality when Velvet calls has made Clea, Luvie and Jiggs feel resentful, betrayed even, and if that makes Bee a weak, pathetic beggar, so be it. She'll never rebuke Velvet for fear of getting even less of her voice, less of her handwriting, less chance of her coming through the front door. And when she does? Bee will give her the best robe, put a ring on her finger, wash her feet and kill a fattened calf.

Clea lays her palm across Bee's forehead. "You OK, Grandma?"

Bee smiles. "Fine."

Clea whispers into her ear about spaghetti, salad and garlic bread.

Bee nods. "Yes, yes, it'll all be ready." Bee pulls a pair of scissors from her fishing vest and snips a long thread on Clea's hem.

"Thanks, Grandma. I'm off."

To God knows where. Bee watches her granddaughter disappear into the front hall. Wherever, with whomever, Clea has softened and Bee's not about to tip the cart prying. Jiggs is in on it. That's all she needs to know.

Clea grabs her backpack and a canvas sack on her way out the door. The day is sunny and warm, every green thing swelling. Yellow tulips peek over the edge of the porch. She runs down the front steps, shoves the canvas bag into her bike basket and cycles down the muddy driveway. When she reaches the deer stand, Jerod and Jiggs are hanging the last of the fairy lights in its blooming branches. She leans her bike against the base of the tree and grabs the canvas sack.

"Luvie has no clue!" she says, climbing up to the stand.

Jerod calls down from a high branch. "Jiggs says you've planned these before?"

"Not this elaborate, but we got them to park next to each other at the drive-through, Jiggs with Pastor Ray and me with Luvie. We sent them both to the concession stand and then Jiggs and I ditched them. Then we sent them both treasure maps and tickets to *The Bodyguard* in Fulton." Clea drops the sack on the wooden platform. "The last stop was dessert—you know that old sign from the Ark? Jiggs made a table out of it. We left a lantern on it, a thermos of coffee and an apple pie—your apples, by the way. Tonight they think they're going on a hayride for an Elks club fundraiser, but Jiggs is pulling the two of them out here with the tractor. We'll park the Buick on the highway so they can get home." Clea looks up at the clear blue sky. "Weather looks good for it."

"F-f-full m-moon." Jiggs slips climbing down from a tree branch.

Jerod catches him by the arm.

Jiggs swings his other arm around the branch and squeezes Jerod's shoulder. "Th-thanks."

Jerod flinches at his touch, but then surprises Clea, not only leaning into Jiggs's hand, but giving it a quick pat. Clea wonders how long it's been since Jerod received an affectionate touch from a man? Probably not since he was seven.

Jiggs climbs all the way down the tree and plugs the fairy lights into an extension cord running to the generator. On top of the generator he's set up a record player and a box of Tony Bennett and Frank Sinatra albums. After checking that both the lights and record player have power, Jiggs hops on his ATV.

Clea calls down to him from the deer stand. "When Grandma gives you the crockpot and stuff, don't forget the tiramisu and birthday candles on my bed, OK?"

Jiggs gives her a thumbs up as he drives away.

Jerod climbs into the deer stand and stares at Clea. "You look real..." He pauses. "Nice."

She blushes. "Kinda prissy, huh?"

"No." Jerod looks away.

Clea smoothes the front of her dress, relieved and disappointed to be released from his gaze. "Grandma sewed it for me." The breeze feels strange on her bare legs. Maybe they look funny? Pale? Knock-kneed? Jerod is staring at them.

He points at her bags. "What else have you got?"

"What *haven't* I got?" She sets up the folding table and chairs Jerod and Jiggs dragged into the stand and then opens the cooler Jerod set up in the corner. Pulling bottles of beer and soda from her bag, she inserts them into the ice. She and Jerod spread a red and white checkerboard cloth on the table, lay out plates, napkins, silverware, candles, matches, lovebird salt and pepper shakers, wineglasses, two bottles of Chianti and a bottle opener. Clea pulls two View-Masters and a box of reels out of her bag. "I thought we'd put one of these next to each of their plates." She hands Jerod a View-Master. "You choose Ray's. I'll choose Luvie's." Clea flicks through the box. "We've got *Naples, 1949, Dolomite Mountains Northern Italy, 1949* and *Discover Pompeii, 1951.*" As Jerod flicks through the Naples reel, Clea finds more. "There's also *Rome, 1949* or *San Remo: The Riviera Italy, 1957.*"

"Where do you get all these?" Jerod flicks through the Pompeii reel.

"My grandfather collected them."

Jerod chooses Rome for Ray. Clea chooses Sam Remo for Luvie.

"What else have you got?"

Clea flips through the reels. "*New York, Hearst Castle, Scenic USA, Castles of Bavaria, Land of Windmills, Natives of Zululand, Hula Dances of Waikiki, Cave of the Winds.*" Clea pulls one out and hands it to him. "You have to watch this one: *Weeki Watchee Spring of the Mermaids Florida, 1953.*"

Jerod takes it and flicks through the reel, chuckling.

Clea flicks through *Water Skiing Thrills, Cypress Gardens*

*Florida, 1955.*

Jerod lowers his View-Master. "You want to travel?"

"Definitely." Clea packs up the other reels. She wants to gobble the globe, go everywhere Velvet hasn't. "You?" She inserts the reels they chose for Luvie and Ray and lays the View-Masters on the table.

"Sure." He sits on the open edge of the deer stand near the ladder. "It would depend."

"On what?" Clea sits next to him.

He gazes into the treetops. "The right companion."

Clea suddenly feels sad the school year has ended. Will Jerod miss their study sessions as much as she will over the summer? "Ninth grade next year."

Jerod nods. "Four and goal."

Clea knocks her knees together. "How long is your gig as a fishing guide?"

"Until the end of July. Want to walk beans in August?"

Clea has never walked bean fields pulling weeds and spraying pesticides, but knows the money's good. "Sure, on my days off from the pharmacy."

Jerod reaches up to a branch and snaps off a leaf. "We'll have to read our list from different ends so we can both check out the books." Jerod made their summer reading list from a list of classics posted at the Henning library.

"Top or bottom?" *Top or bottom?*

Jerod chuckles. "Ladies first."

Clea blushes. "Top?"

"It won't be that easy when we duke it out for valedictorian."

"Depends what you need it for."

Jerod rips the leaf into smaller and smaller pieces.

Clea knocks her thigh against his. "Tell me."

He throws the pieces over the edge of the deer stand. "Even

thinking it is crazy."

Clea watches the pieces float to the ground. "I want to be an artist. How's that for crazy?"

Jerod nods. "That's a good one." He turns and looks at her, his expression serious. "Don't tell anyone, not even the admissions counselor, OK?"

Clea smiles. "They'd have my head examined—not only do I want to be an artist, I want to study in New York." She has a fantasy, set, she guesses, in Times Square: more people enter the crosswalk than currently live in Big Bend, and passing a newsstand, Clea buys *Chinese Vogue* and the cashier doesn't point out that she doesn't speak Chinese or sigh at the vanity of fashion or *tsk* ten dollars better spent on a metrocard or say who does she think she is, someone who thinks she gets to go to the real China? Blank stares. Clea will love New York for them. No one will get nervous when she counts coins at a cash register or teary-eyed if she pauses by a rack of Mother's Day cards. No one will give her free gas or socks or doughnuts or cough syrup or lunch vouchers. Not one in eight million people will pity her.

"They'd have both our heads checked. I want to be a pilot."

"Like my grandfather! Will you join the military?"

Jerod closes his eyes. "I have to go to university first and do really, really well."

Knowing how insurmountable the first hurdle feels, Clea doesn't press for specifics. "You be valedictorian. I'll take the Excellence medal."

Jerod laughs. "You need valedictorian, too."

"I think for art school a portfolio will matter more, so salutatorian and the Excellence medal will do for me."

He shakes his head. "I'm not taking charity."

Clea extends her hand. "Fight to the death?"

He shakes it. They sit quietly for a long time. The breeze rattles the tree's tiny, waxy leaves. Birds chirp. A chainsaw buzzes in the distance. Jerod stares down at her bike, frowning. "That day."

Clea catches her breath. "That day" can only mean one of two things: that day at the Qwik Stop or that day the thing happened when he was seven.

Jerod swallows. "We were goofing around, me and my step-dad's nephew. I built all these bike ramps with sandbags and sheets of ply. We were riding on them by the creek. My mom came down with my baby brother and set him on the grass. She said she had to hold something for my stepdad. He was fixing something. She asked me to be in charge. I remember her words exactly because she hadn't asked me before and I liked the idea of being in charge, especially since the other boy was older."

The wind blows Clea's hair into her eyes, strands catching in her eyelashes.

"Me and the nephew were playing E.T., pretending to outrun the CIA on our bikes." Jerod pauses. "I got the idea to pretend my brother was E.T., so I put him in the basket on the front of my bike." Jerod covers his face with his hands.

Clea's eyes well.

Shaking his head, he crosses his arms. "I'd gone down that ramp a million times, but that day I crashed against the other kid and skidded. I hit a rock." Jerod stares beyond the tree into the pasture. "My brother went flying. I can still see the sky behind him. Then he vanished. I got up, but couldn't find him. I called for him. He wasn't crying. My mom came running with a horrible, the most horrible," he winces, "look on her face. I'd never seen an adult look like that. That's how I knew something bad had happened. She asked where my brother was. I said I didn't know. She ran around and around calling and calling him."

Tears run down Clea's face.

"She crossed the bridge and screamed. My stepdad came

running with a wrench in his hand. I remember that wrench. I was sure he would beat me with it."

Snot oozes toward Clea's lip, but she doesn't move.

"My brother had landed on some rocks in the creek. The other boy said I threw him down there on purpose. I said I didn't, but he kept saying he saw me do it and acted out his lie for them. I don't know if he said it because he was scared our bike crash would get him into trouble too, but once he told that story, he stuck with it and the adults believed him. My own mom didn't believe me. A social worker came and talked about half-sibling rivalry, Freud, Oedipus, Cain and Abel, none of which I understood at the time. It was confusing. My brother there, then not."

Clea nods. Velvet not *here* here.

"My stepdad there, then not. My mother's face looking at me one way, then another," he whispers. "No one looked at me the same after that."

A tear drips from Clea's chin and makes a wet circle on her dress.

"Maybe I was jealous of my brother. He had dark hair like his dad." Jerod smiles faintly. "I called him Ewok."

Clea reaches over and squeezes his hand.

Jerod squeezes back.

They stare into the trees.

*

*That day.* Retelling her own story, saying her mother's name, Clea feels zaps of panic not unlike the many she felt the year after Velvet left—in class, in church, in bed, in front of the TV, but most often in her dreams, where the rooms of the Qwik Stop had uneven floors and odd numbers of corners. There were two Tiny Mites in those nightmares—one chatting with Oscar, doing crosswords and stuffing herself with French fries; the other screaming at her lazy, deaf and dumb twin self to "Get off the chair! Call the police! Get George to chase her! Quick, hurry, faster! You're letting her get *away*!"

Honeycomb strands of light reach through the trees, turning patches of the brown river gold.

Clea kicks the stump of a pine with her heel, chipping crumbly clumps of bark onto the mossy ground. "Thanks for not saying, 'at least this' or 'at least that.'"

Jerod jiggles a handful of rocks in his palm. "There's an 'at least' after what your mom did?"

"There are tons—at least you have your grandma, at least she isn't dead, at least she sends money, but even if I were a disfigured, mentally disabled, abused foster child who's lost all my limbs on a land mine, I'd get an 'at least you have eyes.' People have an 'at least' ready for anything."

"No one ever said 'at least' to me."

"They would if they knew the truth."

They throw rocks into the river, Jerod's skipping, Clea's sinking.

"How did your grandma react?"

"A week later she called the guy who'd been at the Qwik Stop with me and hammered him with questions: Was the driver of the green car short? Did he have grayish skin? A big head? At first her questions gave me the impression she knew the man driving the green car, a boyfriend I hadn't known about, which for a moment made me feel things might still turn out alright, but then her interrogation frightened me: Did the attendant hear a sound similar to that of a tuning fork when her daughter disappeared? Or feel drowsy in the presence of the driver of the green car? Experience an unexplainable time lapse? The gas station attendant threatened to call the police. Grandma told him it wouldn't do any good—the government was in on it, too.'" Clea leans down, picks up a handful of rocks and hands them to Jerod.

He skips them. "In on what?"

"An abduction."

Jerod scrunches his face. "Your grandma thought she'd been kidnapped? By whom?"

Clea sighs. "Aliens, demons, I don't know."

"Were you scared?"

"The idea that my mother had been taken against her will was less upsetting than her *deciding* to leave."

"But after the shock wore off, your grandma didn't believe that?"

"No." Clea wipes mud from her palms onto her jeans and steps backward, jumping onto the hood of the rusty, abandoned truck. "I almost wish she could." Fighting tears, Clea scans the river, the rapids, the treetops, scrambling for a new subject.

Jerod sits next to her on the truck, leveraging his weight against the sagging bumper. "Do you and Jiggs have a roster of dates planned for Ray and Luvie this summer?"

Relieved, Clea shakes her head. "We don't have to. Ever since the Italian extravaganza, they've managed on their own."

Jerod smiles. "Good for them."

"Yeah." Clea stares at Jerod's muddy sneakers next to her sandals. Tomorrow he'll leave for a two-month job as a fishing guide with a second cousin's outfit in Montana. She feels both jealous and relieved for him to have a break from the trailer and the fights that have been raging between his mother and her boyfriend. Luckily Floyd's daughter is having a baby so Clea will have full-time hours at the pharmacy. "When you get back"—she flicks rust wafers off the truck—"will you teach me how to drive a stick shift? Floyd wants me to make deliveries."

Jerod laughs. "You are a terrible driver."

"Jiggs has been trying. Poor guy gets so tongue-tied. I can't torture him or his truck any longer."

"Can I pick my payment?"

Clea hesitates, nervous. "OK."

"I'd like another one of those little books you make."

"Sure." She feels both disappointed and relieved. "What of?"

Jerod eases off the truck. "Surprise me."

Clea jumps down and pats rust powder from the seat of her jeans, wondering how to say goodbye. Should she hug him? "See you round?"

He pauses, then lifts a palm. "See you round."

She should be happy. Summer. No coats. No school. No Queen Priss. The garden planted. All the pies they'll eat. All the vintage clothes they'll alter. All the films they'll watch in the barn. (In exchange for his help demolishing the drive-in, Jiggs scored Ed Hoit's collection of projectors and film reels.) And yet Clea feels grieved watching Jerod's black figure recede through the trees.

Over the past five months she has felt like an empty jar filling with colored marbles. Stories. Secrets. Jokes. Picnics. Plans. Strategies. Schemes. Now that she has a friend, even when she's alone there's a volley between her thoughts, feelings or experiences and Jerod—wondering how he would feel, what he would say, think, do. She takes every photograph for two sets of eyes. When he's ill and misses school or goes to Mead to sell venom, she makes a movie of him in her mind snuggled into his cot with a Louis L'Amour or roaring down in the interstate in the orange Mach 1 chewing red Twizzlers. With Jerod in Montana a new movie will start. All summer, while she trims green beans, removes sheets from the line or rings up Floyd's customers, she'll imagine Jerod baiting lures, cleaning fish, erecting tents, building campfires.

Jerod stops by a boulder, turns and calls to her. "You know

that hole between the caves?"

"Yes?"

"Check it from time to time!"

"OK!"

Jerod waves.

Clea waves, turns, walks thirty feet and hides behind the trunk of an oak, watching him disappear. When the coast is clear, she runs upriver, crosses the fallen tree, scales a wall of pink granite and shimmies through piles of dry leaves and sticks along the ledge to the caves. When she reaches the hole, she looks inside. Something round and dark. A rock? She picks up a stick and wedges it free. A package wrapped in brown paper. She tears it open. A battered paperback: *On the Road*. Tucked inside: an old map of the United States, the land celadon green. Jerod has drawn Big Bend on their state, and next to the black circle, in his tiny, angular handwriting, written *START*.

**Left ankle strap. Now the right. She kicks the gold heels** onto the brown linoleum floor, winces as she draws her left foot onto her bare knee. One, two, three. Breath held, she tears off the Band-Aid. The blister underneath: red, raw, screaming. Five minutes to closing: two customers. Two twenties. She lays them on the table, presidents up, corners aligned.

She checks the time. Limps to the door. Locked. Limps to the curtains. Closed. Listens. Eucalyptus leaves, wind chimes, crickets. Waits. Crashing waves. Fighting cats. Feet throbbing, she climbs onto the seat of the chair, pops open the defunct air-conditioning vent in the ceiling and pulls down a Folgers can.

When she opens the plastic lid: the sweet, sweaty, dirty, metallic smell of money. Reaching in, she removes eighteen loose twenty-dollar bills and lays them in rows alongside the two on the table. Presidents up, corners aligned. She makes a stack and taps the bills once on each side before rolling them tightly, triple twisting new white rubber bands around each end. Her favorite part: slotting the roll vertically alongside the other rolls into the can, the ritual a balm for the blisters, the exhaustion, the guilt for what she's done and all the lies she's told Bee. The lies at first merely loans with which to buy more time, but all these years later, heavy weights, an unpayable debt, pulling her beneath the surface of her life.

How many nights has she fantasized that Bee would appear at her door and take her home? *Mother, why don't you come for me?* But by morning she's always donned uniform, work gloves, tool belt, change purse, sunhat... and now, uncomfortable gold heels. But this can. She replaces the plastic lid and hugs its cool metal sides. This can is going to save her.

# SEPTEMBER

# Whispers erupt like geysers when Clea enters

homeroom on the first day of ninth grade. For weeks she planned her outfit: 1950s white eyelet dress, green canvas military belt, half-bleached jean jacket, red socks, buckskin work boots. Her hair is blow-dried straight, her nails painted Luvie's latest red.

Victoria Fitch whistles as she passes. "Nice dress. Got sick of rug munching?" Queen Priss wears her blue-and-yellow cheerleading uniform, the waist rolled up to make the skirt shorter. Her look has also changed over the summer: hair dyed platinum blond and cut into a chin-length bob. Two of her sycophants have copied her hairstyle, though not stolen their master's thunder going platinum or cutting bangs.

Knowing Jerod will want to sit by the window, Clea chooses a desk by the wall. The stripped, disinfected classroom feels stark and more appropriate for kindergarten due to the paper doll chain their new teacher has strung over her desk. The doll with

Clea's name on it is yellow, Jerod's black. Is it a coincidence or has the teacher been warned?

Waiting for him, Clea feels the anticipation she felt each day he was in Montana, minus the undercurrent of unease, because the night he returned and she snuck him into the hayloft to watch *On the Waterfront* with her family in the barn, Jiggs—she couldn't have expected him to keep her secret forever—carried in an extra lawn chair and called for Jerod to join them. Luvie patted the woven plastic seat and Bee passed him popcorn as if he'd always been around. After that Jerod visited the farm several times a week, often staying for dinner; twice, during his mother's breakup, sleeping on the davenport. Those nights, lying in her bed up in the attic, Clea thought of him down in the living room and couldn't sleep, watching moonlight sink into the floorboards, followed by sunlight traversing the lines on her walls.

Embarrassed by the memory, Clea opens the homecoming packet on her desk, reads the theme—"Lions Past and Present"—and ticks her votes for Spirit Week: toga day (to see Jerod black in a sea of white), heavy metal day (to see everyone dress like Jerod), hillbilly day (to see everyone dress like themselves), superhero day (to wear Luvie's red velvet cape) and pajama day (to see Queen Priss get detention for wearing something inappropriate).

Queen Priss walks around the classroom distributing vote-for leaflets printed on blue, pink and yellow paper. Class President. Freshman Princess. Drum Major. Clea crushes them into balls. Another priss passes out face-paint sticks for the homecoming pep rally; another, tailgate tickets. Clea takes two tickets for Luvie and Ray, imagining the picnic she'll pack for them: barbecued ribs, potato salad, coleslaw, two vintage letterman jackets, bleacher cushions, wool blankets.

"Oops!" Queen Priss pretends to trip, spilling her bottle of

Mountain Dew down the front of Clea's white dress. "It was so pretty, too." She pats the yellow neon liquid with one of her flyers, smearing pink dye into the fabric. "I hope that doesn't stain."

Clea pushes Victoria away—Bee worked on the dress for a week—and goes to the sink at the back of the room. Dabbing the fabric with soap and wet paper towels, Clea watches through the window for Jerod, biting a smile when his Mach 1 roars into the parking lot, AC/DC blaring from its speakers. Despite the warm weather, he crosses the sidewalk in a long-sleeved black sweatshirt, black jeans and black high tops. Returning to her desk, Clea thinks of his sun-bleached hair under the hood and tanned arms inside the sleeves.

Throughout the previous August, buffered by six hundred and forty acres, they walked hundreds of rows of beans, spraying weeds, making up knock-knock jokes, alternate movie endings and lyrics to popular songs. Swatting flies from their heads, they played twenty questions, would-you-rather, two lies and a truth.

Things Jerod left in the hole between the caves: the map, his lines drawn where he wants to go (Colorado, Utah, Arizona, California); venison jerky; a watercolor set; summer sausage; watercolor paper; a library book on book binding. Things Clea left in the hole between the caves: the map, her lines drawn where she wants to go (New York, Massachusetts, Maine); chocolate chip cookies; Bud's flight goggles; canned peaches; aerial photographs Bud took during the war; flipbooks.

Over the summer, Clea has practiced sewing bindings, making quilted covers with Bee and wooden covers with Jiggs. She's experimented with bark, rubber, burlap and plastic. While all of her flipbooks incorporate her photographs, some are hybrids, partly drawn or painted. Some are flipbooks within flipbooks, one sequential series (drawn or photographed) cut and pasted into another. In exchange for teaching her how to drive Jiggs's truck, Clea took three rolls she shot of Jerod running across a field, cut out his figures and pasted them onto a series of photographs she took of a train rumbling through town. Jerod was pleased with his train jumping, inspired by the westerns they watched in the barn.

Clea returns to her desk. Homeroom falls silent when Jerod enters.

"Red rum, red rum," Queen Priss croaks.

Clea shoots her a contemptuous look.

"What? I can't quote a movie I saw last night?"

Jerod sits behind Clea in the last remaining desk.

"Red rum," Queen Priss repeats.

Clea studies Victoria. No blush. No twitch. No awkwardness. No shame. The chilly presence, she decides, of evil. The Halloween after Queen Priss stole her diary, Clea poured gasoline in the shape of a pentagram on the Fitches' front lawn and set it on fire, prescient, clearly, about their daughter's true nature.

"Red rum."

The prissies offer hesitant, but loyal giggles.

"Shut up!" Clea snaps. Do they really have to endure four more years of her cruelty?

"Red rum."

Clea crosses the aisle and squeezes her palms against the sides of Queen Priss's head. "You, demon, are a liar and I reject your spirit of rebellion. I bind and command you to leave this body in the name of Jesus Christ." Clea lets go and returns to her desk. "Sorry. The worst demons can't be exorcised, not even by the Pope."

"Religious freak." Queen Priss sticks out her tongue.

"Tongue tying is a sure sign."

Gaze narrowing, Queen Priss glances between Clea and Jerod,

a look of knowing settling into her face. To the tune of *Grease*, she sings, "Summer lovin', got me a dress."

"Summer lovin'," Clea sings, "naked in vans."

Unfazed, Queen Priss nods toward Jerod. "Met a boy, crazy like me."

Jerod springs across the aisle. Queen Priss screams as he lifts and slams the lid of her desk, papers flying to the floor like startled chickens. Swiveling, he pulls Clea out of her desk, pins her shoulders against the wall, and within the theatre of his black hood, scowls, revealing the full extent of his rage.

Struggling against his grasp, Clea reciprocates with the tears she restrains at home, at church, in school. "Let go! Leave me alone!"

"No." Jerod growls in a voice Clea has never heard. Upper lip kinked, he leans so close she worries and hopes he'll kiss her. He smells of shampoo, toothpaste, bug spray, Lava soap. "You leave *me* alone." With each word of his declaration, he bangs her against the wall, terrifying the class, protecting their secret. "Freak!"

"Psycho!" Clea spits, comforted by the reality show within their farce.

The principal runs into the classroom. "Stenker! To my office!"

Jerod pushes her harder against the wall.

The principal points at the door. "Now!"

With a wink only Clea can see, Jerod lets go of her.

*

"She's *my* queen." Ray strokes the white banner crisscrossing Luvie's gown. "I'm just loaning her to the parade."

Adjusting her elbow-length, black satin gloves, Luvie blows him a kiss.

Bee puts the last stitch in the hem of the scarlet gown Luvie wore as homecoming queen in 1942, and setting her sewing kit on the front hall bench, addresses Clea. "I ironed your band uniform."

Clea helps Bee to her feet. "Thanks, Grandma." Not that it makes any difference, her uniform so old a person would think the school colors are purple and orange instead of yellow and blue.

"You've got your trombone?"

"Yes."

"Your music?"

"Yes." The school hasn't purchased new band music since the early 1970s, their most contemporary piece "Eye of the Tiger."

"Your box?"

"There's no box, Grandma."

"Weren't you making a box?"

Clea blushes. "No."

"You painted it silver."

Clea turns red. "No." She grabs her uniform, trombone case and other bags by the door.

Bee calls after her. "You've got Luvie's clothes for the game?"

"Yes! See you and Jiggs at the parade!" Clea runs out to Ray's Eldorado and jumps into the back seat.

Ray helps Luvie into the front passenger seat to avoid snagging her gown. Once in the driver's seat, he opens the glove box and hands her a plastic box.

"A corsage!" Luvie slips her wrist through the elastic band attached to a cluster of white carnations and baby's breath.

"I've never been to homecoming," Ray winks, "so I wanted to get it right."

Luvie sniffs the carnation. "It's perfect."

Ray turns the ignition. "So in Big Bend, once a queen, always a queen?"

"Heavens, no. This is the first year all the past queens have been invited." Luvie laughs. "They cooked up this 'Past and Present' theme to get more bodies into the parade. Wait till you see it." She rests her hand on Ray's leg as he drives. "There aren't enough kids to be in the band *and* ride the floats, so after the band passes the judging stand and rounds the corner, the kids change out of their uniforms and run back to the floats. In the meantime, Rotary takes over the drum line. That's when you get the vets, police, fireman, church boards, Elks, Kiwanis and the like. When the school floats come out, the party begins. Clea, who's that queen I'm supposed to watch out for?"

"Victoria Fitch. She's only a princess."

"They didn't have that in my day," Luvie tells Ray. "There was only one king and queen."

"Now they have a whole float for the royal couple," Clea explains, "and a second for the court, which Victoria has commandeered and turned into a monstrous swan. The princesses are going to throw rose petals and release doves, only watch out, Luvie. They couldn't find real doves, so your gown could get splattered with pigeon crap."

"I'm on this swan?"

"You're behind it on the lower tier of the royal float."

"And you're mascot this year? That sounds a bit cheerful for you."

Clea rolls her eyes. "If you must know, I'm wearing the *old* mascot costume, but only as a disguise while I set up a prank."

"Ah." Luvie grins. Because no one would ever guess Clea would wear it. "What's homecoming without a prank?" She raises a gloved palm. "Don't tell me what it is. I want to be surprised."

"You will be." Clea has told Jerod nothing about her plan, but warned him to be involved with homecoming in order to have an ironclad alibi.

Ray drives slowly to minimize dust. "Is Jerod in the parade?" He's visited their trailer a few times and invited Jerod's mother to AA.

"He's pulling the freshman float. Note the hood of his car stained with the word *PSYCHO* from the shaving cream Victoria sprayed all over it." Thinking Jerod would believe Clea did it. They at least got a laugh out of that.

Luvie squints. "This the girl who stole your homework?"

"And put glue in my lotion bottle."

"So she's mean *and* lacks imagination?"

"She put crickets in my locker."

"That old trick?" Luvie shakes her head. "In my day, the football team put the principal's car on the roof of the school, tipped all the bleachers and blocked the hallways with so many boxes from the storage room we missed a day of school. I'll never forget homecoming senior year. Bud and Fred Pearlman hauled Dickie Smith to the graveyard and roped him to a tombstone."

Ray tugs his white moustache. "And left him there?"

"Dickie not only stole the float kitty, he snitched on Loretta Day because she wouldn't let him under the float with her—that was the big thing for the boys, you see, getting invited under the float while it was under construction." Luvie laughs. "The lucky ones sure came out grinning! You'll see Loretta in the parade today. Still can twirl a baton." Tilting the rearview mirror, Luvie checks her red lipstick. "No one could find Dickie though. Parents, sheriff, teachers. Next morning, the undertaker heard him screaming. Bud and Fred got kicked off the team and had to rake and fertilize the entire football field. Before they did, they took the yellow thistles Bud's father had cut from his pasture and harvested them with a combine. The following Saturday, they seeded the entire field. Next homecoming, you could hear the players yelling 'ouch' every time they got tackled on the thistles. Now *that's* a prank."

Ray shakes his head. "I thought I'd seen it all in the music business."

Luvie smiles. "Made history."

Clea feels nervous excitement as Ray turns onto the road into town. Jerod has begged her to ignore Queen Priss, but the red rum incident has left her bloated with rage. "Drop me behind the post office?" She'd be happy to spar with Victoria all the way to graduation, but spray-painting *red rum* on Jerod's locker? Tracking red paint footprints through the halls? Smearing red chalk along the walls? Leaving a pile of red pens on his desk?

At Big Bend's first stop sign, Luvie looks around. "Where is everybody?"

"We're a touch early." Clea hops out of the car, grabs her things from the back seat and disappears behind a hedge.

"She OK?" Ray turns onto Main Street.

Luvie sighs. "It's always been hard to tell."

Ray pulls into the lot beside the diner. "Does your highness desire a soda?"

They go inside, sit in a booth by the window and order two 7-Ups. The diner has red-and-white gingham curtains and a wooden display cabinet containing three generations of Haag sporting trophies. "Did you see that?" Luvie points to the blue dumpster next to the hardware store. "That flash of yellow?"

Ray catches the scruffy tail of the old lion mascot. "Stalking her prey."

"With a gas can? What's she up to?" Luvie puts her nose to the window, but loses sight of Clea behind the bakery.

"Don't look so worried." Ray reaches over and squeezes her hand. "I thought you liked pranks."

Sighing, Luvie gazes out the window. "It's you-know-who."

"She coming back?"

Luvie shakes her head. "Has the nerve to write asking *me* to drive Clea out to California to live with her."

"Are you going to?"

Luvie snorts. "Couldn't take care of her here, with family helping! And who does she think I am? Her chauffeur? I'd have to burn all my vacation doing her bidding. She claims she has the money. Hogwash! Even if she does." Luvie gazes out the window. "Clea's doing good in school. She has a friend."

"Are you going to tell her?"

"We haven't decided. Bee's worried about upsetting her, much less her *going*—which, let's face it, would kill Bee—and you-know-who not coming herself, not offering her mother so much as a visit." Luvie's eyes fill with tears. "Oh dear, I'm wrecking my face."

Ray hands her a napkin from the dispenser.

Jiggs's truck pulls up in front of the diner, Bee in the passenger seat. Ray pays for the sodas and they all join the crowd gathering on the sidewalk. Jiggs sets up three lawn chairs along the curb and props Bee's bad foot onto a cooler. Jiggs and Ray debate over which of them should drive Luvie to the royal float, but she declines them both, citing the rarity of being able to saunter down Main Street in her homecoming gown. When Luvie reaches the parking lot of the supermarket where the band waits, she finds Clea in her band uniform, flushed and sweating. "Are you OK?"

Clea forces a grin. "Great." She flips through the miniature sheet music clipped to her trombone.

Luvie raises an eyebrow. "See you at the tailgate."

A parking lot party where people eat from coolers out of the back of their cars? Determined never to be that desperate for entertainment, Clea shuns tailgates, but even if she didn't, she'll be long gone anyway. "Sure, Luvie. See you there." Clea watches her mill down the street greeting and hugging people, holding out her corsage for admiration. The homecoming king, Freddie Grunt, his movements constricted by his father's too-small blue suit, helps queens of years past onto the royal float.

"Would you look at that float?" Queen Priss sidles up to Clea in her velvet drum major dress. "It's more like *Sluts: Past and Present.*"

Clea nods at the outline of the bra showing through Victoria's tight dress. "You're well on your way."

Queen Priss adjusts her feather-capped, conical hat. "It's a shame the sluttiest homecoming queen of all isn't here, don't you think?"

Clea's stomach tightens. How could Velvet stand being one of these girls? Tongue-tied, spinning on her heels, Clea joins the brass section thinking of Peter Dale, glad he and Miss Wright moved away, bought a four-bedroom mock-Tudor and had three kids.

Tuning her trombone to a band mate's, Clea smells diesel fuel on her fingers, but there's no time to wash away the evidence. Raising her baton, the music director cues everyone to take positions. The drum line begins. *Thum thum tukatukatuka thum thum thum tukatukatuka thum thum.* The band plays the school song, to which Big Bend's residents sing *Onward lions, onward lions, fight on for your fame!* The drum line picks up pace—*tukatukatuka thum thum tukatukatuka*—as the crowd gets louder. *Onward lions, onward lions, fight, fight, fight, fellas, fight and win this game!*

Marching in place in front of the judging stand, the band salutes the mayor, Mert Kraas, and then marching on, plays "Louie Louie" and "Evil Ways." At the end of Main Street, the band rounds the corner and stops in front of the Baptist church, where dozens of instrument cases lie open on the lawn. While rotary members take the drums down the street, band members throw their instruments into their cases and strip out of their uniforms and helmets, leaving the lawn looking like the site of a vanquished Roman army. In the costumes they'd worn underneath their uniforms, they run to their respective class floats: grades seven through twelve, each representing a decade between the 1940s and the 1990s.

Shaking out her long hair, Clea runs in the bell-bottoms, striped blouse and burgundy vest comprising her Partridge Family outfit. Onto a hayrack, her class has constructed a bandstand and rainbow out of wood, chicken wire and multicolored crêpe paper. Clea takes her place as Laurie behind an electric keyboard. Jerod's Mach 1 idles, hooked to the front of the float.

As the float rolls forward, Clea's rat heart lurches. She presses play on the boom box, and despite "I Think I Love You" playing full volume next to her ankle, hears cheers up ahead as the first school float enters Main Street: the principal, his nose pasted with zinc oxide, wearing goggles, a life jacket, swim trunks and roller skates, pulled via water ski rope behind a fishing boat pulled by an ATV.

Clea pretends to play the keyboards. Her classmates throw candy to onlookers. "I Think I Love You" segues into "Looking Through the Eyes of Love." Clea spots Bee, Jiggs and Ray watching the parade from lawn chairs on the curb in front of the diner. Bee claps. Jiggs taps his cowboy boot to the beat of the music. Ray chats with Jerod's mother, who stretches her neck, watching for Jerod, taking part in a school activity for the first time. Candy corn lands on Bee's lap. She hands it to Jiggs. Jiggs passes a 7-Up to Ray. Ray adjusts the pillow under Bee's foot. Watching them, Clea feels pride and jealousy, wishing she could feel their contentment, laughing as if nothing in the world could be better than a ragtag parade. Clea waves. Bee waves back, nudging Jiggs, who stands on tiptoe to see Clea, such affection on his face, she feels guilty about her prank.

Too late.

Jerod stops the float in front of the judging stand. Their class dances to "Come On Get Happy," during which Clea catches a backward glance of Queen's Priss's swan dwarfing the royal float. Nervous, she lip-syncs "I Can Feel Your Heartbeat" and "I'll Meet You Halfway" as her class float continues to the end of Main Street. When Jerod parks it in front of the Baptist Church, they all jump down and run back to watch the rest of the parade.

Instead of joining her family, Clea sits on a grass knoll between the phone booth in front of the bank and the judging stand. As instructed, Jerod goes to the curb across the street, edging his way to the front, where, as she planned, his shock and innocence will be on display. If she stands on her toes, she can see the lower half of his face beneath his black hood. Freckled cheekbones. Clenched jaw. Only she will see the smile behind his mask. Only he will know the meaning of her prank. *I believe you.*

Clea crushes a dandelion between her palms to erase the smell of diesel fuel. Breathe. Smile. Act natural. Catching a rubber bouncy ball thrown from one of the floats, she leans down and gives it to Maggie Campbell's towheaded toddler. As the swan float approaches, Vivaldi plays from a boom box.

"Classy," Maggie whispers.

Clea nods, trying to look awed as the swan pulls in front of the judging stand. Head too small, neck too long, it looks like a cross between the Loch Ness Monster and a baby chick, its body constructed from yellow insulation foam. Wearing a tiara and pink taffeta gown, Queen Priss curtsies to Mert Kraas before leading the homecoming court in a waltz around an inflatable baby pool filled with water, lily pads and ducks. As the dance ends, a Bach cello concerto begins. The court bows. Queen Priss climbs a stepladder pushed against the base of the swan's neck and opens the lid of a silver-painted wooden box.

"Doves," Maggie sighs.

"Pigeons," Clea corrects.

Bull and garter snakes stream out of the box. With a startled yelp, Queen Priss flicks one onto a princess below, who screams, starting a stampede. Queen Priss falls from the ladder into the makeshift duck pond and shrieks as squawking ducks flap water onto her dress, makeup and hair. Snakes slither all over the float. Searching for an exit—the swan's high sides make it difficult to escape—the princesses pop the baby pool with their high heels, causing water to rush across the hayrack, soaking the blue and yellow crêpe paper. Dye smeared onto her dress and face, Queen Priss climbs the ladder, crawls over the empty silver box and slides down the swan's neck. As it breaks under her weight, Clea slips behind the bank, her last sight Luvie alone on the royal float, down on bent knee, laughing.

# PART III

# 1998

# MAY

Everything happens faster in the dream. The green car pulling into the Qwik Stop. *Where are you headed?* The numbers flipping on the pump. *For the longest time, I've been trying to figure out how to get there.* The gold tie dancing like a snake. *You're welcome to a ride.* She wants to reply, "No," but her dream self always says, *No kidding?* The dream gains momentum—*I need, please, just until, mechanic, nice man, not long, good girl, think of it as a vacation*—and suddenly she's clasping a brand new seat belt, breathing the green car's minty air. She wants to say wait. *Wait for me.* Chocolate-smeared mouth. Marker-stained hands.

Velvet opens her eyes—heart racing, teeth sore—and gets out of bed, at the end of which lies a flannel robe. Grabbing it, she slips through glass doors onto a redwood deck. This recurring dream has taught her she won't go back to sleep—awake or dreaming her brain plays the entire sequence of panicked decisions and sickening revelations that occurred that day, from her first sight of the green car at the Qwik Stop to the pay phone at the Starlight Motel, where, on the verge of calling Bee for help, she lost her nerve, interpreting gum stuck in a coin slot as a sign that it was too late to turn back.

Crossing the redwood deck, Velvet lies on a lounge chair and pulls her knees into her robe. *Nice man. Good girl.* The dream takes time to fade. *Think of it as a vacation.* She often has it when she's anxious, and the past month she has been as terrified as excited imagining the Greyhound bus carrying her eighteen-year-old daughter to California. *Wait for me.* The sea of glass mixed with fire. How to drown it? Velvet focuses on the crash of waves and tinkle of wind chimes.

*

Tiny rainbows swim the edge of a large chip in the bus's window. Her own *madman road, rainbow road, guppy road.* The May morning Clea boarded the Greyhound bus at Henning, she'd felt so giddy—had Velvet experienced a similar rush in the green car?—she'd almost felt obliged to forgive her. Finally it was Clea's turn to *shamble after* herself *eager for bread and love.* In preparation for their journeys—she to California, Jerod to his uncle's fishing outpost in Montana—they reread *On the Road.* The night before her departure, in the *burn, burn, burn* of the candle, still wearing their blue satin mortarboard caps and opening beer after beer, they celebrated in the deer stand, *mad to talk, mad to live, mad to be saved, desirous of everything at the same time*, laughing, whooping, never yawning, *running from one falling to star to another.*

Now, two days later, two cities from Santa Cruz, listening to the man in the front row recite the Gettysburg address for the hundredth time, Clea's feels it's too much a *madman road.* She has wanted to leave Big Bend for so long, she underestimated how overwhelming, disorienting and frightening the reality would be, and the bus journey that promised amusing *dingledodies* and a poetic *too-huge world* has introduced her to so many unsavory characters, she has been scared of being robbed every time the bus stops and opens its cargo hold. The two nights she checked into roadside motels, strange noises and the close proximity of flirtatious oddballs made it impossible to sleep, nor has she been able to eat, for lack of appetite as much as her loathing of the onboard toilet. At Cheyenne, she almost called home, but after all her bravado, couldn't bring herself to dial Bee.

Clea agreed to this trip and applied to California schools partly to please Bee, partly to have an adventure and partly to relieve her curiosity about Velvet's life—according to Bee, working for a winery, living by the ocean—and also to explore what might heal between them if she were to amend the New York dream to California. Hockney's swimming pools and Diebenkorn's oceanside avenues in mind, Clea had grown not only open to the idea, but convinced, by the time the bus reached the California border, that being near a family member, even Velvet, was the only way she could study so far from Big Bend. Why hadn't she applied to State with Jerod? If she couldn't handle a two-day bus journey to California, how would she cope with day-to-day life on the buses and subways of New York? In Big Bend, her dream felt like a balloon, but without Jerod, a boulder. How will she carry it?

Two days and she already misses him.

*You're grinding the gears! Don't ride the clutch!*

Driving the Mach 1 down the interstate, Jerod in the passenger seat.

*It's all in the wrist snap.*

A snowball fight at the caves, Jerod's cheeks doll pink.

*What is it we're doing again?*

*Skying.*

*That's a verb?*

*It was Turner's—*

*Turner?*

*The English painter. 'Skying' was his term for doing quick studies of the sky. I do it with my camera, and until you get your airplane, you'll do it in your mind.*

They fell asleep in the deer stand, Clea waking to find Jerod's arm around her waist, but they were astronauts, daily counting down for separate missions, and, worried about sabotaging their launch, she'd pretended not to notice.

*Debbie Reynolds? Loretta Young? Barbara Stanwyck, surely!*

*Nope. None would be the gal for me.*

Mortarboard cap askew, he'd set the View-Master and *Movie Stars* reels next to their empty beer bottles and hamburger wrappers, his expression grave, eyes soft, swelling with longing, so vulnerable she could barely return his gaze, the meaning of which was unmistakable. Unsure how to respond—even with graduation behind them, wouldn't giving into their feelings mean one of them losing a scholarship, and with it, a dream?—she'd feigned incomprehension, slipping like a ghost through his disappointment. Regretful of dismissing his feelings, Clea sits upright in her Greyhound seat, rat heart circling.

On the bus three miles outside of Big Bend, Clea gloated over her escape and Victoria Fitch's entrapment—pregnant, engaged to Jimmy Hooper, and, thanks to Johnny's enlistment in the army and Jimmy Sr.'s stroke, stuck on the family hog farm. Now, three hours from Santa Cruz, she feels chastened. Who is she to judge another person's version of happiness? Maybe Victoria and Jimmy are the Bee and Bud of their generation? Maybe she's been watching too many Cary Grant movies, imagining a similarly besuited suitor in New York? Or flipping through too many

Doisneau and Brassai books, studying their ornate staircases, wicker cafe chairs and steamy train platforms, vowing to hold out for kisses that threaten to break necks? In her determination to avoid a Velvet-level mistake has she made a Velvet-level mistake?

Is Jerod her Peter?

Each mile on the bus has torn a scale from her eyes until she sees him the way the girls at State will see him—smart, handsome, a starter on the basketball team and in possession of an academic scholarship. Their current plan: to speak every Friday afternoon at 4 p.m. Eastern Standard time, or, if she chooses California—and she has less than a week to decide, no more extensions—Saturday mornings at 11 a.m. Pacific Standard time. How has she maintained the illusion that a phone booth half a continent away will be a continuation of the deer stand, the caves, the truck? While Jerod joined the basketball team and led Big Bend to its first basketball wins in decades, how did she fail to realize his stigma had receded?

That day the thing happened when he was seven.

Gazing out the bus window—rocky canyon, blue sky, gauze clouds—Clea realizes how that day made him hers. She should be happy for him, going to State, free, the way she will finally be free, in either California or New York, to be a person unabandoned, unashamed, unmarked, but she also misses the old rules that set them apart.

The Gettysburg man starts his third recitation of Martin Luther King's *I Have a Dream* speech. The Greyhound driver yells at him to shut up, but Clea's relieved he's moved onto a new speech. A toothless woman in front of her turns around, shoves a rumpled, grease-stained, empty paper bag in front her face and asks if she wants any. The young man in the seat behind her continues a freestyle stick-and-poke tattoo down his swollen forearm. The woman across the aisle leans over and asks Clea whether she'd like to have her fortune read—her tarot cards are just up in the overhead bin—but Clea politely declines, less out of a disbelief in the psychic's art than a disinclination to hear bad news. Short line of heart. Faint line of marriage. The death card. Ten of cups reversed.

She reaches into her purse—a brown leather binocular bag of Bud's—and pulls out the last surprise Jerod left in the hole between the caves: a set of seven sunglasses he found at a garage sale in Hagan. Opening the battered box, she reads the instructions:

*Color is a powerful mood regulator and our color therapy eyewear is a safe, easy, nonintrusive way to create the mood you desire. Violet facilitates relaxation. Indigo encourages clear thinking. Blue stimulates creative expression. Green counters overstimulation and exhaustion. Yellow lifts spirits. Orange rejuvenates. Red increases vitality and energy.*

Clea slides on the red pair and looks out the window.

Red canyon, purple sky, cotton candy clouds.

\*

Tiny Mite once told Velvet the planets align once every two hundred years, a fact Velvet repeated as she tried to calculate the odds she would, one, pull into the Qwik Stop at all, two, meet a man on his way to the city where George told her Blankety Blank lived, and three, be offered a ride. Wasn't Bee always saying God works in mysterious ways? Tiny Mite also claimed that pebbles cross multiple oceans, and as the green car sped up the interstate ramp, Velvet felt that if a stupid rock could make it halfway around the world, she could make it halfway across the country.

She never planned to stay in California. Her only thought when she jumped into the green car was to make it to Modesto, find Blankety Blank, obtain her child support and return to Big Bend a hero. When she failed to find Blankety Blank, going home felt impossible until she'd achieved something that would justify her impulsivity and the pain she caused, so she readjusted her goal to something higher—making it in California—but the more classes she dropped and years she struggled to find and keep good jobs the more shameful she felt, and the more shameful she felt the greater achievement she needed to face her family, especially the daughter who hadn't spoken or written to her since she left. No longer able to live in Big Bend, nor possessing the strength or courage to leave it twice, Velvet became stuck.

Now, hopefully, she can make amends, Tiny Mite eighteen! Bee has warned Velvet to address her as Clea, a name that never felt right even though Velvet chose it. It had been the title of a book she'd checked out of the library for a book report, but never read. If her memory is correct, the book had been about an artist, so at least she got one thing right.

Velvet looks at her watch. 11:45. She'll leave at noon, drive for an hour and a half to Santa Cruz and collect Tiny Mite—Clea—at the Greyhound station. Velvet is nervous about how to greet her. Should she hug her? Or would that seem presumptuous? But if she doesn't, won't that sadden and offend her daughter? Bee told her that Tiny Mite lies in ditches and treetops by herself for hours at a time, reading and taking photographs. She doesn't date or go to ball games. She wears old clothes, hunts snakes and has a perfect school attendance record. Salutatorian and the Excellence medal. What will they have in common? Talk about? Velvet wishes Bee, Luvie, Jiggs even, could have accompanied her.

Velvet regrets disliking Jiggs, who has been a good surrogate father, teaching her to shoot, drive and use Bud's table saw and woodworking tools. Her father would be proud to know his granddaughter makes wooden photography books, zoetropes and sculptures.

Bee brags about the scholarships Tiny Mite has won—two to California universities and another in New York. Velvet hopes she'll pick one of the California schools, but isn't sure how strongly she should encourage it for fear of appearing desperate and pushing Tiny Mite—Clea—the opposite direction, although she also doesn't want to seem disinterested and get a similar result. Bee has warned her not to expect Tiny Mite to take photographs of them separate or together—Clea doesn't photograph people. Velvet wonders why, but guessing it has something to do with some art theory, won't ask. She would like to give her daughter one of the wind chimes or mosaic pieces she makes with healing stones, shells and sea glass, especially because she often thinks of Tiny Mite while making them, but cringes at the thought of them being judged as art.

Velvet looks at her watch again. 11:58. Taking a deep breath, she rubs a fluorite bead on her necklace. Almost time to leave. Nothing would be worse than being late. Thick mist hangs over the pines in the canyon. Velvet hopes it will burn off before she and Tiny Mite return from Santa Cruz.

Closing her eyes, Velvet feels the gritty weight of her exhaustion. Too anxious to sleep or sit still since Bee announced Tiny Mite's willingness to visit, she has sewn curtains and bedspreads, agonized over recipes, cooked sample meals and cleaned windows and rain gutters. A hawk squawks overhead. She opens her eyes and looks down at the car keys in her lap. She sewed the patchwork skirt for this day, but wonders if Tiny Mite—Clea, Clea, Clea—will find her old and frumpy? Will she even recognize her?

Velvet hopes that if the life she lives isn't compensation enough, she can make everything with Tiny Mite all right, or at least much better, with the contents of the Folgers can hidden in her utility shed. Surely between seeing her mother's home and receiving this gift, Tiny Mite will perhaps not forgive her, maybe not right away, but recognize how hard she's worked and sacrificed for her? And if that's still not enough? Velvet will brandish the only other weapon she has—revealing how many times Bee refused, even when she found the type of housing, school or job her mother demanded, to let Tiny Mite live with her in California. Velvet hopes things won't get that desperate, but Tiny Mite is now an adult. Velvet longs for friendship, envisioning walking and talking on the beach, camping in Big Sur, wine tasting in Napa, attending Burning Man and maybe even working the Half Moon Bay pumpkin festival, where she sells her handicrafts.

A gust shakes the eucalyptus trees surrounding the patio, scattering shadow fish across the white lounge chairs. Velvet looks at her watch. 12:14! Jumping up from her chair, she forgets the car keys in her lap. They fall, bounce off her foot, slip through a gap in the decking and disappear onto the rocky edge of the cliff.

*

The Greyhound bus pulls into Santa Cruz station. Tired, hungry, thirsty, bladder aching, Clea scans the people leaning on cars and milling the sidewalk. She wants to identify Velvet before disembarking, not only to feel safe, but to avoid looking like a lost lamb unsure which way to walk. The bus hisses as it stops. The driver jumps down and opens the cargo hold. The crowd closes around the exiting passengers, but Clea cannot see Velvet.

Wincing, she sits down to let the crowd thin and picks at a dried chunk of banana on her jeans. She had planned to change into a special dress, but the toilet smells vile and she's not supposed to care what Velvet thinks. Closing her eyes, she vows: *I, Clea*

*Marie Baumhauer, will not be swayed by convertibles, palm trees or swimming pools.*

Clea's rat heart rustles and roots as the last passengers exit the bus. Where is Velvet? Has she dyed her hair a different color or gained a lot of weight? The only remaining people by the bus are a Hispanic family and an elderly lady with an American flag on her walker. Would Velvet hang back to look nonchalant? Thinking how typical of her that would be, Clea grabs her backpack, stomps off the bus, and just as she feared, walks around like a lost lamb unsure which way to walk.

"This your bag?" The driver calls from the cargo hold.

"Thanks." Clea carries Bee's yellow vinyl suitcase by the handle, as it's too out-of-date to have wheels. "Is there another place people wait?"

"Ticket office." Slamming the cargo door, the driver climbs onto the bus and shuts the folding door.

Clea trudges toward the main building, bemoaning her large suitcase, a sure sign she's overpacked for fear of looking frumpy alongside her beautiful mother who will no doubt have fashionable clothes to match her glamorous house in her life so fabulous she couldn't leave it for a single visit to Big Bend, not even for Luvie and Ray's wedding, not even for her graduation. This had better be good, Clea thinks, nearly slipping on a hamburger wrapper. Better than manna, better than Oz.

Velvet is not in the ticket office. Clea goes to the bathroom and takes her time combing her hair, brushing her teeth, washing her face and changing into a violet A-line shift of Luvie's. She closes the suitcase's dull brass clasps. Surely by now Velvet is outside waiting for her.

Velvet is not in the ticket office. The bus is gone. Clea circles the transit building with her bags, sweat rings darkening her dress. On the sidewalk, a taqueria sells primary-colored bubbling juices and sugar-dusted churros. A gift shop bursts with T-shirts, beach toys and plastic flip-flops. The sky is a cloudless blue, the palm trees taller than she expected. This is it, the moment where she's supposed to be included in the good life and Velvet is nowhere in sight. Clea wonders whether she should wait near the buses in front of the transit office or out on the main street? She chooses a street bench, and sliding on her indigo sunglasses, studies the drivers of each passing car.

After an hour, Clea wonders whether Velvet is coming at all. Could she have gotten the date wrong? How much longer should she wait? Where should she go? How will she get there? Will she have enough money for the trip home? Bee told her to keep money in her bra and emergency numbers in her shoe in case she gets robbed. Clea can feel the roll of twenties against her breast and folded paper against the arch of her left foot, but the thought of having to use them makes her feel more panicked than reassured. She reaches into her bag and slides on the yellow sunglasses.

Green sky, red sun, orange coconuts.

A blue van pulls alongside the curb in front of Clea's bench. A tinted window rolls down. The driver, a man with a gray ponytail and aviator sunglasses, pokes his head out the window and asks her if she needs a lift. She shakes her head. He says she looks lost. She shakes her head again. He says he knows a place she can crash. Clea picks up her bags and runs to the ticket office. No Velvet. She returns to the area where the buses pull in and out of the station. No Velvet. Throwing her suitcase and yellow sunglasses onto the sidewalk next to a graphitized cactus, Clea collapses onto her suitcase and cries. Why did she get on that bus? Why did she believe Velvet wouldn't screw up? Why did she let a fancy job and beach house trick her into forgetting how selfish and irresponsible Velvet is? Because you never learn, Clea tells herself. You're stupid, pathetic and weak.

Her rat heart circles in agreement.

A black convertible screeches to a halt behind one of the parked buses. A woman with a mousy bun and large sunglasses gets out, slams the door, looks around, and as she runs toward the ticket office, trips several times on a floor-length patchwork skirt. "Oh no!" she whimpers, running past, a strand of purple stones bouncing against her chest. Disappearing into the transit office, she makes high-pitched, muffled entreaties to the staff. Several minutes later, she runs back outside, turns left at the curb, runs a short distance, stops, mutters something, turns around and runs the other direction, glancing at Clea as she runs past. Skidding to a stop in Birkenstock sandals, she tears off her sunglasses. "Tiny Mite?"

Her mother's same blue eyes. Velvet doesn't look like the aloof goddess Clea remembers, but a normal person, attractive still but likably chubby, wrinkly, weathered. Clea wipes her eyes and stands, embarrassed and angry to have been caught crying.

Velvet springs forward as if she might hug her.

Clea crosses her arms. "I thought you weren't coming."

Velvet jumps backward. "I'm so sorry. I lost my keys."

It sounds like a tall tale, but relieved to be found, Clea doesn't complain as Velvet throws the backpack and yellow suitcase into the trunk of the convertible.

*

The black convertible winds down a sunbaked canyon of red, gray and ochre taffy-stretched rock. At a dead end, it turns onto a shaded dirt road that descends through a forest of redwood, pine and eucalyptus. At a fork marked by a wooden sign announcing *Emu Oil For Sale,* it turns again onto a two-tire track. Wildflowers and grass grow down the middle. Cats sunning on the grass scatter before the convertible. The road leads to a clearing with panoramic views of the Pacific.

On the left side of the clearing, a dozen emus pace the edge of a long, rectangular, chain-link pen. A mustard-yellow Dodge Gremlin sits between the pen and a shed constructed from mismatched wood. On the right side of the clearing, at the base of a steep, wooded hill, sits a singlewide trailer hoisted onto concrete blocks. Christmas lights, red geraniums in white plastic pots and an inordinate quantity of wind chimes hang from its roof. A large redwood deck extends beyond the edge of the cliff.

Velvet parks the convertible in the middle of the clearing, leans into the steering wheel and squints—irritated, Clea guesses—that the emu oil salesperson hasn't emerged from the trailer. What does Velvet do with the oil? Rub it into her skin? Cook with it? Drink it?

Velvet smiles apologetically, "I need you to wait here." She doesn't want to leave Clea by herself, but her boss, who lives in a sleek, cantilevered house up the hill, is temperamental and often rude. After the stress of running late, she doesn't want to risk more trouble. She looks at her watch. She was supposed to return his car twenty minutes ago. "I've got to do an errand, but I'll be right back." Popping the trunk, she hops out of the car.

Clea is confused as to why she should wait at the emu oil salesperson's house, but as Velvet has unloaded her suitcase and backpack, gets out and glancing at the large redwood deck overlooking the ocean, decides to wait on one of the white lounge chairs.

Velvet hops back into the convertible. "Make yourself at home. As soon as my boss drops me back, we'll have a nice dinner."

Clea looks apprehensively at the trailer. "Should I tell them I'm here?"

"Help yourself to anything!" Velvet shouts over the engine. "I'll be right back!"

The emus ruffle their dark gray feathers watching the convertible. When it disappears, they stare at Clea. One of them has a bandage around its claw. Clea drags her bags to the edge of the deck, leaving them next to a large, dome-covered BBQ grill attached to the deck via thick chain. Clea climbs the steps, the edges of which provide a display area for shells, candles and pieces of driftwood. Stump stools surround a wooden table topped with a glass-and-stone mosaic in the pattern of a fish. Running her hand over its cool, bumpy surface, Clea heads toward a group of white lounge chairs, mostly inhabited by cats. Choosing an empty one in the shade, Clea brushes pine needles from its seat and lies down.

The sound of tires on gravel rouses Clea from a catnap. Relieved she and Velvet will soon be back on the road, she stands. A brown pickup truck pulls alongside the trailer, driven by a man with a patch of salt-and-pepper hair over each ear. The emu oil salesman, she thinks with dread. He must be desperate for a sale, because when he sees her, jumps down from the truck and bounds up the stairs of the deck. He's slim, tall and tan, the length of his legs emphasized by the shortness of his Hawaiian shorts.

"You must be Clea." He offers his hand. His green polo shirt is splattered with bleach stains. A white crystal hangs from a leather band around his neck. "I'm"—he lowers his voice—"Mitchell."

His pause gives her the impression she's supposed to know him, like he's famous, which annoys her, but she shakes his hand. "Nice to meet you." His irises don't match—one is blue, the other mostly brown with a spot of blue—and he watches her expectantly, as if there's something she's supposed to be doing, but isn't. "Would you mind if I use your restroom?" Anything to free herself from his lopsided gaze.

Bounding off, he seems relieved. "Help yourself. If you need anything, I'll be feeding the birds."

The inside of the trailer smells like incense and cat litter. Kilim rugs, Indian saris, patterned cushions, brass lanterns and large crystals cover every surface. Zodiac magnets on the refrigerator hold two-for-one coupons to a Hare Krishna vegetarian buffet/ movie house and a flier for a workshop entitled Synastry 101. The first door in the narrow hallway leads to a bathroom with pink porcelain fittings and 1970s peacock wallpaper. The emu oil salesman, she chuckles, has a flamboyant side.

After washing her hands with a rose-shaped soap and drying her hands on a macramé hand towel, Clea can't resist looking in the medicine cabinet, the true window, she's always believed, into a person's soul. Among the predictable containers of aspirin, skin lotion and toothpaste sit small brown dropper bottles of zodiac oils—one called *heavenly moon magic oil*—and a home-opathic remedy with a label that reads: *take in the event of a migraine, menstrual pain or gunshot wound.* A green stopper bottle containing Californian poppy extract sits next to a value-size tub of valerian tablets. Clea twists several orange prescription bottles on the top shelf to read their labels. *5 mg Ativan. 20 mg Prozac. 10 mg Ambien. Do not operate heavy machinery while taking this prescription. Two refills remaining. Velvet Lynn Baumhauer.* Velvet? Why does the emu oil salesman have her mother's prescriptions?

Recalling the Indian fabrics in the living room, Clea's rat heart freezes. Bee said Velvet lives in a house overlooking the ocean. Despite the cliffside deck where she just napped, Clea feels there must be some mistake. Velvet couldn't have sacrificed so much to live in a place like this. Dizzy with disappointment, Clea spins the prescription bottles back to their original positions. The only logical explanation, she decides, is that Velvet gave this man her prescriptions (best-case scenario) or is dating him (worst-case scenario), in which case they can break up. On her way out of the trailer, Clea ignores details from her childhood: hair bands tied around the handle of a brush, dainty necklaces hanging from a cabinet knob, mugs stacked into a pyramid by the sink, chamomile tea bags, Little Debbie oatmeal crème pies. *No, no, no, no, no.*

Outside, Mitchell waves her over to the emu pen. The emus eat cabbage leaves and carrots scattered on the ground. Mitchell points at a burlap bag near the door. "Grab that rye grass?"

Clea obliges. The emus are her height or taller, have large black beaks and red eyes. Their feathers brush against her arms. She stiffens. Mitchell shoos them away. Taking the bag, he fills a plastic tub.

"What do you use the oil for?"

"The question is what *isn't* the oil used for?" He fills a long, rusty trough with water from a garden hose. "It's a powerful antioxidant that heals stings, burns, eczema, ulcers, hair loss, arthritis, high blood pressure, scars, insect bites. It's outrageous doctors prescribe poison when emu oil cures nearly everything, but then they're the pawns of pharmaceutical companies, so what do you expect?" Trough full, Mitchell turns off the hose and leads Clea out of the pen. "It's not just the oil that's beneficial, but lean meat. I wanted to grill emu steaks tonight, but Velvet said it would be too weird for your first dinner."

First? There will be more? When she and Velvet only have a week together? Clea forlornly follows Mitchell to the grill. He reaches into a cooler, pulls out two cans of Budweiser and inserts them into foam beer cozies. Clea doesn't want to drink with him, but as she's hot, thirsty, and the beer is cold, accepts, drinking more quickly than she should.

"That's the spirit." Mitchell guzzles, spilling onto his shirt. He reaches into the cooler and retrieves them each a second can. "Don't worry, your mother will be here soon."

His accurate read of her anxiety unnerves Clea. She shrugs. "She's a Sagittarius."

He taps his beer can against hers, misreading her sarcasm. "So very true."

A gray cat jumps off the roof of the trailer onto the top of the grill, sending a domino effect of jingling through the wind chimes strung along the rain gutter. Mitchell shoos the cat away. While he prepares the coals, Clea drifts along the side of the deck and pours half of her beer into a potted cactus plant. When the coals glow red, Mitchell grabs them each another beer, leads her onto the deck and kicks several cats off two lounge chairs.

An overripe sun smashed against the cliffs drips red, pink, purple, yellow and black juice into the ocean. A brown-and-white cat jumps onto Clea's lap, knocking over the beer she set on the deck beside her chair. Already feeling buzzed, she leaves it upturned and pets the cat. The cat purrs. Three other cats lap up the spilled beer. Mitchell sighs. The wind chimes jingle. Clea reaches into her binocular bag for the box of sunglasses and reads the instructions to Mitchell before offering him a pair.

He chooses orange. "Every time I watch this sunset, it's worth it."

Clea slides on the violet pair. "Worth what?"

"Working for him." He nods up the wooded hill. "Her being late, again, but we can't complain and risk pissing off his royal highness, who so kindly lets us pitch our tent on this scrap of his kingdom."

Purple ocean, fuchsia sun, violet cats. "It's not a bad scrap."

Nodding, Mitchell finishes his beer and crushes the can under his flip-flop. Standing, he fiddles with the back of her chair. The cat bounces off Clea's lap and disappears under the deck. "When this chair reclines, I'll give you an adjustment. I was studying to be a chiropractor. I had a partner with a health food store and colonic hydrotherapy clinic who wanted to round out his business with my practice, but the opportunity to invest in the emus came up." Mitchell shakes the chair. "I give up. Lie on my chair and we'll get you relaxed."

Clea grips the sides of her chair, angry Velvet has not returned. "I'm sorry but bone cracking freaks me out."

Mitchell laughs. "Lucky for you, I'm certified in Indian head massage."

Pushing her head against the back of the lounge chair, he rubs the base of her skull. His fingers smell of lighter fluid. Clea feels uncomfortable being touched by Mitchell, but the massage feels surprisingly good, so she takes a deep breath, leans her full body weight into the chair and tries to relax.

"Now we're getting somewhere."

Mitchell works his fist around the sore junction between her spine and head, and then using his thumbs, rubs her entire head, stopping and pressing various pressure points along the way. He massages her temples, squeezes her eyebrows and tugs her ears, working her tight jaw over so thoroughly, she wonders how she previously opened her mouth. His fingers crawl under her hair, slowly circle to her crown and pull downward, giving her goosebumps. Beyond her hairline, onto her neck, the energy changes. She wants the massage to end. Mitchell reaches under the neckline of her dress and rubs her shoulders. Her body stiffens. His hands stop, but despite the awkwardness ballooning between them, he doesn't remove them. She feels it. He feels it.

Velvet feels it as her boss drives his black convertible into the gravel lot. She has wanted to leave Mitchell for years, but not summoned the courage. Furious to see him touch Tiny Mite, the path Velvet needs to take is clear. For the moment, however, she simply wants his hands off her daughter. Reaching over her boss, she toots the horn, and thanking him for loaning her his car, hops out and slams the door.

Mitchell wrenches his hands out of Clea's dress. "God, Mimi! It's about time!"

Clea spins around in her chair. *Mimi?*

Mitchell's shoulders slump. "I mean Velvet."

Clea hurls her mother a fierce, questioning look.

Velvet stares at her Birkenstocks. Whenever she's on the verge of salvaging things, the day gets worse. Her plan was to give Clea the big surprise at the end of the week, but given this awful start, decides a better, perhaps crucial, strategy is to present it this evening after Mitchell leaves for the shooting range. Velvet hopes it will fix if not everything, then surely something significant. Looking up, she claps. "Anyone hungry?"

\*

Velvet hovers near the grill, quilted oven mitts on each hand. "Don't cook them too long."

"Back off." Mitchell feints with his BBQ tongs. "I've *got* it."

"They're supposed to stay pink in the middle."

"How much were these?"

"Shh!"

Alone at the mosaic table decorated with shells, stones, crystals, tea lights, sea glass figurines and exotic-looking brass lanterns, Clea watches sparks float from the grill into the blue twilight. Eucalyptus leaves clack in the breeze, maracas to the steady drumbeat of the surf far below.

"Flip them!"

"Not yet!"

Clea rereads the menu card next to her plate:

*Prosciutto-wrapped ricotta-stuffed black Mission figs with arugula*

*Romanesco with cumquat and tarragon vinaigrette*
*Leek and artichoke quesadillas*
*Salmon empanadas with hoisin glaze*
*Grilled swordfish with mango and cilantro chutney*
*Panna cotta with stewed persimmon and candied fennel*

When she first sat down, Clea could not identify a single food on the menu, but the first four courses have tasted good. Velvet has paired a different wine with each course, showing off the expertise she's gained from her job running a tasting room for the winery owner who lives up the hill. Sonoma, Paso Robles, Los Gatos, Santa Clara, Santa Ynez. Pinot, cab sav, Chardonnay, Semillon, merlot, Zinfandel, fume blanc. Rootstock, varietal, acidity, fermentation, tobacco, tannin, lean, leafy, peppery, pruney, plush, bouquet, barnyard, bricking, browning, breathing, oaking, decanting. All evening, winking, rolling his eyes behind Velvet's back as he fills the glasses, Mitchell has read Clea's embarrassment of Velvet's boasting.

Watching Velvet cook has disoriented Clea, who can't remember her mother so much as buttering toast. The gourmet food, wine knowledge, New Age lingo, cats, and the baby voice with which she speaks to them, make Velvet feel like a stranger until she does something disarmingly familiar like twirl her hair as she speaks, nod as she listens, tug her left earring, jiggle her foot, swirl her food with her fork or double pat her lips with her napkin. Throughout the evening, careening between the familiar and unfamiliar, the irritating and endearing, Clea has fumed, yearned, hated, loved.

Before the first course, explaining her jewelry and the handicrafts with which she'd decorated the table, Velvet gave Clea a smooth, white, round crystal, a worry stone Velvet claimed Clea could rub if she ever needed to feel calm. Clea felt grateful for the gesture and elaborate meal, but while cutting her black Mission figs, listening to Velvet describe a recent class she'd taken in which she'd learned that a person can't create a sacred place within without first forgiving oneself, Clea had thought, doesn't she need *my* forgiveness to do that? Did Velvet think rubbing a rock could erase everything that had happened?

The quesadillas were served. Velvet interrupted Mitchell's display of knowledge about artichokes—one of California's top crops, technically a thistle, aphrodisiac, rich in minerals, vitamins K and C, fiber dense, a sure cure for constip ... to praise the vegetable animals Clea once made for a puppet show. "The sheep were cauliflowers, the hippos eggplants, the yams armadillos, and Jonah and his wife?" Velvet spooned mango salsa onto her plate. "He was a cucumber and she was a pumpkin." A squash, Clea corrected, amazed Velvet remembered. "Clea was always making things," Velvet continued. "A vacuum cleaner into an elephant, underwear into a crown. Remember that camera?" Clea pictured her Polariod Impulse disintegrating in the fire barrel along with the Winnie the Pooh baby album. "She made it out of a box, a tuna can and wad of aluminum foil. Took it everywhere. Adorable." If I was so adorable, Clea thought, why not stick around? The empanadas were served. Velvet announced that she and Mitchell were "pescatarians," except when they made an exception for emu. Clea struggled to chew, disoriented as much by the contradictory feelings roiling in her mind as by the new flavors mixing in her mouth.

Velvet and Mitchell step away from the grill, Mitchell transfering the swordfish steaks onto brightly patterned Mexican plates, Velvet pouring a yellow sauce over each one.

"I hope you're still hungry." Velvet beams, carrying a tray to the table.

Mitchell reaches into the ice-filled cooler next to his stump stool, opens another bottle of white wine and tips it toward Clea's glass.

Velvet tsks him with the same tone she deploys for misbehaving cats. "Stop giving her so much. She's underage."

"Not in Europe." Mitchell winks, filling Clea's glass.

The swordfish is dense and dry, the green flecks in its sauce unlike any herb Clea has ever tasted, but she enjoys it more than the salmon. The lamplight flickers. Waves crash down on the beach. Drinking wine for the first time, eating gourmet food, adeptly debating with Mitchell about Bohemian Club initiations, Kennedy mob connections, Greenpeace tactics, Iran contra secrets, genetically modified crops, Grateful Dead lyrics and the horned sperm in Keith Haring's art, Clea feels a shift from her high school to college self.

Yet another tabby jumps on the table, craning its neck toward Velvet. All evening dozens of cats have circled the table, meowing, rubbing their arched backs against Velvet's legs. To Clea's relief, Mitchell has shooed most of them away, but he swipes this one so hard it lands with a yelp against the metal side of a lounge chair. So far, his annoyance with Velvet has made Clea feel aligned with him, but now she feels sorry for the cat.

"Mitch!" Velvet scoops up the limping cat and cradles it in her arms. "My poor lovey dovey licky lady." Velvet lets it lick her mouth and nuzzle its wet nose against hers. "Remember that calico we had on the farm?"

Clea says nothing. Growing up, she had begged Velvet for a dog, pony, chicken, lizard, anything, but was never allowed a pet. Feeling lightheaded, she sets down her wine glass and fans her warm cheeks with her napkin.

Velvet laughs. "That calico used to meow all night. One time, Luvie poured a bucket of water out the window to make it stop." Velvet breaks off a piece of her swordfish and feeds it to the tabby. A white cat jumps onto the table. A black cat jumps onto Velvet's shoulder.

Mitchell stands, wobbles and steadies himself against the table. "I'm heading to the shooting range."

"What about dessert?" Velvet says to the cat in her cutesy voice.

Mitchell rolls his eyes. "Save me some."

Velvet hides her smile in cat fur. With Mitchell gone she'll be able retrieve the Folgers can from the shed and give Clea the surprise over panna cotta and mint tea. The perfect ending for a trying day. Velvet sets the tabby on the ground, and as she sits up, catches her reflection in her wineglass. Despite the candlelight, she looks haggard, deep lines around her mouth, hardness through the brow.

Clea watches Velvet pause over her reflection in her wine glass, feeling the shame she felt as a kid when her mother admired herself in store windows, car mirrors, gas pumps, cash registers, anything reflective, in front of people, oblivious to their judgment of her vanity. Unable to bear the cats or her confused feelings any longer, Clea stands. "I'll go to the shooting range, too." A change of scenery and fresh air will clear her head.

"No." Velvet stares in disbelief at the woman in the glass: Bee, middle-aged.

Velvet's flat, distracted tone strengthens Clea's resolve. "Can I, Mitchell?"

Shrugging, he heads toward the shed.

Standing to gather the dinner plates, Velvet feels exhausted. She lays the plates on the deck, and watching the cats eat, wonders if breakfast would be a better time to give Clea the surprise. When they're both rested and the sun is shining? Yes, she decides, after Mitchell leaves for work, she'll make yogurt, melon, homemade granola, coffee and orange juice from their trees. And if she couldn't control her daughter at eight, what chance does she have at eighteen? "OK." Velvet feels sad Clea prefers Mitchell's company, but also relieved she'll be able to go to bed.

Hurt Velvet didn't fight for her to stay, Clea stomps to Mitchell's truck. It smells like potting soil, melting plastic and marijuana. The seat is covered in a red-brown-and-blue-striped Mexican blanket. Crystals, a wishbone, several tin ornaments—heart, skull, crucifix, hand—hang from the rearview mirror. Clea opens the glove box and flips through a collection of cassettes. Beach Boys, Pink Floyd, Simon and Garfunkel, John Denver, Van Morrison, Crosby, Stills and Nash. As Mitchell loads three gun cases into the back of the truck, she inserts *Smiley Smile* into the cassette player.

The Beach Boys' upbeat harmonizing lightens Clea's mood as Mitchell drives hairpin dirt roads leading higher and higher into the canyon. Wide-open windows letting in cool, sobering evening air, they pass low wooden fences, barking dogs, houses built into the hill hodgepodge, propped by stilts, woodpiles, elaborate decks. Pine, woodsmoke, barbecue coal. Clea hums along to the music. *Chomp chomp chomp chomp do-do-do do-do-do.* Evergreens, eucalyptus, jacarandas form a canopy over the road. *Bop bop bop bop do-do-do do-do-do.*

Half a dozen turns higher, Mitchell turns right at a five-tier mailbox. The bottom one reads *Ricks Range* in gold, reflective stickers. The dirt road is steep and bumpy, the middle deeply grooved by an uneven stream of water. They pass an abandoned dog kennel and a California Forestry Service trailhead. Clea searches for houses—lit windows, yard lights—but the road is dark, the only illumination from the truck's headlights.

At the end of a long, winding adobe wall, Mitchell turns left into an open gated driveway. Despite the CLOSED sign hanging from one of the gate's rails, Mitchell pulls into an empty paved semicircle containing one other car and turns off the truck. Ticking engine, crickets, frogs, clacking eucalyptus leaves. They get out. The air is cold. Clea rubs her bare arms, wishing she'd brought a sweater.

Grabbing the guns from the truck bed, Mitchell leads her to the door of a low, 50s-era modular home, its walls, trim and door painted the same shade of bark brown. Mitchell pounds the brass knocker. "Rick?"

Small dogs bark. A woman shouts at them to "pipe down!" A man with a large belly, shaggy shoulder length hair and joint to his lips answers the door. He wears women's terry cloth slippers, khaki cargo shorts and a black T-shirt bearing a yellow stage-coach and the letters *WELLS FARGO*.

Rick taps his knuckles against Mitchell's. "Hey man." Scratching a scab on his calf, he looks Clea up and down. "Wow, so you're Mimi's daughter?"

Mitchell coughs. "Velvet's, yeah."

"No kidding." Rick exchanges a look with Mitchell that causes them both to smirk.

"I know you're closed"—Mitchell nods down the hill—"but we needed a breather."

Chuckling, Rick steps to the side and hands Mitchell the rest of his joint. "Have at it." The hallway is paneled in dark-stained, knotted wood.

After a long drag on the joint, Mitchell hands Rick a twenty-dollar bill. "Won't bother your neighbors?"

Rick shakes his head. "Moved two weeks ago." He shoves the bill into his pocket. "No one around for miles." He leads them through the hallway and screen door to a large, spare, dirt clearing containing half a dozen trees, a tall yard light and picnic table. "Tara and I are heading down to Clear Spring Tavern. Join us when you're done?"

Mitchell makes a face that says *I would if I could.*

Rick laughs, wishes them a good evening and shuts the door.

Mitchell offers Clea the joint, and when she declines, continues smoking as he unpacks the guns onto the picnic table. Through one of the large picture windows, Clea watches Tara, long hair, denim sundress and purple polar fleece, washing dishes in the kitchen. She drums her bare foot to the beat of the country music playing on a small radio in the windowsill over the sink. Heartened by the sight of multiple pans and stacks of dishes, Clea helps Mitchell assemble the guns, deciding that when the kitchen light goes out, she'll suggest going to the tavern or ask Tara to call Velvet.

Mitchell loads the guns, flicks the butt of the smoked joint onto the ground, and disappearing into a shed, returns with a line of cardboard bull's eyes. He hands her a set of blue ear protectors and a rifle. He shoots first, missing three, grazing the edge of one and hitting the outer ring of another. Clea hits all five within the central ring.

Mitchell gives her a high five. "Where'd you learn how to shoot?"

"Jiggs."

"Jiggs?"

Clea lowers her gun. "She hasn't mentioned him?"

Mitchell pulls a flask from his back pocket, takes a swig and holds it out to her.

She shakes her head.

They blow the bull's eyes into Swiss cheese wheels. They shoot beer cans, glow-in-the-dark clay pigeons, mannequins, potatoes hanging from ropes, Mitchell swigging whiskey to "loosen him up," "improve his shot," "force him to rely on instinct." The back of the clearing contains an obstacle course—barrels, logs, climbing frames. They crawl through it, Mitchell breathing hard, missing every target, complaining about a past shoulder injury ruining his aim.

Clea stops at the bottom of a hole. "How come you and Rick called Velvet 'Mimi?'"

Mitchell sighs. "Everyone does."

Clea feels stung. Her special name, common. Crawling through a tunnel of camouflage netting, she emerges into the clearing to find all of the house's windows dark. A sinking feeling overcomes her as she lays her gun on the picnic table. Worried about Mitchell's level of intoxication and the long, winding road back to Velvet's trailer, she packs her gun and the spare into their cases. "Let's go."

"Please don't be angry." Mitchell collapses onto the picnic bench and hands her his gun. "She didn't tell me her real name for years, and by then, I couldn't switch, and what kind of a name is Velvet?"

One of Bee's favorite Liz Taylor characters. Clea zips a case shut. "She introduced herself as Mimi?"

"You did."

Clea feels a sickening wave. "*I* did?"

"When you were chasing the car. I assumed that was her name."

*Mimi, wait!* Clea feels breathless. "*You* were driving the green car?"

"I'm not supposed to talk about it." Mitchell shrugs. "I thought she was Amish."

"What?"

"Trying to escape that life, you know, without television, electricity, computers."

"She told you that?"

"Her clothes gave me that impression."

Velvet's Prairie Town uniform. Clea scrunches her face. "You expect me to believe that? You would have known better when you made your plans."

"What plans?"

Shaking her head, Clea inserts the last two guns into their cases.

"Look, all I did was pull up for gas and mention where I was going. She asked me for a ride."

"She just jumped into a stranger's car?" Clea grabs the guns and trudges toward a chain-link gate at the side of the house. Would Velvet have done something that impulsive and risky? Bee and Luvie had always figured she'd met a tourist at Prairie Town and made plans to meet at the Qwik Stop. "Even if she did, who drives away from a screaming child?"

Following her, Mitchell trips on a coiled garden hose. "I wouldn't have done it if I'd known you were her kid."

Clea kicks open the gate. "Who did you think I was?"

Mitchell dislodges a stone embedded in the sole of his flip-flop. "Her sister. She said the guy at the station was a family friend, that he was happy to watch you."

Sister, not daughter. "I had never met that guy before in my life." *Nice man, good girl.* Clea stops on one of the concrete slabs forming a footpath, rat heart spinning. "Think of what could have happened!"

Mitchell runs his hand up her arm. "I'm sorry."

"Don't be." Clea yanks her arm free. "If it hadn't been you, it would have been someone else."

"I'm not an asshole." Mitchell tries to hug her. "What can I do?"

Guns knocking against her legs, Clea glances at the dark house. "Take me home."

"Fine." Snatching the guns by their handles, he stumbles to the front of the house.

Clea catches up to him and holds out her hand. "Give me the keys. I'll drive."

Mitchell throws the guns into the truck bed and raises an eyebrow. "You don't know how to get back."

She considers repeating her offer if he gives her directions, but scared to admit she doesn't know where she is, remains silent.

Clea looks at the dark house. Tara and Rick gone for the evening. *No one around for miles.* Thinking of the phone numbers in her shoe, she runs to the front door, hoping to get inside and call Velvet for help. The door is locked. When she turns, Mitchell is behind her.

He presses her against the door, his breath reeking of whiskey. "I think you and I have the same idea."

She tries to wiggle free. "You need the bathroom, too?"

Laughing, he squeezes tighter. "You know what I mean. Flirting with me all night. Coming shooting in that dress." He kisses her neck.

Mitchell's whiskers poke Clea's skin. All she wants is Velvet. To make it to her. "Not here," she whispers. "At home."

Mitchell pulls away, studying her face.

"I want to do it right under her nose."

His gaze narrows. "You really do hate her."

It's never felt truer. "You have no idea."

Mitchell grins. "She said you're wild!" He runs to the truck, jumps into the driver's seat and starts the engine. The cheery Beach Boys song blaring from the stereo sounds as eerie as fairground music in a horror movie. Looking into the dark forest, she considers making a run for it, but to where? To whom? *No one around for miles.* And if he finds her? And has a gun? Fighting tears, she climbs into the passenger seat and closes the door.

Mitchell sings along to the Beach Boys as he swerves down the canyon. Clea grips her seat belt with one hand and the dashboard with the other. The headlights scrape trees, shoulderless turns, smashed guardrails, sometimes the wrong side of the road. The further the truck descends the greater her panic at what she's started and how she'll get out of it. How can Velvet stand this man? Why would she date him all these years, Clea wonders, and live in a trailer and serve wine and make wind chimes and raise emus and love cats when she could have done all of that in Big Bend, only with me?

*

Mitchell runs over the *Emu Oil Sold Here* sign and hits a tree. Swearing, he reverses the truck and turns onto the two-tire track. Clea removes her seat belt, unlocks her door, grips the handle, and when—just as she feared—she sees no sign of Velvet inside or outside the pitch-dark trailer, decides she has no choice but to implement the plan B she devised on the way down the canyon. Twenty feet shy of the trailer, Mitchell rams the gear into park. Clea hops out, pulls the three canvas gun cases from the bed of the truck and scrambles up the hill.

Mitchell opens his door. "Hey!"

Loose soil and thick piles of pine needles and eucalyptus leaves make Clea's climb slower than she'd anticipated.

Mitchell turns off the ignition and falls out of the truck. "Where's my kiss?"

Clea climbs. With her left hand, she grabs undergrowth and exposed tree roots each time she slips. With her cramping right hand, she clutches the handles of the guns.

"That's cool." Mitchell slurs, fiddling with something metallic in the truck bed. "I like hide-and-seek."

Clea stops and looks down. Mitchell stumbles toward the base of the hill with a flashlight. He trips and curses. The guns slow her ascent, but she doesn't dare leave them behind.

Light flashes through the trees. "There you are."

Clea gazes upward hoping to see another house, but the woods are dark. The churning and crashing of the surf reminds her to stay away from the cliff.

Mitchell pants, struggling up the hill. "I like a challenge."

Clea displaces a rock, slips and twists her ankle.

"It just makes me hotter."

She climbs toward a clump of trees.

"And boy am I hot."

The light gets brighter. Is he gaining on her? Clea vacillates between two strategies: stopping where she's at and using her lead to get one of the guns loaded, or continuing toward the clump of trees and hiding. Feeling exposed in the spare wood, she climbs, hoping to find a place from which she can defend herself with one of the guns.

Mitchell stops, panting. "Enough is enough!" He pinches his side. "I'm getting annoyed."

When Clea reaches the clump of trees, she runs around panicked, wondering where to hide. Several redwoods have trunks wider than her body. A fallen log is half decomposed. Both spots make her feel either too exposed or trapped. She looks up, wondering if she should climb one of the trees.

"Naughty girl."

How would she climb a tree with three guns? Even if she could reach the lowest boughs, she doesn't have time.

"You're going to get punished."

She climbs a ramp made by a fallen tree up to an outcropping of boulders surrounding a cluster of dead trees.

"And you're going to like it."

Mitchell's flashlight bounces around the clump of trees she abandoned minutes before. She runs around the trees looking for one with a hole or split through which she can position one of the guns.

"Getting hotter."

Clea crawls inside a half-rotten redwood tree with just enough height for her to pull the guns in with her. There is not, however, enough room for her to load one of the guns without holding it outside her hiding place.

"I can hear you."

She pulls several branches over the opening in the tree, regretting not having loaded one of the guns. If Mitchell finds her, she'll be trapped.

"Hotter."

Clea can hear him breathing. Leaves swish as he walks around the tree.

"You're here somewhere."

Clea wills herself not to hold her breath. Light flashes around the leaves two feet from her foot. The footsteps cease. The light slowly moves toward her foot stopping an inch from her toe. She fights her instinct to move.

The light disappears. "This isn't fun anymore." Footsteps crunch. "You can come out now."

Clea stays still.

Mitchell sighs. "I'm sorry if I scared you."

Keep breathing, Clea tells herself. Keep it soft.

"Come on, Clea. I was just kidding."

Footsteps again. Faster. Is he running around the tree?

"You're freaking me out now. I'm really worried."

The footsteps stop. She stays still.

"Bitch!"

Thump. Breaking glass.

"Lying bitch!"

Mitchell whacks tree trunks with what sounds like a branch. Swish of displaced leaves. A belch. Grumbling, he slides down the hill. After what feels like an hour, she hears the yowl of a kicked cat followed by the slam of a door. The forest resumes its sounds. A gust shakes the trees. An owl hoots. The tide, which seemed to pause during her ordeal, continues its onslaught against the cliff. She removes the branches from the opening of her hiding place. Her body aches from crouching so long. Stepping out of the tree, she stretches a few times, shakes out the numbness in her legs and retrieves the guns. The clouds have cleared since she hid. The moon is a dried dandelion.

She picks up the broken flashlight, and as she flings it over the cliff, wonders what she should do. Go to the trailer and alert her mother to what's happened? Go to the trailer and call the police? Go to the trailer, trust Mitchell is sleeping off his booze and try to sleep? What if he isn't asleep at all, but waiting to ambush her? Should she stay in the forest? Hide under a log and sleep? She hasn't slept for two nights and now wonders if she should *hide under a log and sleep* so her mother's boyfriend won't attack her? The man, it turns out, who was the accomplice to her greatest humiliation? She's given up her summer with Jerod for this? Forget California. New York, too. *I, Clea Marie Baumhauer, swear to go to State, even if they don't offer an art major, even if I can't start for a year, even if I have to take out a student loan that takes ten times ten thousand years to repay so help me God.*

Unzipping one of the rifles from its brown canvas case, Clea loads it with the last three bullets in the side pouch. She returns the case and two other guns to her hiding place and covers the opening with branches. Gun over her shoulder, she slides through the loose soil and leaves down to the trailer. The driver's door of the truck is wide open. One of the emus has escaped and paces outside its cage. Clea bypasses the trailer's main door and climbs onto the deck. Looking through the window, she tries to see whether Mitchell is in bed, but the curtains are drawn, blowing in and out with the breeze. The sliding glass door is partly open. With the tip of the rifle, Clea pushes the curtain aside and slips inside.

Still dressed, Mitchell snores on the bed, arm around Velvet, leaf-caked flip-flops dangling from his muddy toes. Velvet sleeps on her back, arms around her head, purple tie-dye nightgown twisted at her knees. They have some nerve, Clea thinks, sleeping with abandon when she's terrified to walk around without a loaded gun.

Piled high with wadded tissues, cucumber slices and sleeping pills, Velvet's bedside table and all the anguish it represents ignites guilt and distress in Clea, followed by an urgent need to make everything OK for Velvet in order to make everything OK for herself. How to stop feeling crumbly until Velvet feels solid? Exterminate this maddening, illogical need to comfort her tormentor? End the torture of loving the one she hates? Clea steps closer to the bed. What kind of mother takes sleeping pills when her eighteen-year-old daughter isn't home safe? Clea raises the gun and aims it at Velvet.

Velvet sleeps.

Mitchell snores.

Curtains billow.

Wind chimes tinkle.

Through the gun's viewfinder, Clea gazes at Velvet, thinking *maybe*. She imagines pulling the trigger, Velvet's body jerking from the impact of the bullet, blood staining the sheets, wiping her fingerprints from the gun, slipping it into Mitchell's hands, tiptoeing out of the room and calling the police. She imagines recounting a scene of drunken domestic violence, watching Velvet's covered body being carried out of the trailer on a stretcher, red lights swirling around the yard, Mitchell being handcuffed and shoved into the back seat of a squad car, a policeman draping a blanket over her shoulders.

Something metal crashes in the yard.

Clea takes a step closer to the bed, half hoping Velvet will awaken and see her, and know, finally, the extent of her daughter's rage and power. *I could*. Velvet rolls over and sighs. *But I won't*. Clea lays the gun down in the bed between them. Walking backward, she slips onto the deck, the curtain rubbing against her cheek. A cat runs under a chair. The escaped emu sniffs the grill.

Wind chimes tinkle.

Crossing the moonlit yard, Clea goes to the utility shed to get a carrot with which to lure the emu back to its cage, but, when she enters, picks up a feedbag and spills it all over the floor. She does the same with the alfalfa pellets and kicks over the veggie bucket. She pulls a large box of washing detergent from the shelf over the washer and dryer, knocks it over, and as it spills, works through the entire shelf, opening and upturning every cleaning agent, toolbox, nail can and matchbox she encounters.

Clea stops. A red coffee can sits at the back of the shelf. She stares at it for a long time remembering the identical one she found in the basement of the farmhouse when she was a kid. Her mother's secret ashtray. Grabbing it, Clea decides to return to the trailer and spill cigarette butts all over Velvet and Mitchell's doped bodies. Halfway across the shed, she lifts the lid and peeks inside.

Money.

Clea removes one roll and peels white rubber bands from each end. Presidents up. Perfectly aligned. Twenty twenties. Her rat heart rouses. Ever since that day at the Qwik Stop, she has only imagined two possibilities: Velvet too poor to send Clea out to California to live with her or all of her money invested into a better life, one that would be a comfort for Clea to join. Clea digs into the money rolls—five layers deep, the can full—as astonished by the amount of money as by the fact that she ever trusted that a woman who abandons her child at a gas station with a stranger was going to *share*. Velvet *hoarding* money? While she, Bee, Luvie and Jiggs ate the old food from the deepest shelves in the basement? Monitored gas gauges and electric meters? Counted food stamps, coupons and toilet paper squares?

Clea reseals the lid and runs to the trailer, the emu trailing behind. Entering through the main door, she shoves the can into her backpack and zips it shut. As she gathers the few things she'd removed from her suitcase, the emu taps the door with its beak. Heart pounding, she snaps the suitcase and—to avoid making further noise—leaves the door open, running, catching in her last backward glance sight of the emu stepping into the trailer.

# AUGUST

# Asphalt molten, the clouds boiled. It's a wonder the

fences and telephone poles don't curl like wilting flowers toward the scorched grass, although not once in sixteen hundred miles has she rolled up the windows and tried the air conditioning, preferring the brusque scrubbing of the wind, which together with the heat in her cheeks, throb of her temples and trickle of perspiration through her bra and waistband, solder her to the landscape, mitigating her anxiety, because the closer she gets to home the more she fears it's a hologram sustained by the humid air.

She presses the accelerator. Sixty, sixty-five, seventy. The car shakes. The dashboard squeaks. Bugs explode onto the windshield. The tires, it feels, melt toward their rims. Will she make it the last twenty-one miles? Seventy, seventy-five, eighty. Lights flash in the rear window. Red, yellow, blue. She bangs the steering wheel with the heel of her sweaty palm. Not now. Not this close. She can't afford to fill the tank again, much less pay for a speeding ticket. Eighty, seventy, sixty. Swearing, she decelerates onto the interstate's shoulder, and, worried the car won't restart if she kills the engine, rams the stiff gear into park.

She aims the rearview mirror at herself—hair wind-whipped, cheeks burned, eyes bloodshot, every wrinkle caked with dirt—thinking of the comb and lipstick in her backpack, but there's only time for untying the T-shirt wrapped around her head and mopping her face with it. The engine ticks under the dented hood. Two passing vehicles pepper her doors with gravel. A wasp enters the passenger window, hovers near the headrest and exits a back window. This is how it will be, she thinks. Slow. Familiar. Space between details. Overwhelming feelings flooding each space. It's inescapable now: she will have to feel everything.

She readjusts the mirror. A state trooper in a short-sleeved tan uniform, brown felt hat and black leather boots expands in it as he approaches. Her right leg shakes. Though the car idles out of gear, she presses hard into the brake. What if he searches her vehicle? She places a hand onto her knee to still it. What if she gets arrested? The trooper stops and crouches behind the car. Shaking the bumper? Tapping the lights? She holds her breath. What if he searches the trunk? Please don't search the trunk. Please. Standing, shaking his head, he pats dust from his hands. She exhales as he approaches her window. Act natural. Smile.

"Afternoon." He says it with no trace of friendliness. Though perspiration dots his forehead and nose, the rest of him—slicked dark hair, trimmed goatee, polyester shirt, metal badges, mirrored aviators—looks dry, creaseless, polished.

"Afternoon." Her leg shakes.

He hooks his thumbs into his thick black leather belt. "Do you know your speed back there?"

She presses her palm against her knee. "Sixty-seven?"

He bends down so close she can smell his cologne, Fahrenheit, embarrassing not because of the sudden intimacy, but because she can smell her armpits. "Eighty-two."

"I'm really sorry, officer." Seeing the medusas reflected in his mirrored lenses, she abandons her normal strategy of flirtation for one of heartrending honesty. "I have a family emergency." Sniffling and rubbing her eyes, she pauses, as if struggling for composure. "You see—"

"License and registration." He thrusts out his palm.

She leans over and presses the release button of the glove box, but it doesn't open. "It's stuck."

Standing, the trooper shifts his weight to one leg and gazes down the interstate, tapping the wad of keys attached to his belt. "I've got all day."

Fighting real tears, worried that if she cries she'll never stop, she shakes the knob. Does this car even have registration? She left in such a hurry she didn't think to check. She bangs the plastic door of the glove box with the side of her fist until it falls open. Digging through maps, cassettes, lozenges, tissue packets and candy wrappers, she finds an orange plastic sleeve containing yellowed papers. "This must be it." She should have said *this is it*. Think. Stay calm.

The trooper opens the envelope. "Is this your vehicle?"

Should she lie? "No." Her leg shakes. Pressure to knee.

"Is," he pauses to read, "Mitchell T. Bell aware of your use of his vehicle?"

"Yes," she lies. Please don't search the trunk. Please.

Frowning, he hands her the orange plastic sleeve. "License."

Hands shaking, she returns the sleeve to the glove box, takes the wallet from the front pocket of her backpack and reluctantly passes it to him. Please let me go with a warning. Please.

He leans backward to read it, its laminated surface reflecting the sun. "Velvet Lynn Baumhauer." Lowering his aviators, squinting, the trooper studies her. "Velvet? Is that really you?"

*

Watching a cowboy lean against a trash can to light a cigarette she has to laugh at herself, having likened fleeing to Montana to escaping into a Robert Frank contact sheet, despite the exact same cowboys, guns, motorcyclists, lunch counters, American flags and Fourth of July parades populating her world back home. She reaches into the front pocket of her backpack and bounces her remaining change—two nickels and a penny—in her sweaty palm. Eleven cents won't buy her a newspaper, lollipop or even a call to the farm. Pleased, Clea shoves the change into the back pocket of her cut-off jeans. Returning home stone broke had been half the challenge and the fun.

Running up the dark canyon from Velvet's trailer, waving her arms at the first set of white headlights to break through the mist, her only thought had been Bee, but by the time Clea settled into the tweed back seat of a brown K-car belonging to an elderly couple, bakers on their way to work, another thought crossed her mind, and by the time the wife, her white bun trapped in a black hairnet, asked where she was heading from Santa Cruz, Clea pronounced: Montana.

Now, sitting on her yellow suitcase in a slice of shade outside the Henning bus station, feeling the immensity of her journey, Clea questions whether she really did it all by herself. Would she have had the nerve to ride the bus, unannounced, all the way from Santa Cruz to Missoula, Montana, hitchhike to both Bozeman and Jerod's uncle's fishing camp, and then ask his uncle for a job, without the fuel of hatred and Velvet's can of money in her backpack, daring her, taunting her to open it and take just one roll? Not once has she unsealed its lid. She hasn't needed to. It's like a chunk of kryptonite, weakening her mother, but protecting and strengthening her, emboldening her to share her feelings with Jerod, to let one week in Montana stretch into ten.

The moment Jiggs pulls his truck alongside the curb and toots the horn, Clea's faltering self-congratulation disintegrates into guilt. He swivels out of the driver's seat so slowly and robotically—is something wrong with his back?—that she calls, "I've got it!" and heaves the suitcase into the bed of the truck. Inside the cab, Jiggs hugs her long, hard and enthusiastically, but something feels different. He's lost weight, but there's more. Exhaustion? Distraction? When they last spoke on the phone, he mentioned some crisis at the farm, something broken. Did he fix it? Is he angry with her? Saddened she went to Montana instead of Big Bend? Disappointed she's been gone all summer?

Clea suddenly feels exposed sitting in the passenger seat of the truck wearing nothing but short cut-offs, a tank top and flip-flops, worrying Jiggs can sense the change in her body, because it does feel different, like her skin is etched with Jerod's fingerprints, her ribs replowed by his fingertips, her lips reshaped by his. The entire bus journey from Bozeman, Montana, to Henning, South Dakota, the summer replayed in her mind like a long flipbook—nights in Jerod's tent, mornings in the river, lips, mouths, hands, like hundreds of birds, landing on her head, neck, back, arms, knees, thighs, chest.

Exclamation marks back in her life.

A thought bubble rises over her head: *I can levitate!!! Fly!!!!!!!!!*

On the highway, the roar of wind through the cab makes conversation difficult. Clea slides down into her seat, hoping to sleep. Jiggs reaches over and squeezes her hand. "At h-home, we we n-need to to t-talk."

Can he sense she's a superhero in red patent boots? "Of

course." Embarrassed, dreading a mortifying talk about the birds and the bees, Clea looks out the passenger window to hide the grin she hasn't contained since the moment she arrived at the fishing camp, crept through the forest and snuck up behind Jerod, waiting for him to set down his chainsaw, remove his deer hide gloves and massage his palm before springing forward and covering his eyes with her hands. She didn't have to say, "Guess who?" He didn't have to turn around. His hands shot to hers. She pressed her forehead into the space between his shoulder blades. Their fingers interwove.

*

The blunt force of it. Not *is that you*, but *is that* really *you*? So she *is* unrecognizable. Having her fear confirmed feels like a horse kick to the chest. Studying her, the trooper's blue eyes flash through recognition, disbelief, happiness, curiosity and disdain, landing on a smug twinkle. This is how it will be, she thinks. This is how everyone will see her, and can she blame the remaining residents of Big Bend for glorying in her demise when she treated them all with condescension?

"Billy Grover." She tries to sound pleased to see him. He asked her to the harvest dance freshman year and she dropped him last minute to go with Peter. "How have you been?"

"Can't complain." He pushes his aviators onto his face. "Got a ball and chain, two rug rats and a mortgage. You?"

Broke. Unemployed. Estranged from her only daughter. "I'm great."

"What've you been up to?"

Everyone will ask. Should she concoct something satisfying or say it like it is? "This and that."

"So you're back?"

She forces a smile. "Looks like it." And because that sounds too final. "For now. My mother's unwell."

He nods. "I heard she took quite a tumble."

"Broke her elbow, wrist, three ribs, hip and leg."

He winces. "Sorry to hear that. Please give her my best." Widening his stance, he reinserts his thumbs in his belt, a trooper again. "This vehicle is barely roadworthy. I'll have to escort you into town."

A police escort into Big Bend. Velvet restrains a laugh. At least he's not giving her a ticket, or worse, searching the trunk.

"Go straight to Hagan's and tell him I sent you. You remember his garage?"

Velvet nods.

"Good to see you, Velvet."

"Good to see you, Billy."

With a slap to the roof of her car, he returns to his patrol car. He pulls in front of her and she follows his flashing lights and sirens for twenty-one miles. Sixty, seventy, eighty, eighty-six, the mustard-yellow Dodge Gremlin shakes keeping pace. Billy Grover. Stalker and arsonist by eighteen, now a show-off cop. Who could have guessed? But then here she is, approaching Big Bend with nothing to show for ten years' absence, a greater failure than when she left. She was supposed to change, but the opposite happened: Luvie is sober and adheres to marriage vows; Jiggs lives in the farmhouse and has an online admirer; Bee smokes pot; Clea dates a murderer.

When Bee told her why Clea went to Montana, Velvet was outraged the relationship was allowed to build for so long. What if he pushes Clea off course? What could be worse than her daughter ending up like her? Youth spent, going backward? Velvet's sole remaining comfort is that Clea will do everything better, and with a local boy in the way, she worries she'll lose that hope, too. Why didn't Bee tell her sooner? She would have been on the interstate years ago, and yet if she's honest, she has mixed feelings for Jerod Stenker, revulsion and fear, but also, given her hunger for grace, jealousy and even admiration, because if someone like him can redeem himself, doesn't that improve her chances?

The exit for Big Bend appears. When she veers onto it, Billy waves out his window and continues down the interstate. Velvet feels a twist in her stomach as she slows toward the stop sign at the end of the exit ramp and the Qwik Stop comes into view. It looks exactly the same, but smaller, despite looming so large in her nightmares and regrets. But then everything looks smaller: the rusty white grain elevators, faded green water tower, excavation company, implement center and billboard for Prairie Town, a *CLOSED/FOR SALE* sign running across it in a diagonal line.

She used to assume life could only get bigger, bring more opportunity, more experience, more knowledge, more people, more memory, space and air, but the contractive shifts she's felt since coming up empty-handed in Modesto, the frustration of striving harder only to lose ground, have made her wonder if instead of endlessly expanding, life is a constant reapportioning, one part contracting to accommodate another part amplifying, and she's relieved to feel, as she drives down Main Street, despite the cracked concrete, empty flowerpots, boarded-up storefronts and lack of pedestrians, a sense of amplification and gratefulness for her purpose here.

The bank and post office still operate. The Crow Bar and funeral home look open for business. The diner is *UNDER NEW MANAGEMENT*. The old boarding house has been converted into a gallery/coffee house/internet cafe. She'd worried that without Peter, Big Bend would feel emptier and more claustrophobic than ever, but to her surprise, it feels dilapidated and sleepy, but benign. This is how it will be, she thinks. Smaller, as long as her mother is alive, but she feels sure about her choice.

As she passes the faded Lions, Kiwanis, Veterans and Elks club signs at the edge of town, Velvet's stomach clenches. On the washboard road out to the farm, passing the turn-offs to the dunes and the caves, the still-standing Haverton homestead, blinking red radio tower, Henderson mailbox, Beel Junction and string of *WHY DIE?* signs, her nerves remind her of the first time she experienced an earthquake: teacups rattling in their saucers, pots jumping on their burners, plates vibrating in their rack, forks, spoons, knives sliding off the counter and crashing onto the floor.

\*

Groggy and overheated, Clea wakes as Jiggs turns the truck into the driveway. She vows to her reflection in the passenger window: *I, Clea Marie Baumhauer, will not, under any circumstances, inquire about Velvet.* Throughout the summer, Bee has written Clea letters encouraging her to call Velvet, but Clea has refused on the grounds that she can't bear one more excuse. Bee insists Velvet wants to hear her voice to know she's OK, but Clea knows Velvet just wants her money. Clea has reveled at the thought of Velvet's torment over her missing hoard. The one person she's told about the money: Jerod. Their one disagreement: his insistence that she return it, although Clea assured him Velvet could have it any time—taking a penny from her mother would feel like owing her a dollar—but she'd have to come all the way to her dormitory in New York and beg for it.

In front of the farmhouse, scattered across the brown grass, lie towers of cardboard boxes, appliances on their sides, shelves piled ad hoc, dress dummies, ironing boards, clothes racks, crocks, jars, clothes, cots, tents and gas masks. "Jiggs, what happened?"

He parks the truck. "B-b-burst p-pipes."

"In the basement?"

He nods.

Clea imagines her grandmother's last supplies for the apocalypse drowned like Earth during the Flood, the life raft rising like the Ark toward the kitchen. "How come no one told me?" Jiggs had told her something broke, and as usual, downplayed it. She should have pressed for details. "I'll help clean up the rest."

Jiggs eases himself, hand to lower back, down to the ground. "Y-your your g-grandma."

Clea can't wait to see her. "Leave the suitcase, Jiggs. I'll get it later." Grabbing her backpack containing Velvet's can of money, Clea jumps down from the truck, and though Jiggs raises his hand, calls to him, "I'll be right back! I'll make a pot of coffee and we'll get all caught up!"

Bounding up the bowed wooden steps, Clea enters the house, which smells of mold, rot, dust and mothballs. Mildew-spotted cardboard boxes and bulging black plastic bags fill the front hall. Propping the front door open with the decapitated gnome Jiggs has been using as an ashtray, Clea sidesteps boxes and bags to the staircase, its steps lined with shoe boxes filled with loose change, old photos, pink plastic hair curlers, sermon notes, sympathy cards, food coupons, magazines, phone books, wooden spools, elastic waistbands and old Mary Kay cosmetics. Upstairs the landing is crammed with more boxes, plastic baskets heaped with clothes, piles of shoes and an ironing board stacked with warped, water-logged books. The floorboards creak as Clea approaches Bee's room.

"Velvet!" Bee gasps. "Velvet?"

"It's me, Grandma." Clea peeks inside the room. Does she smell marijuana? Bee lies on the bed, her bruised foot propped on three pillows, her good leg covered in a white cast and held aloft by a metal pole at the end of the bed. "Grandma!" Clea runs around the bed and touches the cast on Bee's left arm. "What happened?"

A pink line of recently removed stitches runs diagonally across her forehead. "I had a little fall."

The frailty of Bee's voice shocks Clea. Both of her eyes are ringed with purple bruises. "Where? How?"

"Tripped at the top of the basement stairs."

Clea sits on the wooden chair by the bed. "Trying to clean out the basement."

Bee nods until pain stops her. "I couldn't find Bud's letters. Jiggs has been overwhelmed. The water was six feet high before we realized."

"When did this happen?"

Bee gazes at the ceiling. "Two weeks ago?"

"Why didn't you tell me?" With shame she remembers her last conversation with Jiggs from the leaning phone booth in Bozeman: babbling about all the exciting things she was doing in Montana without asking him any questions, ending the call, her change running out, with rushed information about her arrival date and time in Henning. "If you'd written me a letter, I would have come right away."

"It's been busy. The surgery alone—"

"Surgery?"

Bee whispers. "The old hip gave out on me."

Clea feels disoriented by the onslaught of alarming information. "Where are Luvie and Ray?"

Bee brightens. "On tour! In Sturgis ministering to those gangs."

Clea frowns. First Bee thought Clea was Velvet, now this outlandish story? Is Bee lucid? Are painkillers to blame? "What are they doing?"

"Managing a Christian country band. Left a month ago. They said to say goodbye. Their last show is in New York, so they'll bring you home for Christmas."

"Luvie knows you fell?"

"I don't want to spoil it for her. The church formed a committee to help."

This sacrifice seems excessive, even for Bee. Something doesn't add up. Clea scans the bedside table—medications, throat lozenges, a mug holding a toothbrush and toothpaste, water bottles stuffed with bendy straws, a remote control, its buttons labeled with stickers. An unsmoked joint lies on the base of the lamp. A white enamelware bedpan pokes out from under the bed. The bed is so full of Bud's coats, newspapers, books, tablets and pens that Bee occupies less than a third of its space. More piles of newspapers and boxes from the basement cover the floor. Clea glances at a stack of letters near Bee's hand. Written in thin, spidery handwriting and addressed to twenty members of the State Senate, they argue in favor of the legalization of medicinal marijuana. "Grandma, would you like me to mail these?"

"Please."

Clea squeezes her grandmother's hand. "I'll be right back with some tea." She gathers the letters, and when she meets Jiggs on the stairs, holds them out to him. "Am I reading correctly?"

He grins.

Clea chuckles. "Luvie and Ray are on some kind of tour? Until Christmas?"

He nods.

Astounded, Clea shakes her head. "Jiggs, I'm so sorry you've been dealing with this alone."

He waves a hand like it's nothing.

As the situation sinks in, Clea considers her options. Should she contact Luvie? How quickly could she come? Orientation at

NYU begins in two weeks, class in three. Even if she were to skip orientation, she'd only gain two and a half weeks to help, and even if she could clean this mess in that time, she can't leave Jiggs alone with Bee in such a weak state. Panic and disappointment tear through her imagining calling student services to inquire about a deferment. Anger flares as she gazes at one of the portraits lining the stairs, Velvet in a rainbow shirt, glitter lip gloss and silver barrettes. Absent as usual. Shirking her responsibilities. Probably at a wine tasting or transformation seminar, in the lotus position, obliviously chanting. Should she call her? Tell her how bad things have gotten? Clea looks into her mother's twelve-year-old eyes and vows: *I, Clea Marie Baumhauer, will get a deferment for a semester, a year even, before asking you for help.*

Jiggs's cough and quick, nervous glance at Velvet's portrait makes Clea guess he wants her to contact her. "We don't need her, Jiggs." The can of kryptonite in her backpack glows a brighter shade of green. "I'll stay until Grandma is better." At any cost—the intensity of her anger, the destructiveness of the only option that feels viable, carries a rush not dissimilar to the moment she kissed Jerod or pushed her NYU confirmation letter through the slot in the Bozeman post office. Though excruciating, the rush feels like movement, which promises change, which heralds relief, only it's short-lived, because even in the moment she feels powerful, she despairs the outcome. In these rages she feels like a miner fleeing an explosion—the route up and out, anything beyond her immediate survival, irrelevant, only that she escapes. The sacrifices she has to make for Velvet! Clea stomps down the stairs, a miserable, self-appointed saint.

Jiggs blocks her. "Sh-sh-she's c-c-coming."

Clea brightens. "Luvie?"

Shaking his head, he glances at Velvet's portrait.

Clea gasps. "Here?"

He nods.

"You called her?"

His expression says *Are you kidding?* He jabs his thumb toward Bee's room.

It makes sense. Clea gone. Luvie gone. Jiggs too distracted to intervene. What better opportunity for Bee to force Velvet home? Despite kindness being one of her grandmother's best traits, Clea feels maddened, not only by her certainty that Bee will never punish Velvet—that she'll act as if she never left—but that Velvet, who was supposed to travel twenty-three hundred miles to claim her money, will now get away with half. Clea takes another step toward Jiggs. "When is she coming?"

He glances at his black digital watch, then her, his eyes apologetic. "A-an-any m-minute."

He's been trying to tell her since collecting her at the Henning bus station, but she's either brushed him off or fallen asleep. Panicked, she bounds past him to the front hall, grabs the binoculars from their hook on the back of the closet door and runs onto the porch. There. A mile north of the mailbox. Flashes of mustard yellow through the leaves of the corn.

*

Twenty, fifteen, ten, five. Velvet pumps the accelerator, but after two rattles and a bang, the Dodge Gremlin shudders to a stop half a mile from the mailbox. Turning the ignition, the starter crank churns progressively slower until it quits. She tries it again. Dead. Leaning into her seat, blowing upward onto her sweaty face, she laughs and then cries, her failure so complete, she can't even make it home. The windshield is so caked with bugs and wiper smears she can barely see through it. The pile of crumpled paper bags on the floor of the passenger seat reeks of hamburgers and rancid fries.

A fly gorges itself atop the straw in the soda can in the cupholder. The hot plastic seat sticks to her back. Her legs cramp and eyes sting and yet she's hesitant to get out. Outside the car: so much sky, land, and even bigger, the void of her absence. The thought of someone driving by and finding her in this state finally motivates her to click on the hazard lights and open the door.

Velvet grabs the backpack from the passenger seat and gets out, denting the door with her wooden clog as she kicks it shut. She limps to the trunk, lifts the hatch and heaves a heavy canvas duffel bag onto the gravel. Lifting the trunk's felted base, she reaches under the spare tire and pulls out a gallon-sized plastic bag of marijuana. When they last spoke, Bee mentioned that Luvie's "special cigarettes" had had a positive affect on her pain, breathing and "morale," so Velvet took Mitchell's stash along with the Gremlin.

Velvet stuffs the stash in the backpack, slings it onto her shoulders, and looping the duffel's rope handles onto her forearms, heaves them down the road. Crickets. Locusts. Gnats. The corn grown. The sun low. The road looks narrower than she remembered it. The corn shorter. The sun smaller. She's sad to see that her father's clown head mailbox has been replaced by a galvanized tin rectangle embossed with the letters USPS, but brightens at the sight of the gladioli, poppies and dahlias potted in old paint cans beneath it. Velvet opens the mailbox, and finding it empty, turns into the driveway.

Clea stands in the middle of the driveway, feet apart, clutching the straps of her backpack. Velvet had thought she was still in Montana. She would throw down her bags and hug her daughter if not deterred by Clea's scowl and crossed arms. "Oh, you startled me." After two months of seeking contact this is what she says to her daughter? Velvet opens her mouth to add, *I'm so relieved to see you.*

"Don't come any further." Clea takes a step forward, shocked by the sight of Velvet, hair snarled, dress filthy, face caked with dust. She looks like a sharecropper in a Dorothea Lange photo, like she's aged ten years in as many weeks. Don't, Clea wills herself. Don't start feeling sorry for her now. "We both know why you're here."

Velvet blinks. She needs a reason? "I'm here to care for Mother." She almost adds, *So you can go to college.*

"Is that the story you're telling yourself? I know it's the one you're telling her. I understand why, but it's not the one you're telling me."

Velvet feels breathless. This child, towering a head above her, is far fiercer than the tentative, wounded, passive-aggressive one she collected at the Santa Cruz bus station ten weeks earlier. Velvet raises a palm in peace. "I don't blame you for anything that happened with Mitchell."

Clea snorts. "You don't blame *me*? How generous."

"We broke up, as we should have done years ago. I'm sorry you ever had to meet him. I'm sorry I—"

"Left me in the hands of a rapist?"

Velvet drops the duffel onto the gravel. "What?" Mitchell told her Clea had gotten drunk, come on to him at the shooting range, and ashamed of her behavior, split to avoid facing her mother.

Clea's hands fly away from her shoulder straps. "He got stoned and drunk and assaulted me at the driving range! Almost killed me on the way home! Chased me up the hill!" Rage balloons in her chest recalling the horrors of that night—the icy swish of Mitchell's footsteps, the uselessness of the disassembled guns, the claustrophobic tree trunk. "I had to hide from him!"

Velvet feels pathetic. How could she have believed him? Someone who stole from her and shamelessly lied about it? "I didn't know."

"Because you were sleeping!" Clea cries. "Passed out cold. I saw the pills."

Velvet stares at Clea. Her heaving daughter is a lion she's terrified to draw near. "I believe you." Velvet had woken with a loaded gun against her head. Mitchell claimed Clea had done it, but that she hadn't believed. Did he point it at her daughter? The thought fills her with panic. No wonder Clea fled. With shame Velvet remembers taking two ten-milligram doses of Ambien. "I'm so deeply sorry. I want to understand every—"

"I have nothing more to say to you!" Clea's lower lip shakes. She hates herself for wanting to accept Velvet's apology. "You only ever make things worse!"

Velvet throws her backpack on top of the duffel and holds out her arms. Having no clue what to say or do makes her want to storm her daughter, peel back her skin, climb inside her, breathe her breath, gobble her scent, ransack her thoughts, blast her heart open with a barrage of buts: but I was young, but I was heartbroken, but I was rash, but I was ashamed, but I was scared, but I was broke, but I was naive, but I was tired, but I was lost, but I was depressed, but I was overwhelmed, but I asked and asked, and no matter how much money I saved picking oranges, stocking shelves, cleaning houses, frothing lattes, painting fences, canning artichokes, sewing hems, pouring wine, baking bread, waiting tables, counting change, scanning groceries, stuffing envelopes, painting nails, delivering mail or dealing cards in a low-cut leotard and gold vinyl heels, Bee always said no, but that would sound like an excuse, and worse, cause more hurt. The last thing Clea or Bee deserve. Mothers, Velvet muses, swallow as many buts as their children. "Please give me another chance, Clea. I'm here to help." Her last card, now that her hoard in the Folgers can is gone, stolen by that son of a bitch Mitchell when he realized she was leaving him.

Unable to bear her mother's Florence Nightingale ruse, Clea

yanks off her backpack, unzips the main compartment and pulls out the heavy can that's been inside it all summer. "Here." She shoves it into Velvet's arms. "Take what you came for and leave. It's cruel coming to Grandma under false pretenses."

"Is this...?" Velvet stares at the can. "Is this...?" Could it be?

Clea narrows her eyes at her. "Your precious? Yes."

Velvet jumps up and down, kissing it.

Clea watches her, disgusted.

"Mitchell *sent* it to you?" Velvet shakes the can. It doesn't feel like he took very much. "When? How?"

"Mitchell had nothing to do with it." Clea feels powerful saying it. "*I* took it."

Velvet furls her brow, confused. "You?"

It feels as good as Clea expected. "I didn't spend a single bill." She awaits her mother's wrath, eager to retaliate, but Velvet covers her mouth with one hand and cries, her face distorted with a hard-to-read smile.

"But that's too perfect!" Velvet rushes at Clea and tries to hug her.

Bewildered, Clea pushes Velvet away. "What?"

Velvet laughs. Here it is—finally—the moment toward which she's labored. "Clea, the money is for you. I saved it"—she almost says *so you could come and live with me in California*—"to pay for college. I was going to give it to you during your visit"—she almost says *but you left me*—"but Mitchell and I drove you away."

Clea tilts her head. "You expect me to believe that?"

Velvet reels. "You don't believe I could do it?"

"You're covering up for the fact that while we struggled, you hoarded money for yourself and I caught you. If it was for me, why hide it in a shed?"

"So Mitchell wouldn't find it!" And use it for his pyramid schemes, bullets, pot or booze.

"You haven't heard of a bank?"

"I needed to look at it, roll it myself. It kept me going." Velvet shakes her head, incredulous. "I thought Mitchell stole it." When she discovered it missing, and failed to retrieve it, she drove him off the property with a hoe. His acquiescence, despite his protestations that he hadn't stolen it, strengthened her resolve. Now she knows his guilt stemmed from another crime. She wants to get to the bottom of that, but later. "It's all just as well." Velvet closes her eyes, savoring the relief of having him out of her life. Could she have done it if Clea hadn't taken the money? She'd failed half a dozen times, gotten lonely or depressed or failed to save a deposit for her own place. Opening her eyes, Velvet beams at her daughter. "Thank you." She returns the can to Clea's hands. "It's yours. Do whatever you want with it."

Clea feels helpless, like she's fallen to the bottom of a deep hole. The green aura has drained from the kryptonite. Her rat heart has abandoned her. Remembering the billowing white curtains and tinkling wind chimes at Velvet's trailer, she thinks of the loaded gun she pointed at her mother, the cold trigger she stroked thinking *maybe*. She has told Jerod about Mitchell and the money, but not the gun. The thing that happened the day he was seven was an accident and misunderstanding, but what she thought about doing would have made her the real thing. What if Velvet knew? What if anyone knew? Her shame triggers fresh anger. Why couldn't Velvet have saved rolls of twenties in Big Bend? Why stay away ten years and then foist this overwhelming gift onto her? Does accepting it mean everything is forgiven? What is the price of forgiveness? Her dignity? Her rat heart? She's always hated it, and yet, could she survive without it? Achieve and create? The thought makes her feel skinless, afraid. "I'm sorry." Clea hands the can back to Velvet. "I can't."

Velvet's heart drops and splatters between her feet. "But—"

"You'll need it." Clea almost adds *to take care of Grandma*, but overwhelmed and confused, turns and walks toward the farmhouse, sad not to hear Velvet's footsteps behind her, relieved not to hear Velvet's footsteps behind her, hating her, loving her, the journey to the porch steps the same old seesaw between yearning and fury. Her rage could fill the landscape ten times ten thousand. She leans down to pick up a rock, and by the time she throws it, realizes what anger gives her: exoneration. Without it, what does it mean, what she did with the gun? Who would she be?

Velvet fills with sadness watching Clea walk away. Should she run after her? Or give her space? Her own child, a stranger. *I hate Mimi! Mimi is mean.* Velvet looks down at the can. How could she think money would compensate for all she's done? *What kind of mother are you? I can't believe I ever wanted you to have my children.* Should she stay? *Shame on you, Velvet Lynn Baumhauer!* Or would it be better for everyone if she left? Maybe she's been gone too long? Maybe it's too late to come home?

Climbing the porch steps, Clea vows: *I, Clea Marie Baumhauer, will not turn and look at Velvet.* She longs to see her, dreads to see her. Jiggs stands in the front hall, grimacing. Clea shakes her head at him. *I can't talk about it right now.* Nodding, he follows her to the base of the stairs, wringing his hands as she ascends.

"Velvet!" Bee calls. "Velvet?"

Clea silently climbs the ladder to her attic room and lies on the unmade bed. Has she driven Velvet away? What has she done? To her grandmother? To Jiggs? To herself? Downstairs, the front door opens and closes. Velvet entering or Jiggs leaving? A long silence. Footsteps on the stairs. Clea lies still, eyes alert, listening.

"Velvet!" Bee calls. "Velvet?"

The creak of the top step.

A whisper. "Mother?"

A bleat. "Here!"

Pulling her knees into her chest, relieved, Clea cries along with them.

*

Metallic thunder. Wind-jumbled Pearl Jam. Steeling herself, Velvet steps to the attic window, and gazing toward the road, watches a caterpillar of dust stretch above the corn. An orange hot rod, black stripe down the middle of its hood, turns into the driveway and tears down the gravel, spewing loose rocks into its billowing wake.

Slam of the screen door. Flash of white. Clea, in a crocheted dress that once belonged to her, shoots out of the farmhouse and runs toward the car. Though it hasn't stopped, she inserts her bare arms through the driver's open window. As the car brakes she pushes her head inside. A tanned arm reaches out and pulls her torso inward until her legs dangle out the window, the car like a robot sucking in a mouthful of spaghetti.

Suffocating pain in her chest. Fear she might choke. Over the years Velvet has convinced herself that she never possessed that kind of love, that she and Peter were like any hormonally charged teenagers, perhaps more grandiose, but watching Clea's legs disappear into the car, hearing her buttocks honk the horn as she kisses the driver, Velvet feels the sting of recognition and stupefaction at what she has lost. A sea of glass mixed with fire rises over her heart. How to hold her child's happiness, and her genuine gratitude for it, alongside her own grief? Her child's success, a future at which Velvet can only gape, alongside her own failures? How to temper the regret that compels her to run out the kitchen door and gasp for air?

There are gifts. The shimmer and downswing of her daughter's hair, as well as her acceptance that it is Trent's, when Clea bends down to pick up a box. The way Clea jumps to her toes while telling a funny story. Blushes when Jiggs tickles her. The gentle humming with which she combs Bee's hair. Her laughter as Jerod kicks open the car door and they emerge, still entwined.

Marvel at her child carries a bitter kickback: awareness of lost time. She fretted about it in California, but that alternate reality fed a fantasy that everyone in Big Bend had paused, that everything there could be not merely restored, but improved, if she could make the California dream work. The gag-inducing truth is that the total gain for all of her effort, plus the serendipity of Clea finding the Folgers can, is one week of her daughter's childhood, the last week before she embarks on her adult life.

Throughout the past week, caring for Bee, cleaning the house and packing Clea's suitcases, Velvet has deferred to Clea and Jiggs on all schedules, systems, menus and decisions, from which boxes go to the dump to what temperature Bee likes her bath. Velvet knows she is an intruder, and accepting that she must earn her place, makes herself available, works tirelessly and follows instructions without question. As she ascends and descends the stairs all day, passing crisp portraits of her former selves, she feels like a ghost, but doesn't panic: each day with her family reinstates a fraction of herself, and she trusts that in time, and it may take a lot, she'll reemerge whole and as distinctly different as the bright-eyed schoolgirls lining the stairs.

Slam of the front door. Velvet leaves the attic window, skirts Clea's unmade bed—with her off to college today, Velvet will sleep in it tonight, maybe every night—and tiptoes to the door. Jerod's footsteps are loud and echoing on the stairs. Velvet doesn't like the feeling of him being in the house—ungenerous, she knows, given Clea's feelings for him and that fact that he is driving her all the way to New York, settling her into her dorm room and driving back to State with only two days to spare before the start of his own classes. Jealous, Velvet climbs down the ladder and listens to the reunion in Bee's room.

Laughing at Jerod's broken-bone jokes, claiming osteoporosis isn't what it's cracked up to be, Bee fawns over him. Handsomer and taller than ever! So brave to drive across the country! She wouldn't cross the street to go to New York. Will he promise to make sure Clea doesn't live near hoodlums or gangsters? He must call her now and then from State. He and his mother must join them for Thanksgiving. By then she will be able to make his favorite pumpkin bread. Will he promise to eat enough at State? She apologizes for not having made him any lettuce and peanut butter sandwiches for the journey.

Clea joins the conversation, Jiggs laughing, as usual, most loudly at whatever she says. Unable to hear everything, Velvet creeps along the cleared hallway still smelling strongly of the white vinegar with which she scrubbed it the day before. She cranes her neck. Through the opening in the door she can see Bee lying on the bed in her best pink nightgown, Bud's fishing vest over it, holding hands with Jerod, sitting on the chair beside her. Clea stands behind him, arms locked around his neck. Jiggs watches from the foot of the bed.

Bee reaches into one of the piles stacked on her bed and hands Jerod a box of newspaper clippings. "Make sure she reads these during the drive."

Clea leans forward and reads one of the headlines in Jerod's lap. "Grandma, that stabbing happened in Uruguay."

Bee taps the edge of the box. "You think these nuts can't board a plane?"

Jerod nods. "We'll read them all."

Pointing to the floor, Bee instructs Jerod to take a pile of yellowed newspapers folded to the crossword section. "For years

I've tried, but for the life of me can't finish them. Your professors, though, they'll know the answers. You can each take half."

Suppressing a grin, Clea knees Jerod in the back.

He elbows her in the hip. "Yes, ma'am. We'll make sure to finish them."

Bee pats his hand. Reaching into one of the pockets in her fishing vest, she pulls out a glass mustard jar. "Take this, Clea." Reaching over Jerod's shoulder, Clea obeys. "An insurance policy should you ever find yourself in a pickle."

Clea shakes the jar. "These aren't teeth?"

Bee nods. "My grandmother gave them to my mother. She made the additions she could and passed them on to me. Now it's yours."

Velvet, despite not wanting the jar of teeth, can't help but notice her omission from the succession.

Clea frowns. "Our ancestors pulled people's teeth? Before they buried them?" Repulsed, she releases the jar into the box on Jerod's lap.

Bee tsks her granddaughter. "In my day, we didn't turn up our noses at perfectly good gold. Now take that jar to New York and sell them to a jeweler to help pay your expenses."

Jerod stands. "That is so kind of you. Clea will do that." He leans down and kisses Bee on the cheek. "Get better. I'm counting on that pumpkin bread." With a promise to come for Thanksgiving, Jerod gathers Bee's gifts into his arms and heads to the door.

Embarrassed to be caught eavesdropping, Velvet jumps away from the door and holds out a hand to Jerod, shoving it into her jeans pocket when she realizes his hands are occupied. "Hello, I'm"—she almost says *Clea's mother*—"Velvet."

"Jerod." His gaze is intense, but not unkind; in fact, where she expected to find judgment, and possibly disgust, she finds a knowing compassion. "It's good to see you here." He nods farewell.

Watching him descend the stairs, holding Bee's junk as if it's fine china, fills Velvet with affection.

Jiggs leaves Bee's room with another bundle of newspapers. Shutting the door behind him to allow Clea and Bee privacy, he follows Jerod to the front hall, where Clea's suitcases await loading into the Mach 1. Hoping also for privacy with her daughter, Velvet remains on the landing. When Clea emerges from Bee's room, eyes swollen from crying, Velvet wonders if enough goodwill has been created for her to hug or comfort her?

Clea wipes her tears with the back of her hands. "Thanks for taking care of Grandma." She couldn't leave otherwise, not when Bee's better, perhaps not ever.

Velvet shakes her head. "You don't have to thank me."

Clea smiles. Throughout the past week, Velvet has been disarmingly deferential and empathetic, leaving Clea, as now, speechless. Clea had assumed Velvet would stay only until Luvie and Ray returned, but now that Luvie knows everything and has given Velvet her blessing to stay, Velvet's plans are to live in Big Bend indefinitely. Clea is also grateful Velvet managed to save the money in the Folgers can. Knowing Velvet has plenty with which to care for Bee makes it easier to leave. Clea would like to acknowledge the fact, but doesn't dare revisit the subject of the can or the money, lest it raise the shameful subject of the gun, which Velvet attributes to Mitchell. Clea leans down and picks up the backpack and camera lying at the top of the stairs. "So I'll see you at Christmas?" She says it cheerfully, hoping her tone will convey what feels too awkward to articulate. *It will be nice to see you.*

Velvet nods, trying to suppress her disappointment. She'd hoped to join Jiggs for the send-off at the porch, but this seems to be it. "I'll look forward to it."

Clea slings the backpack onto her shoulders and loops the black camera strap around her neck. "Well," she grins, "I guess I'm off."

Velvet stares at her tiny reflection in the uncapped lens lying against Clea's chest. She knows Clea doesn't photograph people, yet wants to shake her and tell her that one day those are the only shots she'll care about. "Good luck, Clea."

"Thanks." Clea hesitates.

Velvet hopes they might yet embrace, but with an awkward little wave, Clea skips down the stairs, and because Jerod and Jiggs have already cleared the front hall, goes straight out the front door. Velvet waits until the screen door has bounced shut before going down to the living room and peeking through the lace curtains fluttering in front of the open window over the davenport. Jerod loads the last suitcase and slams the trunk, remaining behind the car so as not to interrupt the farewell taking place on the porch. Velvet tries not to feel jealous watching Clea and Jiggs embrace.

"Salty."

"Sw-sw-sweetie."

Velvet looks forward to the moment they pull apart. As planned, Jiggs reaches into the back pocket of his Wranglers and hands Clea a manila envelope.

She taps him affectionately on the shoulder with it. "What's this?"

Velvet grins. Two nights earlier, she and Jiggs stayed up half the night starching and ironing twenty-dollar bills, trying to make them look bank fresh, but the next day, worried Clea would know the money came from the Folgers can and not accept it, Jiggs drove to the bank in Henning and exchanged the twenties for hundreds, and because he didn't believe Clea would believe he could have saved more than four thousand dollars, declined half the rolls Velvet tried to give him. It thrills Velvet to watch Clea slip the envelope into her backpack, to know that she won't be like her, arriving in a strange city without money.

Jerod joins Clea and Jiggs on the porch, and with a few more hugs and handshakes, the group parts, Jiggs going into the house to check on Bee, Jerod and Clea walking toward the car. Clea laughs to herself at the thought of Jiggs believing he'd convinced her that he'd saved the money in the manila envelope. To her surprise, she feels peaceful accepting Velvet's money. Turning, Clea scans the farmhouse, and trying to imprint it onto her memory, notices Velvet in the corner of the living room window.

Clea lifts her camera to her eye and zooms onto her mother's face.

Velvet waves.

Clea takes her picture.

# ACKNOWLEDGEMENTS

Jan Sue Warren, storyteller, Louis Warren, homesteader, Craig Lawrence, childhood prankster, Ross Olson, snake wrangler—I am deeply indebted to you.

For support moral and editorial (and not an insignificant amount of room and board) thanks to: Arabella de Beaupuy, Simon Burke, Eric Carpenter, Kim Cole, Matthew D'Ancona, Ashley Pearson Erol, Catherine Ingram, Chad Lange, Mary Ellen Mann, Alexia Paul, Julie Richards-Carpenter, Sarah Schaefer, Diana Kazuko Singleton, Catherine Taddei-Ehrke, Bart Tarman, Linda Tarman, and more Warrens: Ralph, Andrea, Stuart, Julie, Todd, Ruth.

Special thanks to Campbell Brown, Chris Kydd, Lina Langlee, Alison McBride, Janne Moller, Daiden O'Regan, Thomas Ross and Henry Steadman at Black & White Publishing, and the whole team at Peters, Fraser + Dunlop, particularly my determined agent, Laura Williams, fierce champion, discerning editor, steadier of frazzled nerves, knitter of beloved donkeys.

As for my wolf pack, deepest thanks to my husband, Santiago, trusted reader and first believer. And to Dámaso, Caio and Ignacio, who have no memory of me not working on this book, thank you for so graciously sharing your mother with a town full of imaginary people.